# CORVID WINGS

# CORVID WINGS
## THE AMETHYST WRATH
### BOOK TWO

### DEE MANNINE

This book is a work of fiction.
Characters, names, incidents, and places are the product of the author's imagination and are used fictionally.
Any resemblance is coincidental.

Character art illustrations by Anas Arzaq
(Instagram: @anasarzq)

The scanning, uploading, and distribution of this book without permission is theft of the author's intellectual property.

Copyright © 2026 by DeeMannine
All rights reserved

IBSNs:
979-8-9930749-2-4 (paperback)
979-8-9930749-3-1 (hardcover)

# CONTENT WARNING

This story contains mature themes and sexual content that may not be suitable for all readers.

Content warnings include, but are not limited to:

Explicit brutal abuse, character death, references to miscarriage, domestic violence, profanity, infertility, references to sexual assault, gore, spiders (arachnophobia), and violence.

A note from the author:
This book includes a chapter containing elements of domestic violence. You will see an asterisk * at the top of chapter 22. I avoided going into *excessive* detail, but the content is mentioned. I advise anyone sensitive to the subject to exercise caution.

Help is always available.
National Domestic Violence Hotline
800-799-7233

# DEDICATION

*For those who I didn't scare away with Corvid Whispers.*
*You're pretty freaking cool.*
*Thanks for entering this chaotic mind of mine.*

*-Dee*

# CONTENTS

| | |
|---|---|
| Author's Note | xvii |
| Prologue | 1 |
| **PART FOUR** | |
| Chapter 1 | 5 |
| Chapter 2 | 11 |
| Chapter 3 | 17 |
| Chapter 4 | 31 |
| Chapter 5 | 39 |
| Chapter 6 | 47 |
| Chapter 7 | 59 |
| Chapter 8 | 67 |
| Chapter 9 | 89 |
| Chapter 10 | 93 |
| Chapter 11 | 103 |
| Chapter 12 | 109 |
| Chapter 13 | 113 |
| Chapter 14 | 121 |
| Chapter 15 | 125 |
| Chapter 16 | 135 |
| Chapter 17 | 141 |
| Chapter 18 | 147 |
| Chapter 19 | 155 |
| Chapter 20 | 163 |
| Chapter 21 | 171 |
| Chapter 22 | 177 |
| Chapter 23 | 185 |
| Chapter 24 | 195 |
| Chapter 25 | 203 |
| Chapter 26 | 207 |
| Chapter 27 | 219 |
| Chapter 28 | 227 |

## PART FIVE

| | |
|---|---:|
| Chapter 29 | 239 |
| Chapter 30 | 247 |
| Chapter 31 | 259 |
| Chapter 32 | 267 |
| Chapter 33 | 273 |
| Chapter 34 | 279 |
| Chapter 35 | 289 |
| Chapter 36 | 297 |
| Chapter 37 | 303 |
| Chapter 38 | 309 |
| Chapter 39 | 317 |
| Chapter 40 | 327 |
| Chapter 41 | 335 |
| Chapter 42 | 351 |
| Chapter 43 | 357 |
| Chapter 44 | 367 |
| Chapter 45 | 371 |
| Chapter 46 | 379 |
| Chapter 47 | 385 |
| Chapter 48 | 391 |
| Chapter 49 | 397 |
| Chapter 50 | 403 |
| Chapter 51 | 409 |
| Chapter 52 | 413 |
| Epilogue | 421 |
| Afterword | 427 |
| Acknowledgments | 429 |
| About the Author | 431 |

# GLOSSARY

Locations
- Amanita Copse: The giant mushroom forest where the Vatte live
- Camp: A rehabilitation center where humans are sent when they are chosen from a Wyrd or for misbehavior
- Dracamora: Unknown
- Dreadspire Crater: Volcanic region where Jotnar cross into Tuath
- Gardvord: Plant science division
- Heath Forest: The Hailec-infected forest northeast of the Camp
- Joro: The human city enclosed under a dome
- La Uma's Lair: Where La Uma resides
- Mt. Ebenveil: The mountain where the Wisps reside
- Noctrya: Somnuim's realm
- Palatium: The central building of Joro
- Tuath: The Lycanthrope realm
- Umbrea: The Fae realm
- Umbrea Castle: The castle within Umbrea
- Xyberus: The world

Beings
- Amaru: Snake Shifters
- Corvid: Ravens Shifters
- Dark Witch: Witch who serves Supay
- Dragor: Non-magical lizard humanoids employed by the Monster King
- Fae: Beings with mist magic who reside in Umbrea
- Gnashing Flora: Non-magical man-eating plants
- Hailec: Magical, zombie-like monsters that transform themselves to attract their prey
- Human: Non-magical beings
- Jotnar: Non-magical giants
- La Uma: Monster in Umbrea
- Lionne: A creature that is half lion, half dragon
- Lobison: Monster guardians of the Umbrea forest
- Lycanthrope: General Shifters: Wolven and Bear
- Mother Goddess: The Divine Creator
- Mungder: Non-magical, octopus-like monsters that inhabit bodies of water
- Solios: The Solar Sovereign
- Supay: The Deathly Sovereign
- Unipaca: Magical alpaca with a horn
- Vatte: Beings with earth magic who live in the Amanita Copse
- White Witch: Witch who serves the Mother Goddess
- Wisps: Magical beings of the Mother Goddess

Roles
- Advisor: A person who works under Lord Mordred
- Rozzer: The guards of Joro and the Camp
- Rozzer Captain: The captain of the Rozzers
- The Rising: A rebel group of Joro.
- Traverser: Humans whose job is to venture outside of the city
- Umbra Council: The Fae who serve as counselors to King Ael

Characters
- Ael (eye-el): King of the Fae, aka Cahir
- Arzhel (arz-hell): Ojore's cousin
- Askold (as-cold): Joro Rozzer
- Benny: Seda's brother
- Cahir (cuh-hear): Seda's best friend, aka King Ael
- Chief Vidar (vi-dar): Vatte chief
- Elco: Lionne
- Esper: Seda's co-worker
- Ferona (fer-oh-nuh): Roya's Corvid sister
- Feich: Roya's Corvid brother
- Fran: Head Housekeeper at Umbrea Castle
- Jason: Seda's father
- Kalon de Somnium (kuh-lawn): Guardian of the Last Sleep
- Lucja (luke-juh): Daughter of Chief Vidar
- Luelle: Umbra council member and spy
- Meir (mare): Umbra council member
- Misandra: Cahir's mother
- Mordred: Lord of Umbrea
- Neoma: Daughter of a Fae lord
- Orion: Son of Lucja
- Ojore (uh-JOR-ray): Citizen of Joro and friend of Jason
- Praxis: Umbra counsel member and captain of the Umbrea guard
- Roya: Warden of the Corvids
- Ruel (ru-el): Joro Traverser
- Sacha (sach-ha): Lobison leader
- Sara: Seda's mother
- Seda (say-duh): Citizen of Joro and main character
- Sephyr (seff-her): Corvid
- Seren: Joro Traverser
- Supay: The Deathly Sovereign
- Suza: Maid at Umbrea Castle
- Tahti (tah-tee): Fae witch
- Teivel (tee-vul): Joro Advisor
- The Monster King: Ruler of monsters
- Vira (veer-uh): Corvid
- Yepa: Lycanthrope leader

# CORVID WINGS

# Author's Note

*Corvid Wings is the second book in the series, The Amethyst Wrath. It is highly recommended to read Corvid Whispers prior to starting this one, as this book immediately picks up where the first left off.*

The amethyst wrath is growing,
beneath the azure sky.

A monster lies with a crystal,
That it hoards under its watchful eye.

Birds caw loudly in the misty air,
Foreboding the destruction of the dome.

The key must find all four,
But death has been lurking… for one to return home.

# PART FOUR
## UMBREA

# CHAPTER 1

Kalon de Somnium<br/>(A very, very long time ago)

The eclipse of darkness descended the heaviest when loss consumed the heart.

The ceiling looked exactly as it always did, covered in cobwebs, with the slight breeze swaying their threads like ripples in water. Kalon watched a spider crawl through its network of fibers, gradually creating its intricate maze.

He eagerly watched an insect trap themselves within and grinned with excitement. The black spider lunged for its prey, swiftly wrapping it into a tight ball and sinking its fangs into its meal.

This had been the most entertaining thing in months. He had lost interest in tormenting the sleeping being of Xyberus with nightmares after learning the news.

The hand resting on his chest twitched, and he silently groaned to himself for slipping. He looked away from the tempting display above to the Fae lying beside him in his bed, her messy hair tangled from the night before.

He wanted her to go. His mistake only deepened the pain.

She shifted from the blankets and sat up, turning to look at him. Her long, brunette hair was unlike the starlight hair he longed for.

"Sleep okay?" she asked, stretching her arms in front of her and yawning.

"Fine," he replied shortly, not wanting to engage with her. If he said anything more, she would be impossible to stop.

"Last night was amazing." She looked at him with anticipation, yearning for something he refused to provide. He could sense waves of desperation coming from her as she pulled the blanket off, exposing her naked body for him in the cool air. "Would you like more?"

She leaned in to kiss him.

He averted his face, feeling irritated at the gesture. Kissing was clearly forbidden, and she knew that. He made that clear before he crossed the line.

She paused, her body stiffening beside his. "What's wrong?"

"I messed up," he whispered softly, feeling the pain of the truth tearing at his heart. He didn't care if she heard or if it hurt her feelings. She knew he belonged to someone else, and her ongoing efforts to get close to him during the months she was there were increasingly irritating.

"She's dead. I highly doubt my premonition was about *her*," the Fae snidely responded, cruel ire laced behind each word.

Kalon's neglected heart fluttered in pain like a whispered song fading into the void, with no one around to hear the aching melody.

The brunette got out of bed and seethed, "I'm over this."

She grabbed her clothing from the floor, stormed to the

doorway, and paused before exiting. "I'm going back to Umbrea."

She stared at him for too long, clearly hoping he would argue her departure.

When he didn't answer, she sighed and shook her head as she left the room. He listened to her muttering profanities as she descended the hall.

*Finally*, he thought when silence greeted him once more. She had been around for too long, trying her hardest to seduce him. She had foretold that the stone had been jaded, the tree fell, and the guardian had been captured.

He already knew these things, as they had happened long before her arrival.

He frequently considered sending her away but hoped her premonitions of yanantin would offer more details—such as a location, a time, or *anything* else that could help his search—so he allowed her to stay in Noctrya.

He permitted himself just this one mistake, this single chance to reveal anything more. But none occurred.

He stared at the ceiling and watched the spider drain the life from the bug, feeling as though his own was depleting with each passing day, month, and year that *she* was gone.

He lay there for a long time, yearning to smell the long-forgotten scent on his pillows, missing the vibrant violet eyes that healed his darkness, and recalling the smile that brightened his dismal world.

He continued to watch as the spider rebuilt its web, wishing he had a way to mend his soul the same.

"Immortal Kalon de Somnium," an Amaru, one of his shape-shifting, shadowy snakes, said as it slithered into his doorway, flickering in and out of sight. "Tahti stole from you as she left."

He didn't respond. He already knew what it was, and he

didn't really care. He could torment the Fae witch when he felt like it.

Nothing of true value was left for him here. His only focus was to find *her*.

Kalon turned over in bed, closed his eyes, and began his endless search through countless minds, always searching, always coming up empty, but never losing hope.

She would eventually return, and when she did, he would find her.

# CHAPTER 2

<u>Jason</u>

The sun's crushing heat pounded against Jason's exposed skin as he exited the stage and moved through the Palatium doorway. He felt a wave of relief as the cool air enveloped him in the shadowy hall, muffling the sounds of cawing birds when the door closed behind him.

The Corvids appeared to follow him wherever he went now, as if they were watching and waiting.

If only one would come close enough, maybe he could speak to it.

This week's Wyrd went as successfully as it could have gone. They gathered ten more citizens without any chaos erupting. The Monster King was pleased with the results and the recent announcement, declaring that he, Jason Arbor, was the new lord of Joro.

Holding a position of power felt strange. But was it truly authority?

No, it was merely a facade—he still answered to the Monster

King. To the citizens of Joro, being their lord was a guise concealing corruption. He lacked real power. But it didn't matter. His true goal was to help the Darkened however he could.

Weeks had gone by since his children and friends from the Rising vanished. Each night, he prayed to the Mother Goddess, hoping for their safety, but, as always, there was no response and no sign that she had heard.

He thought about Benny's cheerful outlook on life and Seda's reticence. What monsters were they facing out there in those woods? And where did they go? He knew Ojore, Seren, Askold, and Ruel would do everything in their power to protect his children. He just prayed that his friends were also safe.

He devised these plans alone, well, not entirely; he worked alongside Mordred to get where he was, and the Monster King was none the wiser.

*For the best,* he thought, even as anxiety gripped his throat, tightening its hold while he thought about his children, causing him to stop his ascent on the dark stairs and gasp for air.

Long before meeting Sara, the Oracle had told him that a key would be born. She had said he needed to assemble a team to help this 'key' save all of Xyberus. She predicted that one day, a moonlit child would become part of his life, joining his future White Witch wife. That they must raise her by the name of Seda and that he needed to work with Mordred to protect her, as she would lead them to the Darkened.

He worked tirelessly to climb the ranks at Gardvord so he could gain an audience with Mordred. He also did everything he could to teach his children obedience, aiming to keep them safe in this hellish society, with the understanding that one day, *everything* would change.

Maybe that was a mistake.

He passed a few Rozzers watching guard along the stairway,

who regarded him warily. Their trust in him was wavering and new.

He finished climbing the stairs, and before pushing open the door, he ran his hand over his pocket, feeling the device within.

He pushed open the worn, wooden door, quickly hiding his emotions behind a neutral expression.

He knew who was already waiting on the other side.

"That went well, Lord Jason," the Monster King said to him from the opposite side of a magic, floor-length mirror that leaned against the wall. He studied Jason carefully, clearly looking for any weaknesses or signs of betrayal.

Mordred used to be the Lord of Joro, and he was more than willing to give up that position of power to Jason, even if it meant enduring torture from the Monster King. But his betrayal made Jason's job all the harder. Jason had tirelessly held off any further violence toward Mordred from the hands of the Monster King since the initial episode. But it was becoming increasingly difficult to distract him from such events.

"Yes, it did," Jason replied nonchalantly. "The selectees have been gathered and are making their way down to the Camp as we speak."

The Monster King puffed on his veilroot smoke, exhaling it through the mirror into the room where Jason stood. Jason hated the smell of veilroot, for it was the smell he associated with the darkness of this world, and held his breath as the smoke billowed around his face.

He hated this man.

"You've been doing well so far. Come through. It's time we took another finger from Mordred. He's only lost one, and I have a sudden appetite for Fae."

If the Monster King continued this torment, the dawn would hesitate to crest over the mountains, and eternal cold would sweep across the lands, casting the planet into everlasting darkness.

Jason swallowed his disgust and hesitation before walking toward the mirror, cautiously stepping through the glass. It rippled against his skin like water and placed him into the Camp, alongside the Monster King.

As he stared at the expectant, hungry expression on the Monster King's face, he offered another silent prayer for his children, hoping they were safe... wherever they were.

# CHAPTER 3

### Seda

Seda opened her eyes, focusing on Cahir's outline through the misty, pink fog around her. The pink haze gradually cleared, and she saw him holding onto a woman's thigh from high on a dais. Cahir was staring at her with wide eyes, the same green eyes he had stared down at her with false love and emotion for years. She noticed that he looked different than before. He had grown taller and broader, his face now framed by a hint of rugged facial hair. His skin tone had subtly changed, glowing with a jade undertone, and he had tattoos along with more defined features than when she last saw him.

He wore a tall, three-spiked golden crown with a diamond-shaped hole in its center.

It took her weeks to get to this place, and his betrayal scorched her heart into a ravenous fury. Her escape from the Camp, the long journey to the Wisps, and finally reaching Umbrea took her through dark, haunted woods, where she learned to defend herself and others. But most of all, that journey taught her that the life she knew had been a lie, and that she had to believe in *herself.*

Cahir had been her best friend for years. She had isolated and strapped herself to his side, leaning on him for emotional support, only to discover that he had been lying the entire time she knew him.

He wasn't who he pretended to be.

He was someone and something else entirely.

And it wasn't just him. Kalon had also entered her life, taking her first kiss and her moonstone necklace, then disappearing into the darkness of the Amanita Copse unnoticed. She needed that stone back.

Elco roared beside her, shaking the ground beneath her feet.

*Elco was now her best friend.*

Fuck Cahir. She and Elco had been chained together in the Camp, not only learning how to find themselves and survive in that dark place, but also discovering what true friendship was: loyalty, support, trust, and above all else, *honesty.*

Cahir shouted for everyone to stop, quickly releasing the woman's leg he was holding, and held up his hand to the guards rushing toward her and Elco.

Seda's eyes slowly scanned the woman he was touching and noticed her breasts were exposed for everyone in the room, just moments before for *him*. A sudden, intense pain pierced her chest, and a swift, overwhelming wave of rage engulfed her.

He *was* fucking all kinds of women, Kalon was right when he told her that. How *dare* Cahir act like he's upheld moral standards all these years?

Without any hesitation, her powers flowed through her arms, and sparks of electricity flickered from her fingertips.

"You lied to me!" she snapped at him as everyone murmured around her display of power. "You *LIED* to me!"

The Fae surrounding her began to murmur in hushed tones.

*"Is that a monster?"*
*"She looks human."*
*"How does King Ael know her?"*

Cahir quickly stood from his throne, raising his hands in an apparent attempt at mock surrender. "Can we talk, please?" His green eyes begged her to accept, looking so familiar, so trusting. Seda watched him with a broken heart, consumed by betrayal.

She wouldn't trust him; she couldn't. He broke that. *He broke her.*

A beautiful woman, with the same skin tone and pointed ears as everyone else in the room, whispered something into Cahir's ear. She wore a silky red dress, and her hair was in a long blonde ponytail. Seda narrowed her eyes, her anger simmering like a fueled inferno, causing her magic to vibrate violently in her chest.

A dark cloud formed in the ballroom, sparking against the ceiling.

She didn't know what to do with the surge that pulsed from within and threw her hands at the window above Cahir, wanting it to scare him as she discharged a violent arc of electricity that shattered the glass in every direction.

The room erupted in screams.

She smiled as she watched the glass shatter, noticing how Cahir and the others on the dais had to cover their heads to protect themselves.

The guards rushed toward her, colliding with each other as Elco's mighty roar echoed through the room, stopping them from their approach.

"I said *STOP!*" Cahir shouted at everyone. He looked back at Seda, his eyes softening. "Seda, could you please pull your powers back in, and we'll find somewhere private to talk? *I can explain everything."*

The woman with exposed breasts casually tucked them back in and looked at Seda with raised brows as she brushed glass off her shoulder. Her eyebrows slowly relaxed, and a smile spread across her lips.

Seda slowly looked between the woman in red silk and Cahir. Did she want to talk to him? So far, everything she had argued with herself on her journey here without him had been true.

"What do you want to do, moon-flutter? I'll follow your lead," Elco asked, his body tightening around hers. He watched the guards with baited interest.

When had he eaten last anyway?

She waited a few moments before answering Cahir, allowing the people in the room to wonder as they watched their king nervously fidget.

"The Wisps sent me here. I have a lot of questions for you, *King Ael*," she shouted, sarcastically emphasizing his title and name.

He winced at her use of his true name, and Seda smirked as the Fae in the room murmured over her mention of the Wisps. She watched him slowly descend the dais and head toward a door on the far side of the room.

She would have her revenge. The shattered glass wasn't enough.

"This way," a woman's voice said from beside them, and Elco snarled, flashing his sharp fangs as he turned to see who it was. The woman in the red silk gown appeared at her side, guiding her to follow Cahir out of the room. "Your friend is welcome to join you."

Seda's slitted eyes followed her as she walked away. She grumbled and moved away from Elco's protection, walking beside the woman and smiling as the guests watched her leave, enjoying the fear on their faces.

She glanced back at the woman and felt venom rise at the sight of her. Was she one of Cahir's whores? She regarded her beauty, which enraged her. She had long, golden hair and pointed ears adorned with earrings.

Seda didn't wear fancy dresses or stylish jewelry.

She bit the inside of her cheek and silently scolded herself. Why should she feel any animosity toward this woman regarding that liar? He was dishonest, and if this woman desired him, she was free to have the lying bastard.

With a devious smirk, as if she had just uncovered some juicy gossip, the woman looked at her. "That was quite a grand entrance. I've never seen anyone make Ael fidget like that before. Please do it again?" She raised a perfectly manicured eyebrow at Seda.

Seda noticed that the woman didn't give Cahir a title when she referred to him, as if she were close to him.

"And who are you?" She tried to hide the sharpness in her tone, pretending she didn't care, but her emotions were a tangle of currents. The woman chuckled, and Seda clenched her fists as sparks of electricity flickered across her knuckles.

The woman glanced at Seda's glowing hands, her face paling. "I'm Luelle. I've been friends—only friends—with Ael since childhood. I'm also one of the three advisors here in Umbrea."

"Seems like he has quite a few *friends*. Did you know he made me feel like I was his *only* friend? Did you know he lied... for years?" Her tongue moved of its own accord.

Sure, she occasionally missed him during her journey, but seeing him with these wretched women upon arriving changed that. She held back the vibration of her simmering magic that wrapped around her throat, choking her.

"Ael doesn't claim to be friends with just anyone. If he says he's your friend, he means it." Luelle turned away from her, and Seda rolled her eyes.

Luelle was obviously a fool for believing anything that man said.

The ballroom door closed as they left. Elco followed, snarling at anyone who dared to come too close. Mostly, people dropped their wine glasses with muffled shrieks as they hurried away from her path.

When they entered the hall, they saw Cahir waiting a few doors away, holding a door open. "I can take it from here, Luelle. Please give us some privacy." He looked at Seda, his cheeks flushed, and then back at Luelle. "Can you please see to it that Fran sets up that room for her in the East Wing? She knows which one."

"The East Wing?" Luelle asked, the corner of her mouth curling upward.

"Yes. And make sure there's room there for Elco, as well." He cleared his throat and quickly glanced at Seda before looking away.

Luelle politely stepped aside, allowing Seda to walk through. Seda glared at him as she walked past, hoping her eyes stabbed him in his stupid face as she entered the small, brightly lit room with a large table.

She looked back at Elco and said, "You wait here, too, please. I'll be out shortly. This room doesn't look big enough to fit you."

Elco stared at her and puffed out his chest. "I'll stay at this door until you come out. Call me if you need anything. I *will make myself fit* if I have to," he replied.

She nodded in response and entered the room, choosing not to sit at the table and instead standing in the far corner with her arms crossed over her chest.

Cahir stepped in, and Seda glanced at him, taking in his new appearance. He must have grown a foot in height between his human and Fae forms. His teeth and ears were pointed, and his skin had that slight luster of jade to it.

She didn't know him at all.

Anger simmered beneath her skin, and hot tears began blurring her eyes. She looked away, unable to handle his betrayal any longer.

Cahir walked to the table and sat down, his chair squeaking under him. He took his crown off and set it aside, placing his hands on the table with his palms facing up. She glanced back at him and glared, a single tear quickly falling from her left eye.

"I'm sorry, Seda. I have more to say, but I want to be sure you hear that first, in the middle of this, and for the rest of your life. I'll never forgive myself for hurting you. *Ever*. I've broken your trust, and I'll do *everything* to gain it back, if you'll allow me," Cahir said as he stared at her.

The single tear that slipped free felt like molten glass sliding down her cheek and onto her clothing. She stared at his stupid palms on the table next to his stupid-looking crown. She took a deep breath and choked out, "I trusted you with everything I had, and the entire time you were lying to me. You played me like a fucking fool." She laughed and aggressively wiped the remnants of the tear from her cheek. "It feels like you ripped my heart out and stomped on it when all I had for you was love and trust. Why? What was it *for?*"

She looked away from him, unable to meet his dishonest face, expecting more lies in return.

He replied softly, "To save Umbrea."

She ground her teeth together, feeling a twitch in her jaw.

"How did being friends with me save your kingdom?" she seethed.

She stared at a small mark on the wall, keeping her focus there instead of on him.

He sighed. "It hasn't."

She looked back at him and sneered, "What do you mean, 'it hasn't'? Are you saying that all those years of your fake friendship were for nothing?"

"It was never fake, Seda. I've always been your friend. From the moment I met you at the Gardvord."

She let out an angry sob, pressing her clenched fist over her mouth as she remembered the day he had entered and announced he was the new member of her division. Seda had been alone in that department before, and she felt anxious about having someone else with her. Being alone with a man in the same room had caused her to break down and collapse. Cahir had run up to her, catching her just as she was about to hit the ground. When her vision had cleared, she panicked and scratched him for touching her. He apologized repeatedly, moved his desk to the opposite side of the room, and didn't speak to her for a week. One day, he came in with a honey cake and a cup of coffee, placed them on her desk as he walked by, and said nothing. She had hesitated too long before poking the cake and taking that first sip, but eventually she gave in. The next day, he brought her another cup of coffee and another honey cake.

"No, we were *not* friends on that first day," she corrected him, looking back at her favorite spot on the wall.

Cahir smirked, and she quickly looked back at him, scoffing in return. The familiar dimples she remembered so well showed, and her heart lurched.

"From the first day. I could see how you needed someone in your life who just flowed through your waves the way you needed," he said.

She watched him, tears blurring her vision. "Tell me everything, Cahir. I want the truth."

He didn't correct her on his name.

She could see him nod through her impaired vision and hear him take a deep breath before he said, "It started thirty years ago. Tahti, the Oracle witch, called for me, saying a 'key' was born. A key that would save Umbrea, a key that would save all of Xyberus. I was foolish back then and thought she was insane. How could a 'key' be born? I didn't care what happened in the lower half of Xyberus as long as Umbrea was safe, and it was until a few years ago. A Jotnar found its way past our borders and tore through a small village. The Fae brought it down and disposed of the body, but another came. We worked alongside the Lycanthropes to secure our borders and formed a fragile alliance with them, but that's a story for another time."

He paused and watched her. She listened while she glared at his open palms on the table.

"After that, I went to Tahti again and asked her to recount what she had told me. She said that I needed to travel to Joro to find you and the Dark Stone, but first I had to visit the Wisps. So I did." He took a deep breath, ran his hands down his face, and placed them back on the table. "The Wisps, as you may or may not know, require a payment to grant a wish. I wished to find you. They transformed me into a human, told me I wasn't allowed to tell you anything about this world outside of Joro, about who I really was, about any of it. They also said I wasn't allowed to lie to you, Seda. Throughout that entire time, I never lied directly. And it was hard, so fucking hard navigating around that. If I broke my deal with them, I could've been banished back here." He placed his hand over his chest. "I'm truly sorry that I had to tell you partial truths to hide the full truth. I tried so hard, so many times, to confess. Especially towards the end, when your safety was at risk and my time as a human was running out."

Seda braved stepping away from the wall and walked up to the table. She pulled out a chair a few spaces down from him and sat down. She stared at him, at the honest look on his face, at the way his palms remained upright on the table. "Was any of it true?"

"What do you mean?" he asked.

"It... you told me you loved me. You told me we would be together, always. We were trying to have a *baby*, Cahir."

He looked away from her and clenched his fists. "I would never *force* you to have a child, Seda. Not when you didn't know the truth about who I was or why I was there. That part wasn't true. Joro was forcing you to conceive, and it didn't *feel right*." He ran his hands through his hair, messing up the perfectly laid waves. "You were never provided with my... semen." He looked away from her, his cheeks reddening, and lowered his head.

Seda's jaw dropped, and her voice pitched. "What?"

"I never placed my semen in the cup, Seda. I wasn't comfortable putting you in that position." His words came out whisper-soft.

Her temples pounded as rage surged through her once more. "Are you fucking kidding me?!" She looked away from him again, feeling the heat rise to her cheeks and a faint tingling of electricity dance across her forehead.

Her mind was torn with mixed feelings. She felt relief that she had never gotten pregnant, because it meant she would have missed discovering this other world and would have stayed within Joro. She also might never have unlocked her power.

The other part of her was filled with anger—angry at herself and at him—and she concentrated on that, taking deep breaths.

"I was selected for the Camp because I never had a child, Cahir. It was *my* choice to do that, not yours! You should have told me you weren't comfortable, and I would've found *someone else*," she seethed.

Her heart raced, and she saw him look at her throat, watching as her pulse beat rapidly.

He looked away. "You deserve better, Seda. You deserve better than me."

She jumped from her chair and pointed a sparking finger at him. "You're damn fucking right I do! I saw and went through horrible things in that place, Cahir. I was almost raped again! I was attacked by a fucking Jotnar! I witnessed a friend of mine give birth, *alone*, and heard her cries for her baby. I had to listen to them beat her and watch as they dragged her and her lifeless baby away." Her voice cracked as her tears welled again, electric shocks emitting from their silken drops.

Cahir was silent for a long time before he said, "I'm sorry, Seda. But I'll *never* force you to have my child. The rest of what you asked was true."

"The rest of what?" she snapped, throwing her hands in the air and shooting a spark at the ceiling.

Cahir looked up at the spot, the ceiling now blackened. "That I'll always be by your side, if you want me to be. And that I love you. I was always telling the truth about that. You are and have been my *best friend* in this entire fucked up world. You mean everything to me."

His *friend*. Was that not what she had told him countless times? Why did it sting now when he said it? She winced.

"Will you tell me what the Wisps told you?" he asked, seemingly trying to change the subject.

She wiped the tears from her cheeks and chin with the back of her hand. She sat back down and waited for several heartbeats, watching that same stupid spot on the wall, unsure how to start.

She took a deep breath and wiped her nose again, her gaze shifting back to his. "They told me I needed your help to find all four stones and achieve harmony with them. That's why I'm here, *the only reason*." She watched with satisfaction as he forced himself to swallow.

A knock interrupted their conversation, and they both looked toward the door. An older man with a long gray beard and the woman who had exposed her breasts when she arrived, casually walked in.

Seda tensed. Flashes of her nude form in front of Cahir swirled through her mind, and a wave of nausea curdled within her stomach.

Seeing her felt like someone was stabbing her in the chest with a dull knife, the soft blade bruising her heart.

She suppressed the feeling and narrowed her eyes, refocusing on her anger instead.

They both bowed, and when they rose, the old man asked, "King Ael, I wanted to check on you. Is everything okay?"

"Why is *she* here?" Cahir asked the older man sharply.

The older man hesitated, looking between Cahir and the woman. "I came to see Seda with my own eyes, Sire, because I want to get to know her better... so I can research her powers more effectively. And since Neoma is also new to the castle, she wanted to meet Seda too, to make her acquaintance."

Cahir glared at Neoma before looking back at the older man. "We're having a private conversation, Meir."

Meir bristled, quickly masking a face of anger. He apologized, and they turned to leave the room when Cahir said, "If Seda wishes to make friends, *she* can choose who she wants to see, not have them forced on her. You and I need to talk, Meir. I was told some interesting information earlier, which explains a lot of the recent behaviors I've been noticing lately."

Meir played with his fingers. "Yes, Sire. I—"

"I'll spend time with her," Seda interrupted. She could make her own decisions, and if Cahir was going to spend his time with this woman, as his 'friend', she should get to know her better. She unfortunately needed something from Cahir now. Playing nice was in her best interest, even if it wasn't sincere.

She told herself she didn't care whether Cahir or this woman were truly her friends.

The older man offered Seda a gentle smile.

She looked at Cahir, who had wide eyes and furrowed brows. "Umm.. as you wish, Seda," Cahir said.

Someone knocked on the door again, causing another scowl from Cahir. Luelle entered with a stout woman wearing a blue dress and an apron. *"Your Highness*, we've found suitable accommodations for Seda and her Lionne. May we please lead them to their rooms?" Luelle asked sweetly.

Cahir stood and turned to Seda, looking at her with a gentle expression. "May we continue this conversation tomorrow over breakfast? I need to return to the ball to ensure everything is settled with the crowd... and Seda." He paused. "I truly am sorry. It will *never* happen again."

She wanted to believe him, but she didn't trust the words coming from his mouth and desperately needed some time alone to reflect.

She didn't respond as she followed Luelle and the woman out of the room, meeting Elco again. A small Fae girl sat beside him, braiding a small section of his mane. "Everyone loves to play with that luscious hair of yours," she said with a smile.

Elco muttered and stood on all fours. The girl hugged him and then left, casually skipping down the hallway.

They followed the women through the castle to their rooms. The music from the party grew quieter the farther they went, and Seda wondered if Cahir was sitting back on the throne with Neoma again.

# CHAPTER 4

<u>Seda</u>

They walked quietly through long hallways where the gentle candlelight illuminated the vine-covered ceilings that appeared to reach the sky. Seda ran her fingers over Elco's scales, noticing his little hairs standing with her touch and feeling his rumbling purrs through her palm.

She bit the inside of her cheek as her mind wandered to her brother and the friends she had left behind at the Wisps. Did they know where she and Elco went?

They passed through a pair of wooden double doors that stretched from floor to ceiling, with a sign reading "East Wing" in ornate, scroll-like lettering. At the end of the hall stood another pair of large double doors, with smaller entrances leading toward them along the corridor.

Seda felt a tingling sensation on her back and reached up to scratch, but she couldn't reach the spot where her skin was irritated.

Luelle stopped at the fourth door and looked at them.

"This room is designated for Elco. We had to move some furniture around to fit him comfortably, but the bed is large enough."

Elco looked curiously at Seda as Luelle opened the door. Inside, a massive bed, big enough for ten people, lay in the center of the room, with a patio door on the opposite side.

They walked in, and Elco strolled to the door. "Can you please ask them to leave this open so I may fly freely?"

Seda looked at the women. "Will Elco be allowed to roam? He wishes for the exterior door to remain open."

Luelle and the woman exchanged a hesitant glance.

Luelle cleared her throat before she asked, "Does he intend to eat the citizens of Umbrea?"

Elco growled, staring at Luelle with slanted feline eyes.

"He'll not harm any citizens. I assume you have plenty of deer and other animals around?" Seda asked, ready to argue if they turned down Elco's request.

"Yes. But please let him know he's not allowed to eat the livestock either. That'll cause problems." Luelle looked between them, eyebrows raised.

Seda looked at him and chuckled. "You got that, Elco?"

"No citizens and no livestock. They never said anything about pets," he grumbled.

Seda sighed and shook her head. "He agrees."

Luelle nodded and unlocked the doors, and the fresh night air entered the room. Small floating green orbs blew in, like fuzzy bubbles flitting through the air.

Seda gasped. "What are those?"

"That's our Umbrean magic, miss," the other woman answered. "It's nothing to fear. Just floats around the air as it pleases. We're a magical and plentiful realm."

The orbs surrounded Seda, gathering on her skin and tangling through her hair. A sense of peace and love gradually filled her, warming her from within and making her feel whole again.

"I've never seen them react... to anything," the woman gasped by her side.

Luelle stared at Seda with wide eyes. Seda held out her hand, and the little orbs twirled around her fingertips like fireflies dancing through moonlight.

"You've always been special, moon-flutter," Elco said. "Will you be okay while I explore the area?"

"Yes, Elco. I think my room will be near, right?" Seda looked at the women, and they nodded, their mouths open in awe as they watched the orbs flit around.

The woman in blue cleared her throat and said, "You'll be in the room across the hall, the door straight on the opposite side of this one."

The orbs gracefully left Seda and continued their aimless drift through the air around them. Elco walked to the doors and spread his wings wide when he exited onto the expansive patio, scattering the glowing orbs.

He flew off into the night.

"Follow us, miss," the woman said to Seda as she held open Elco's door for her. Seda walked out and across the hall while Luelle pushed open the door meant for her. She entered and inhaled a deep breath of the heady lavender aroma. It was beautiful, unlike anything she had ever seen before. The large bed was draped in green silk, with soft pillows and four elaborately carved posts that rose to the ceiling.

The sparkling stars and the enchanting orbs drifting across the night sky were visible through a glass ceiling that spanned the entire length of the room. Luxurious mahogany furniture was carefully arranged throughout the room.

The woman turned to Seda. "My name is Fran, and I am the head housekeeper here. If you need anything, please let me know. My team will be coming by periodically to check on you and prepare you for your days. You're a guest of the king and will be treated as such. Please let me know if you encounter any issues, dear. Your closet is full of clothing to pick from, and the bathroom is through that door there." She pointed to the door on the left side of the room. "A hot bath has been drawn for you." Fran bowed slightly at her waist and walked out the door, leaving her and Luelle behind.

Luelle watched Seda with furrowed brows. "You aren't human, not Fae, not a Lycanthrope. What are you?"

"I don't know. I was raised believing I was human. Maybe I am just a human," Seda answered with a shrug. "Can you tell me what to expect here? How are the people? How is Cahir?"

Luelle looked at her and chewed her inner cheek, turning her head to the side and staring out the window. "Cahir... Did you know *Cahir* was the name his mother called him? He never allowed anyone else to call him that after she passed. He took his given name, Ael, after her passing."

Seda didn't know that. She had only ever known him as Cahir.

Luelle continued, "People here are kind, *usually*. Right now, the women are acting like stupid fools because they think that Ael will be picking a wife soon."

A sudden pang of hurt shot through Seda's chest. He was a king—an unwed king. She should have expected this, but it never occurred to her.

She silently scolded herself for the fleeting feeling, reminded herself that she was upset with him.

Who cared who he married?

Luelle watched her intently. "Since you're here, I'd be cautious around women you don't really know. Not of me, of course. I'd rather die than try for his hand."

"That other woman offered to be my friend—the one who

was half-naked on top of him when I arrived." Seda tried to hide her barbed tone.

"Hmm..." Luelle paused and chewed her cheek once more. "I'd be wary of that one. Let me know if you'd like a tour tomorrow. The library might be a good place to find information about your powers. I know Meir was trying to find some, but I'm not sure if he's had any luck. He hasn't mentioned it."

Luelle walked to the door and turned back. "Is there anything else I can do for you tonight, Seda? Are you hungry?"

"No, thank you, Luelle. I'll be fine," she responded with a forced smile. The unease of this new place and these new people kept her hunger from surging, despite the meager food from her trip.

Luelle offered a small smile before walking out of the room and shutting the door behind her.

Seda sat down on the bed and looked up at the night sky. This place was beautiful. She felt comfortable in this room, but she was nervous about why she had been sent here. She needed to find the information and the stones to return to the door and the Wisps.

She went to the bathroom and noticed a large tub filled with foaming water, surrounded by dozens of lit candles that flickered across the walls. She had never taken a hot bath before, and a smile crept onto her lips.

After she removed her filthy clothing from her sore body, she dipped a toe into the steaming hot water. She slowly eased herself into the tub, savoring the heat that burned against her skin, wrapping around her like a blanket.

Goosebumps erupted on her arms, and she sank further into the water, dunking her head and letting her hair soak up the suds. She popped up and grabbed a bar of soap, lathering it all around herself. How long had it been since she had a proper shower? Her last one was at the Camp, and that felt like weeks ago. She shivered at the memory of Alexi watching her, but pushed aside the uneasy feeling and washed her hair, then grabbed the conditioner—a luxury in Joro—and ran it through her tangled strands.

The irritation on her back returned, and she smiled when she spotted a long washcloth. She reached for it and scrubbed it between her shoulder blades, letting out a small sigh.

She sank back into the water and rinsed the conditioner from her hair, remaining within until her skin began to wrinkle. When she got out and drained the water, she spotted a fresh toothbrush and a small jar of toothpaste on the counter. She rushed over to them, excited to thoroughly brush her teeth.

With a towel tightly wrapped around her, she walked back into the bedroom, exhaustion hitting her like a tidal wave. The thought of looking through the closet for something to wear sounded exhausting.

Dropping the wet towel onto the floor, she climbed into the silken sheets and nestled into the plushness of a bed for the first time in what felt like forever, closing her eyes and quickly falling asleep.

Sweet dreams of familiar snakes wrapped around her soul, comforting her, whispering sweet nothings into her ears, and softly caressing her body.

# CHAPTER 5

<u>Ael</u>

The rest of the ball was fucking boring. The housekeepers did a great job cleaning up the broken glass, and thankfully, Neoma was nowhere to be found. After Ael walked back in, a line of women formed to talk to him, but he announced that he was not seeing anyone for the remainder of the night. He sent them back to enjoy their evenings, noticing the many pouting faces at his command. He didn't care. All he could think about was Seda.

What was she doing now? When he found out from the witch that she would be arriving soon, he organized for her to be within his wing of the castle, a couple of doors down from him. He wished for her to have the best room there—the one that was once his mother's when he was a baby—and the finest selection of soaps, shampoos, and clothing. She deserved all that and more. He even chose a toothbrush and toothpaste he believed she would prefer.

Was she in the bath now? He couldn't pull his mind away

from her. She looked vicious when she arrived, and shifted uncomfortably in his seat, desire burning under his skin. He focused on the punch bowl, watching the boring Fae that were gathered around it, idly talking.

Praxis silently joined him, both watching the crowd dance and eat. Ael thought about how Seda had glared at Neoma, and was confused when she agreed to spend time with her.

When the clock struck three in the morning, and the crowd was thoroughly drunk from wine, he excused himself and headed back to his room.

The halls were quiet with the staff either in the kitchens or serving guests. He walked through the large, double doors of his wing and caught himself pausing outside Seda's room, listening for sounds within.

He wanted to knock and say hello, to make sure she was okay, and to see if she had everything she needed.

He hesitated as he lifted his hand. It would be impolite to wake her if she were asleep. But what if something had happened and no one was around to hear?

He swallowed down the hesitation and forced himself to knock, anxiously waiting for her response.

Silence only responded to him.

He waited a few more moments before knocking again, this time cracking her door open and peering inside.

"Seda? Are you here?" he asked, his voice just above a whisper.

This was definitely a bad idea. She was so upset with him earlier. Entering her space might cause her anger to bubble over, leaving him a charred mass in the room.

He slowly entered the candlelit room and found the bed empty. A flutter of anxiety stirred in his stomach. Where was she? Was she okay?

A sound came from the bathroom, and he quickly turned toward the opening door.

Seda emerged... completely naked.

She gasped, her body freezing like a deer caught in the crosshairs when their eyes met.

He struggled to look away, but like a starving man tempted by a platter of desserts, his eyes slowly drifted downward.

He inhaled a ragged breath as he took in her full breasts, the peaks of her nipples firm from the cool air. The soft mound at the apex of her thighs and the supple curves of her hips epitomized her perfection.

The air thickened, and his breath stalled, his chest tight with her fresh lilac scent. He felt his pants tighten with desire as his body immediately responded to the breathtaking sight of her devastation before him.

He wanted to reach out and touch her, longing to feel her soft skin within his own, but like a rubber band snapping back quickly, he turned away, trying to hide the evidence of such carnal desires.

"I'm sorry," he choked out, finally releasing his breath. "I only came in to check on you and became concerned when no one answered."

Seda's trance fractured, and she grabbed a throw blanket from a side chair, quickly wrapping it around her body.

He hesitantly glanced back at her.

"Since when do you not knock?!" she snapped, her cheeks flushed pink even in the dark of the room.

Her eyes widened with shock when she glanced down at his pants, his firm length unfortunately still visible with his body turned to the side. He went to apologize again, but a faint scent filled the room, growing stronger the longer he stood there.

He had never smelled that from her before, and its sweet aroma overwhelmed him.

His cock jerked.

He needed to leave her room as quickly as possible before his dick took over his thoughts and reason.

"I... I'll leave you to it." He rushed out of her room, closing the door behind him and leaning his back against it, inhaling ragged breaths. He should have known not to intrude. He always gave Seda the space she needed in their tiny apartment back in Joro.

Her being in Umbrea was no different.

But her unique scent...

A faint, flickering sound from the doorway of the two large doors separating the wing from the rest of the castle caught his attention, and he quickly glanced toward them.

"Who's there? Show yourself!" he demanded.

No one appeared.

He walked to the doors and looked around. It was empty. He waited a few moments to hear the sounds of breathing or movement, but when none came, he shook his head. It was late, and he needed to rest and take a cold shower. He would have Praxis post guards here tomorrow.

He turned around and walked to his bedroom, closing the door behind him.

His cock aggressively strained against the confines of his pants as he entered the bathroom and stripped off his clothes, slowly easing into the cold, running water.

Just as he had on all previous occasions, he let the freezing temperature shock his body.

Seda was absolutely *beautiful*.

He had never seen her nude body before. The closest he had come was that day when Roya busted through their window, and he walked in with her in a huff, only wearing that damn towel.

That fucking towel that he thought about too often after.

The fucking towel that made him ache for her.

The Hailec in the forest was way off when it pretended to be her in the woods.

*Seda was divinity itself.*

Was she mad at him or was she not?

Her scent tonight, though. Was it her arousal? It had to be. It was like the first bite of cake, the rush of endorphins, the craving to have more.

He thought about the full shape of her breasts, about the soft-looking hair between her thighs, and the thickness of her hips. He wanted to grab them and squeeze them between his palms.

His erection throbbed, and he groaned as the cold water washed over him, the years of agony fighting against his control.

He waited a few minutes, trying to think of anything other than her, but visions of her continued to galvanize his restraint.

He reached down and grabbed his cock firmly, slowly running his fingers over the beads of precum escaping the tip.

He paused and fought with himself.

He hadn't earned her trust, and he felt guilty even placing his hand there. But he *did* feel better about being honest. It was the first time in years that he no longer felt as if he had something to hide. Like a heavy weight had been lifted from his chest, Seda knew who he truly was now. The complicated past of hiding it from her was over.

The smooth sensation weakened his knees, and he supported himself with his other hand against the wall. He slowly and firmly stroked up his length, his throat emitting a growl behind his clenched teeth.

He cupped his palm over the tip and rested his forehead against the shower wall, fighting with himself one last time.

*Fuck it.*

He turned on the hot water and sighed as the heat soaked

into his skin, dense steam rising around the walls. He slowly and firmly stroked himself up and down.

It felt so fucking good, like her lightning striking him in the eye of a storm, with every assault electrifying his core. It had been years since he had done this, since he had felt this type of sensation. He stood in the shower, with lips parted, and eyebrows furrowed, savoring the warmth of the water and the silky friction.

He tried not to quicken his pace, but it felt so fucking addicting to give in to this craving, to this consuming torrent of pleasure.

He daydreamed about her heavenly smell just minutes before.

The thought of making her orgasm and the possible sounds she might make caused him to shudder and stroke himself harder.

He ran his tongue across his lips and inhaled deeply while dreaming about how she might taste and the way her clit would feel pressed against his tongue.

The silky sensations were overwhelming, finally easing the years of tightly wound tension with each unyielding caress.

His abdomen tightened, and he gazed down, staring at the enlarged head of his cock—swollen, supple, and ready.

The thought of her sucking on it, with his cum dripping from her beautiful, full lips, was the final indulgence, the capstone to this rhapsody.

A growl erupted from his lips as he threw his face toward the ceiling, his legs buckling beneath him. Waves of tingling heat swept through him like a blazing storm, tearing through every nerve from the very core of his being.

He crashed down with the water hitting the top of his head, his climax breaking him open, uncoiling the tension and angst of years past.

He fucked his fist as hard as he could, not wanting it to end, never wanting it to end, feeling like he found himself in heaven, with her on his mind, and allowed his cum to paint the walls of the shower.

*Seda is mine,* was his final thought.

The only thought that mattered.

# CHAPTER 6

<u>Seda</u>

Seda jolted awake in the darkness, where distant screams and gurgling sounds echoed around her. Her breath caught, and she felt a shiver run through her body.

A slow drip hit her arm as the heavy smell of copper and iron filled the air. Her wrists felt heavy as she slowly stood on unsteady legs, reaching out her trembling hands to explore her surroundings, with the sound of rattling chains clinking as she moved.

As the distant screaming grew louder, she backed away as far as she could, her head hitting the wall behind her, and she slipped on something slick.

She curled into a tight ball, the only way she knew to protect herself.

Footsteps echoed as an orange glow lit up the area. Seda peeked out from under her arm and saw that she was trapped, chained in a dungeon deep within a long, dark hall lined with cells. A small, metal bed stained with old, dark blood sat beside her, with a bucket placed near the bars.

Panic began to seize her throat, and her breathing became labored.

"Looks like my albino-freak has finally woken up."

SEDA SHOT UP IN BED, sweat coating her forehead and dread wringing its ugly claws across her chest. Daylight streamed through the windows as Seda gazed at them, panic still rushing through her in a relentless assault.

She inhaled deeply, reassuring herself that it was only a nightmare. She wasn't in the Camp anymore. She was in Umbrea. She was *safe*.

She ran one hand over her face, rubbing her eyes and exhaling slowly through pursed lips. Her other hand ran over her heart, feeling the racing beating below the soft material of her nightgown.

After Cahir left the night before, she made sure to find something suitable to wear from the massive closet. She glanced upward through the glass ceiling, watching the green orbs floating and fluttering amongst the clouds.

*I'm safe*, she reassured herself.

A gentle knock sounded at her door, and she quickly turned to it, choking out, "Yes?"

The door swung open, revealing a small, wiry Fae woman with messy hair. "My name's Suza, and I've been instructed to serve as your lady's maid during your stay here at Umbrea. Breakfast is almost ready, and King Ael is waiting for you." She moved to the closet doors and entered.

Seda noticed the angry scowl the woman made as she turned toward the closet. "There's no need. I'm fully capable of dressing myself," she stated.

"Nope, I'm to assist you," Suza replied firmly as she stepped out. "I've been instructed to help you in all the ways you might need." She held out a lavender gown with a built-in corset and a long skirt.

*So much for that,* Seda thought.

"Do you happen to have any pants in there?" The thought of that constricting dress sounded awful, especially with her still racing heart, and it wasn't that long ago she had to wear another uncomfortable dress.

Suza glared at Seda, eyes slitting into small open seams. "*No.* When you dine with a king, you *dress* for a king."

Seda didn't care how she looked for Cahir. She angrily got out of bed and moved toward Suza and the horrible gown. She muttered as the woman placed the gown on the chair beside her and waved her fingers for Seda to remove her nightgown.

"I'm not comfortable dressing in front of others. You need to leave while I put this on," Seda said as she crossed her arms over her chest and pointed her nose higher in the air.

The woman tried to argue with her, but she stayed firm. This woman wouldn't tell her what to do for every small thing. She had this choice, and she decided not to be naked in front of this snide Fae.

Suza hissed and stormed out of the room.

Seda waited for the door to close before pulling the dress over her hips and sliding her arms into the sleeves. She called for Suza, and the woman entered the doorway, wearing a scowl and quickly sliding her tongue across her lips.

"Turn around," Suza said with a commanding tone.

Seda turned, and Suza forcefully tugged on her dress, tightening the corset and making it difficult for her to breathe.

Suza lit a candle flame and began heating a curling rod. "Sit down, I need to do your hair."

The corset's tightness caused Seda to sit uncomfortably on the vanity stool. She looked in the mirror and gasped. Her hair was badly knotted, and it also shimmered more than usual.

Perhaps it was because it was finally clean? Maybe it always looked this way, and she never paid attention. Or maybe there was something in that conditioner she used?

She should have brushed her hair after her bath, but was so tired she forgot. Her hair was undeniably knotted from her journey and the tornado of Wisps.

"Do you know why your hair sparkles?" Suza asked her as she reached for the disaster atop her head.

"Don't know," Seda replied nonchalantly. Even if she did know, she didn't care to discuss it with her.

Suza aggressively brushed her hair, causing Seda to cry out several times in pain. However, when she finished, Seda was impressed with her work. She tried not to judge the poor girl for her own hair.

"This looks nice," Seda said when she was finished. Her hair had been pulled into an updo with long, loose curls hanging down, framing her face.

The woman harrumphed, blew out the candle, and walked to the door. "Of course it does. Come with me. I'll take you to the dining room."

"What about Elco?" Seda asked.

"Your friend is currently outside the castle, likely biting into the wolves that keep appearing," Suza replied.

Seda followed her through the castle, trying to remember the path so she could take it herself next time. When they reached the door, Suza knocked and opened it. The scent of coffee reached Seda's nose, making her mouth water.

Seda entered the room, and Cahir rose from his chair. Luelle, Meir, Neoma, and another man she didn't recognize sat beside him. When they saw Cahir stand, they also stood and waited for his orders.

Cahir was all smiles and looked refreshed, as if he had gotten hours of sleep. She was undeniably mad at him, especially now since he appeared to have slept well, and she hadn't.

A smile slipped across her lips, remembering how he reacted

to seeing her naked. He had run from her room like a frightened deer. So much for being this all-powerful king.

Unfortunately, something dormant had stirred deep within her last night when she saw how he had reacted to her. She suppressed the feeling.

*You're mad at that liar,* she reminded herself.

Today, though, his dimples and bright smile were on full display, accenting his pointed canines. His chestnut hair was tousled and hung over his forehead.

"You look beautiful, Seda. Welcome in," he said, mistaking her smile as politeness.

"Thank you, *Cahir*," she responded. She decided to continue using the name she knew. Fuck calling him King Ael. No way in hell was she about to do that.

"You're excused." Cahir looked at the wiry woman next to Seda, and Suza quickly bowed and left the room. "Seda, you've met Meir and Luelle, but I'd like you to meet Praxis." He pointed to a muscular, Fae man standing next to him, and he smiled at her. Seda noticed that he had left Neoma out of the introduction. "Praxis is my captain and my third advisor on the council."

"I apologize for last night," Praxis said as he approached her and extended his hand for Seda to shake. He shook her hand firmly, and she noticed him staring down at her chest, which was unfortunately showing too much cleavage from the wretched dress.

She cleared her throat. "It's fine. I assume I would've acted the same way if someone shattered my massive windows, too."

He smiled brightly at her and glanced back at Cahir, who was watching her with an almost predatory gaze. He wasn't staring at her breasts like he did the night before, or like Praxis just did, but instead focused solely on her eyes, which was slightly uncomfortable in its own way. She returned her gaze to Praxis and the others.

"It's nice to meet you. And nice to see you again," she politely said to everyone else in the room, even to Neoma.

Luelle huffed, "*King Ael,* may we please sit back down, and can we eat now? I'm *starving,* and these look amazing."

Cahir gave everyone a nod, and they all sat down except for Cahir. He gestured for Seda to come and sit next to him, pulling out her chair as if he were a gentleman. She hesitantly walked over, wishing instead to sit on the opposite side of the table, and begrudgingly sat down. She looked down at the table and the food on display.

Her eyes widened.

"Honey cakes and coffee?" she asked, her excitement slipping free.

"Honey cakes and coffee," Cahir answered with a dimpled grin.

She picked up a fork, digging into the warm cake and feeling the buttery, sweet texture melt in her mouth.

"Mmmmmmmmm," she softly moaned. It had been so long since she had one of these, and these were even better than the ones she remembered in Joro.

Cahir's hand tightened on his fork for a moment, and he shifted in his seat. Seda took another bite and sipped some of the sweetened, hot coffee.

"So, Seda, tell us about yourself," Praxis asked from across the table, drawing Seda away from her thoughts of Cahir.

She looked over at Praxis, and his rugged smile lit up his face.

"Well, I was raised in Joro by adoptive parents. I have a brother and worked in Gardvord with Cahir. I also recently escaped the Camp."

"How'd you escape the Camp?" Luelle asked as she bit into her own honey cake.

"Well, I had a little help from Elco and a surprise," she said, holding up her hands.

"How the hell did you befriend the Lionne?" Praxis asked. "I've never in my hundreds of years of life seen one, but I've heard ancient stories."

Thoughts immediately raced through her mind. *Hundreds of years? Hadn't Kalon seen one at some point?*

She swallowed another bite of honey cake and wiped her mouth. "We were locked in the same area at the Camp. We talked and became friends." She glanced over at Cahir. How old was he?

Meir looked at her with what almost looked like mock confusion and asked, "You can understand him, Seda?"

She nodded. He pulled out a notepad from his knitted sweater pocket and jotted something down. "What else can you do?"

"Just the purple electricity that you saw," she responded.

"She also has the loyalty of the Corvids," Cahir added.

Meir gasped as he glanced between Cahir and Seda. She noticed his eyes shift toward Neoma before he said, "The Corvids have no loyalty to anyone except themselves." He jotted more words down in his notebook.

Seda thought about Roya, Ferona, and Feich. Why had they wanted to protect her? She hoped Roya and Ferona were heading to Umbrea alongside her brother so she could see them again. She really missed Benny.

Cahir reached under the table and gently placed his hand on her knee, softly squeezing it. He whispered to her, "I'm sure they're on their way here now. Roya wouldn't stop at anything to stay close to you."

She tried to shift away from him, but he kept his hand where it was. She glared his way as she took another sip of her coffee. The warmth of his palm on her knee caused her cheeks to flush in frustration.

Luelle looked at her and asked, "What do you think, Seda?"

"What?" She wasn't paying attention. Cahir lightly squeezed her knee again and smiled down at her.

Luelle cleared her throat and looked between Cahir and Seda with raised brows. "Would you like to explore with me after breakfast? *King Ael* was just about to kick us out. He wanted to have a private conversation with you. But I'll wait outside if you'd like to."

"Oh, yes, please. I'd love that," she answered as she felt her cheeks heat again in embarrassment. It was obvious Luelle knew where his hand was. She took her fork and inconspicuously stabbed it into his hand, but he didn't remove it from her.

The others got up and excused themselves, quickly bowing to Cahir before leaving the room. Cahir waited for the door to close and for them to be alone before he turned her direction.

"That hurt," he said with a devious smile.

"It's *my* knee. Not yours." She tried jerking her knee away again.

His large hand clamped down with firm determination. "No, Seda. That's where you're wrong."

"*Excuse me?*" She felt anger ripple through her chest, and her power flared in her eyes when he smiled in response.

Cahir wasn't her fucking king. Who did he think he was?

She pressed her palm against his hand and emitted a small spark, causing him to quickly pull back his hand and hiss in pain.

"*No*, it's mine," she said with a defiant smile, but he grinned back at her like he held a secret she didn't know. She flared her magic again in her palms, readying to electrocute his stupid, dimpled face.

She inhaled a deep breath to steady herself. He was purposely agitating her, just like when he would fall asleep at work and wake up with what he thought were funny jokes. Sadly, she didn't have any mandarins to chuck at his face.

"How old are you, Cahir?" she asked, remembering what Praxis had said of his age and changing the subject.

He paused and averted his eyes briefly before turning his gaze back to her. "I'm three hundred and five."

"Three—" Seda stammered, her mouth falling open. "How are you still alive? And why do you look no older than thirty?"

"Aging looks different for the Fae," he replied with a shrug.

"You're decrepit," she snapped in annoyance at yet another falsehood he had given her, wanting it to sting a little bit, to hurt him in any way she could.

He laughed loudly, and she tried to hide the smile that his sound of laughter made her feel in return by pursing her lips and narrowing her eyes.

He rubbed his eyes and said, "In human terms, I guess I would be. But not in Fae. And you definitely aren't human either. Humans don't have magic like yours."

Her nerves prickled at her neck. What if she were just a fluke of a human?

"So, all four stones. Where do we start?" he asked.

She let out a relieved breath, allowing her shoulders to sag slightly. He wasn't going to make finding the stones difficult, at least. "Yes. Luelle mentioned you had a library. I want to visit—"

"Where's your necklace?" he interrupted, his eyes drifting over her exposed collarbones.

Seda instinctively touched her neck, longing for the chain's comfort. Cahir's eyes tracked her fingers grazing along her throat.

"Kalon stole it from me and left the group in the middle of the night," she said, and watched as Cahir's eyes widened.

"He *stole* it from you?" Cahir asked in a slow, quiet voice, causing chills to run down her spine. "How did he get it from you? Did he hurt you?" His gaze met hers again, anger simmering behind his storm-filled, emerald eyes.

"No. I don't know. I was asleep, and he was on the floor next to me." She made sure to add that part in, even though she wasn't sure why she felt the need to.

She reconsidered her stance. If Cahir was going to parade his women before her, she could do the same.

"It was after we *kissed*," she said, trying to hide her smirk. "And suddenly, I wake up, he's missing, and my necklace is gone. Someone saw him taking it in the middle of the night when he left."

Cahir's eyes darkened, and a low growl vibrated from his throat. "He put his *lips* on you?" The smallest bit of green magic expelled from his nostrils.

"...Yes." The hair on the back of her neck stood as she watched the magic escape him.

He watched her nervously bite her lips, and his eyes flared.

A painfully long and awkward silence stretched on before he finally cleared his throat and spoke, his voice rough, "That must be one of the stones. I've never seen one like that before. That fucker has probably been working for Mordred the entire time."

Nothing Kalon did made sense. He was kind and gentle with her. She had a fleeting moment of doubt when she refused to kiss him further, but nothing else he did suggested he was working for Lord Mordred or the monsters. Something about Kalon just felt... different, too. She wasn't sure what it was. But it was almost like she had known him much longer than she actually had.

She shrugged and said, "I don't know. I think researching the stone might be a good first step, though. Maybe I can find something written about it in the library."

Cahir continued watching her mouth before shifting his gaze up to meet hers. He cleared his throat. "I think that's a great start. I'll meet you there this afternoon. I have a few things I need to finish up first, but I'd love to help you look."

Seda nodded, eager to learn more about the stones and to potentially discover more information about herself.

She still felt the lingering warmth of his hand on her knee and perhaps also liked how he responded to Kalon's kiss.

# CHAPTER 7

<u>Seda</u>

Seda strolled with Luelle around the castle. The interior, both lavish and vibrant, was vastly different from her small, dusty apartment back in Joro. Everything was absolutely breathtaking, and everyone seemed to be in a joyful mood. The servants and guests joked and laughed as they went about their day, and children raced through the halls, their magic freely used. She saw women using their magic to clean, men moving heavy tables with it, and children flying paper airplanes farther than expected. They all used the same green mist as Cahir, which emanated from their palms to move objects. It was the most interesting thing she had ever seen, second to the magic of the Vatte in the Amanita Copse.

Seda's dress was still too tight, and her breathing felt restricted, causing her to ask Luelle to pause several times to catch her breath. They slowly stepped through the large front doors and into a green, grassy field lined with rows of colorful roses. Seda could smell the salt in the air from the nearby ocean, a smell she had never experienced before. It was fresh and alive, wild and free. Joro air was stuffy and constricting, and she suddenly felt the weight of the vast world around her.

"The roses were planted for Ael's mother," Luelle said as she pointed to the colorful assortment beyond.

Seda's interest piqued at the mention of Cahir's family, and she looked over to the roses in the distance, perfectly manicured and displaying a rainbow of colors. "They're beautiful," she replied. "What happened to her?"

Luelle pursed her lips as she stared into the distance. "She passed when Ael and I were children."

She wanted to ask more, eager to learn about Cahir and his past, but held back from pushing.

Seda spotted Elco lying in the grass, with children placing small flowers from the field into his mane, and pointed him out. Luelle smiled, and they walked closer to him.

When they neared, Seda said, "Yet again, I find the Lionne with children and flowers in his hair."

Elco opened a lazy eye at her and huffed warm air around them. The children giggled. "I'm where I want to be, moon-flutter. Don't disrupt them."

"I heard that you were eating wolves?" she pried.

"They taste like chicken."

"Well, I'm glad that you've stuck to your word and aren't eating the Fae." The same little girl from the night before looked up at Seda with wide eyes, and the flower she was about to place into Elco's hair fell to the ground. She ran away, glancing back at them as she hid behind a nearby green bush.

"Don't scare them away," Elco complained. Seda laughed and walked over to the bush, peering around it.

"Elco's nice, sweetie. He loves the flowers and how fancy they make him look. He won't hurt you, I promise." The little girl looked at her with big, brown eyes and hesitantly walked back over to Elco. She picked up the dropped flower and placed it in his hair, giving Seda a broad smile after she positioned it perfectly.

Elco purred under the touch, murmuring something about happiness and how it felt like his heart was melting its thick layer of ice.

"Would you like to see the gardens?" Luelle asked Seda. "It's through the hedge maze."

"Sure." The two left Elco behind as his purrs rumbled across the grass. Luelle led her through the large hedge maze, and they came out on the other side. Rows of lush gardens greeted them, and the little green orbs fluttered all around the plants.

"The essence makes our plants grow stronger," Luelle answered her silent question. "Umbrea's produce is unmatched in all of Xyberus."

Seda watched the orbs. "I see that. Back in Joro, we had a plant science division called Gardvord. Cahir and I worked there, studying the decline of produce being harvested."

Is this what Joro was missing? Magic?

"And what did you discover?" Luelle asked.

"Nothing. Plants need sunlight, good soil, pollination, and water. We couldn't find anything that could explain the decline."

Luelle looked at the plants alongside Seda, and the two watched as the orbs fluttered around. Like little bees kissing the tops of flowers, they bounced around, almost as if playing through the fields.

"Life needs balance. Nature needs love," Luelle stated as she stared at the garden.

Seda glanced over a distant tree line and saw a thin plume of green smoke rising into the sky. "What's that?" she asked.

Luelle rolled her eyes. "That's that nasty witch, Tahti. She's always brewing up something that stinks up the air. Be careful if you go there, Seda. That woman may be an Oracle, but she's heavy-handed with her broom. Last time I went, she hit me over the head with it. I had a bump for hours."

"You said she's an Oracle?" Seda asked, intrigued, recalling her discussion with Cahir. "I'd love to talk to her."

Luelle huffed, "We can go there if you want, but I'll stay outside if she allows you in."

"Do we have time?"

Luelle looked up to the sun and back at Seda. "We'd have to be quick."

They walked through the trees while pine needles crunched beneath their feet. Tahti's cabin slowly appeared, and the smell of roasted meat and chemicals drifted around them. Luelle paused at the white picket fence gate and turned to Seda. "This is as far as I go. I'll be right here. I strongly dislike that woman."

Seda paused, sensing anxiety beginning to creep up her spine, but she inhaled a restricted breath and moved toward the front door.

Loud screaming came from inside the cabin, and the door swung open.

"Your presence isn't welcome here!" someone yelled.

Seda quickly jumped back, and Neoma ran out backwards, a broom smacking the woman on the head.

"*OUCH*! You fucking mean, old thing!" Neoma yelled before spinning around and colliding with Seda. They both fell to the ground, with Neoma landing on top of her.

The door loudly slammed shut.

"I'm sorry, Seda!" Neoma exclaimed as she rose and brushed the dirt from her dress. Her dark hair was a mess, with bits and pieces of the broom tangled within.

Seda was gasping, trying to catch her breath with the stupid dress blocking her airflow. Neoma extended her hand and helped Seda to her feet.

"What are you doing here?" Seda asked her.

"Yeah, what *are* you doing here?" Luelle asked from behind. They both looked back at her as she picked at her nails, not staring at them as she spoke.

"I... I wanted to see if she could give me a... *a love potion*," Neoma fumbled.

"A love potion for whom, exactly?" Luelle asked as she narrowed her eyes at her.

Neoma fidgeted with her dress and said, "Umm... my brother. It was his one ask for me when I came to the castle."

"Is that so?" Luelle said slowly as she stared Neoma down, her eyes narrowing further.

"Yes. Well... it was nice seeing you, Seda. Maybe we can catch up later? I plan on joining you guys for dinner tonight," Neoma said.

Seda looked at her in bewilderment. Why would she lie about a love potion? Was it for Cahir? It was clearly not the truth. What else could she want from this witch?

"Yes, I'll see you tonight," she replied hesitantly.

"Sorry about knocking into you. She really got me good with that broom." Neoma walked up the path and slowed as she passed Luelle, who watched her pass. After she cleared the area, she picked up her pace and ran through the trees, quickly disappearing through their camouflage.

"I don't believe her," Seda whispered to herself.

Luelle tilted her head and glanced at Seda. "Me neither. No one admits to using a love potion. That's embarrassing, to say the least. And they also don't last long enough to make a difference." Luelle rolled her eyes and continued picking her nails. "You sure you want to go in?"

Seda nodded and tried to take a deep breath to gather the courage to knock on the door. She raised her hand, and the door swung open again. A short, wrinkly woman stood there, staring intently at Seda.

"*Finally*," the witch said to Seda, looking up. "I've been waiting for you."

"You have?" Seda asked nervously, fidgeting with her dress.

The older woman moved aside, and Seda bravely stepped in, closing the door behind her but not before glancing back at Luelle to ensure she wasn't leaving her alone.

# CHAPTER 8

<u>Seda</u>

The room was dark and musty, wrapping Seda's exposed skin in a dense cloud of humid air, while a bubbling cauldron simmered with thick green liquid at its center. Tahti looked at Seda and grinned broadly, revealing sharp, stained teeth.

Trying not to be rude, Seda smiled back and averted her gaze as she looked around the room. Her eyes caught on disgusting bottles of brown liquid with floating body parts on the shelves. She tried to suppress her gag and covered her watering mouth with her hand.

"You are the key, young Seda." Seda looked over at Tahti, and Tahti blinked, her eyes clouding to a milky white.

Seda gasped and took a hesitant step back toward the door, grabbing for the handle.

She felt the cool metal and took a deep breath to steady herself. She was here for questions. She could be brave and had seen worse before. She released the handle and quietly asked, "What do you know?"

Tahti watched as her hand retracted from the door, and a smirk formed on her lips. "You are the key to saving Xyberus. You're the only one who can open the door." She took a step closer to her, and Seda bristled.

"What does that mean? The Wisps told me I need to find stones and harmony. Would you know what I need?"

"I would know of the stones, but the harmony is up to you." Tahti backed away from her and limped toward the boiling cauldron. She collected spit from deep in her throat and spat it into the liquid. A plume of green mist rose into the air, revealing images of four glowing stones, each with a different shape and color.

Seda lurched forward when she saw the stone from her necklace in the image. "I was right! My moonstone!"

"You will need the Stone of Protection." She pointed to Seda's stolen moonstone. "The Stone of Love," she said, pointing at an anatomical heart-shaped ruby. "The Stone of Peace," she continued, indicating the diamond-shaped sapphire. "And the Dark Stone. The Dark Stone is the Stone of *Power*."

Seda moved closer to the images, feeling the cool mist brush her cheeks and a foreign smell, not entirely unpleasant, filled her nostrils. She examined the stones. She had only seen one of these before. "Where would I find these?"

"One was already yours, but you still need to find the others. King Ael tried to get the Dark Stone for you but failed. That stupid fool." Tahti crinkled her nose in disgust.

"Lord Mordred has it," Seda replied.

Tahti furrowed her eyebrows as her blank eyes stared intently at her. "He does not, child. Mordred is not the abuser of the Stone of Power."

For a moment, Seda thought she had misheard. Thoughts

raced through her mind. If Mordred didn't have the stone, then who did? "Who has it?" she asked.

"The Monster King," Tahti replied as she raised her hand and touched the mist with her fingers, swirling it around in the air. She waited for Seda to part her lips to ask who that was before she cut her off. "Don't know. Don't ask."

Where could the rest of these be? She needed to find Kalon and get hers back. Anger surged through her body, and her palms lit up when she thought about him stealing from her.

"Now, now, child…" Tahti looked at Seda's palms. "You need to practice conserving that. It's not unlimited, you know."

"I didn't know that." Seda looked at her palms and drew her power back in, letting them return to their natural color. All her practice during the trip to the Wisps was paying off. She knew how to call on it easily. All she had to do was think about what made her angry. To pull the power back in, she needed to breathe calmly and stay grounded.

"All magic has limits. You must conserve and use only what you need. This is a good practice. The orbs you see flying around here can help you recharge quickly, but they do not exist in other parts of Xyberus. When you leave here, you'll only have so much to give, and recharging your reserves without them takes time."

"Why do they only exist here?" Seda asked. She remembered how the orbs moved around her and the sense of completeness they left behind.

"It was the Mother Goddess's first gift to Umbrea before she created the Fae," Tahti responded with a shrug.

Seda looked out the small, crooked window at the green orbs flying around. "Is there anything else I should know?"

Tahti blinked again, and her eyes reverted to their natural color. She screamed and tore at her hair. "Please go, child. I can't endure this so many times in a single day. Please *go*."

Seda rushed out the door and slammed it shut behind her, muffling the screams inside. She leaned against it, her heart pounding wildly in her chest, and inhaling restricted breaths of the fresh outdoor air.

Luelle watched her from the gate. "Unfair." She pouted at Seda.

"What is?" she asked.

"She didn't hit you with the broom," Luelle responded.

Seda nervously laughed, glancing back at the door, and walked toward Luelle.

LUELLE AND SEDA stopped at the library doors. Seda was eager to get inside and see if she could find information on the stones that Tahti had mentioned.

"You sure you'll be okay in there alone?" Luelle asked her.

She responded with a smile and said, "Yes, I'll find my way around."

"Good, I have something I need to follow up on. I'll see you tonight at dinner. You should change out of that miserable dress. You can't breathe in it. Ael said he asked the chef to make something good," Luelle said as she winked at Seda.

"I'd love to wear anything except this thing." She looked down at the constricting dress with a frown.

Luelle laughed and inclined her head toward Seda's chest. "I noticed several Fae looking there today. Even a certain king of mine."

Seda chuckled nervously. She hadn't noticed Cahir watching her, but he was adamant about his hand on her knee.

"I'll see you later," Luelle said as she walked down the hall, whistling and bouncing her ponytail as she left.

Seda turned around and opened the thick wooden door to

the library, and her eyes widened in awe. Three stories of books greeted her, with floor-to-ceiling stained-glass windows casting a soft green light into the room. The rich-toned wood of the shelves and tables all matched, and the most enormous chandelier she had ever seen hung from the center of the room, hundreds of sparkling candles lit, the wax slowly dripping onto a large table at its base. Multiple Fae were inside, seated at the many tables and quietly reading.

She approached a desk where an older woman sat. The woman looked up at her curiously, glasses resting low on her long nose. "I haven't encountered a human in ages. What brings you here, young lady? What can I help you find?"

"I was hoping you could point me toward mysterious stones? Specifically, any information about a moon-shaped stone," Seda asked.

The librarian pursed her lips and placed a finger on her chin before muttering something and smiling. She walked around the counter. "I'm not sure if this is what you're looking for, but I'll lead you to the section of crystals and similar items. Perhaps you can find something of interest there. If not, feel free to come back to me, and we can look around some more."

She followed her up to the third floor and down several aisles, noting the row numbers as she passed. The librarian stopped at a section of the bookshelf, and Seda browsed through the titles.

*"The Properties of Crystals."*
*"Where to find Gemstones."*
*"Gemstone Hunting."*

None of them looked quite right, but she thanked the woman who quietly left the area. Seda searched through the bookshelves, muttering in frustration. None of the books looked remotely helpful, but she didn't want to return to the librarian and ask for more help.

She slowly walked around the library, searching for the history section and examining the titles on each shelf. She turned a corner and bumped into someone carrying a stack of books and scrolls, which covered their face. All the items fell to the floor.

"I'm sorry," Seda said as she bent down to help pick up the fallen items. She looked up, seeing Meir, and a strange feeling crept up her spine. "Oh… hello."

He responded with an eerie smile. "Hello, Seda. No worries. I tend to overload."

She looked at the fallen items. They were all texts and scrolls written in a foreign language. She noted the word *custos* on several titles and handed him a couple.

She suppressed the shudder she felt from being so close to this man, and asked, "Maybe you can help me? I was looking for the history section. Can you point me in the right direction, please?"

"Yes. Follow me. I have some questions I'd like to ask you, if that's okay? I'd love to learn more about your powers."

She helped him gather the remaining scrolls, carrying some for him as they went. They moved farther into the second floor and found a table to place the items on.

"History's all in here." He waved his hands around him toward the alcove of books. There were hundreds of them. "It's a rather large section."

She reached for a book title as he sat back in his chair, adjusted his glasses, and looked at her. "Do you love King Ael?"

Seda hesitated, almost dropping the book. Why would he ask that? She paused before responding, "He was my best friend in Joro, my only true friend there outside of my family."

Meir looked at her without saying anything, slowly chewing

his thumbnail and watching her. "How did your powers emerge?"

"Umm..." She wasn't sure how much she wanted to share about herself or her past, but she said, "I defended myself at the Camp and it just... happened."

Meir continued watching her with his hand under his chin, listening to her words. "And what happened then?"

"Well, the man died. He was electrocuted. Elco disposed of the body for me before anyone found out."

"Have you ever experienced anything weird or strange that might have indicated you had a power before this? Has anything traumatizing ever happened to you before?" he asked, his eyes widening in anticipation and a slight smirk cresting his lips.

"No and ... no," she lied. She didn't feel comfortable telling him the truth about Michael and Alexi all those years ago. The fewer people who knew, the better. She didn't want anyone to judge her or think less of her, and she really didn't want people to pity her. She had grown so much since being at the Camp and living in Joro. She no longer cowered or cried in fear. She didn't want to be seen as weak, even if it made no logical sense. It was her business and her business only.

"And King Ael said that the Corvids are loyal to you?" he asked.

"What do you mean by loyal? Roya and Ferona have said that they have protected me for years. I had no idea they were watching over me." She felt this conversation needed to end, and fast.

He smiled brightly and pressed, "Loyalty, like you telling them what to do, as if they are your servants."

Seda's sudden burst of laughter caught Meir by surprise, and his bushy eyebrows flew up. This felt like too much. First, he was asking her private questions, and now he was making assumptions. Roya and the others weren't tied to her in any way, and she didn't give them commands. They were... *mysteriously*... protecting her. She turned to face the window and watched the shadow of the green orbs outside dance around behind the colored glass. "I don't command the Corvids."

His slitted eyes met hers. "Interesting. Perhaps you could? Have you tried?"

She needed to escape these questions and this man. "Thank you for showing me where the history section is, Meir. It was nice to see you again. I'll see you tonight at dinner, right?" She wanted to leave quickly. That same creepy sensation was rising up her spine again.

"You don't want to look around?" He held his hands out toward the books lining the shelves around them and smiled at her.

"Oh, I'll be back. I have a few things that need to be completed. Thank you for showing me where the section is, though."

He studied her before saying, "Then, yes, I'll see you tonight. Neoma will be there, too. As you know, she's also new."

"Sounds good," she replied as she retreated towards the staircase leading to the exit of the library. She exited through the doors, leaving that intrusive man behind and fighting the oily feeling he left her with.

She headed to her bedroom, walking past the large, double doors to the East Wing, and noticed two guards posted at her door. She paused and looked at them. "Hello, my room is behind these doors."

The guard with brown hair and a long beard looked at her and chuckled. His gaze flicked to the other guard with trimmed black hair and a narrow face. They both smiled.

"Is something funny?" She narrowed her eyes at them.

"No, Seda Arbor. Nothing's funny. We know who you are, and King Ael has told us to wait for you and guard your door.

Please don't electrocute us," the bearded guard said, and they both laughed.

"May I please enter my room?" She scoffed at their lack of good humor. They stepped aside, and she walked in. What was Cahir worried about that she needed guards at her door? Especially those two? She went inside and reached around her back to pull the laces of her dress. They wouldn't budge.

She spent a few minutes trying to untie them and had just begun to pull at the laces, tightening them in the process, when a knock on her door drew her attention. "Yes?" she asked with irritation, trying to breathe through the constricting corset.

Cahir opened the door and entered, smiling at her as he always did—sincerely, cheerfully, and frustratingly charming. He noticed her tied-up fingers in her laces and paused his steps into the room. "Should I leave?"

"No... no, don't go. Can you please help me loosen these? I've been trapped in this damn dress all day, and I desperately need to get it off." She turned away from him and listened to his footsteps as he slowly approached her.

She felt the tickle of his breath brushing her neck as he leaned down and gently touched the laces. Goosebumps rose on her arms and shoulders, and he paused behind her. The room seemed to close in as she focused on the amplified sound of him and the sensation of his warm fingers.

Why had he stopped? Did he notice her goosebumps? He slowly started to gently tug at the bottom lace above her backside and gradually loosen it from her back, his fingers softly grazing the skin between her shoulder blades.

Her heartbeat quickened, and she felt that warm, tingly sensation start low in her stomach again.

"You have small bumps on your back," he said as he brushed along her skin once more.

So he did notice.

After he finished, she inhaled a deep breath. The sweet relief of not being constricted was like a breath of fresh air, and she moaned as her top loosened and the shoulder straps fell off. She heard his breath hitch behind her and turned around to look at him. He was bent over her, staring down at her neck, and his rich, green eyes met hers, their noses almost touching. Heat surged deep within her as she looked into his eyes and then lowered her gaze to his lips. She licked her own, and his eyes followed the movement.

"Seda, I—" he began, reaching toward her, but then someone knocked on the door. He swiftly pulled back.

Seda cleared her throat and quickly rushed to the closet, away from Cahir and whoever was waiting outside. She stepped into the room, easing the door shut behind her, and stood listening, her breath caught tightly in her chest.

"Come in," she heard Cahir say.

She silently reprimanded herself for having *any* feelings when he was near, reminding herself that he was a liar. But seeing his reaction to her empowered her, giving her a newfound strength she hadn't realized she possessed. What if she could use this for her own benefit?

"Oh, Sire… I wasn't expecting you here. I just came to see if Seda was available for a walk." She could hear Neoma's voice from the door. Jealousy curled her stomach as she remembered Neoma's breasts exposed for Cahir when she arrived at the castle.

Had Cahir made love to that woman? Did he touch Neoma gently, the same way he just touched her? Did he cause her goosebumps to rise on her arms?

"Seda had a long day today and is resting before dinner. She'll see you then," he said to Neoma.

She heard the door close and quickly changed out of the dress into something comfortable, putting on a shirt and soft shorts from the dresser. She stepped out of the closet and saw Cahir sitting in a chair near the window. He looked down at her legs and back up. A half smile appeared on his lips, with his dimple catching the light from the window.

"That's the Seda I remember," he said approvingly.

Feeling awkward and a little angry at herself for caring who Cahir touched, she changed the subject, "I met Tahti today."

Cahir tensed and asked, "Luelle took you there? Be careful of Tahti, Seda. My mother passed away with her present."

Curiosity piqued within Seda. She didn't know anything about Cahir's past or family. "What happened to her?"

Cahir stared out of the window, his eyes tracking a singular green orb outside. His voice came out in a whisper, "My mother was the light in my dark childhood. I have vague memories of her. I remember hearing her scream, and then I remember crying beside her casket." He bit the inside of his cheek.

Seda stood, stunned and frozen, unsure how to react. Cahir had never once talked about his family before, and admitting that last bit must have weighed heavily on him, because he slumped and placed his hands over his face.

"I'm sorry, Cahir," she replied.

He looked up at her and struggled to smile. "Tell me how the visit was with Tahti."

She released a breath. "She was... interesting. She shared something that could be valuable, though." She moved further into the room and sat on the bed's edge, feeling her legs grow weak from the weight of the prior topic.

"What was it?" he asked.

"She told me about the four stones. She didn't tell me where to find them, but she told me what they are." She reiterated what Tahti had told her about the stones and that she had gone to the library to find more information, but had been unlucky in her search. She left out running into Meir there and his weird questions. Cahir sat there and watched her talk, not saying much in return, just listening intently.

"I know what the Stone of Peace is and where to find it," Cahir said after she finished her story.

Seda perked up. "Where do I find it?"

"It's the Umbrea Stone, gifted to my father shortly after the war with the monsters. It was once inlaid into the crown, but it was stolen when I was a child. Now they say that La Uma has it."

"Who's La Uma?" Seda frowned. How was she supposed to get not only a family heirloom, but one held by someone else?

Cahir hesitated before saying, "She's, unfortunately, a monster that lives north of here. She mostly sticks to herself, thankfully."

"*What?* How did she get it?" she asked as anxiety coiled around her. How was *she* going to get it from this beast?

"I'm not sure. But, it's believed that La Uma only hunts men." He looked away from her. "We should talk to Tahti once more to ask her what she knows of her."

How would they get the stone out of her hands? And why would he give her a family heirloom like that once they had it back? It had to be valuable, judging by the size of the hole in his crown, and it must have had sentimental value to him.

"Tahti told me Mordred doesn't hold the Dark Stone. That the Monster King does. Do you know who that is?" she asked.

Cahir furrowed his brows. "Mordred isn't the one in charge down there?"

"No... apparently he isn't," Seda replied as she bit her lower lip. "How will I get back into Joro with these stones anyway? And how will I even find the Stone of Love? I can't just sit around here and wear pretty dresses, Cahir. I need to find these stones so I can help the people of Joro."

Cahir sat there for a long moment before sighing. "We'll find it. We can research together tomorrow. I went to the library earlier looking for you, but Meir said that you left."

Seda nodded, not wanting to talk about Meir.

"I need to get going, but I'll see you tonight. We'll find them. Also, don't worry about the guards at the door. They're just there for protection—mainly for my peace of mind rather than yours. I know you can handle yourself now. I'm so proud of you." He rose to hug Seda but hesitated, choosing to walk to the door instead.

He looked back at her and gave her a small smile before leaving the room and closing the door behind him.

Seda lay back on the bed and thought about the events of the day. Breakfast was a surprise. She reflected on how kind it was of Cahir to bring honey cakes and coffee, as if it were another apology, a way to remind them of how they first became friends.

Could she really trust him, though? Probably not. Not trusting Cahir was definitely the best plan. She just needed to tread carefully and play this part effectively.

She needed his help to get the Stone of Peace. That must have been what the Wisps meant by sending her here, saying she needed his help. He at least knew where one was.

She reflected on Luelle and how much she had enjoyed her company earlier. She was genuinely fun to be around, and her rebellious spirit felt like a breath of fresh air after meeting people in Joro. She also thought about Neoma walking out of Tahti's cabin, claiming she wanted a love potion from her, and how Neoma had come to her door not long ago.

She really didn't like or trust that woman. Something felt off. Why did Neoma want to be friends with her? And finally, she considered Cahir willingly offering to help retrieve the Stone of Peace alongside her, something clearly important to him and his kingdom.

She sighed and looked up through the ceiling at the orbs and the sky. She sat there for a long time, deciphering shapes from the passing clouds, when someone knocked again at her door.

*Please, gods, don't be Neoma,* she thought.

"Come in," Seda called out with a groan. The door opened, and Suza walked in, her hair an even greasier mess than it had been this morning.

Seda pursed her lips. She should have included her in her prayer.

"I'm here to get you ready for dinner," Suza said curtly as she walked over to the closet and threw open the doors. She stepped inside, ruffled some things around, and walked out with a silky green dress.

"Does this one tie really tight, too?" Seda asked.

"No, but I can find one that does if you want." She waited for Seda to respond, and when Seda shook her head, she walked over to her. "Now, I know you said you don't want me to dress you physically, so I'm going to turn around and wait for you to put this on." Suza turned around, preventing her from arguing in response.

Seda ground her teeth together as she glared at the woman's greasy head.

As Seda undressed and pulled the gown over herself, she continued to glare daggers at her, hoping her eyes could fry that messy hair further. She thought she saw a flicker of something, like she had something stuck in her hair, but she looked away, no longer wanting to focus on the mean Fae before her.

When she was done, the woman turned around, and her eyes flashed when she saw her in the gown. "Let's do your hair. Hopefully, you didn't tangle it all up again."

She sat down on the vanity stool, and Suza worked on her hair. She was gentler this time, or maybe it was because Seda's hair wasn't such a disaster as before. She styled her hair to cascade down her back, placed an emerald hairpin in her hair, and stepped back, admiring her work. "If anyone deserves to be a queen, it should be someone as beautiful as you, even if you are a human-*thing*."

Seda was about to respond curtly, saying she had no interest in being a stupid queen, when Suza made her get up and walk to the door. "What about my shoes?"

Suza ran to the closet, grabbed some matching, silky green flats, and handed them to Seda. She slipped them on and followed the woman into the hall. The guards did a double-take when she walked out, and the guard with the beard cleared his throat and nudged the other in the arm. Both of them straightened up and stared ahead.

Seda followed Suza through the halls and paused at a full-length mirror. Her dress was stunning, unlike anything she had ever worn before. It reached her ankles, with a slit running up her left thigh. The neckline was low and hugged the curves of her body she usually kept hidden.

This dress was too much to wear to dinner tonight. She grasped the fabric between her fingers, the green silk feeling too thin, unable to shield her from what lay ahead.

She inwardly groaned and continued following her lady's maid, letting the distance grow between them as they walked, not wanting to enter the dining room looking like this.

Suza silently pulled open the dining room door and waited for Seda to approach. The laughter and chatter in the room fell silent as everyone turned to Seda. She glanced around at the people in the candlelit room and awkwardly waved. Her gaze drifted to Cahir and noticed his parted lips frozen in wordless astonishment.

She knew this dress was too much.

Luelle reached across the table and lifted his chin for him, and he quickly cleared his throat. "Seda, please sit here again." He gestured to the seat next to him on the right.

She briefly considered walking to the other side of the table to spite him, a form of defiance against his command, but decided against it and walked to the chair he suggested. She sat down and fiddled with the silk of her dress, her ears burning with embarrassment as everyone silently watched her take her seat, their faces bathed in the candlelight's glow.

"What are we having tonight, Sire?" Praxis broke the silence. He kept gazing at Seda, then back at Cahir. She tried to shift lower in her seat, attempting to hide herself as much as possible under the table.

"I know what *King Ael* wants," Luelle joked, and Praxis laughed in agreement. Luelle wiggled her eyebrows suggestively between Seda and Cahir.

"Show some respect!" Meir scolded Luelle with an angry, red face that resembled a tomato, and his thick eyebrows furrowed in frustration.

Luelle exaggeratedly mimicked his expression, silently moving her lips and furrowing her brows, while Seda fought back a smile at her brazenness.

"Duck and roasted potatoes and some other things," Cahir replied to Praxis, ignoring the argument and not denying the insinuations.

"Seda, would you like to go for a walk tomorrow morning?" Neoma asked politely. Her dress was low-cut, nearly revealing her breasts. Seda felt a bit more comfortable with her own outfit after noticing hers.

Seda saw Praxis's eyes lingering on Neoma and let out a sigh of relief that his attention wasn't solely on her.

"How did your potion work for you, Neoma?" Luelle asked as she took a sip of wine, her blood-red lipstick leaving a mark on the crystal.

"Umm…" Neoma started.

"What potion?" Meir interrupted, sharply looking at Neoma.

"Oh, we saw Neoma leaving the witch earlier today. Did you have a nice conversation with her?" Luelle took another sip of her wine and exhaled loudly. "Something about... What was it again?"

"Just a beauty tincture," Neoma replied quickly, readjusting her top. Praxis noticed the movement and watched her breasts rise and fall.

Luelle rolled her eyes and took a deep drink. She roughly set the glass back on the table, the crystal clinking loudly against the wood and spilling scarlet liquid.

"Is there something you want to say, Luelle?" Cahir asked.

"No, *Sire*. Nothing." She smiled sweetly between him and Neoma. "Nothing at all." She let out a deep sigh and rolled her eyes once more.

The doors opened, and servants entered carrying trays of food. Roast duck and potatoes, garlic green beans, fresh buns, and other delicious dishes that Seda couldn't name.

Her mouth watered.

Cahir placed his hand on Seda's exposed knee again and gently brushed his thumb back and forth. She wanted to pull away, but that effort was futile last time. Her cheeks burned with irritation as she casually reached over to fill her plate with food.

She took a bite of the warm, buttery bread and licked her lips. It was so soft and lightly sweetened, *perfect*. She slightly lifted herself from her seat to reach the potatoes, and as she did, his hand shifted higher on her thigh.

Seda glared at him, but a warm heat spread low through her. She sighed to herself and went back to her plate. She didn't move his hand away when she sat back down. Instead, she placed her palm over his and encouraged him to keep rubbing his thumb back and forth.

*Fine*, she thought. She could play this game, too.

She heard a faint growl coming from him, too soft for anyone else to notice, and she smiled. She was feeling gleefully spiteful.

She took a bite of the roasted duck and purposely moaned as she chewed. His hand subtly tightened on her thigh.

"This is delicious," she said as she looked at him with hooded eyes and slowly licked her lips. He watched her mouth with a starved expression. "You look hungry. Do you want to try the duck?"

"You mean does he want to *fuck*—" A hiccup. "You?" Luelle slurred, inebriated from the wine. She held up her glass in the air, and a servant walked over and poured more for her.

"Unacceptable!" Meir shouted at Luelle. "You will show respect for your king, or you can leave this room!"

"Meir, I can handle this, thank you," Cahir interjected. "Luelle, that was impolite. You may leave now." He smiled at her and inclined his head toward the door.

Luelle gave him a little wink, stood up while holding her glass, and grabbed two more fresh buns from the table before leaving the room and slamming the door behind her.

"Is she always this crude?" Neoma pouted as Luelle exited through the doors. Seda caught her staring at Cahir's arm placement on her lap and smiled to herself while hiding her smirk through a sip of wine.

"That's her middle name, after all," Praxis joked. Cahir chuckled in response.

"Is it really?" Neoma asked, her face clearly forced into a look of shock.

"No, it's Crina. But I like Crude more. Fits better," Praxis said, and both he and Cahir laughed again.

Cahir's hand slid under the split in her dress, caressing the soft inner part of her thigh. Goosebumps spread across her legs as Cahir gently rubbed them, causing a slow ache to spread through her core.

"Seda, will you be in the library tomorrow?" Meir asked her sweetly, as if he were a father figure in her life, wanting to help. She noted that the tomato-red in his face had faded.

Cahir slowly moved his fingers higher, gently tracing the hemline of her underwear, and Seda struggled not to whimper.

"Um..." She couldn't focus as Cahir's warm fingers were so close to her sensitive skin, choking out a strained, "Yes."

"Perfect! Perhaps I can meet you there tomorrow, and we can explore some history, as you had wanted to do today. Maybe after your walk with Neoma?" Meir said excitedly.

Cahir's hand was dangerously close to slipping under her underwear, and she had to hold back a groan from escaping her lips.

"Yes, sounds nice," she said, masking a soft moan, and picked up her glass of wine again to focus on. The warm liquid pooled in her stomach, and her vision started to blur.

"Seda won't be able to meet you tomorrow at the library. We're working on something together," Cahir said.

"Oh?" Meir asked, raising an eyebrow. "Is there something I can help with?"

"No, but if that changes, I'll let you know. Thank you, Meir, for always being so... *helpful*." Cahir's face was set in a perfect mask of neutrality as his fingers lightly explored the edge of the thin fabric, getting dangerously closer with each stroke.

She shifted in her seat and slightly parted her legs, granting him access. She had never done anything like this before in her life, and the thought excited her. She was being reckless, but she didn't want to stop. Her body was throbbing, and she felt desire, something she had never really felt before, at least not in this capacity. She had never allowed herself to feel things like this, and that ache deep within was all-consuming.

Cahir's hand froze, and he didn't accept the invitation. He

remained close, but didn't move his fingers where she now wanted them.

Seda felt a slight drop in her heart and looked over at Neoma, who was staring at them with wide-eyed curiosity. Others didn't see what was happening, but it was clear something was going on if they paid attention, and Neoma *was* paying attention.

The doors burst open, and four guards rushed inside. They bowed quickly and stood up, looking at Cahir. One guard said, "Sire, there are guests who have just arrived. They're requesting an audience immediately."

# CHAPTER 9

<u>Luelle</u>

That dinner was terrible, like saggy balls. Praxis's saggy balls.

Luelle chuckled to herself at her hilarious humor as she walked through the empty, old servants' halls. She made her way to the spot where she had previously seen Meir and Neoma screwing and sat in the chair that her fabulous self remembered to set up for her future, more fabulous self. She sipped her wine and munched on her bread, waiting for someone to arrive.

Ael knew she was planning her escape from the dinner. They had talked earlier about Meir's and Neoma's strange behavior, and Ael had asked her to keep a close eye on the two. She was glad that her fake, drunken act fooled them, allowing her to escape and get early access to watch the room. She really hoped someone would spill the beans tonight. They were both acting so damn weird. She could feel that they were hiding something. Meir never just took anyone in because they hadn't seen the castle before. The whole situation was suspicious, and Ael knew it too.

A few minutes later, just as Luelle was about to doze off from boredom in the uncomfortable chair, she heard the door open roughly and peeked through the hole.

*Ugh... No!* she thought, fighting back an audible groan.

Neoma and Praxis were roughly kissing. He had his hand inside her tacky dress and was roughly squeezing her breast. Luelle rolled her eyes.

*That man would fuck anything that walks.*

They fell onto the bed abruptly, making it squeak. Praxis tore off his shirt and ripped Neoma's dress open from the front.

"Hey, I liked this one," Neoma playfully chided him as she wiggled her body, letting her overly large breasts sway back and forth.

"I like it better this way," Praxis said as he dove face-first into her chest. Neoma let out a fake moan, and she reached down and peeled her underwear off. Praxis lowered his face to her core and blew on it.

Neoma fake moaned again.

*Ugh, this woman. And why do men fall for fake moans? Stupid idiots.*

He smashed his head between her thighs, and she cried out like it was the best thing she had ever felt.

*I know for a fact he sucks at this,* she thought, covering her mouth with her hand and fighting the urge to laugh loudly at the display.

A faint chuckle escaped silently as she watched Praxis try his hardest with his short tongue to eat Neoma out. He stopped, stood up, and ripped his pants off. His extra-large cock sprang free, and Neoma gasped.

Luelle smirked when she saw his balls, just as saggy as the last time she saw them.

*His cock is his only saving grace, sweetie.*

Praxis spread Neoma's legs apart and shoved himself in hard. Neoma moaned loudly, and her eyes flared open wide. Praxis fucked her quickly, grunting loudly through each thrust, and Luelle was about to pack up and leave when she saw Neoma reach over to the side table and grab a small, glass vial of green liquid.

Luelle paused and watched with bated breath. Was that what she received from the witch? Praxis's grunting was loud, and the bed was rocking against the wall roughly. Neoma was struggling as she poured a small amount onto Praxis's back, and his body shifted into the perfect form of Ael, slightly shorter, but still Ael.

*What the fuck. This fucking weirdo!* She thought as her anger bubbled over.

She watched as Neoma hid the vile with the remaining green liquid under a nearby pillow, turning her attention back to Praxis. She moaned loudly and forced Praxis over, climbing on top of him and sliding his cock back into her. She rocked her hips quickly and fucked him hard, her moans finally real. Luelle noticed the dark wing of a tattoo on her back that she hadn't seen before.

Luelle bit her nails, lost in thought. This woman was causing problems. She knew Ael had feelings for Seda, and she could tell Seda felt *something* in return. They just needed time to work things out. She quite liked Seda and didn't want to see her hurt.

She needed to find Ael and tell him what she had seen as soon as possible.

Luelle turned away from the gross scene and ran through the darkened corridor.

# CHAPTER 10

<u>Ael</u>

A el quickly left the dining room and followed the guards to the front doors. His mood had soured with their distraction. It was the first time he had been that close to Seda, and he really wanted to go back to her. Her aroused scent lingered in his senses.

He felt her invitation when she parted her legs, and he *really* wanted to accept it, but like the love-drunk fool he was, he hesitated. If he had touched her there, he wouldn't have been able to control himself and would have thrown her onto the table, taken her as a meal, and sent everyone out of the room.

When the front doors of the castle appeared, he saw five people standing nearby, staring awkwardly at the castle's architecture. Their weathered look, with torn clothing and muddy skin, indicated they had traveled quickly to get here.

Roya, Ferona, Benny, Ojore, and Askold had come for Seda. They all turned toward him when they heard his thunderous steps, and Benny and Askold gasped at his changed appearance.

Roya marched forward, unfazed at seeing him in his Fae form. Her usually pristine hair was a tangled mess. "Where is she?" she seethed.

"Holy shit, man, *you're huge*," Benny said as he approached him and gave him a big hug. "Please tell us that Seda made it to you? We lost her at the Wisps."

"Seda's here, and she's fine," he replied as he bent down low to return Benny's hug, glancing at Roya.

Askold looked at him and awkwardly bowed. "King Ael."

"Get up, you fucking fool. His name's Cahir," Ojore snarled at him. Askold shot back up to his feet, shuffled around, and decided to hold his hand out to shake Ael's.

Ael shook his hand firmly. "It's nice to see you again, Askold. And yes, *Ojore*, it's King Ael. You'll show respect and call me by my given name while you're in *my* kingdom."

Ojore's face swelled in anger.

"I need to see Seda," Roya said impatiently, interrupting the men. "We need to confirm she was unharmed. We came as fast as we could, but these idiots slowed us down." She looked at the others with narrowed eyes.

"She's doing well. I can take you to her room. We were wrapping up dinner. She and Elco arrived in the middle of a ball. They made quite an impression," Ael said to everyone with a smile as he remembered the rage Seda carried when she arrived.

"Has she tried to murder you yet?" Benny joked, reaching up to slap him on the shoulder. "She wanted to when you left. I'd never seen her so mad before."

Ael held out his hands and spun around, showing how healthy and unharmed he was, and Benny laughed in response. "I knew she wouldn't."

Seda *did* want to hurt him when she had arrived, and he knew it. In fact, he thought she still might want to. He truly wished to make amends to her for everything.

Ael turned to one of the guards and asked them to fetch Fran to arrange some rooms for their guests.

"I've never seen anything so grand. This place is amazing. Why the hell would you leave it to live in Joro?" Askold asked him as Ael led them to a sitting room near the front doors.

"You know why," Ojore snapped at him, clearly in a particularly sour mood, more than usual. A servant entered and brought them some whiskey as they waited. They obviously needed it.

Everyone chose a seat and sat down, except for Roya.

"Did Seda tell you what the Wisps said to her?" Ferona asked, sighing in relief as she plopped down in her chair.

"She did," he responded.

"Go on…" Roya said curtly as she waved her hand in the air and paced around the room. The woman was always only business. When did she ever take time for herself?

*She obviously needs more time with Benny,* he thought as he watched her stomp around.

"Not here," Ael replied in a calm tone, not wanting to discuss the details of Wisps where prying ears might be listening. Roya huffed and finally chose a spot to sit.

"Where's Feich?" Ael asked them. The room went quiet, and everyone stared silently at the ground.

"Our brother died with honor, protecting the one he chose to protect," Roya responded, grabbing her glass and taking a long sip of her whiskey.

"I'm so sorry," he said as he looked between Roya and Ferona. "He was a good man. May the Mother Goddess carry his soul." The two thanked him in return, and Ferona wiped away a tear that slipped free.

"I take it you heard about Kalon?" Benny asked, staring into the fireplace in the room, trying to change the subject.

"When I get my hands on that bastard—" Ojore snarled.

*We're at least on the same page about something,* Ael thought.

"Make sure to do it in bear form," Ferona joked as she tried to lighten the mood. Ojore glared at her at first, but then nodded in approval, clearly thinking that was a good plan.

So he was a bear shifter. Thinking back, it was pretty clear which Lycanthrope type he was. The anger should have been the most obvious clue.

"Yes, I've heard about Kalon. He stole something we need to get back." Ael took a sip of his whiskey, savoring the burn as it went down his throat. Not only had he stolen her necklace, but he also placed his fucking lips on Seda. He intended to get back *both,* even if it meant cutting the man's mouth from his face.

Ojore wasn't going to lay a finger on Kalon. He would give that gift to Seda and watch with a smile as she roasted him to a crisp. He smirked into his cup and took another drink. That fucker was going to pay. He tried to get close to Seda, and she was *his.*

He would much rather see him suffer at the hands of her than Ojore.

"We need to get back a necklace?" Askold groaned. "I know it was sentimental, but how will we even find the guy?"

"Not here," Ael reiterated, and Askold looked down at the floor, his cheeks turning pink with embarrassment at forgetting not to discuss details.

"Sire." Fran approached with six other servants, and they bowed deeply. When they straightened, Fran asked, "How many rooms will we need, and which wing?"

"Ferona and I can share, and we demand to be close to Seda," Roya commanded.

Ael sighed. "Do all of you want to be near Seda?" He looked at the group of exhausted people before him.

"Well, I don't wanna be alone in my own wing," Benny told him. "Wherever Roya and Seda are, that's where I am."

Ael turned to Fran. "East wing. Four rooms." Fran quickly headed off with the other servants. His usually almost silent wing was about to get incredibly noisy.

Ojore finished his whiskey and stood up to pour another from the crystal decanter. "Have you heard from the Lycanthropes?"

Ael shook his head, and Ojore quickly drank his glass in one large gulp, hissing from the burn. "I'm concerned about them," he stated.

Ojore had a point. It was pretty strange that they wanted to meet and then left when Praxis tried to make contact at the wall. "I'll see what we can find out. Trade is expected to happen within the next couple of days. They're leaving tomorrow."

Ojore nodded at him and reclined in his chair. The group talked while they waited for their rooms to be ready.

Luelle ran into the room, panting from her quick pace. "I need to talk to you, Ael." She paused and looked around at everyone else. "Who the hell are *these* people?"

"It can wait." Ael stood and introduced the group to Luelle. She looked at everyone and evaluated each one.

"Two Corvids, a Lycanthrope, and two humans, huh." Luelle chuckled. "What a mix that is."

"How did you know I was a Lycanthrope?" Ojore asked.

"The musky aroma of a wild animal," she said with a shrug.

Ojore frowned, sniffed himself, and sighed as if he didn't care about his smell, but his burning cheeks revealed his embarrassment.

Askold stood and approached Luelle with a cheesy smile. "Humans can have a lot to offer, you know." He looked Luelle up and down and grinned at her. "You're *beautiful*. I've never seen such a stunning goddess before in my life."

Luelle laughed so hard she almost toppled over. "Humans

sure do have some balls, don't they?" She looked to Ael for agreement, and he chuckled.

"Oh, I *do*. I was hoping to run into a Fae beauty, and fate was on my side," Askold said in mock defense as he sat back in his chair and looked at her.

"Shut up, idiot," Ojore snapped irritably. "Why don't you just go wank one out in the bathroom and stop embarrassing yourself?"

Askold grinned wider and wiggled his eyebrows. She smiled back at him and said, "Thank you for the compliments. I do so *love* them. Unfortunately, I don't care for men." She winked at him and sat on the armrest of Ael's chair, looking over at Ferona and smirking.

Ael rolled his eyes at Luelle, and Ojore's jaw dropped. A servant walked by, and Ojore tried to catcall her, but she gave him a dirty look and flipped him off. Once she realized Ael was in the room, she apologized, bowed, and continued with her tasks.

Everyone burst into laughter, except for Roya. "How much longer?" she demanded as Fran approached.

"The rooms are ready. Please follow me," Fran replied.

They followed her as she guided everyone down a long hall and up winding stairs. Benny kept admiring the castle and complimenting the architecture and decor. Askold walked alongside Luelle and tried to strike up conversations with her, but she shifted away from him and closer to Ferona, who smiled in response with a blush to her cheeks.

When they reached the East Wing, Ael asked the guards if Seda was in her room, and they nodded. He knocked loudly to make sure she knew he was there, and he heard her reply, letting them in.

When the door opened, his heart fluttered in his chest at the sight of her. Seda stood there, wearing the same shirt and shorts again, looking just as she had when they lived in Joro.

*Fuck, she was waiting for me,* he realized.

She saw her friends and screamed in excitement as she ran to the door, throwing herself at Benny and hugging him tightly. "Benny! I'm so glad you're okay!"

Roya approached Seda and bowed her head, "I'm glad you're safe, Seda."

"I'm so happy you're here. I was worried about you guys," Seda said.

"What did the Wisps tell you?" Ferona asked eagerly again after the door closed.

Seda repeated what she told Ael and what she learned from Tahti. Everyone remained silent as they listened.

"So, we truly need to get that necklace back," Benny said as he sat beside Roya, placing his hand on her knee. "Sorry, Seda. We should've gone after him. How do we locate Kalon?"

"What if we ask that witch of yours?" Ojore suggested.

"What if we ask Elco to hunt him down again?" Ferona asked at the same time.

Seda shook her head at both of them. "Tahti said she couldn't help locate the stones. And I'd prefer not to ask Elco to do that again."

"Well, sounds like we know how to find one of them, at least," Benny said.

Ojore groaned loudly and slapped his knees as he stood. "*Another fucking monster.* It's late, and I'd like to shower and rest. I'm glad to see you're safe, Seda. What's our plan for tomorrow?"

"We'll meet for breakfast and figure out our next steps," Ael responded.

"I'd like to go with the others for the trade route if possible,"

Ojore said. Ael looked at him for a moment before nodding his head.

The group rose and said their goodbyes, with Ojore leaving first. Roya and Ael remained behind with Seda.

"Thank you, Roya, for coming and continuing to help with this. I'm very thankful for your friendship," Seda said to her with a beautiful smile that lit up her face.

Roya blushed at the compliment and bowed her head. "It's in our nature." She left the room, and Ael remained behind. The two of them stared at each other, feeling like it was a silent battle of who would speak first.

"Is there something I can help you with, Cahir?" she asked, giving in.

"Yes, there is," he replied, a smile forming on his lips. "Dinner was great. The buns were so soft."

She nervously fiddled with a strand of her hair, and he noticed a blush creep across her cheeks. His gaze caught on that freckle he loved so much on her chin.

He desperately wanted to kiss her, but he didn't know if she was ready yet. "I'll leave you to it, then. Good night, Seda." He winked at her.

Her face fell slightly, but she quickly masked it with a polite smile. Ael approached her and gave her a small hug, pressing his nose into her hair and softly breathing in her clean, fresh scent. She faintly reciprocated the hug.

"Good night, Cahir," she said as he began to walk out of the room. He exited and closed the doors, nodding to the guards before walking to his own room. As Ael closed the door behind him, he leaned against it. He shouldn't have left. Maybe she would have wanted him to stay? Should he go back?

No, he wanted to kiss her when the moment was right, and right now he wasn't sure if she wanted him that way yet. He also shouldn't have touched her the way he did at dinner without doing things the right way first. When she opened her thighs for him earlier, he fought with all of his strength not to slip a finger higher and brush it against her. He wanted to feel her soft, intimate skin so bad it was like fighting a Jotnar alone. What was more important to him, though, was that he wanted her to know he was serious about her.

He wanted all of her. Her mind, her body, *and* her soul. He needed her like he needed air, but he had to control himself and stop letting his fucking dick take charge when she was around. She needed to know she was his and he was *hers,* and he would burn the fucking world to the ground for her if she asked him to.

He would do anything for her. *Anything.*

And even after all of that reasoning he just gave himself, it didn't stop him from remembering her smell for him or the feel of her soft thighs.

He walked to the bathroom and turned on the hot water. Showers were becoming his new favorite thing.

# CHAPTER 11

<u>Seda</u>

"It's time to get up!" Suza thundered to Seda as she looked down at her sleeping on the bed. Seda had slept terribly, staying up all night thinking about how to find the stones, fighting tears for how horribly people were treated at the Camp, and how much she wished she could help quickly. She needed to do more. She needed to find these stones as soon as possible.

She stared up at Suza and noticed her hair looked freshly washed and that she appeared refreshed.

Seda groaned and threw the blanket over her head. "I need more time to sleep."

"Not gonna happen, Seda. I have been instructed—"

"To get me ready, yes, yes," Seda finished for her. She pulled the blanket down just below her nose and looked up at the blue sky through the glass above.

"Yes, um… exactly."

Seda climbed out of bed as Suza walked to the closet. She

returned carrying a cotton dress that looked shockingly comfortable. "No corset today?" Seda asked.

Suza smirked. "If you want one, there are plenty of them in there."

Seda quickly shook her head and waited for Suza to turn around before putting the dress on. The dress was a light lavender, airy and not constricting at all. A much better choice than the last one.

When they left the room, the guards from yesterday had been changed out with two she didn't recognize. They tilted their heads at her before shifting their focus back towards the opposite wall.

The door next to hers flew open, and Askold tumbled out.

"Seda! Good morning!" Askold exclaimed as he approached. "Nice dress!"

"Morning, Askold. Thank you. Did you sleep okay?" Seda politely asked as he stepped beside her.

"Sure did. Feel like a billion food tokens," he replied with a grin and a wink.

Another door opened, and Roya and Ferona stepped out, appearing as if they hadn't slept well all night.

"Everything okay?" Seda asked them.

"There's something we need to discuss," Ferona said with a downturned mouth.

"Have you heard from the Corvids?" Seda asked.

Ferona and Roya nodded.

"Your father's been promoted to Lord of Joro. No one has seen Mordred since," Ferona said.

Seda gasped. "How's that possible?"

"We don't know yet. But we'll try to find out," Roya added.

Luelle walked up the hall and met them. Seda noticed Luelle smile at Ferona and step alongside her.

"Does Benny know?" she asked the Corvids.

"Yes. We told—" Roya began, but was rudely cut off by Suza.

"Let's go!" The mean woman snarled at them.

"Damn, calm your chonies." Luelle rolled her eyes at her. "I just got here. We can leave now."

Seda turned to follow Suza, who was giving them all dirty looks as she gestured for them to hurry their pace. Seda's mind was racing. Learning her father was now the Lord of Joro and knew what was going on in the Camp made no sense. It wasn't like him at all. He started the Rising, after all.

When they entered the room, everyone else was already there. Benny sat next to Praxis, who sat beside Neoma, who sat next to Meir, who sat next to Cahir.

Cahir motioned for Seda to sit beside him again.

She walked over and sat in her chair, recalling last night and him touching her dangerously close. Heat bloomed in her belly, and Cahir looked at her quickly. She locked her eyes with his, and they stared at each other for a long moment.

"I don't know about all of you, but I slept like a rock." Luelle broke the staring contest and smiled at Neoma, as if she were hiding a secret. "How was *your* night, Neoma?"

"Uneventful," Neoma replied too quickly.

Praxis quickly glanced at her with wide eyes, his jaw falling open. Then he muttered something under his breath.

"Is that so?" Luelle pressed, smirking at Praxis.

"Didn't you learn your lesson last night?" Meir scolded Luelle. "You embarrassed yourself and got kicked out of this very room."

"I recall that rather fondly," Praxis chimed in, and Luelle glared at him.

"Where's Ojore?" Seda asked, just now realizing he wasn't in the room.

"He left early this morning to join the others on the trade route," Cahir answered.

"He went to see the Lycanthropes already?"

Cahir nodded in response. "He's concerned about his people and wanted to check in. The group left earlier than expected for him."

"What happened?" she asked.

Everyone in the room had quieted down and was listening to their conversation.

"We don't have any information. Everything will be fine. He'll return soon," Cahir said.

"Seda, did you sleep okay?" Neoma asked sweetly from Praxis's side. Yet again, her dress was a tad too revealing, and she caught Meir looking over at her.

*Gross. Meir's a pervert, too,* she noted.

Neoma glanced at Cahir and smiled softly, pretending to stretch and drawing attention to her chest.

"I slept fine," Seda answered shortly. She desperately wanted to look over and see if Cahir was looking at her overly apparent attempt at attention, but didn't want to make it obvious.

Did she care? The overwhelming feeling of jealousy made her stomach turn. She swallowed it and told herself she didn't. Not at all. Let him look.

"*Sire*, I really need to talk to you after breakfast," Luelle said as she munched on a biscuit that was smothered in gravy.

"Whatever about?" Meir asked.

"It's for King Ael to know." She shrugged as she took another bite.

"This is a safe space—" Meir started, and Cahir raised his hand in the air to stop him.

"When breakfast is over, we can talk," Cahir responded. Seda saw Meir scowl into his cup, his eyes darkening.

The rest of the meal was uneventful. Cahir never placed his hand on Seda's knee. In fact, he looked rather stiff sitting next to her. Was it because his attention was on Neoma? She tried several times to get his full attention, but he refused to respond. She felt upset and angry at herself for even trying.

She looked over at Neoma, who was laughing at everything Cahir said, and her mood soured even more. She kept giving him baby doll eyes and adjusting her top. Not once did Seda look towards Cahir. She felt livid.

When breakfast was over, everyone filed out of the room except Neoma, Luelle, Cahir, and Seda.

"Seda, will you walk with me to the gardens?" Neoma asked with an eager expression.

Seda really didn't want to walk to the gardens with her. What she wanted was to electrocute her pretty face and turn it into fried eggs.

"Sure," she responded curtly.

She said a brief goodbye to the others and followed Neoma out into the hallway, closing the door behind her while avoiding eye contact with Cahir.

# CHAPTER 12

<u>Ael</u>

"You saw her do *WHAT*?!" Ael exclaimed as Luelle told him what she had seen Neoma do to Praxis the night before.

"She poured a green liquid onto him while she was fucking him, and he turned into almost a direct replica of you," Luelle reiterated.

"Are you sure you saw correctly?"

She looked at him with a what-the-fuck expression, "Yes, Ael, I saw Praxis shift into you unknowingly."

He knew Neoma was after him. That much was obvious. He also noticed that she was flirting with him during breakfast. But wanting him and changing who she was fucking into him was something else. He felt… *violated*. "Follow her. She's up to something more than just desiring me. I can sense it. If anything suspicious happens, find me immediately. I won't delay your coming to me next time, even if the castle is on *fucking fire*. I also don't trust her with Seda. She's pushing to be around her too much. Follow them, and make sure everything's okay."

Luelle nodded, got up from the table, and pushed her chair in.

"Luelle?" Ael stopped her from leaving.

"Yes?" She turned around and looked at him.

"Keep an eye on Meir, too. He brought her here, and something really seems wrong with both of them."

"Will do." She left the room, and Ael remained sitting at the table, feeling disgusted by what he heard. He wanted to talk to Tahti and see if she had given her the potion. Why would she give her something like that? What sort of games was that tricky witch up to now?

He got up from the table, looked at the clock, saw he had some time before he had to hear petitions in the throne room, and made his way outside to find the damn witch.

HE MOVED QUICKLY along his usual path to her cabin in the woods. As he approached, he noticed the usual smoke stack from the fireplace was gone. He navigated through weeds that had grown over since his last visit, brushing aside the overgrowth to reach her door. He pushed through and knocked loudly.

Usually, he would hear rustling, grumbling, maybe some cursing, but now only silence responded. He knocked on the door once more.

When no reply came, he tried the handle, and it opened smoothly.

His eyes widened as he looked inside. The cabin was empty —no stack of pots against the far wall, no cauldron bubbling with the lingering smell of chemicals in the middle. It was a completely barren room with only an empty cauldron at the center.

The weight of absence pressed heavily around him, the stale air thick as forgotten memories. It seemed no one had lived there for decades. He cautiously entered and surveyed the space. Cobwebs decorated every corner of the walls, while a thick layer of dust covered the floor.

*What the fuck?*

He felt like his mind was playing tricks on him, so he walked back outside and looked at the cabin again, checking to make sure he was in the right place.

The small, shanty-looking cabin he knew so well came into view. He walked back inside through the curved front door and went to the small kitchen, opening the cabinets to look for any sign that she had been there, but they were lined with even more dust. He went into the bathroom, looked around, and had to push his way through cobwebs that blocked the entrance to the small room.

He scratched his head in confusion and walked over to the empty cauldron she usually brewed in. Inside was a weathered-looking book. He picked it up and examined the blank pages.

Tahti was gone.

# CHAPTER 13

<u>Seda</u>

"The gardens here are so lovely, don't you think?" Neoma asked Seda as they walked along paths lined with colorful roses, bordered by a tall brick edging. She wasn't really looking at the flowers. Instead, she focused on the two Corvids that flew high in the sky above them, their shadows dancing across the ground below.

"Yes, they're beautiful," Seda grumbled, not even staring at the plants. She didn't want to be walking around the gardens with Neoma, and she found it increasingly hard to stay polite. She kept thinking back to how Neoma had been watching Cahir, and how he seemed distant from her that morning.

Jealousy dragged its ugly claws through her body, stabbing through her like the rose thorns that were likely on those bushes. She thought about how Cahir had been up close and personal with this woman the night she arrived, and her fists clenched tightly together.

"What do you like to do for fun?" Neoma asked, obviously not getting the clue that Seda was over this wretched walk.

"I don't have hobbies. I wasn't allowed such frivolities in Joro," she stated bluntly.

"That's a shame. But now you're here! I love to embroider. Would you like to try sometime? I brought some materials with me."

"I don't think so." That sounded boring as hell.

"Oh! Look at this one! It has a honey-colored eye!" Neoma exclaimed as she examined a red rose.

Seda had no idea what the woman was talking about, so she stepped closer and peered at the colorful assortment of roses before them. Each rose featured gentle, curled petals surrounding a glassy eye with long, black eyelashes. Every flower switched its focus from Neoma to Seda as she neared, watching her warily.

"These roses are sentient?" she asked, curiosity piquing and forgetting her previous irritation with the woman. "They're *beautiful*."

"Just another monstrous plant. Probably sapient. Beautiful but disgusting creatures. Their tears can burn your skin if they're not plucked from their bushes," Neoma said with a cheerful tone. "Would you like to pick a bouquet for your room?"

Before Seda could object, Neoma reached out and yanked roughly at one of the stems, revealing red sap that slowly oozed out.

The other flowers tried to shy away from her touch, but she kept reaching out and plucking the roses, their eyes closing and lashes trembling as if in pain as they were gathered into a bouquet.

Could Neoma not see that she was hurting them? Anger

surged back through Seda as she glared at the saddened florals in Neoma's hand.

"You're hurting them!" Seda yelled, her heart sinking as she watched the flowers struggle to escape Neoma, their roots deep in the soil, holding them back.

"Stop trying to escape from me! You were planted here just for this, you foolish things!" Neoma snapped as she tussled with the plants. She glanced at Seda. "These are *monsters*, Seda. Don't tell me you feel sympathy for beastly creatures, do you?" She raised her eyebrows.

This woman was ignoring the room—or the garden—and Seda's patience was already paper-thin. She took a deep breath to steady herself. No, she didn't have sympathy for *monsters*. She remembered the Gnashing Flora from her journey and swallowed down her pity toward the flowers. That plant had tried to eat her and killed one of her friends. She thought back to the blistered body of Seren and pursed her lips.

Her anger finally shattered, and she looked away from the pitiful plants, clenching her sparking fists.

She shifted the topic and blurted, "What do you want from the king?"

Neoma paused mid-way through picking another rose. She glanced at Seda and roughly snagged the stem without looking at it. "I want *nothing* from him."

"It seems otherwise, Neoma."

Neoma fluttered her eyelashes and sighed. "I mean, he *is* incredibly handsome, and I heard he's amazing in bed. Have you *seen* those muscles? I bet his cock is just as intimidating."

Seda ground her teeth together and looked away. She wanted to strangle this woman, but she refrained and chose not to respond. At least Neoma was being honest for once.

"Do you love him, Seda?" Neoma asked as she aggressively yanked another scared flower from the bush.

"He's just my friend," she replied matter-of-factly.

"That's not what I meant, and you know it." Her voice was thick with fermented honey. Neoma placed the flower next to the others in her pile and grabbed another just as forcefully.

Seda allowed the silence to surround them before muttering, "I do have love for him."

Neoma looked at her with lips pressed in a bloodless line before smiling sweetly, a hint of cruelty flashing through. She reached down, picked a small purple rose, and placed it above Seda's ear. She could feel the red sap oozing into her hair, and tensed when Neoma's finger grazed along her ear. "This one matches your eyes. You're so beautiful, Seda. You shouldn't fall for that stupid man's charms. I'm sure there's someone better for you out there."

This woman was utterly confusing. If she didn't want anything from Cahir, then what was her goal? She followed her as they continued along the path. Neoma finished gathering her large bouquet and pulled a red ribbon from her pocket, tying it around the flowers. "Perfect," she said as she held out the bouquet to Seda, the blood red sap slowly dripping from the bottom.

Seda reached for the flowers, and before her fingers touched the bouquet, her vision blurred.

The sky darkened as thick fog enveloped her. The cool, sandalwood-scented mist brushed against her skin, and her breath billowed around her in small clouds.

All she could see were the roses that had fallen on the floor and were bleeding dark blood, with a large crimson pool spreading around them.

The distant sound of violent screams echoed as footsteps crunched on the gravel nearby. Seda instantly activated her magic and looked around, sparks dancing along her fingertips.

The setting felt oddly familiar.

"Who's there?" she called into the fog. "Neoma?"

"There you are," a deep, male voice echoed with silk through the fog. Where had she heard that voice before?

"Who are you? What do you want?" she asked, raising her hands in preparation in case someone suddenly rushed at her.

"The better question is, *do you know who you are? Do you remember yet?*" he asked in response.

Seda felt something slither across her ankle, and she looked down. Black, wet snakes began writhing all around her, just like all of her dreams from before.

This time, she jumped back and screamed as the creatures tightly coiled around her calves. She heard the deep, chuckling voice as it said, "You usually love them. Don't move too quickly... They have an intriguing bite. You may never want to leave if they do."

"What do you want?" she asked once more, scanning her surroundings, but the fog was so dense she couldn't see anything.

"I have something *you* want," he replied with a deep, rumbling laugh, ignoring her question.

Seda's eyes widened as a large man emerged from the mist. He was clad in black snakeskin armor and wore a cracked skull mask with vibrant eyes that peered through it, as if looking into her soul. She felt her heartbeat quicken when she stared into his familiar eyes.

He slowly walked up to her, and she looked up at the color of seafoam that she knew so well.

Her breath came out in a whisper, "Kalon?"

He gently extended his hand and carefully plucked the purple flower from above her ear, holding it up so she could see. The flower had tears falling from its petals, mixing with the red sap seeping from its base.

Anger clouded her vision. He stole her necklace, toyed with

her heart, and kissed her. He pretended she was important—someone worth getting to know better—and she was *furious*.

"I want my necklace back!" she shouted as electrical shocks slithered up her arms.

"Soon," he replied with a shrug, his voice carrying a playful lilt.

"What does that mean?"

He dropped the flower onto the ground, and a snake quickly coiled around it.

"What do you want?" She stepped closer to him and narrowed her eyes, catching sight of the black moth tattoo on his neck. He was playing games with her.

"I want my guiding light back."

"I don't know or care what that means. Give it back!" She didn't even think before she unleashed the magic from her palms, aiming straight at his heart. Lightning struck his chest, and sparks trailed along his body and over his mask.

He chuckled as the electricity swarmed across his body. She threw another blast at him, hitting his chest once more, but he spread his arms wide and groaned. "Oh, Seda. I feel so *alive!*"

Seda lowered her hands. Her magic wasn't affecting him. Why wasn't it hurting him?

"Where's my necklace!?" she seethed.

The largest snake Seda had ever seen came into view and lunged for her with murderous fangs drawn.

"I'm coming for you," was all she heard before the dark claimed her once more.

ROYA WAS OVER SEDA, lightly slapping her cheeks as her vision returned. She looked around and saw she was back in the rose garden, lying on the gravel pathway. On all fours, she swiftly backed out of Roya's arms and bumped into Ferona behind her.

"There was a giant snake, and I saw Kalon!" Seda shrieked, looking around for the enormous serpent.

Roya and Ferona exchanged glances, and she saw Neoma standing there, holding the bouquet of red roses still, looking down at her with furrowed brows and wide eyes.

"I didn't see a snake," Neoma said, and she looked around the ground nervously in case one might pop out and bite her.

"It was a huge snake! Bigger than... than... *Elco!*" she exclaimed.

"Seda, there was no snake here. Are you okay?" Roya asked with concern as she ran her hand along Seda's forehead.

"I saw it! And I saw Kalon! I also saw your roses covered in a pool of blood!" Seda yelled and stared at Neoma's bouquet, which was fresh and clean. No crimson blood covered her hands, only the small droplets of red sap from their bases. Neoma glanced at the bouquet before looking back at Seda.

"You fainted, Seda. We saw it," Roya offered gently.

"Let's get her back to her rooms," Ferona suggested as she stared at her sister, waiting for approval.

Roya nodded, and the two Corvids assisted Seda to her feet. Her legs trembled, nearly causing her to fall again. They supported her by shifting her between their shoulders and guided her back to the castle, leaving Neoma alone in the garden with her bouquet.

Was it just a nightmare?

She reached up to touch the purple flower on her ear, but it was gone.

# CHAPTER 14

### Luelle

Luelle nearly jumped out of her hiding spot when Seda collapsed, but she stopped when Roya and Ferona flew down and shifted. They frantically hovered over her and gently slapped her face to wake her up. Seda awoke quickly and freaked out, exclaiming that she had seen someone and a large snake bigger than the Lionne. The Corvids assisted Seda in getting up and led her back toward the castle.

Luelle remained frozen where she was hidden, watching Neoma with narrowed eyes. She had heard her lies to Seda about not wanting anything from Ael. Seda didn't know what she had seen the night before, and the woman looked visibly angry that Seda had left.

After Seda and the Corvids were out of sight, Neoma threw the bouquet on the ground. She stomped on it five times, crushing the delicate flowers into the grass below and screeching loudly toward the sky.

*So ladylike,* she thought with a roll of her eyes.

Neoma seemed to be hyperventilating, and her face flushed with anger. Luelle hid her smile behind her palm, trying her hardest not to laugh loudly at the scene.

She watched as Neoma stomped off towards the hedge maze and walked in. Luelle rose from her hiding place and followed the angry woman at a safe distance.

She carefully approached the first corner of the maze and saw Neoma speaking with Meir, with dark insects fluttering around them. Her breath hitched, and she quickly pressed her body against the bush behind the corner, trying to listen to their conversation.

"Did she touch it?" Meir asked Neoma.

"No. I'm working on it," Neoma replied.

Their voices were barely audible, so she tried to move closer, but a stick snapped under her foot. Luelle froze, a cold shiver running up her spine as she held her breath.

*Fucking rookie,* she scolded herself.

"Shh! Someone's here," Meir whispered.

She heard their footsteps approaching rapidly. Luelle swiftly left the maze and took shelter behind a large water fountain, waiting for them to exit. Her heart pounded quickly in her chest as she focused on steadying her breath.

She peered over the stone ledge of the fountain and watched. Luelle and Meir strolled casually back through the garden toward the castle, wearing nervous stares and glancing around periodically.

She couldn't follow them now and groaned over her mistake.

Luelle watched until they were out of sight before hearing a low growl behind her, causing the water in the fountain to quiver. She slowly looked over her shoulder and saw Elco staring at her, molten eyes narrowed.

"Good kitty," she said, slowly rising and lifting her palms in front of her. Elco's growl rumbled deeper, as if offended at the endearing reference. He obviously needed a stronger name.

"Easy there... *tiger?*" She swallowed against his menacing presence, then cleared her throat and straightened, steadying herself. "I wasn't following Seda. I was following Neoma because I don't trust her. And you shouldn't trust her or Meir. They're up to something that might harm her," she tried.

His eyes opened slightly from their narrowed glare, shifting to where Meir and Neoma had walked away. He nodded his head once and expanded his wings, quickly taking off into the sky. The sudden gust of wind made her ponytail whip around and hit her painfully in the face.

"Ew, jerk," she muttered quietly so only she could hear, worried he might turn around and eat her.

She dusted herself off, adjusted her ponytail, and left the gardens to find Ael.

# CHAPTER 15

<u>Seda</u>

Roya and Ferona helped Seda to her room. The walk was long, and her legs barely held her up, but the two Corvids didn't complain once as they supported her. They passed through the long halls and reached the large double doors that separated the East Wing from the rest of the castle. When the guards saw them, they hurried over and helped get her into bed.

She was exhausted, and her head pounded like someone was hitting it with a sledgehammer. When her head hit her pillow, she closed her eyes, trying to block out the midday sun blazing through the ceiling windows.

She continued thinking about her dream. Was that just a nightmare about Kalon? Had she truly passed out and dreamt the whole thing?

Ferona hurried into the bathroom, returning with a cool, wet washcloth, and placed it on her forehead. Seda thanked her, closed her eyes again, and drifted into a deep, peaceful sleep.

Hours must have passed because, when she woke, she opened her eyes to candlelit darkness. Someone was crouched on the floor next to her bed, with their forehead resting on her mattress.

"Cahir?" she choked out in a dry voice, noticing his fresh white shirt that made his skin look radiant, even in the dimly lit room.

He rustled and looked up at her with furrowed brows. "Are you okay, Sed?"

She touched the back of her head, and the faint throbbing was still there, but it had eased significantly. "I think so."

"Tell me what happened, please?" Cahir asked as he reached out and touched her arm.

"I apparently passed out."

"But Roya said you saw something?" he pressed.

No one else had believed her. Why would he?

She sighed. "Apparently, I passed out and had a nightmare. You'd think I'm crazy."

"Never," Cahir said with a small smile.

She remembered him saying this to her before, and smiled at the memory. She shifted on the bed, but the movement worsened her headache, making her wince in pain.

"Okay…" she started, "I've had dreams of snakes since childhood. When Neoma handed me her bouquet, the air shifted. It turned dark, foggy, and cold. Dozens of black snakes surrounded me, and a man emerged." She winced from the pounding in her head, and Cahir quickly grabbed her glass of water that was waiting on her side table. He handed it to her and encouraged her to keep going, but she took a deep sip from her glass.

"What did this man look like?" he asked.

"He wore black, scaled armor and had piercing seafoam-colored eyes. When I tried to electrocute him, my magic didn't affect him, and a large snake attacked me. That's when I woke up to Roya and Ferona over me."

Cahir thought for a moment, "Hmm..." He was silent for a moment before asking, "Want to look for any references to that in the library?"

She probably should have phrased that differently. He likely didn't catch the eye color reference, and honestly, maybe it was just a dream.

Seda brightened up at the thought of going to the library with him. "Can we go?"

"Would you like to eat something first? Dinner was hours ago, but yes, we can go."

Seda pushed herself out of bed. She was still wearing the soft cotton dress that Suza had picked out for her. She ran her tongue across her teeth, looking down at herself. "I'd like to freshen up first."

"Of course, I'll be outside waiting." He left her room and closed the door. She went to the bathroom, quickly brushed her teeth, and looked in the mirror. Seeing her hair looked a mess, she quickly brushed out the tangles so it wouldn't be too much work for Suza.

When she finished getting ready, she made her bed so it would be tidy when she returned, and made her way out the door. Cahir was standing outside, talking to the same two guards who had been posted there earlier. All three of them looked at her.

"Shall we?" Cahir asked, extending his arm so she could take it.

She was too tired to fight him on this and was excited to go to the library, so she accepted his outstretched arm.

They walked down the hall, and she felt the warmth of his arm against her skin. She peered up at him. It was still a bit of an adjustment getting used to his new height. He looked down at her, and her heart fluttered involuntarily. She quickly looked away and noticed that they weren't on the same path to the dining room as usual.

"Where are we headed?" she asked.

"To the kitchens."

Her headache had eased, and she tried to tamp down her eager excitement to learn more in the library. They walked down a long hallway and through ornate double doors. The lantern-lit kitchen was empty of Fae, and Cahir led her to a table filled with cured meats, strawberries, cheeses, and crackers.

She picked up a strawberry, and the juice burst in her mouth. Cahir watched her eat the berries, observing intently as the pink liquid dripped down her lips. She licked at them, enjoying how his eyes flashed when he saw her tongue.

"I have a surprise for you." He cleared his throat and looked away from her. "But you'll need to close your eyes when we get there." He led them into a storage room where dozens of shelves were lined with dry goods.

"Close your eyes," he told her.

"What are we doing in the pantry?" she asked, wary of what could be a surprise in this room.

"Shh… you'll see," he said.

She huffed, closing her eyes and fighting the urge to peek. She heard rustling, the sound of a jar opening, and an acidic smell hit her nose. What was he doing? He placed something cool and wet into her hands, and she opened her eyes again.

"What is—" She looked at her palm, and a fermented egg was in her hand, dripping yellow liquid down her fingers. "Ewwwww!" she yelled.

She smashed the egg against his chest, vigorously rubbing the yolk into his white shirt. He laughed and tried to get away as she rubbed the egg on him, quickly turning his back to her to shield himself.

She saw a jar on the ground and grabbed another egg, smushing it onto the back of his shirt. She accidentally kicked the jar over with her foot, spilling the liquid and the rest of the hard-boiled eggs across the floor.

"How dare you place that disgusting thing into my hand!" she yelled, laughter slipping free, as she rubbed it harder into him.

The egg chunks on his back fell off his shirt in large clumps. She reached for another one on the floor, but when he turned to stop her, he slipped in the liquid and crashed to the floor, bringing her down with him.

Seda fell onto him, their chests pressed together, with their noses just inches apart.

He held her waist securely and gently squeezed. Seda's breath hitched, and suddenly the storage room felt much smaller. They looked into each other's eyes as silence took over.

Seda's heart began to thunder in her chest.

"I thought you liked those," he whispered breathlessly.

Heat flickered low in her belly, and she watched Cahir's eyes darken.

"You know I don't. Now we're stinky," she whispered back.

"Not at all," he said, his gaze sliding down to her lips. Her heart fluttered again. "You're so special to me, Seda."

Doubt slithered into her thoughts, and she pulled herself away, settling beside him on the floor. "If you want to spend time with Neoma, I'd understand. As your friend, I'd support you if that's what you wanted. I think she's... *okay*, I guess."

He shifted to sit alongside her and paused, glancing at her with wide eyes. "I want *nothing* from that woman, Seda. I never have and I never will."

"But I saw you with her when I arrived, and the way she was flirting with you today—"

"She throws herself at me, and I reject her. She isn't for me. She isn't the one I want," he interrupted as he sat beside her. He pressed his leg against hers and reached down to gently touch her hand, tracing his index finger over it and repeatedly drawing a heart.

She glanced at her hand before shifting her gaze back to his. "Then who…" Her words fell quiet.

A long silence followed, and he pulled on his neck with his hand before answering, "*You*, Seda."

Seda felt her mind go blank as she stared into his eyes. He continued tracing his finger over her hand, and it tickled slightly, but she didn't move it; she couldn't.

"I've wanted to tell you for so long. The last thing I want is to lose your friendship even more than I already have, but I need to express this. I promised you honesty. You've been my closest friend, the person I look forward to waking up next to in that tiny bed alone in our apartment because you're there on the other side of the room, the one who makes me laugh and makes every moment feel special, even when you get upset and threaten me." He smiled at her, and her heart fluttered like a butterfly trapped in a glass, desperately trying to break free.

"I… I *love* you, Seda, more than anything in the world. My love knows no bounds. I'll help you find all the stones. I'll help you burn this Monster King and others to the ground. I'll seek revenge on those who hurt you and innocent others. You're my best friend, my entire heart, and you ignite my soul with a fury that rivals the sun. I'd do all of these things even if my feelings were never echoed. You have me, Seda. From now until the end of time."

Her hand flew to her lips, and her eyes widened. She had no words, no way to respond.

"I..." she started, feeling a tear slip free. She thought she loved him, too—more than a friend. He had been her haven for years, the silent calm amid chaos, the steady ground holding her broken pieces together. But... he lied to her. What if he was lying now, too?

He reached out and gently cupped her cheek, wiping away the stray tear with his thumb. He slowly leaned in and tentatively brushed his full lips against hers, seeking silent permission, allowing her the chance to say no.

His lips were warm, and she noticed him trembling against her. Was he as nervous as she?

She felt the soft glow of her magic awaken within her chest. She opened her mouth for him, and the rush of emotion caused her to close her eyes as she lost herself in the moment.

His kiss felt like magic—like she was flying through the clouds, watching from far above. His kiss felt gentle and caring, and a determined flame began to grow within her, refueling the emotions she had allowed to fade.

She returned his kiss, leaning into him more tightly, and softly moaning into his mouth.

He slowly pulled away from her, and she opened her eyes, gazing into his. His face was inches from hers, and she could see the purple glow from her eyes light up his own.

She pulled back, afraid she had hurt him with her magic, remembering how Kalon's kiss ended with a spark to his lips, "I'm sorry."

"Don't apologize. Ever," he rasped as he watched her mouth with a hunger she had never seen on him before. He smiled at her, gently touching his lips with his fingertips, and her heart warmed as her favorite dimples showed on his cheeks through his trimmed beard.

"Can we do it again?" she asked, her voice hesitant. She might not trust him completely yet, but she was willing to try.

"Fuck yes."

His lips met hers once more, and they both tumbled to the floor.

Seda forgot about the chaos around her. She forgot about the stones, the Camp, the monsters, Kalon, and her terrible past. The only things on her mind now were the fullness of his lips, the joy in her heart, and the fire consuming her soul.

# CHAPTER 16

<u>Ael</u>

H*oly. Fucking. Shit.*

This was more than anything he had imagined. It was a seismic shift—an awakening as the burning flames of hell ravaged him with fiery passion. Her lips were ambrosial, tasting like mint and strawberries, and he couldn't stop himself from pulling her closer and feeling her warmth wrap around him. She enveloped him, body and soul, until nothing else seemed to exist. It was a silent collision of longing, time, and friendship that had magically transformed into more.

They kissed each other until he felt his lips swell. Then, ever so slowly, Ael ran his tongue across hers, and when Seda reciprocated, he lost all sense of control. She was his addiction now—more than ever.

Seda was on top of him, fully clothed, and pressing her lips to his with a burning passion. Her arousal surrounded him in the air, and he struggled not to take things further in the dark, cramped room. His cock strained against his pants, and Seda shifted, just barely brushing it against her as she adjusted over him. A small moan escaped her parted lips, and he instinctively pushed up and ground against her, desperately craving more and getting dangerously close to going all in.

She shifted onto him again, and when she rose, he growled as he pulled her back down onto his throbbing cock one more time. He savored the feel of her warmth through the clothing, silently cursing her underwear and his pants for blocking their skin from touching.

His breathing felt ragged as he reached under her dress and cupped her hips in his palms, squeezing them for the first time and feeling the soft, supple skin he had longed to touch for years.

"Ahem." Someone cleared their throat as a bright light filtered into the storage room. They quickly moved apart and stared at the doorway.

Fran stood at the door, holding a large bowl and lantern, looking down at them. "Are your rooms not up to standards, Sire?" she asked with a slight grin that she quickly tried to hide behind a scowl.

Seda quickly stood, revealing the bulge in his pants with her absence. Fran didn't stare as Ael stood and brushed the egg off his clothes. He looked at Seda, noticing the mess tangled in her hair and all over her dress, and fought back a smirk.

"The rooms are fine, Fran. Thank you for asking. We'll be leaving now." He grabbed Seda's hand and led her out the door.

Seda turned around and apologized to Fran for the mess.

"It's no problem, dear. Although maybe next time you guys could choose something less... acidic?" Fran's laugh escaped her, and she placed the bowl on a small table, reaching for a mop.

"I don't think we should go to the library looking like this," Seda said. She looked up at him and laughed loudly as she picked a chunk of egg off his shoulder.

"I suppose not. But it would be rather funny to dirty that place up, wouldn't it?" Ael replied, his grin spreading across his face. This was the happiest he had felt in years, perhaps even forever.

"I don't think Meir would like that."

"Oh, he'd love it the most out of everyone." He laughed at the thought of Meir fuming about egg on his beloved books.

"We could transfer this mess onto those fancy, strange scrolls he's looking at," she said, her grin widening at the suggestion.

Ael paused and looked at her, their hands still intertwined. "You said he was looking at scrolls?"

"Yeah. When I ran into him at the library, he was looking at scrolls written in another language. Not sure what they were."

"No one's allowed to look at those," he stated with furrowed brows. "Let's get cleaned up and go see."

Meir knew the scrolls were off limits. How did he even get in there? Only the royal family had the power to enter and view those ancient texts.

They walked with fingers intertwined through the halls. When they turned a corner, Neoma bumped into Seda, knocking her back.

"Oh! I'm *so sorry*, Seda! I didn't see you there," she said to her with a mock expression of shock on her face. She let her top loosen, pretending to catch her breasts to hold them steady, as if Seda was the reason they slipped out.

Ael narrowed his eyes and sneered at her. "You'll do better to ensure that *your* clumsiness doesn't harm others, *especially Seda*."

"I'm so sorry, Sire. I—" she began.

"Bow for your king," he commanded, cutting her off. His

magic flared with anger, and green swirls of mist curled around her neck, forcing her to the ground, pressing her face against the stone floor.

The color drained from her face as she was thrown down, and her dark curls spread out around her.

"What's wrong? Thought you liked this position from Meir and Praxis," he casually said.

She began to stutter as she tried to defend herself. He tightened his magic's grip around her neck, causing her to flinch and her face to turn a shade of red. He waited for it to grow darker, not wanting to hear her anymore.

Seda placed her hand on his arm, asking him to stop and let her go, but her voice felt distant. He glanced at Seda and saw her pleading eyes.

His gaze shifted back down at Neoma, and he seethed, "You will leave this castle and never return."

He released his magic from her constricted throat, and she gasped for air. He retook Seda's hand and led her through the halls away from Neoma.

He saw in the wall's reflection Neoma get up and glare at them.

She was no longer welcome in the palace. She wasn't allowed around Seda. He didn't have the patience anymore to figure out what game she was playing with Meir. Meir would be a harder person to handle, but he wanted them both gone after what Luelle had told him earlier.

When they reached Seda's door, the guards glanced at them before quickly looking away.

"I'll meet you back out here in a few minutes," he told her, gently raising her wrist to his lips and softly kissing it. Seda's cheeks were slightly flushed, and she turned around to walk into her room, closing the door behind her.

"Eggs, sire?" the bearded guard asked with a slight smirk on his lips.

"I rather like them," he replied with a shrug. He went to his room and walked to the shower. He now had a new drive to help her find these stones and understand their meaning. It was her wish to fulfill, and he would do everything he could to make her happy. Always.

# CHAPTER 17

<u>Seda</u>

When Seda's door closed, she rushed into her room and flung open the bathroom door, undressed, and jumped into the shower. Cahir's magic was impressive. Seeing Neoma on the ground begging had scared her, and she didn't want him to hurt Neoma, but it felt nice to see him defend her, to see him prove the things he told her in that storage room were true.

She wanted to be the only one he desired.

A smile spread across her face when she thought back to their kiss and his declaration of love.

A fire within her, the same one she had stamped down, flared to life, growing stronger the more she thought about it. How many years had they wasted avoiding each other? His gentleness with her, his protectiveness, his respect for her—everything should have been evident, but she was so blind to it.

Years of dealing with her own trauma blinded her to his affection.

*But he lied.*

She shook her head at the thought. It was out of his control. She knew how tricky the Wisps could be. She understood that now.

She jumped out of the shower and hurried to the closet to grab some clothes. She slipped into shorts and a tank top, then brushed her hair. Looking in the mirror, she saw that her hair had more random glittering strands, like the twinkling of starlight, with a few strands of purples and blues scattered through.

*Strange. It's changing even more now.*

She grabbed her shoes and stepped through her door. The guards were stationed there, eyes on her with smirks cresting their lips. One snickered something about eggs, but she ignored them and walked to Cahir's door.

She knocked, and when no one responded, she knocked again.

She opened the door and walked inside. The room was impressive. A bed larger than Elco's was placed in the center of the room, covered with green silk sheets and throw pillows. His bed was perfectly made, and the tall windows behind it were lit, revealing the beauty of the land beyond. She moved toward the windows and looked out.

Vast landscapes of jagged cliffs, ending in a battlefield of chaotic waves, crashed against the rocks a hundred feet below. Low-hanging clouds brushed against the cliffsides, hugging them as if the sky was trying to wrap them in warmth from the cool ocean air.

She could hear the running water in his shower and decided to grab a blanket from the bed and step outside. The sea below carried the whisper of salt, a fresh aroma that reminded how immense this world truly was.

As the wind tore through her hair, she sat on a plush chair and gazed across his kingdom to the west, where the ocean lay no claim upon the land. Verdant landscapes and the twinkling of the green essence, like fireflies scattered across the land, fought for triumph against the sparkle of the stars. She inhaled the fresh, salty air and sighed. The essence swirled around her and settled on her skin, softly tickling her once more.

Umbrea was beautiful, its charm not only in its lush scenery but also in the peaceful atmosphere that enveloped everyone here. Unlike Joro, where citizens faced punishments and restrictions on their essential resources. Food, shelter, and safety shouldn't be hard to find. It was *wrong*.

If the Jotnar had a reliable supply of food from Joro, why were they trying to break the dome? It didn't add up. She saw firsthand how people were treated in the Camp. The Wyrd was just an excuse for cruelty to kill and control.

She thought about Mordred. How old was he, anyway? When she was a child, he was the lord then, as well. How long had he been running the city prior to her father? If the lord wasn't the one in charge, then who was this Monster King pulling the strings?

She refused to believe her father was intentionally hurting people now that he was the lord. There was more at play that she didn't understand yet.

Warm hands gently rested on her shoulders as she gazed into the distance. She looked up and saw Cahir standing behind her, smiling down with a tenderness of love she hadn't allowed herself to see before.

"It's beautiful here, Cahir," she said as she looked across the land to the distant mountain range beyond, bathed in soft moonlight.

"This could be your home, too," he replied. "We could stay here... together."

Seda hadn't thought about that. She had no plans when she escaped the Camp; her only goal was to find safety. Peace sounded nice. She had finally found the safety she had been searching for.

For several heartbeats, she breathed in the fresh air, allowing the silence to settle.

Her journey to the Wisps and meeting with Tahti had taught her more about herself than she had realized. She was called a key, someone, or *something* necessary for the safety of all of Xyberus.

She thought about Joro and how living there only taught her fear. She tensed when she remembered the painful cries from Esper in the Camp.

The others who lived there deserved to live in a place like this, too.

Remaining in Umbrea was a childish hope.

"I can't. I'm needed for things I don't even understand yet," she finally whispered.

Cahir stayed silent for a moment. He gradually took his hands off her shoulders and let out a sigh. "I wish things were different."

"Me, too."

He gently touched her hair and twirled it around his fingers. "This is changing," he said of her sparkling strands.

"Yeah, I've been noticing that as well." She collected a handful of it and admired it in the moonlight's glow.

"Would you like to go to the library now?" he asked, extending his hand to her. "I have a book I'd like us to see when we get there, as well."

She accepted his offered hand, and they left the patio, heading toward where she hoped to find answers.

# CHAPTER 18

<u>Seda</u>

Cahir carried a weathered book as they walked, one he had picked up from his bedside table before leaving.
When they entered the library, they began in the history section, where Seda was last with Meir. Most of the books were covered in a thick layer of dust as they pulled them from the shelves and sorted through them on the table. They were surrounded by a diverse range of options, including the history of the Fae, historical recipes, and stories of monsters.

Nothing in that section was quite right, and Seda sighed in frustration. The only interesting option here was the book he had brought, which he was looking through.

"Nothing here helps. What's that one about?" she asked as she plopped roughly into the chair beside him, causing it to squeak.

He sighed. "Tahti seems to have gone missing. But I found this book in her house."

"She's missing?!" Seda gasped.

"Yup. Went there to talk to her, and her house was empty, as if she hadn't lived there in years. The only two things left were her cauldron and this book."

Where would Tahti have gone, and why was she missing? She had just seen her not long ago.

"What does it say?" Seda asked as she scooted her chair closer to him, feeling the warmth of his leg brush against hers.

"All of the pages are blank," he replied. He handed her the book, and she opened it.

"They're not blank," she said, reading the scribbled words scratched through each page.

"What?" Cahir looked over the book again. "What do you mean?"

"They aren't blank." She pointed to a page. "This one's a spell of remaking."

She looked up at Cahir, whose mouth hung open. He closed it and cleared his throat. "What else does it say?"

She flipped through more pages, each inscribed with a different spell. Some were gruesome, others sweet. She saw a page about a love potion and chuckled to herself.

"Well, shit, Seda. I suppose this book's for you," Cahir replied as he ran his hands down his face.

"We should see if anyone else can read it. It can't be just me."

"Who knows. A lot of crazy things seem to happen for you." He smirked and sat back in his chair. "Let's go to the Royal Alcove. Nothing else here seems like it's going to help us."

"Is that where the scrolls are kept?" Seda perked up.

"It is."

They returned the books they had taken out to their original locations, except for the one Cahir had brought, which Seda kept, and he held out his hand for her to take. The familiar, comforting warmth of his hand reminded her of their time in

Joro, of their hands entwined as they walked the dusty roads together. The memory felt like so long ago.

Cahir led her down the stairs to the main floor and stopped in front of an empty bookshelf. She looked at him with confusion and was about to ask what he was focusing on when he released some of his magic from his palms. It spread through the empty shelves, filling them like smoke through the air. The bookshelf slowly swung open like a door.

A small room came into view. Cobwebs lined the ceilings, and an unlit candle chandelier hung from the ceiling. The scent of old books drifted from the room.

"Umm..." Seda hesitantly started.

"Don't tell me you're scared." Cahir looked at her with a glint in his eye. "I promise you there aren't jars of fermented eggs in there."

She smacked him in the arm and confidently strolled in. "There better not be, you just cleaned yourself up."

He smirked at her, and her heart fluttered in her chest in response.

After Cahir lit the candles on the chandelier, Seda spent a few minutes examining the old shelves filled with both books and tightly bound scrolls, all covered in a thick layer of dust. There were random fingerprints on the shelves, as if Meir had forgotten to disguise his tracks. But everything appeared to be in place, with no noticeable gaps within the shelves.

Most of the items were written in a different language, so she wasn't sure where to begin.

A small black book caught her eye. It was decorated with gold-pressed lettering on the cover. "A History of Magic," she read aloud.

Cahir lifted his head and rolled up the scroll he was reading through. She brought the book to the table and sat down in the chair next to him.

He shifted closer to her and looked down at the gold font. "That looks promising, at least."

She opened the book and went through the summary.

*A historical account of magic's origins and evolution over thousands of years, tracing its birth from the two high gods to its inheritance by mortals. Throughout history, magic has allowed Xyberus to flourish. In this book, we explore the early stages, from the rise of the Mother Goddess to the creation of other magical beings. These beings, both mortal and eternal, have fought wars across the land, spreading magic deeper into the world of Xyberus. Combining arcane theory and history, A History of Magic is a comprehensive guide for those seeking to learn more about the origins and development of magic.*

She quickly turned to the first chapter on the Mother Goddess and read it.

"This is amazing. I had no idea anything like this existed. Do you think they have chronicles like this in the Joro library?" Seda asked Cahir excitedly.

Cahir sneered. "I highly doubt it. That place is so subservient and controlled, they probably don't have anything on magic there at all."

She hummed and kept reading. Each chapter described the different beings and their magical powers. One focused on Supay, the god of death, and his attempt to take over the mortal world millennia ago. The image on his page featured a black moth with a skull inlaid into the center. There were pages on guardians and mystical beings, with one chapter devoted to the Vatte and their earthen magic. A passage describing magical beings cursed for their greed and condemned to live as golden trees caught her attention. Unfortunately, most of the text lacked accompanying pictures.

She paused when she flipped the page, and the familiar image of a black snake appeared.

Seda gasped. "It was him!" She pointed to the picture on the page, and Cahir leaned over to look as she read aloud.

*Somnium, the Guardian of The Last Sleep, was once considered a myth. Now, he rules over Noctyra, a land in the distant eastern regions of Xyberus. There are a few accounts of his encounters, and he is hard to locate. As a result, little is understood about his complete magical powers. What is known is that he can read minds and induce terrifying dreams, resulting in pain and death. The most divine creation of Supay, he has snake familiars but appears as a demonic, armored figure. Somnium is seen as cruel and selfish, thriving on inspiring fear and horror in the sleeping realm of beings.*

While other chapters of this book spanned multiple pages, Somnium's chapter was just a single page featuring a detailed image of a large, black-scaled snake with elongated fangs. The same fangs Seda remembered when she passed out in the rose garden.

"What does he want from me? I thought all the gods fled?" she asked.

"Apparently not all of them," Cahir replied. She looked up at him and watched as he bit his lower lip.

"There's something else, Cahir…" Seda started.

Cahir's emerald eyes locked onto hers, and she inhaled sharply. Should she tell him her assumption? He didn't catch her reference to the eye color back in his bedroom, and trust went both ways. She was *trying* to tread down that path with him again.

"I believe this is Kalon." She pointed at the image.

Cahir froze, going deathly quiet, and his face shadowed under the light.

Silence lingered for a moment before he finally spoke. "He said he had something you wanted. It's the Stone of Protection he stole from you."

A clock chimed in the room three times, causing Seda to jump, but Cahir remained unaffected by the sudden noise.

"We should probably head to bed. I have some things I need to take care of tomorrow and am expecting Praxis back with the trade crew," Cahir responded while anger radiated off of him.

Seda went to place the book back on the shelf when Cahir gently took it from her hand. "I'd like to read more about this."

Cahir's anger was palpable, and she could feel his heat of fury like a simmering woodstove warming an already hot house.

"What should I say to him the next time he comes to me in my dreams? My magic didn't affect him," she asked nervously. She wasn't sure why he was so upset. Yes, Kalon had stolen her moonstone and provoked Cahir on their journey to the Wisps, but this sudden change of demeanor was… unexpected. Perhaps telling him was the wrong choice, after all.

"You can stay in my room. I'll wake you up if you start tossing and turning."

She hesitated to accept his offer because of his emotions, but she didn't want to be alone. She also feared it would be too apparent that the idea of lying next to him, feeling safe in his arms, and possibly kissing him again, excited her. But was it really so wrong to feel excited about something like that? She genuinely wanted to experience it again.

She looked up at him and smiled. "I'd love that."

He tucked the book under his arm and blew out the candles, bathing the room in darkness once more.

# CHAPTER 19

### Ael

Ael took steadying breaths as they walked back to his room. His mind was racing. She mentioned having dreams of snakes all her life, and Kalon had been especially interested in her from the moment he saw her arrive in the dunes. He also spoke of Seda as if he had known her for a much longer time than he actually had.

Kalon had to be Somnium.

The image of the Gnashing Flora writhing in pain flashed through his mind. That was so sudden, and no one had done anything to stop the monstrous plant from its attack. It had to have been Kalon's magic. Also, Kalon didn't have the same dragon tattoo as the other Rising members.

It all made sense.

Well, mostly. How did he know Seda before meeting her? Had he sensed she was special from the moment her beautiful soul entered this world? Or was it something else?

One thing was sure, though: Kalon couldn't have her. Seda belonged to him.

They entered his dimly lit room, where Seda sat on the silken sheets, fidgeting with her fingers. He could tell she was nervous. Hopefully, it wasn't because of his reaction to Kalon and his anger that he couldn't swallow down in the library.

He sat beside her and held her hands to calm not only her but himself as well. She looked up at him, her beautiful, storm-filled eyes meeting his.

"I'm sorry I got upset, Sed. That man can't be trusted, and I'll do everything I can to stop him from getting to you." He took another deep breath.

Seda bit her lip, anxious tension radiating from her posture, and his eyes tracked the movement.

They were close in proximity and alone on his bed.

His cock involuntarily firmed, and he silently scolded himself. He knew he shouldn't be thinking about that when she was worried about Kalon or Somnium, whatever the fuck his name was, haunting her dreams.

"There's no need to feel nervous, Seda. I'll be here if he comes for you."

She hesitated and blushed brightly, "Oh… yes. Thank you."

He reached for the blankets and pulled them back, patting the bed for her to get in, and she slid under the covers. He crawled in from the opposite side of the bed and looked into her eyes, their faces just inches apart.

She hesitantly reached up and gently ran her fingers through a strand of his hair, the feeling, once again, rushing straight to his pants. He pretended to reposition himself on the bed, creating more space between them, and let himself ache without her noticing.

He could tell from the pulse in her throat that her heartbeat was racing. He didn't want her to be so scared. He would always protect her, even if it were just making sure she woke up from a nightmare into the safety of his arms.

Her eyes darted between his and then down to his lips. "Umm… can we kiss again?" she asked.

*Fuck. Yes.*

His lips parted into a smile, and he said, "Sed, you never need to ask. I'll kiss you whenever. Even if I'm burning alive, I'll kiss you."

She gently pressed her soft lips against his, moaning when he returned the gesture. He wrapped his hand around her neck and pulled her closer, firmly holding her face to his.

Her desire swept through the air as he groaned into the softness of her mouth, gently biting her bottom lip.

He adjusted and leaned over her, pressing her into the mattress with his hand still wrapped around her, softly licking her lip to soothe the bite he had just given.

Their lips remained connected, and he never wanted it to end.

*Fucking mine*, he thought.

Anticipation swarmed through him as she reached for his hand and guided it under her shirt. He inhaled sharply when his fingers brushed the soft skin of her breast and hardened nipple.

He throbbed, feeling himself swell as his desire blew out of control. He tried not to, but his kiss grew rougher, more uncontrolled, and he rolled her nipple between his fingers. Her eyes shot open, and she moaned into his mouth. He splayed his fingers and gently squeezed her breast within his palm, kneading the soft tissue. She was so fucking soft.

She pulled away from him and lifted her shirt over her head, allowing her full breasts to spill out between them.

A low growl vibrated from his throat as he looked down and admired the perfection that lay before him. He couldn't stop himself, didn't want to stop himself, and he bent down lower and sucked a nipple into his mouth, his cock aching and straining against his pants as she moaned.

He swirled his tongue around and sucked on it, letting it pop loudly when he released it from his lips.

*So fucking perfect.*

"Oh my *gods*, Cahir," she gasped.

"Repeat my name. I only want *my* name coming from that perfect fucking mouth," he commanded as he smiled wickedly above her nipple and blew onto it.

She had never felt this before—never felt someone love her the way she deserved—and he was going to give her *everything*.

He slowly reached his fingers under the hemline of her shorts and ran his fingers over her underwear, groaning when he felt her soaking through the material. Ever so slowly, he slid his fingers under and ran them around her clit, growling when he felt how soft she was.

She gasped under him, her body trembling. He pulled them out and sucked them into his mouth, finally savoring her taste for the first time.

*So fucking divine. So fucking mine.*

He circled his fingers around her again, around and around, painfully slow, loving how her body shuddered in response.

"Oh... *Cahir*," she moaned and pressed her hips into him. He teased her entrance and swirled his fingers over her opening.

Her breathing became labored, and she grabbed onto his shoulders firmly. He pulled his fingers away and ran them over her clit again, loving the feeling of the skin he had dreamed about touching so many times before.

He was so hard and groaned as he pressed himself against the mattress, allowing himself this one, only this one, bit of sensation. His focus was solely on her. He continued to rub his finger around her and sucked her nipple back into his mouth, synching the swirling of his tongue to the swirling and pressure of his fingers.

He looked up at her and saw the pure bliss on her face as she watched him, her jaw slightly open and her bright eyes fixed on him.

He could do this all night. He *wanted* to do this all night. The smell of her was dizzying, electrifying. He released her nipple from his lips and slowly kissed his way down her stomach.

She was rocking her hips against the rhythm of his movements, and he pulled his hand away. He heard her groan, wanting more, and he smiled to himself.

She was completely unaware of what was coming next.

He pulled her shorts and underwear off and spread her legs open, groaning loudly when he saw her for the first time. Beautiful and glistening, just for *him*. He couldn't help the moan that escaped him as he looked at how swollen and ready she was, and he licked his lips in anticipation.

He looked back into those glowing violet eyes, so wide they illuminated her chest.

"W-What are you doing?" she asked, trying to close her legs.

He parted them once more and grinned at her when her eyes widened further.

"I have been starved, Seda." He didn't let her react before he leaned in and ran his tongue along the center of her, sucking her into his mouth and humming in pleasure. She tasted better than he had imagined, better than anything he had ever experienced before, surpassing even the richest of honey cakes. He firmly pressed his tongue against her clit, swirling it around and feeling her whimper under him.

She gasped, and her hips began to move in sync with his tongue as she pressed into him. He peered up and saw her head thrown back, gazing at the ceiling as she basked in the feeling of being worshiped for the first time in her life.

He slid his fingers into her, pressing them back and forth against the sensitive area inside, slowly sliding them in and out.

She cried out and rocked herself against him harder. Supporting himself with his elbow, he firmly pressed his hand on her lower abdomen to hold her down.

He noticed her breathing change, her body trembling, and he couldn't help himself any longer. He ground his cock against the mattress and moaned back into her. He slowly thrust himself into the softness below, through his pants, pretending it was her, matching the same rhythm of her hips.

She screamed his name into the darkness of the room, her fingers digging into the mattress, and she exploded in a bright purple glow, lighting up the darkened room.

He ground himself firmly into the mattress once more, and fire erupted from within. He felt the rush of warm cum fill his underwear, and he moaned loudly into her pulsating core while still focusing on the movement of his tongue to ensure her high lasted as long as possible.

Kalon may have had her first kiss, but he had the gift of her first orgasm, and it would belong to *him* for-fucking-ever.

She was angelic, a divine being sent from the stars, and he was created to worship her… *forever.*

A loud crash shattered the bedroom door, flooding the room with warmth. Ael instinctively shifted in front of Seda and activated his magic into a misty shield, protecting them from the flying debris.

He heard the sound of her sizzling storm igniting behind him, but she was his to protect.

A deep, red glow entered the room through the dust and mingled with Seda's purple, bathing it in vibrant magenta.

Ael watched as jagged, snarling teeth neared his face in the dim light, with blood and fur caught between them.

Elco growled deep in his throat, causing the room to shake—threat and promise of violence visible on his menacing face.

# CHAPTER 20

<u>Seda</u>

"I heard you screaming, moon-flutter. Are you injured?" Elco growled through clenched teeth, narrowing his eyes at Cahir amid the smoke still billowing from his nostrils. "Just say the word, and I'll devour him."

"Everything's fine," Seda gasped, still recovering and out of breath. "You're not allowed to eat him, Elco."

She felt Cahir tense against her, and his magic thickened around them. She reached up to brush along his back, trying to calm him and the situation.

"Are you certain? I've never tried Fae, but I hear it's quite delicious."

"*No*, Elco, and I'm not injured. Quite the opposite, actually." She felt her cheeks heat. Did she really admit that out loud?

Elco's eyes shifted from Cahir to her and back again. He slanted them further and pressed his nose against Cahir's shield, smushing it into the green layer of mist that prevented him from passing—an obvious threat.

"Tell him this shield will do *nothing* to stop me. Tell him if he ever hurts you, *ever*, he'll be mine to savor."

She cleared her throat. "I'll tell him. I appreciate your concern, but I'm very much okay."

He growled once more and slowly backed away, leaving the room. The guards who were watching over Seda's door came rushing in, gasping. Cahir quickly grabbed the blanket and threw it over Seda.

"Sire! We tried to stop him, but he knocked us over!" They glanced between Cahir and Seda and quickly looked away, one running a hand over their neck. "I see both of us and the Lionne have intruded. Our apologies. If you don't need us, we'll be on our way."

"Find someone to fix the doors," Cahir commanded. "We'll move to her room for the remainder of the night."

They both bowed and exited the room.

"I should find my clothes," Seda said. She didn't want to walk the hallway with others outside, only to be draped in a blanket.

Cahir shifted off the bed and stood guard at the broken doorway, unaffected by the visible bulge in his pants, while Seda searched for her clothing. She found them on the floor and shook out the wood shards.

Cahir grabbed a fresh pair of underwear and picked her up bridal style, carrying her over the mess into her hallway. She looked over and saw that Elco had not only busted down Cahir's doors but also his own. Roya, Ferona, Askold, and Benny stood in the hall with their mouths hanging open. Roya and Ferona had their claws out and ready to fight.

"I'm okay! It was just a misunderstanding," she told them, noticing Benny's smirk forming. Both Ferona and Roya quickly looked down at Cahir's bulge, their eyes widening at the realization of what happened.

Embarrassment burned her cheeks. She heard multiple Fae running down the hall to clean up the mess, but Cahir walked through her doorway and slammed the door shut behind him, muffling the noise in the hall. He laid her on her bed and carefully removed her shorts and underwear again.

"There might be more debris in those," he said as he stared down at her, a devious smile forming across his face.

"Uh-huh… *sure*," she replied with a forced laugh, trying to move past what just happened and the embarrassment burning through her stomach.

She watched him as he gazed at her with love, the green orbs fluttering above through the glass ceiling, emphasizing his eye color.

Seda had no words to describe what she had just experienced. Was this what sex was supposed to be like? Her only experience was vastly different.

She hadn't touched herself or felt those sensations before. She always refrained from anything in that regard, ever since she was younger. Sure, she had imaginary crushes on the men from her books, and she loved the excitement that brewed low in her stomach when she reached the chapters where the main characters shared a kiss, and sometimes more, but this was completely new.

She loved it. She wanted *more*.

"Wow…" she breathlessly whispered to Cahir, who was watching her with a dimpled grin. Her heart melted as she got lost in his beautiful emerald eyes. "What about you?"

Cahir removed his shirt and lay next to her on the bed. She couldn't help but stare at the defined muscles of his abdomen, trailing her eyes lower, and noticing his rather large erection pressing against his pants. A wet spot was clearly visible through the fabric.

"I may have enjoyed that a lot, as well," he said with a wide grin.

Her eyes went wide. "How—"

"You're so fucking perfect, Sed. You have no idea. I feel like I'm in heaven right now."

She felt a blush creep across her chest and cheeks as he shifted himself closer to her on the bed. He nuzzled into her, and she hesitantly reached down and touched his length through his pants.

He hissed into her ear and shifted away from her. "You do that, Seda, and I'll want *more*. We need sleep."

He adjusted himself near her again, and she slowly ran her fingers down the ridges of his stomach, watching as he shuddered and the muscles of his stomach clenched. She trailed lower and brushed her fingertips over the top of his erection once more, and he hissed again, this time not moving away.

She looked into his burning eyes, his pupils dilated, and licked her lips. He caught the moment and watched as her tongue slid across them. She slowly swirled the tip of her finger around his hardened length, and he groaned, pressing his eyes closed. She continued to swirl her fingertip, trying to catch it every time it jerked away.

He opened his hooded eyes, and his lips parted. She adjusted herself and kissed him as she continued to circle her finger over him, and he whimpered into her mouth.

He slowly pulled away from her and tenderly kissed her forehead. "As much as I want this, it's late, and I need to stay alert for you."

Cahir shifted off the bed and pulled his pants down his hips, changing into the clean underwear he brought with him. Seda's gaze fixed on his narrow waist and muscular backside. She grinned. It was so firm.

He climbed back into bed with her, and she rested her head on his chest, listening to his heartbeat.

They lay in bed, holding each other tightly, their souls intertwined like tree roots beneath the earth. Seda pressed her nose to his chest and inhaled his cedar scent as his fingers gently stroked her hair. The comforting touch of his hand made her eyelids feel heavy.

She fought sleep, worried that Kalon might come back into her dreams, but she felt safe surrounded by Cahir's protection. If he chose to join her dreams, Cahir would wake her up.

"Sleep. I'm here. I'll *always* protect you. You're fucking mine, Sed. He can't get to you," he said to her.

Seda closed her eyes and leaned back against his chest, listening once more to his rapid heartbeat, the pounding drowning out all other sounds. She gradually fell asleep to his steady rhythm in her ears, finally feeling safe once again.

DARKNESS SURROUNDED *Seda as the wind tore through her hair. She could see the glimmer of stars above her, twinkling like heartbeats through the sky.*

*She could hear the sounds of people screaming and birds cawing in the distance, and pushed muscles she didn't recognize further toward the chaos.*

*Then, people were running around her as fires enveloped homes, as Jotnar tore through the village, snagging people with wild fervor and eating them whole.*

*She felt the burning sensation of rage radiate from her chest, and pain tore through her soul.*

*The world was cruel and unbalanced.*

*She glanced back, seeing Somnium a few steps behind, clad in his armor and skull mask. He was taking down the Jotnar two at a time, tormenting their minds with nightmares and making their bodies writhe on the dirt roads. Blood seeped out of their noses, and then their bodies lay frozen on the ground, death claiming them into the pits of hell.*

*He looked over at her, at her chest pulsating violently and her hair alight.*

*She heard him scream and saw him run toward her, tearing off his mask, and revealing wild eyes with fear etched into his features.*

*A bright purple light exploded around her... and then the scene shifted.*

*She was in the damp cell in the Camp, fighting against Alexi as he pressed her into the mattress. She felt anger surge through her body, and she shoved him away from her.*

*Alexi's body flew across the cell, jolting with violent electrical shocks.*

"Next time, don't toast for so long, please."

# CHAPTER 21

<u>The Monster King</u>

The Monster King's nostrils were assaulted by the acidic smell of urine within Mordred's cell as he stood before the bars.

The stupid, betraying fool had given up no further information after this last session, where he had lost his fourth finger. Each time they did this, they drew out the pain, sawing through each finger more slowly.

Nevertheless, the bastard refused to provide anything of use.

"There's no point in doing this," Jason said from beside him. "He isn't speaking. He likely doesn't know anything else."

The Monster King slowly moved his gaze from Mordred to look at Jason. So far, Jason had followed every request of his without hesitation, but he was starting to wonder: every time they tortured Mordred, he tried to stop him from pushing further.

He narrowed his eyes at Jason, whose constantly neutral face showed no indication of caring. Did this man not care about anything? Or was he that good? Was he working alongside Mordred somehow?

"Besides, your informant is about to arrive here soon. We should get out of this disgusting cell. I'm tired of the smell," Jason said, his face still neutral in appearance.

He had a point. The informant was about to arrive any minute. He had received a letter indicating that the informant had been following Seda and her 'friends' and had an update to share. This informant was the only reason he knew about Seda in the first place.

"Fine," he gruffed.

They walked away from Mordred and exited the long hall. The Monster King inhaled the fresh desert air as they left. It had been weeks, and the stupid, fucking Jotnar hadn't come any closer to breaking down the dome. He desperately wanted a fresh veilroot smoke, so he strode ahead of Jason and headed to his office, Jason following him like the fucking puppy he was.

When he opened the door, his informant was sitting in a chair waiting for him, looking like he had flown through the night to reach the Camp.

"Ahh... at last, we meet again," the Monster King said as he approached his desk, reaching for the veilroot and a piece of paper within his desk drawer. He watched Jason's eyes widen as he recognized who stood before him.

*Interesting... How did he know of him?*

The informant didn't respond. He was a quiet one, which often irritated the Monster King. He looked back over at him as he licked the paper and rolled up the smoke.

"Jason, I need a light," he commanded.

Jason walked over and lit the match for him, which he easily could have done himself, but it was better to watch him do it.

He inhaled the veilroot, and the calming sensation spread to his fingertips.

"What did you learn? Where's the moonstone?" he asked the informant.

"It was stolen," he replied.

Anger surged through his temple, and he ground his teeth together. "How did it slip past you?"

"I had some assumptions that one of the people traveling with us wasn't who they claimed to be. And now I have reason to believe that this person, Kalon, is actually who you call Somnium."

The Monster King's eyes widened, and he paused, with his veilroot smoke grazing his bottom lip. No one had ever seen Somnium's face before. He was elusive, appearing only in armor and a mask.

"How did you figure this out?" he asked as he inhaled once more, watching the informant through narrowed eyes.

"We were in a fight with a Gnashing Flora, and suddenly the plant started to writhe into itself, like it was having a painful nightmare. I'm aware you suffer from the same?" his informant asked.

Yes. Yes, he did. He had one just this morning. He desperately wanted to kill that fucker, Somnium. He loathed having someone control him—someone more powerful than he and able to withstand the magic of the Dark Stone.

"What does he look like?" He blew smoke into the room.

"He's tall with dark olive-toned skin, long black hair, and the brightest blue eyes I've ever seen."

He knew about the piercing eye color. He could see them behind the mask every time he arrived to pick up the children they had gathered for him.

"And how did he steal the stone?" He inhaled the smoke again and blew it out through his nostrils, glaring at his informant with hatred for Somnium.

"He tricked Seda by kissing her and stole it from her neck in the middle of the night," the informant said with birdlike eyes that flicked between him and his smoke.

The Monster King looked over to Jason, who was fidgeting. Jason pretended he didn't care about Seda, but obviously, he did, given the nervous anxiety that rolled off his body.

He looked back at the man before him. "And where is Seda now? Is the Lionne still with her?"

"Yes, they're in Umbrea. I nearly got caught sneaking through her corridor at night. King Ael seems interested in her. He lived in Joro for many years, passing as a human named Cahir."

He heard Jason gasp, and he looked over at him while pursing his lips.

"Do you know of him, Jason?" he seethed, studying him intently.

Jason nodded, his face returning to its usual dull, neutral stare. "Yes, Sire. He was trying to conceive with Seda while they were in Joro. I had no idea he wasn't human."

*Fucking fool,* the Monster King thought.

The Monster King sneered and looked back over to his informant. "And why should I continue to trust someone who's betraying their own kind?"

"Not all of us are loyal to her. My sister's an idiot for thinking she could be anything more than the pathetic person Seda truly is."

"What's your name again?" The Monster King stepped back to his desk and leaned against it.

"Feich," the informant replied.

"And how did you get away from this group you were traveling with?" he asked him.

"I faked my own death. They all believe I'm dead."

The Monster King studied him for a long time. He walked

over to him and looked up into his dark eyes and moonlight skin.

"Do you know what I do to betrayers?" he asked while pulling out the Dark Stone from his pocket. The deep burning sensation he often felt when he touched the stone ran up his arm, giving him a sudden burst of powerful energy, just waiting to be used.

"Yes, I do. I'm not a betrayer. I'm loyal to only what's best for the Corvids."

The Monster King grinned and placed the stone back into his pocket.

"Gather the Corvids who aren't loyal to Seda and report back to me as soon as possible. Be discreet. We don't want word of this traveling."

Feich nodded, stood from his chair, and walked out of the office.

When the door closed, the Monster King looked over to Jason. "I'm having trouble trusting you, Jason. You've been lenient with Mordred's punishments, and now I discover that King Ael of the Fae has been living under our noses for years. Someone who, apparently, was close to you."

He walked to the door, opened the creaky metal, and called over a few Dragors.

When they walked in, he said to Jason, "I apparently need to remind you who's in charge around here. And it's *not* you. Let's hope this lesson never has to happen again."

The room darkened as the door closed, and the Monster King smiled as Jason began to scream into the dimly lit room.

# CHAPTER 22

Ael*

(300 years ago)

"Cahir, darling, *please* stop flying that thing so close to my work," Ael's mother, Misandra, pleaded with him as he flew his paper airplane with his newfound magic. They were in her dark room, as they usually were, while she focused on her important work—something related to a different kind of magic she often mentioned.

"But mama, I *booorreedddd*." He dropped the plane mid-flight, and it landed on the stone floor with a soft thud. He roughly sat down in the chair, pouted, and crossed his arms, making sure to furrow his eyebrows especially hard at the back of her head. He glared at her long black hair streaked with white. Ael was bored with being in this room and wanted to go outside and play with Luelle.

A slight smile touched his lips, but he kept his brows furrowed as he thought about Luelle and the funny trick she played on one of the maids. She was a couple of years older than him and his bestest-best friend in the entire world, even if she sometimes teased him.

His mama's back was still turned away from him as she reviewed her papers and picked up some funny-smelling leaves. "I can sense how you're staring at me, Cahir. You know I have the eyeball on the back of my head."

He quickly masked his anger as she turned around and looked at him. "It's not polite to make mean faces at people." She furrowed her brows and pouted, exaggerating his own expression just moments earlier.

Ael couldn't help but laugh at the silly-looking expression, and she ran forward, swooping him into her arms and kissing him all over.

"I sorry, mama," he choked out through laughter. She began tickling him, and he struggled to breathe through the happiness that swelled within him.

When she stopped, he reached out and tried to tickle her back, but she quickly ran away from him. He chased her around the room, bumping into her amethyst crystals and knocking them over. When he finally caught her, his mighty wrath descended upon her, especially with tickles to her neck, where she always laughed the hardest.

"Stop, Cahir! I give in! I give in!" she said through ragged breaths. She pulled him into a big hug, and when she finally released him, she looked into his eyes, which mirrored her own emerald gaze. "You are the best little boy in the entire world. Do you know that? I love you so much."

He nodded his head as he gently reached for the dark bruise under her eye. How was she always getting hurt? "I wuv you more. To the moon and back."

Luelle always teased him about how he said 'love', and he winced when he realized he said it wrong—again. It was the best he could do, though, and Mama didn't seem to mind.

She cupped his hand in hers and reached forward to kiss him on the forehead.

He felt around her head, searching for that mysterious eyeball she always talked about. He could never find it. "Where's the extra eyeball, Mama?"

"Only adults can see it, Cahir. It developed as I grew you in my womb and was made *extra special* so I could always keep watch over you."

He wasn't entirely sure about that because sometimes he stuck his tongue out at her, and she didn't notice.

"Let's go find your father." She reached out her hand, and they made their way out of the dark room, through the dark halls, and back into the main hallway.

The castle was so big and so tall, and not long into their walk, his legs felt tired. She pulled him up and carried him the rest of the way, and he nestled into her warm arms, pressing his ear to her chest and listening to the steady rhythm of her heartbeat.

When they crossed the familiar double doors to his parents' wing, he heard loud sounds coming from his father's bedroom.

His mama stilled.

"Is Daddy okay?" Ael asked her, noticing how her heart had quickly changed its beat.

She didn't respond as she slowly set him down. "Stay here, Cahir." Her face looked serious, and it frightened him. His mama was never serious. Only Daddy was serious.

He tried to ask again, this time whispering, "Is Daddy okay, Mama?"

"Stay *here*," she reiterated, and Ael stood frozen in the hallway, watching with wide eyes as she neared his bedroom.

She flung the door open and marched in, slamming the door behind her.

Ael heard screams and the shattering of glass. Suddenly, the door swung open, and a maid hurried out. She was the same maid Luelle often played tricks on. The maid was unclothed and dashed past him, vanishing down the corridor.

*Ewwwwwwww,* he thought. You only got naked when you took a bath. He shifted his eyes back onto the now open door and took a hesitant step forward.

He heard louder sounds, and the sudden scream made him lurch forward. As he entered the room, he saw his father standing over Mama. Blood dripped from a cut on her face, matching the blood on his father's hand.

He felt so scared. She was hurt. He needed to protect her. He *loved* Mama.

"Cahir..." she choked out when she saw him, her eyes going wide.

Ael tried to run toward her, but Daddy turned around, and the familiar look of anger met Ael, stopping him in his tracks. The only things his daddy wore were the crown on his head and the blood on his hand. Why was he also naked?

Guards and the mean witch, Tahti, rushed into the room.

"Get him out of here *NOW!*" Daddy shouted at the guards. The guards grabbed Ael, and he screamed in response, kicking his legs wildly.

He had to protect Mama and help her.

He broke free from their grasp and ran to her, embracing her tightly. Blood covered his hands, arms, and shirt as he held her close, longing for his own body to shield her from further pain.

"Mama..." he cried into her. He could feel her heart pounding rapidly beneath him. Mama was frightened. He had to be brave and strong. It was not right that Daddy hurt her!

His father quickly walked up from behind and painfully yanked him away from her. He struck his father with all his strength, but his father remained unfazed.

*Daddy should never hurt Mama!*

He screamed as the guards seized him again, this time holding him more tightly. He kicked and yelled at the guards, but couldn't break free.

Tightly clutching him, they carried him away from Daddy's bedroom, quickly shutting the double doors behind them, leaving Daddy, the witch, and Mama behind.

He heard his Daddy say, "It's time."

His Mama's screams echoed once more through the hall, and he reached out with his hands, trying to grab for the door that got farther away with each step, watching in horror as Mama's blood covered his arms and hands.

THE DARKENED clouds in the sky parted, and a waterfall of sunlight filtered through, casting its rainbow of light onto Mama's closed casket where she lay within. Everyone stood there in mourning as the magical essence swirled around them all, dancing up along the cliffside where the casket was placed.

The box was tightly closed, and Ael couldn't see her. He wanted to be close. What if her box fell over the edge into the raging waters of the ocean below?

Tears ran down his cheeks. His mama was his favorite person in the whole world. He didn't know someone could 'pass away'. What did that even mean?

Daddy said she would never come back.

This was a new pain for him, one he didn't understand or know how to handle. Before this, the worst thing he had felt was when Luelle tripped him, and he fell into the gravel, causing his blood to pool on his knee.

Mama helped him then, gently brushing away the small rocks and cleaning him up. Mama wasn't here now to help the hurt.

This felt different. It hurt more.

He stepped closer to her casket and dropped to his knees, pressing his ear to the box, trying and praying to hear her soothing heartbeat through the wood.

Only silence greeted him.

"It's time to get up, Ael," Daddy sternly said behind him. "It's time to *grow up*."

He cried into his hands and collapsed further onto the ground, pressing the side of his face to the rocky ground below, feeling the kiss of sunshine heat his other cheek.

"Fucking disgrace," his father said of him as he and everyone else walked away.

Ael lay there alone as he firmly pressed his eyes closed. He cried out loudly, perhaps to no one specific, or to anyone who would listen, or even to the heavens, the earth, and the depths of hell itself.

This pain felt like his heart was dropping into his stomach, and it hurt so very much.

A soft hand pressed against his cheek and lightly brushed away a tear.

He cracked open his eyes and saw the blurry image of Luelle kneeling beside him. She leaned down and hugged him tightly, her long golden ponytail draping over his shoulder.

"I'm so sorry, Cahir," she whispered.

Ael sat up and angrily brushed the tears away from his cheeks and forced his tongue to move how it was supposed to, "I *love* my mama. Only she could call me that name. My name is *Ael*."

Luelle paused before she said, "Okay, Ael."

She sat alongside him, grabbing his hand into hers and rubbing her thumb back and forth over his palm.

They sat there, with hands tightly intertwined, as the clouds thickened once more and rain began to trickle from the sky, blending with the pain sliding down their cheeks.

They allowed the rain to soak through their clothes and listened to the deafening thunder rumble across the earth.

They sat there until the sky darkened, the clouds parted, and the twinkling of stars glittered above.

And there they remained... both trying to understand what death was at such a young age and how to cope with the loss of such a special person.

Luelle didn't release his hand once.

# CHAPTER 23

<u>Luelle</u>

Luelle awoke in her uncomfortable chair in the dark hallway. Last night was dull, and Neoma had no visitors in her room. She spent most of the night watching her sleep under the plush blankets, wishing it were her lying on that soft-looking bed instead of sitting in the damn chair.

She needed to find someone to bring something more comfortable to spy from, but Ael was the only one aware of her presence within these halls.

Maybe he could carry another in for her.

She sighed and slowly stood from the seat, quietly groaning as her joints felt stiff from hours in the same position. She glanced one last time through the hole and saw Neoma still asleep.

Yesterday, after she saw Neoma and Meir together in the garden, she rushed to Ael as quickly as she could, and Ael promised that Neoma would be leaving the castle as soon as possible.

For whatever reason, she was still here.

Where was Ael anyway? What time was it?

She moved through the dark halls and stopped at the end of her favorite tapestry, listening for anyone on the other side.

Carefully moving aside the hanging rug, she peeked out and saw that the morning light filtered through the windows. She let out a sigh of relief when no one was around and slowly slipped out.

She began walking down the open corridor, and after turning a corner, she accidentally bumped into someone and stumbled backward.

Meir stood there, staring at her with angry eyes. "Where have you been, Luelle?"

She plastered a smile on her face, despite wanting to smack him, and stood back up. "I should be asking you the same question, Meir."

Their eyes stayed locked as they studied each other.

He broke the silence. "Last night, that damn Lionne almost attacked our king, and *you* have been missing."

He had to be lying. Elco wouldn't just attack Ael.

"Where's King Ael now?" she asked.

"In the dining room." He squinted at her, clearly trying to find a break in her facade.

She fought the urge to laugh at his face. He looked so funny when he was all mad and red.

Deciding she could mask her smirk at his expression with sarcasm, she said, "Perfect. I'm heading there now and will check in."

She let out a purposeful, annoying laugh, hoping it would piss him off more.

His eyes darkened completely for a moment, causing her to freeze.

She slowly stepped away, squeezing past him as he watched

her go. She shook her head, dismissing it. She wasn't sleeping, and her mind was playing tricks on her.

She could feel his eyes boring into the back of her head and chuckled when she remembered how Misandra would tell Ael that story about her secret eyeball on the back of her own.

When she entered the dining room, everyone else was there. An open seat next to the beautiful Corvid woman, Ferona, remained, and she gladly took it, looking over at the gorgeous creature and winking at her.

She noticed a faint pink tint spread across Ferona's cheeks, gliding over her moonlit skin.

Both the Corvid women were absolutely stunning. They looked identical except for their accent colors, but Roya's demeanor was too abrasive for her. She could also see that she had a thing for Benny, who was sitting next to her with doe eyes.

*Can't blame the man for being obsessed,* she thought.

"Welcome to breakfast, Luelle. You look like shit," Ael said, chuckling, as everyone fell silent when he spoke. His hand was yet again on Seda's thigh, and she looked... like she slept *really* well.

"Why, *thank you.* I slept rather poorly. Neoma's still here, by the way, snoozing like a baby in that cloud-like bed of hers." She grabbed the serving spoon to dish herself out a portion of chopped fruit and plopped it onto her plate.

Ael narrowed his eyes but didn't respond. He simply tapped his finger on the table, clearly annoyed by the news.

"Same for us," Askold chimed in with a smirk. "There was a lot of noise last night."

Benny cleared his throat, and Luelle looked at him. His eyes started to water as he held a napkin over his lips to conceal his smile.

"What exactly did I miss?" she asked as she looked between Benny and Ael. "I heard there was an incident with the Lionne?"

"Oh, just Seda experiencing her first *orgasm* while Elco thought she was injured from all the screaming." Benny's voice was muffled through the napkin, but his eyes sparkled mischievously as he looked at Seda, who was visibly pale.

"Benny!" Seda began, but her sudden yell caused her to choke on her breakfast.

Ael's face quickly changed from flabbergasted at Benny to concerned over Seda, and he began to pound on her back, trying to help clear her airway.

Seda took a deep breath and, with watery eyes, glared daggers at her brother.

*Damn, I did miss a lot,* she thought as her lips curled into a smile.

Ferona cleared her throat beside Luelle, and she glanced over, their eyes meeting for a moment, but Ferona quickly looked away.

Ael changed the subject while he ran his hand up and down Seda's back. "Ojore and Praxis should be back today."

Benny and Askold sat up straighter in their chairs.

"Do you know what time to expect them?" Benny asked.

"Before lunch," Ael replied.

Luelle let out a sigh, expecting Praxis to return with a new excuse to bother her, likely bringing up his dick again in the process.

She regretted all those times she had drunk too much wine and wished she had someone to spend time with. For whatever reason, Praxis was always available.

A shudder ran through her at the memory. He truly was terrible in bed, which was such a shame given his cock was so large. But without his awful lovemaking, she never would have allowed herself the freedom to discover the beauty of a woman. She had always been attracted to them, but never took that first step until after spending time with *him*.

She supposed she was thankful for his terrible lovemaking and shrugged to herself.

"I have a book that I'd like you guys to read the contents within," Seda said, holding out a worn leather book. She handed the book to Ael, who didn't try to read it, then handed it to Benny.

Benny opened the book and flipped through the pages. "It's blank. What is it?"

"Pass it along, please," Seda asked him. Benny shook his head as if his sister were crazy, then handed the book to Roya.

Roya opened the pages, her eyes squinting. "You really can't see this?" she asked Benny.

Benny grabbed the book back from her and flipped through the pages once more. He shook his head. Roya took the book back from him and handed it to Ferona, who opened it and agreed she could see its contents as well.

Ferona handed it to Luelle, and their fingers briefly touched. The touch was soft, and she flexed her tingly fingers.

Ferona quickly looked away again, heat creeping along her cheeks once more. Luelle's lips curled into a faint smile, and she opened the book, seeing the pages lined with various, disgusting-looking spells.

"Where did you get this?" Luelle asked Seda as she peered over the book.

Seda preened. "Cahir got it from Tahti. Apparently, she's missing, and the only thing she left behind was this book. He cannot see what's inside either."

"So..." Luelle started, but stopped, thoughts circling her mind. She knew Tahti was gone; Ael had told her so yesterday. It didn't make sense that the old, mean thing would vanish, but she honestly didn't care. Good riddance. No more bumps on her head with her gone. "This must be her Book of Light. Sounds like men cannot see what's within."

"I told you it wasn't just me!" Seda exclaimed, her preening finally exploding, and pointed her finger at Ael's chest. He smiled down at her, like she was cute for telling him so.

Luelle had never seen Ael so enamored before, and it made her heart swell for her friend. He deserved to be happy.

He also deserved to hear 'I told you so' more often.

"Why would that mean, old witch, leave her book behind?" Luelle wondered aloud as she flipped through the pages of chicken scratch.

No one answered.

"We need to plan for taking back the stolen Umbrea stone for Seda," Ael finally said.

Luelle gasped and set the book down. "What do you mean? La Uma has that stone. No one goes up there unless you have a death wish. Your father never came back, Ael."

Ael dismissed her with a wave of his hand. "We should reach there in two days. Luelle, I need you to stay and oversee everything as lead advisor."

Luelle protested. "*No*, Ael. You cannot go. Your father never came back!" She felt her stomach tighten. She couldn't lose her friend. And what if he was gone again for years? He had only recently returned from Joro.

She didn't want him to leave again.

Ael narrowed his eyes at her. "Luelle, I'll be leaving with Seda. *I will return*, and *you* need to watch the castle while I'm gone. Can you do that for me, please? As my friend, I trust your judgment to handle things while I'm away."

Luelle flared her nostrils and narrowed her eyes back at him, feeling a small burst of magic escape from her nose as she exhaled.

She didn't want him to leave.

Luelle angrily jumped from her chair and slammed her palms on the table. "If I do this, Ael, I'll need a way to communicate with you. Something is brewing under these stone walls, and if you're gone, who can stop it from happening?"

"Praxis and the guard," he replied.

Roya cleared her throat, and everyone looked at her. "Ferona can stay here with you while we go with Seda. We can communicate back and forth. I'll call in other Corvids to see who's nearby and willing to join."

Luelle's eyes moved from Roya to Ferona, who smiled at her in response.

Perhaps being stranded at the castle with someone intriguing like Ferona wasn't such a terrible idea.

"Fine," she snapped, sitting back into her seat with a loud thud.

"What do you intend to do about Neoma?" Luelle asked as she picked up her fork again and looked at her plate, the food suddenly seeming much less appetizing. She set the fork down and stared at Ael.

"After we leave breakfast, let's go to her room and make sure she leaves. I'll call in a few of the guards to help with this since she seems to think my commands don't mean shit," Ael responded. "I also want Meir there, as well."

Luelle smiled. "Not sure where he was headed, but I saw him on the way here."

"Probably the library," Seda chimed in.

She was right. He was probably going to the stupid, dull library.

For years, Luelle thought Meir was just a boring, old advisor who always followed the rules. But recently, it seemed there might have been more to him than met the eye.

The doors flung open, and Praxis collapsed into the room, gasping and out of breath. Everyone stopped what they were doing and looked at him. He jumped up, met Ael's eyes, and rasped out, "The Jotnar have attacked the Lycanthropes. There was no trade deal. Ojore's missing."

# CHAPTER 24

<u>Ael</u>

"What happened?" Ael asked as he stood from his chair and rushed to Praxis, helping him into an empty chair. "Where's everyone else?"

Praxis was gasping, as if he had sprinted the entire way home from the wall. He took a deep breath and looked at everyone with wild eyes. "We got to the wall, and there were dead Lycanthropes scattered around. We made our way to the other side to check for any survivors, and a Jotnar was lurking around the corner, waiting for anyone else to arrive. We all fought him with everything we had and took him down, but we lost many in the fight. Ojore, that grumpy asshole, didn't fucking listen to us and went off in his own direction, toward Tuath."

Praxis reached for a glass of water and gulped it down, droplets slipping past his lips and dripping onto his shirt. When he finished, he wiped his mouth and said, "We had just a few survivors and returned as quickly as possible. Ael, I believe now is the time to get involved with them. If the Jotnar are attacking on their end, it won't be long before they turn their attention here as well."

Ael looked up at Roya before locking eyes with Seda. "We need those stones," he stated.

"What do we do about Ojore?" Benny asked nervously.

Roya sighed. "We should split up to explore what more we can discover in Tuath. I propose accompanying Ael and Seda to La Uma. Ferona will remain here with Luelle. Askold, you'll go with Benny and any others interested in heading to Tuath."

Benny stood. "Roya, you know I don't want to split from you."

"You and I both heard that La Uma doesn't like men, Benny. Ojore needs your help in Tuath. When we leave here, I'll call upon the Corvids to see if we can get additional help. They will allow us to communicate."

The room was silent as everyone thought over Roya's suggestions.

"I think that's a good plan, Roya," Seda spoke, breaking the silence.

Ael glanced at Seda. Joining her on the trip to the monster north was risky, but he couldn't separate himself from her. His priority was to protect her at all costs, even if it meant he had to confront La Uma alone. He would do it... *For her.*

He placed his hand on Seda's warm thigh once more, and she glanced at him. He would stay with her. He had to.

"We leave first thing in the morning," he said to everyone. "But first, Luelle, come with me to find Meir and Neoma."

Ael glanced up at the birds flying above as they walked along the long hall towards the Western Wing. He could hear Luelle's footsteps in her silken flats as they walked alongside each other. His neck prickled when he noticed how she kept glancing at him.

"So..." she started, and he groaned. He already knew what she wanted to talk about. "First orgasm, huh? What were you doing wrong all those years if she never had one?"

He ground his teeth together and lied through them, "Searching for the Dark Stone."

"Mmmhmmm," she replied, obviously not believing him. He looked over at her, and she was smiling from ear to ear, her face bright. "How long have you wanted to do that?"

Damn, she was persistent, and she wasn't going to stop until he gave her some information. "For far too long."

"Did you two—"

But he interrupted her. "*No*, Luelle. We didn't. And I don't wish to share the details. It's disrespectful toward her. If she wishes to share, you can ask her."

She rolled her eyes and grumbled, "Fine. But I *am* happy for you, friend. Honestly, I haven't seen you swoon over someone like this before. I can see how special she is to you."

He couldn't help but smile in response. "She really is. I'd do anything for her."

They stopped when they reached the Western Wing, and Ael looked around at the hallway filled with doors. "Do you know which room she's in?" he asked.

"Nope. It's one of these, though. Let's knock until we find her."

They stopped at the first door, and Ael pounded on it. When no one answered, he opened the door, and they both walked in.

"This isn't it," Luelle said as she eyed the furniture around the room.

They left the room and kept knocking and opening doors, once walking in on someone changing. The woman screamed when they strode in, but quickly apologized when she realized who was in her room.

When they left that room, they both laughed, and Luelle said, "She apologized to us!"

When they finally went in through the last door, Luelle stopped in the doorway, staring at the furnishings. "This was it."

They looked around at the pristinely made bed, the neatly arranged furniture and accessories, and the absence of anyone in the room.

"Are you sure?" Ael asked as he walked into the bathroom and looked inside. The bathroom was just as empty as the main bedroom. He looked over at Luelle, who was nodding her head and chewing her lip.

"Well, one problem down, one to go," Ael said with a sigh as he ran his hand over his face. He needed to find Meir now and wasn't entirely looking forward to that conversation.

Actually, he didn't need to find Meir at all. Meir would come to him.

He hardened his face into iron and turned to Luelle. "I'll be in the throne room. Tell the guards to find Meir and bring him to me."

He turned and left the empty room, leaving Luelle behind as she stared at the painting above the bed, her focus fixed on the tiny hole.

AEL LISTENED to the tapping of Luelle's shoe as Meir and Neoma were pushed before him. The guards found them fucking in the garden maze, and leaves were still tangled in Neoma's dark hair.

"Your Highness... *Please*," Meir blubbered before him.

Ael ground his teeth together while Meir begged for forgiveness. "You were made aware that Neoma was no longer allowed on the castle grounds. You've also been conspiring against me for unknown reasons. I no longer trust you, Meir."

"We were just saying goodbye, Sire," Meir begged. "She was on her way out of the castle as you caught us."

Ael shifted his gaze to Neoma, who was glaring at him with darkened eyes.

"Neoma, you're never allowed back at the castle. Meir, you are suspended from your services for three months. I don't know what the two of you have been up to, but it's not welcome here."

Meir gasped and fell onto his knees, begging Ael from the floor and looking up at him sitting upon his throne.

"Guards, escort them off the castle grounds. Don't let them come back in. Meir, after three months, you may request an audience." He glanced at both of them before turning his attention to the guards. "Take them out."

Ael watched as they were both led away from the throne room and waited for the double doors to close behind them, leaving only himself and Luelle behind.

Luelle cleared her throat and said, "About gods-damned-time, Ael." She raised her eyebrow as she looked at him sitting on the throne.

He sighed. "Yes, about gods-damn-time." Ael stood from his chair, ran his hand over his face, and stepped down the stairs. "You should be fine now while I'm gone. Please ask Ferona to contact us if anything happens."

He looked back over his shoulder at Luelle, who smirked before sinking into the throne in his place.

"I'll keep everything under control, Ael." She wiggled her eyebrows and idly picked at her painted red nails before crossing her legs as Ael opened the door to leave.

"Ael?" she asked, and he paused halfway through the door. He looked back over his shoulder at her. "Come back, please."

He turned away from her and left the room.

# CHAPTER 25

<u>The Monster King</u>

The wind picked up, and gusts of sand assaulted the Monster King's exposed cheeks. He inhaled deeply, catching the metallic scent of blood.

There were fewer inmates now. Somehow, pregnancies had started to rise within Joro, and as a result, there were fewer and fewer citizens to choose from. Even women in the Camp were beginning to expect more frequently.

He watched as a Dragor yanked a man through the sand, leaving a trail of blood behind. What used to bring him so much joy no longer did. He needed *more*.

At least there would be more children to offer Somnium.

Fucking Somnium. He was expected to arrive today for his collection. He ground his teeth together in agitation. He looked at the two cages filled with women and their babies, soft cries and moans coming from both.

The Monster King smirked, an idea forming. He would offer less to Somnium today, despite the numbers being up.

He yelled at the Dragors to return one of the cages filled with people to their cells.

The sound of footsteps drew his gaze over his shoulder, and he saw Jason.

*Another fucking puppet*, he thought.

Jason's torture revealed nothing. He now wore a fresh scar along his right cheek that was swollen with stitches, and as a result, his long beard had been half-shaved.

"The dome has cracked, Sire," Jason said to him as his attention held on the trail of blood in the sand.

The Monster King's eyes widened, and he felt his heart start to pick up its pace. "It finally cracked? Have they been able to gain access?"

"No." Jason shifted his feet in the sand. "The dome cracked, and they attacked it another dozen times before giving up."

Anger bubbled through him. "Tell them to continue attacking!"

"Yes, Sire." Jason turned around and walked away.

*Finally*, he thought, *we're getting close.*

# CHAPTER 26

<u>Seda</u>

The castle walls seemed familiar—cold and gray—as Seda rested on the black furs covering the bed. She curled up and brushed her hand across her face, wiping away tears that had unexpectedly fallen.

A door opened, and someone walked in. She tightly closed her eyes and dug her face into the pillows, feeling herself wanting to hide her emotions from them.

She felt the bed shift, and a warm hand rested on her shoulder.

"We'll keep trying," she heard them say.

A vaguely familiar sadness enveloped her, and she felt her stomach tighten as a cry erupted from her lips.

"It will never happen," she choked out through muffled sobs.

She felt their hand tighten on her, and the shock that this person might also be upset made her heart fall even further into the recesses of her now-empty soul.

Then she heard her mother's voice in the growing darkness, and a slight flare of love began to pulse within her heart. "*Once upon a time, there was a magical Fae who wished to be more...*"

SEDA GASPED as she awoke and sat up in bed, gripping the emerald-green, silken sheets between her hands. The feeling of dread curdled deep within her. She frantically scanned her surroundings and relaxed when she saw Cahir asleep beside her, exhaustion evident on his face. The sheets had been pulled down, barely covering the lower half of his body. She watched the bare skin of his stomach muscles ripple, and his closed eyes move back and forth, as if lost within a dream.

They had stayed up late the night before, planning their trips with the others, and Cahir had insisted on staying awake as long as possible by her side. Kalon had not entered her dreams since the incident in the garden, and she wondered when the dreams of snakes would return.

Instead, she was having vivid dreams of unfamiliar things, unknown places, and unrecognized feelings.

What were they? Premonitions? Fear of things to come?

She lay back down on the bed and stared up at the glass ceiling, watching the green orbs and clouds float by, their pink hues drenched in the morning glow.

She shifted on the bed, and the sheets rubbed against her irritated back. She reached her arm around to scratch it through her nightgown, and pain flared through her.

She hissed as she ground her teeth together.

Cahir stirred next to her, and he opened his eyes, staring at her with pursed lips. "Is everything okay? Did you have a bad dream?" he asked as he quickly rubbed his puffy eyes and sat up in bed, returning his attention to her.

Was that a bad dream? It felt... *sad*. But nothing had happened to cause fear, and Kalon wasn't there to torment her.

"No dreams of Kalon," she replied.

He adjusted himself and looked at her, running his hands through her hair. "Your hair..." he started.

She looked down and lightly grabbed the section of it that had fallen over her shoulder. Glittering stands of white with iridescent purples and blues rested on her fingertips.

"It's changed more," she noted, dropping the strands when pain flared through her back once more. "Hey, can you look at my back again, please? It's really hurting."

He nodded, and she turned around, loosening the laces on the front of her nightgown and allowing it to slip free from her shoulders.

He gently brushed her hair away from her back and gasped, causing her to flinch when his fingers gently ran over her sensitive skin.

"What is it?" she asked, turning back to stare at him.

"Something's growing out of your back. It..." He paused and chewed on his bottom lip.

"It what?"

He cleared his throat. "It's... *feathers*."

"What?!" She jumped out of the bed and ran to the vanity, turning around and looking over her shoulder into the mirror.

Glistening, black feathers, no larger than her pinky finger, met her eyes, and a soft gasp escaped her astonished lips.

How could she have feathers?

Cahir walked up to her and rested his hands on her shoulders. "They almost look like Roya's."

She looked up into Cahir's gentle gaze, and a small smile played across his lips, the points of his teeth slipping free. "They're beautiful, Seda."

She wasn't sure how she felt about this. Her back was red

and sore to the touch. The strange dreams, her hair changing color, and now feathers?

"I want to talk to Roya and Ferona," she finally said, looking back into the mirror and staring at them once more.

Cahir touched his finger under her chin and directed her face back to his. She stared up into his eyes, and his voice was barely a whisper as he said, "Sed, you're so fucking magical."

He bent down and pressed his lips to hers, and heat began to build through her core.

She released the fabric of her nightgown, letting it puddle to the floor, and felt the cool air of the room sting her exposed skin. She balanced on her toes to wrap her arms around him and pressed her lips to his.

A groan escaped him as he wrapped his hands around her thighs, feeling her bare skin, and lifted her up so she didn't have to strain to reach him. Seda wrapped her legs around him and felt the heat and muscle of his abdomen against the increasingly sensitive area at the apex of her thighs.

"I need to brush my teeth," she said between breaths.

"No... You fucking *don't*," he replied as he nipped her lower lip.

He sat on the edge of the bed, positioning her over him, and she felt his rigid desire press into her through his pants. She couldn't help herself and wiggled herself over him, causing him to groan as he attempted to kiss the top of her head.

His fevered lips met her own once more, and he ran his warm tongue across hers. His palm clasped over her breast, and he gently squeezed it, kissing her as if she were the source of all life.

She felt herself throb and tighten in anticipation, and she ground into him once more.

"Fuck." His voice was rough as he breathed into her.

She reached between her legs and pressed her palm against

his hardened length, loving the sensation of power she felt as his body responded to her this way, knowing she could bring this king to his knees if she wanted.

He adjusted and pulled his cock out of his pants, and they quickly stared into each other's eyes, both questioning if they should go further.

Was she ready for this?

She felt ready. She wanted him. She needed to replace her painful memories with something special she could share with someone she cared about.

She needed him inside her more than anything else in the world right now.

He carefully eased her onto the bed.

"I don't want to hurt you," he said as the silky fabric of the bedding caressed the sensitive skin on her back.

"You won't hurt me." Her back didn't matter right now.

She saw the pleading look in his eyes, the way he continued being so gentle with her—so cautious. She didn't want that. She wanted them to claim each other in ways only they could share.

His breathing became heavy and strained. She stared back down at his length that pushed through the hole in his pants. "I want you, Cahir," she whispered breathlessly, and he groaned in response.

He held onto himself and lightly rubbed the head of his cock against her sensitive flesh, slowly sliding it up and down between her, grazing it against her clit. Her eyes flared at the contact, the feel of his warm, silky skin against hers, and she began to lose all sense of control, grasping at his hips for more.

"I want you forever, Seda." His voice was rough as he slid his length up and down, causing her body to shudder in response. "Until my body turns to dust and my soul wanders through the ends of time, I want you."

That same tension from the other night began to build within her, and she moaned as he continued to glide against her.

More. She wanted more. She needed *more*.

"Look what you do to me, Sed—only you. You're the air that prevents my lungs from collapsing, the source that continues to beat my heart. Every breath I take belongs to you."

She stared down between her legs, at his now darkened cock slowly sliding up and down between her, at the bead of cum forming on the top.

"More," she moaned, and he bent over her, continuing to glide himself between her legs as he kissed her with claiming vigor. He released her lips with a ragged breath and pushed himself back up, looking down at her with awe, like she was everything he said and more.

His pants fell to his ankles before he lined himself up at her entrance.

Cahir glanced down between them, at his hard length throbbing against her, begging for entry. His chest heaved, with his pulse pounding visibly in his throat. His hooded gaze shifted back to hers, looking for her final approval.

"Please," she pleaded, urging him on, hoping he wouldn't cease. She bit down on her bottom lip.

He watched her mouth with a deep, hungry gaze, his pupils expanding with her permission. He slowly circled his cock around her entrance, emitting a moan at the feel of their bodies so close.

"You're so fucking beautiful, Sed," he whispered breathlessly, the words caressing her spine and making her shiver.

He slowly pushed himself in, just an inch, and she felt her body stretch around him, felt herself open to him willingly, causing her to gasp in pleasure.

"More," Seda begged. "*More*," she demanded.

Cahir leaned over and pressed his full lips into hers in a

ragged, rushed kiss, like he was fighting against himself, and ever so slowly slid himself the rest of the way in. He remained seated, giving her time to adjust, then let out a rough growl. She lost herself in the feel of being filled by him, of feeling him everywhere around her.

Seda's magic erupted from within, causing the room to glow with shimmering violet hues. This was everything, this was an explosion of freedom—her want, her body... *her choice.*

She felt him trembling against her as he pulled himself out and slowly pushed back in as pleasure tore through every fiber of her being.

"You're so fucking *tight*." His voice cracked as he pulled back out with excruciating slowness.

"Faster, Cahir," she demanded, grasping for his hips to guide him back in.

He hesitated, fighting against his restraint, his breathing labored. His movements slowly became more measured, and he slid back into her with firm thrusts. He reached down between their bodies, running a warm finger across her clit in agonizing circles. Each thrust of his thick cock matched the swirl of his finger.

"Are you okay?" he breathlessly asked as he slowed.

"Yes. Oh, gods, *yes*. Don't stop." She couldn't control the moans that escaped as tightness began to build through each thrust that only deepened the pleasure every time. Her breathing began to stutter, and she moved her hips against his, feeling every inch of him, every hot stroke of the pleasure he gave to her.

Pulling back from her, he met her eyes with a hooded darkness that made her quiver. His gaze drifted downward where their bodies intertwined, moaning as he continued to not only seek his own rapture but also to gift her one in return.

The heat of her pleasure felt like it was cresting over her own mountain that she had set for herself, and she finally reached the peak, breathing ragged breaths through each stride to the top. She screamed his name as waves of her orgasm tore through her, alighting every nerve in her body. She refused to avert her gaze from his as every pulsating flare exploded, wanting to brand his image into this moment—forever.

She felt his muscles tighten as the rhythm of his movements grew in intensity. Matching his pace, she rocked her hips against his until he released a ragged, almost painful breath and groaned, telling her he loved her in a cracked voice that didn't sound like his own.

For several heartbeats, and when their bodies finally stilled, he slowly pulled out and lay on the bed beside her, pulling her close and nuzzling his nose into the crook of her neck.

This was everything she needed—sharing this moment, this feeling, this love—with him.

He whispered into her, "I didn't hurt you, did I?"

She turned and kissed his forehead. "Not. At. All."

They lay there, staring into each other's eyes, their hearts beating in sync as the tension slowly relaxed with each ragged breath.

"Forever, Seda. I'll never be the same." He pulled her face closer to his, kissing the tip of her nose and wrapping her soul in a comfort she didn't know she needed until now.

He smirked, and she caught sight of the dimples that lit up his face. "We should get ready and go see the others downstairs." He shifted off the bed. "Interested in a shower and that toothbrush now? I'll head down there to say hello. I don't want to wash this off me quite yet."

His smile was devious as he winked at her, and she let out a small laugh. "Yeah, I guess." She reached for the warmth of his hand, and he led her to the bathroom, where she kissed him goodbye, leaving her with a feeling of soreness deep inside. As she cleaned herself up for the journey ahead, the feeling of freedom and liberation washed over her.

*Her body... her choice.*

☾

SEDA WALKED out of the bathroom wearing a towel and into the closet when Suza knocked on her door and waltzed in, barely giving Seda the chance to respond.

"Oh, good, you're clean," she replied with a smile. "This should be an easy morning."

Seda rolled her eyes at the woman, who looked shockingly well put-together. "Suza, I can get myself ready."

The woman ignored her and strode into the closet, pushing past her. "I heard you are to wear clothes that are good for travel, and I refuse to let you leave in the garbs you came here with. Disgusting."

"I wasn't going—" Seda tried to say as Suza started grabbing clothes off their hangers and throwing open drawers from the dressers lined within the closet.

Suza grumbled as she threw items onto the ground, and squealed when she pulled out light pants that shimmered with coordinating armor. "There they are. I knew I put these in here somewhere."

The pants looked too small to fit over Seda's hips, and she groaned. "I want to wear something comfortable," she replied as Suza held them up for her to see. "Also, armor... really?"

"What you *want* is something that can protect you," Suza said as she narrowed her eyes at her. "There's a matching shirt and cloak around here somewhere. The armor is for protection, Seda."

She tossed the pants toward Seda, who caught them between her hands and felt the strange texture between her fingers. The pants were lined with a thin layer of fur and stretched when she pulled at them. Maybe these weren't so bad after all.

"Aha!" Suza said, grabbing the matching cloak and shirt from a hanger in the deep recesses of the closet. "Don't worry about this mess. I'll clean it up after you leave. I know you don't like messes."

The mess in the closet wasn't the first concern Seda had, but it was a thoughtful gesture, and a small smile crested her lips.

"I'll be right outside the closet when you're ready." Suza walked out of the closet and closed the door behind her, leaving Seda to stare at the unique fabric of the clothing she had chosen for her.

She dropped her towel, grabbed a fresh pair of underwear from the dresser, and pulled the clothing on. She had to wiggle herself into the pants, but they slid up and clasped, fitting against her like a second skin.

She pulled the shirt over her head and winced when it brushed against the sensitive skin of her back, but was pleased to find it backless, letting her back feel the cool air of the closet rather than being confined.

She grabbed the cloak and walked out.

Suza was waiting for her at the vanity with a brush in hand. Her mouth hung open when she saw her. "A true queen," she said as she eyed Seda approvingly.

Seda looked down at the armor that was now covering her. How did this make her like a queen? More like she was heading into battle.

The woman was mad, insane, crazy... everything she did didn't make sense, but Seda sighed and walked over to the stool and sat down.

Suza carefully moved her hair over her shoulder and inhaled when she saw the feathers on Seda's back. "They're finally coming in," she said.

Seda furrowed her brows and looked over her shoulder at the woman. "You knew about this?"

Suza tsked and told her to turn back around, slowly dragging the brush through Seda's still-wet hair. "Yes," she finally replied, but gave no further information.

"Tell me what you know," Seda demanded, turning around once more to look at the woman. She felt her irritation grow, and her chest began to vibrate. She was tired of secrets and lies, and if this wretched woman knew something about her, she wanted the information *now*.

Suza rolled her eyes and sighed once more. "You're growing wings, Seda. Wings like the Corvids. You're their queen."

The world tilted for Seda, and she felt herself get dizzy under Suza's scrutinizing stare. A queen? A Corvid queen?

"Wha—" she began to ask, but the world, once again, dimmed into darkness.

# CHAPTER 27

<u>Kalon de Somnium</u>

K alon's mind was lost in thought as the nearby Amaru murmured about needing to leave for the collection. In one hand, he held Seda's moonstone necklace, watching it catch the light from the wall-length windows next to him while seated on his throne. The sparkles were intrinsic to her—vivid and unpredictable, and the stone grew brighter with each day that passed.

Her magic was growing.

Stealing the necklace from her while in the Amanita Copse and sneaking away late into the night had to be done. She hated him for it. He could feel her wrath each time he visited her, but it was necessary. He knew she wasn't ready, especially with how she had pushed him away.

A traitor lurked in her group, someone who he realized almost too late was working against her. He couldn't just whisk her away with him, though. She needed to see the Wisps and gather her information slowly, or else it would be too much, and her magic would threaten to explode around them.

His world seemed to sway when his lips touched hers, as if the ancient rhythms of the world were torn between now and before.

She was everything to him and had been for over a millennium. He missed her so much while she was gone, and now that she was back, she didn't remember him. Pain cracked like frozen waters through his soul every time he thought about her lack of memory of their life before, of *them*.

He knew that asshole Ael was weaning his way into her heart, trying to take his place, and there was nothing he could do about it. He had been plaguing the man's dreams, sending him nightmares of Seda and himself locked in passionate embraces, hoping, praying that the dreams would stop him from pushing forward with his claim upon her.

But they hadn't. They only made it worse.

He could sense Ael's every thought and whisper. Seda dominated his feelings, and the dreams Kalon sent only deepened his love for her. He was a problem, but he didn't want to hurt the man physically. No, he couldn't do that. Seda was attached to him now, despite his own desire for her; despite his love that had only deepened over the years she was gone.

He couldn't harm Ael. He wouldn't, because that would also hurt her.

He could only pry into his mind and listen to his obsessive thoughts, only allowing himself to torment his dreams. Ael was providing what he could to protect Seda as her powers grew. And if that meant allowing this man to get close to her, if she wanted it, she could have this fun... *for now*.

The serpent prattled on nervously before him, and Kalon growled, "I'm aware we're at max capacity. *I don't care.* We collect more. We collect them *all*."

He had been collecting humans for hundreds of years, placing them beneath his castle into the hidden, cavernous, sapphire city of Noctrya, safe from the pits of hell above.

The pitiful Monster King was a lowly man, obsessed with power—a small man with a big complex, obviously making up for other areas of himself that he lacked.

*Probably a tiny dick,* he thought as he smiled at his own joke.

"As you wish, Sire. We must leave, the collection has already started," the black, slithering serpent said before him.

Kalon tucked the moonstone necklace into his pocket and stood from his cold throne. He glanced over once more, for the thousandth time, to the empty, spider-silken throne beside him, and snapped his fingers.

A black, magical air whirled around him and the Amaru, spinning around them like a tornado of nightfall that fused to his very being.

Kalon inhaled deeply as the air settled, drawing in the dust and squinting through his mask as he stared at the ever-burning sun of the desert. He could hear people crying and moaning as his vision cleared, and he looked at the Monster King standing before him, with two Jotnar behind, their enormous forms trying to present a clear threat.

The Jotnar never took part in these events, but their presence caught Kalon's interest. What torment did this man have planned for him today? What measly attempts would he try on him this time?

"You're late," the Monster King seethed. "I don't like being made to wait."

Kalon smirked from behind his mask at the small man, at his trimmed beard and rounded stomach. "I come when I fucking want to," was all he said in response.

The Monster King pulled the Dark Stone from his pocket and let the sunlight reflect off the ground.

"You know that doesn't affect me," Kalon said through his mask, rolling his eyes in frustration. He was constantly flashing that stupid stone. Kalon wished he could torment the man with nightmares and steal it from his person. But the stone could not be touched, not by him, at least.

Everything the dark magic touched was poisoned, except for… Seda. She was the only being walking this planet who could withstand the powerful magical pull of the Dark Stone. It could control her when used by another, yes, but only she could touch its cold surface and not be drawn into its lure.

The Monster King smiled brightly, wrinkles creasing across his gnarled expression. "No, but what you fail to see is that this stone controls everyone else. *Everyone.*"

He squeezed the stone, and oily magic coiled around his palm. The two Jotnar behind lurched forward in pain, narrowing their eyes at Kalon and his Amaru. They flung their hands forward to grab him, and Kalon's magic descended upon them, causing the two Jotnar to stumble. Their eyes rolled to the back of their heads as their minds turned into muddled nightmares. Large, heavy hands fell to the ground, and their bodies convulsed as drool dripped from their parted lips and blood oozed from their bulbous noses.

He looked at the Monster King and laughed loudly. "Give it up, old man. Your plan didn't work."

The Monster King growled and stomped his foot into the sandy earth below. He squeezed the stone harder, the whites of his knuckles catching against the brightness of the ground.

The Draggors within the Camp courtyard began to circle him, the color of their eyes flooding into crimson orbs.

*This fucking man,* Kalon thought. He could only cause nightmares in him for short periods of time, the Dark Stone protecting him from progressing further and just killing him entirely. He had tried countless times before, but the stone was always there, always protecting what it also soiled.

What was he trying to prove anyway?

Kalon snapped his fingers, and the Dragors crumpled to the ground, leaving only the Monster King seething before him. He took a step forward, easily stepping over a fallen Dragor, and walked closer to the small man. *"I am here to collect, Tievel."*

His name, not the Monster King. No. He would no longer call him by the fake title he invented over a thousand years ago. A title that shifted the planet and caused a tear through the harmony of his world.

His eyes caught on the small group of children and women before him. They cried out in fear as his gaze landed on them in their locked cage.

"Where are the rest?" he seethed, realizing this was a smaller group than usual.

The Monster King sputtered as his face turned a deep shade of crimson. "You have the moonstone, and I want it!"

*Ahh, so this is what this is over,* he thought.

Feich must have told him he stole it.

Kalon smirked, even though Teivel could not see it behind his mask, and he pulled the moonstone out of his pocket, holding it up in the air.

Tievel's eyes flashed, and the ground began to rumble, causing sand to shift beneath Kalon's black boots. He jumped back as giant cacti burst from the ground, their pointed tips growing long and deadly, threatening to entrap him.

Tievel squeezed the stone within his palm, grinding his teeth together as he hissed incoherent words through the air. His voice was melodious and echoed deeply through the courtyard, penetrating Kalon's ears and causing his head to throb.

Kalon put the moonstone back in his pocket and snapped his

fingers, revealing the same dark tornado that had formed over the area. He transported the people out of their cages, his Amaru, and himself... safely back to Noctrya.

The last thing he heard before the night whisked them away was Teivel muttering and cursing his name.

THE CAVERNS WERE alight with twinkling glowworms that lit the walls in a rainbow of fluorescent colors. Kalon looked up and inhaled the damp air, smelling the scent of fires, cooking meals, and *safety*. He could hear children below playing and running through the streets, their joyous melody echoing through the cavern walls.

As he stood upon the dark cliff face, peering down into the depths of the city below, he watched as life flourished. The sapphire-encrusted cave walls glistened in the pockets of sunlight filtering through the holes in the earth far above.

They had erected thousands of buildings here in their time. Humans were creative and innovative, finding ways to collect the glowworms' fluorescence to power the city with twinkling lights that lit their houses in vibrant colors.

His gaze was fixed on the distant training camps, where men and women, dedicated to their survival, sought revenge against the evils of the world and the terrors unleashed.

Kalon turned to his transparent Amaru. "Find these people some meals and homes. I'll be back later. I have something I must attend to." He pointed to the group of women and children who were crying in fear and wore dazed expressions from the transport.

He turned his gaze once more toward the training camps and smiled. She was going to need all the help she could get.

Not only had he successfully built an army for her, under the guise of evil, but he was also collecting all the children he could get his hands on, slowly rebuilding society... *for her.*

# CHAPTER 28

<u>Seda</u>

The heady sandalwood air around Seda was misty once more, and she immediately knew where she was. She could see snakes slithering around her and hear the distant cries of people.

"*Come out, Kalon,*" she seethed. "Give me my necklace!" She looked all around her, only seeing the glistening black snakes surrounding her every step. She took a cautious step forward, trying to avoid stepping on one in case it sank its fangs into her.

"I'll give it back soon," came his husky voice.

Kalon appeared through the mist, moving slowly with purposeful grace. He wore a torn black tunic that accentuated his muscular abdomen, his corded arms bearing black snake tattoos that swarmed up to his shoulders.

She narrowed her eyes at him, hating herself for noticing his stupid chiseled face and the breadth of his shoulders. He was now just a symbol of betrayal.

"Where is it?" she asked with an undertone of acid, taking another step forward.

"It's in Noctrya," he replied with a smirk, and her eyes lingered on the cruel perfection of his lips, the same ones he had kissed her with. She sneered with disgust. How could she have fallen for his tricks?

"Why am I here?" She flared her magic once more, allowing it to churn and spark along her fingers.

He looked down at them and smirked. "Oh, Seda, please electrify me again. Last time it felt so good I almost ca…"

"Stop!" Seda yelled, feeling rancor churn in her stomach. "Why am I here?" she asked again. "Why did you steal my necklace?"

He stepped closer to her and slowly raised his hands to her hair, running his fingers through it, his smirk fading as a look of seriousness overtook his features.

"Your hair's finally changing back," he said, his words holding a tenderness she didn't want to understand.

His touch infuriated her, and she quickly pulled away from him.

He sighed. "I had to, Seda. The moonstone's yours. It always has been. It's a part of *you*. You had someone in your group who was about to betray you. He was getting ready to steal it. Despite what you may think, I'm not the bad guy here."

"What do you mean, 'you aren't the bad guy'? You stole it from me!"

"As I said, I had to," he said with a shrug.

She thought about what he said and who possibly could have been betraying them. Electric shocks radiated across her chest, and she felt her eyes flare in anger.

"Who was it?" Her sharp whisper came out tight with seething frustration.

He smirked again as he gazed down at her, his seafoam-colored eyes gleaming with delight. "There she is."

"No more games, Kalon! Who are you accusing?"

He sighed, ran his hand over his face, and pulled the moonstone from his pocket, causing Seda's eyes to flare once more. "I thought you said you didn't have it!" She reached for his hand, but her touch glided through him, as if he were made of smoke.

"I'm not truly here, Seda. I only pretended your magic hit me last time. This is just a dream, and I'm in control within its illusion, but nothing is physically real."

Her lips parted, a soft gasp of surprise filtering through her.

"One of the Corvids, Feich, was about to betray you and his kind," he said. "He's working against the purity of this world, and right now it's alongside that Monster King, Tievel."

Seda's world felt like it was turning on its axis. She began to feel dizzy, and she gasped once more, grasping her throat and struggling to breathe.

"Feich? And Teivel?" she breathlessly asked, feeling shock ache in her heart over Feich. "How do you know? How do I know you aren't lying?"

"I can hear thoughts if I want to," he replied with a shrug. He reached down and gently touched her shoulder. "You are growing your wings back," he said as his light touch caressed one of the feathers on her back. She winced, expecting there to be pain, but none came.

"I'll never cause you pain, Seda. Even in these wild dreams. I'm sorry for kissing you and leaving in the night." He reached out his hand for her, and she reached for it, forgetting that she could not touch him.

His hand brightened, and the magic of the dream allowed her to feel the warmth of his calloused hand within hers.

She rose, and he handed her the moonstone. The stone's glitter was now amplified, sparkling vibrantly around her.

"As I said, this is yours, Seda. I'll give it back to you when I see you."

Her brows knit together as she stared at the stone, his words circling her mind. "Tievel is the advisor in Joro. He's... this Monster King? And you said Feich was working for him?"

"*Is*, Seda. Feich is alive. And he's trying to form an army of Corvids against you. Those who no longer remember and do not trust who you are."

"Who am I?" she asked.

"You're their queen," he replied. "...And so much more."

"How do you know all this?" she asked.

"Because you have been *reborn*, Seda. You once walked this planet, a very long time ago. You must touch the Stone of Peace, remember who you are, and focus on what's important. A ravenous wolf wearing a man's skin is lurking and hurting the innocence of this world."

"Why didn't you tell us about Feich?" She felt herself pulse, an angry inferno growing within her. The dreams she'd been having lately weren't dreams at all.

They were memories.

"Would you have believed me? I've said too much," he noted as the painful power radiated through her very being. "I cannot say more. Get to the other stone, Seda. Embrace the dreams I'm not giving you, for they are your own. Your moonstone is safe with me, I promise."

Darkness began to fill her vision, and the mist started to blur.

"Be careful with King Ael, Seda. I'll see you soon," was the last thing she heard before she was swept away into oblivion.

Seda's eyes flared open, and the room was cast in a pulsating purple glow. Suza stood over her, smacking at her cheeks and begging her to wake with tears forming in her eyes.

Seda jumped up from the floor and narrowed her eyes at the woman. "Who are you, Suza?"

The accusation caused Suza's body to flicker, revealing a black snake beneath. Her body quickly shifted back into the form of a Fae, and she took a hesitant step back.

"You're working with Kalon," Seda said as her eyes widened.

"I…" Suza started, audibly gulping. "I am. Somnium is my master."

Seda's chest was violently vibrating within her, and there were sharp stabs of pain flaring through her nerves, tearing apart the fibers of her being.

"You need to cool down, Seda," Suza said as she quickly turned and ran to the bathroom, returning with a cool washcloth and placing it on her forehead. "You have to cool down, or you will explode, and all of this will be for nothing."

"What do you mean?" Seda asked as another painful flare tore through her.

"Deep breaths, *please*," Suza begged.

Seda struggled to sit back down on the vanity stool with pain ripping through her body. She took deep breaths through each stab.

"In through your nose, and out through your mouth." Suza kneeled before her, showing Seda how to breathe. Seda followed her instructions, wincing every time another round of pain flared through her chest.

The throbbing began to ease, and Seda stared at the woman before her. It all made sense who she was, what she was. But why was she here?

"Wh—" she began to ask, but Suza stopped her.

"Not right now. Someone's coming." Suza looked to the door, and Cahir flung it open.

He ran to her side and kneeled beside her, causing Suza to step back into the recesses of the room.

"Are you okay? I heard you scream from down the hall when I was coming back to check on you," he asked as his eyes searched hers.

Seda smiled up at him, barely wincing as the last bit of pain flared through her.

"I'm fine," she rasped. She reached up and cupped his cheek in her hand, gazing into the worry that filled his eyes and offering a small smile. "Let me finish getting ready with Suza, please. I'm close to making my way down. I'll tell you with the others."

Cahir's eyes shifted between hers, and anger started to simmer beneath them, casting dark shadows. "It was Kalon, wasn't it?"

She nodded, but she didn't want to say more right now. She needed a few minutes alone to process the information Kalon had given her. "Almost ready. I'll see you in a few."

It was a dismissal, and she could see that he knew it for what it was. The muscles in his cheeks flexed with the grinding of his teeth, but he kissed the top of her head and walked out of the room, softly closing the door behind him.

She waited for a few moments before sighing and turning to Suza. "You can do my hair, but you need to *talk*."

Suza bit her lip and hesitantly nodded, glancing down at Seda's glowing chest before taking a step closer.

When she approached, she picked up the brush and began, once again, to pull it through Seda's hair.

"Somnium teleported me to Umbrea, with the sole intention of assisting you as much as I could and also to try and lure King Ael away." She shook her head. "Unfortunately, I'm not the prettiest of Fae women in my disguise, I suppose. I don't have beautiful, shining hair and amethyst colored eyes, like you."

Seda narrowed her eyes at the woman but allowed her to continue, remaining silent.

"With each passing day, I got better at my disguise, but I was too late anyway. King Ael only has his eyes set on you, Seda. I couldn't lure him away, despite my attempts." With gentle touches, she pulled the brush down her hair.

Seda's hands were tightly wrapped around the edge of the stool, squeezing it firmly, but she took a deep breath. The woman was being truthful, and she wanted to hear more. "Why does Somnium want Cahir away from me?"

"Som—" she sighed. "Somnium knew you *before*," she said quietly. "That part of the story is not mine to tell."

Silence fell between them. Suza began to braid Seda's hair into a tight braid, concentrating on her work. "If it's okay with you, I'd like to join you guys on this trip," she said, breaking the silence.

"Why?" Seda asked.

"I promise you I'm not trying to go after King Ael anymore. I failed at that part of my task. But, I want to do everything I can to assist you so that I won't have failed in everything."

Seda studied her, watching how her form now flickered between both Fae and snake, and she sighed in response. "Okay."

Suza perked up and smiled brightly, transforming her face into something quite lovely. What was once a face full of snide expressions was now radiant and beautiful. The ice surrounding Seda's heart began to melt, and she fought her smirk. "You know," she started, trying to sound angry still. "Maybe if you showed that expression more often, your wooing might have worked."

Suza laughed loudly, and the sound was contagious, making Seda chuckle and cover her mouth.

"You're likely right, but I didn't really want to woo him, Seda," the woman said.

Seda reached up and cupped her hand within her own, staring into her eyes. "Thank you for telling me. Honesty means a lot."

Suza beamed under her praise, and the snake within her flickered, revealing lustrous black scales that reflected the light.

Seda looked down at Suza's ragged dress. "Do you have anything else to wear? You can find something in that massive closet if you don't."

"Oh, may I please?" Suza asked excitedly. "This is all I have."

Seda nodded, and Suza entered the closet. She could hear her rummaging through the clothing.

This trip... She needed to explain everything to everyone in the dining hall, but she was nervous to share what she had learned, especially the part about Feich.

Anxiety flared through her when she thought about the new information and Kalon's plea for her to stay focused.

Finding the stones was important. The people of Joro were important. Doing whatever she could to destroy the corruption of the world *mattered*.

All of it felt like too much, too quickly, and she felt her magic flare back to life unwillingly as her mind continued to churn.

Destroying the Camp was important. Bringing balance into the world was needed. She needed the stones. She needed to get back to the door.

Seda was the key.

Agonizing pain ripped through her body, tearing through her back muscles and shredding through her skin. Seda screamed as her chest vibrated a glowing storm of pulsating purple, throbbing through each heartbeat. She felt her back muscles tense, and the sound of a rustling storm blew through the room.

She dropped to the floor, panting for breath, crying through the pain as tears slipped down her cheeks. She felt new muscles she didn't know existed tense. A heaviness pressed her further into the ground.

Suza ran out of the closet, clothing in hand, and dropped her items on the floor. She rushed to her side and knelt, "Oh my gods! They're *here!*"

Seda looked up at Suza, whose wide eyes were filled with wonder as she gazed over Seda's shoulders.

Seda lifted her eyes with a hesitant breath, and twilight rose to meet her, unfolding around her like a quiet revelation. *Wings*, massive wings, the color of midnight with white, beating sparkles like stars etched into every feather, blanketed around her. A moonlit dust floated around the room, blowing out from each feather as if caught in its own wind.

Seda had wings.

# PART FIVE
## THE DIVIDE

# CHAPTER 29

### Ael

Everyone sat around the dining table, discussing their upcoming trips and waiting for Seda to arrive. Roya had successfully gathered two Corvids to aid their cause: Vira, who was a tall, moonlit woman with a pointed nose, and Sepher, who was as dainty as the other two Corvid women, but her eyes were filled with a fire that rivaled Roya's.

"Has anyone told Elco you guys are leaving?" asked Praxis as he plopped two breakfast sausages on his plate and smothered them with thick syrup.

"Seda did, and he refused to listen to the warning about males going to La Uma. He wishes to remain at her side," Ael replied while sipping his coffee, his eyes frequently darting toward the door.

"He's a damn fool just like you." Roya glared at him.

He opened his mouth to speak, but Luelle interrupted him, saying to Praxis, "Why do you have to stay? Why can't you go with them?"

"Because our king thinks you need help here, *obviously*," he replied with a wink. "Besides, what if you get lonely? And what if Meir comes back with Neoma? You'll need some actual strength around here."

Luelle slammed her fork on the table and glared daggers at Praxis. "The only thing you'll do is fuck her in the bushes! Even knowing what she did to you with that potion!"

Praxis shrugged. "As long as it's outside the castle walls, I see no problem with that. I'll be whoever she wants me to be."

"Maybe La Uma doesn't care about male animals. Maybe it's just *men*," Askold said, bringing the conversation back to Elco, as he shoved pancakes into his mouth, the jam on top spilling past his lips and dripping down his chin.

Ferona narrowed her eyes at him, watching the mess he made on his shirt. "Why do you have to eat like a pig?"

He smirked at her, a chunk of pancake stuck to the syrup on his chin. "But don't you remember, Ferona? You said all men are pigs. I'm just living up to the name." He took another big bite and chewed with his mouth open, glancing over to make sure Ferona was watching.

"Besides," he said before he took a big gulp of coffee. "We're going on two separate missions, and who knows when I'll get to eat something like this again? It could be weeks!"

Ferona let out an audible gag at his disgusting display, and Luelle chuckled as she stared at her.

"I agree. Men *are* pigs," Luelle said with a reassuring nod and made sure to shoot Praxis one more glare.

Askold feigned mock shock before digging back into his plate.

The doors swung open, and Seda hesitantly stepped inside, shadowing the doorway and making the whole room fall silent. Askold gasped loudly.

She wore armor that accentuated her curves, but her wings...

they had grown. Folded up, they were taller than she was, and glittering starlight pulsed with what appeared to be each of her heartbeats.

Roya's mouth hung open, and she dropped her fork sharply on her plate. "They're here..."

How had she grown her wings since seeing her? He was just upstairs with her—not even twenty minutes ago.

Her skin looked pale, as if she hadn't slept in days. Whatever Kalon did to her... Ael's anger surged. That fucker was going to pay.

Seda was carrying a cloak in her arm, and when she looked at Ael, she smiled at him and made her way toward the empty chair beside him. She struggled to sit down with her wings, but furrowed her brows and strained, slightly parting them so she could sit.

He could feel the tension radiate off her, and he wanted to reach out and touch her, but she looked like she had seen a ghost.

In a way... He supposed she had. This was all so new for her. What magical being had wings like that? Nothing in the library had shown anyone like this, not even that book he stole and read through countless times, always stopping and glaring at the image of a snake.

He looked down at her, expecting her to talk, but she reached for the honey cakes he had ordered and poured coffee into her cup, saying nothing.

"So..." he pried, glancing up at her beautiful feathers, refraining from reaching out and touching them.

The door opened once more, and the maid, Suza, walked in, wearing clothing made for a... journey, not her usual maid's dress.

"What are y—" Ael began to ask Suza.

"She's coming with us," Seda replied as she took a large bite of her honey cake.

"Why?" Ael asked.

Everyone in the room fell silent, staring at the maid, their gazes slowly shifting to Seda.

"I have a lot to tell you all." Seda swallowed and offered a strained smile.

Suza sat down at the table, hesitant to make a plate.

"You may eat." He waved his hand to her, and she beamed at his approval. This was the same maid who tried to throw herself at him, and he didn't like her.

"Kalon visited me," Seda started, and Ael's gaze quickly shifted back to her. "Things aren't what they seem."

"What do you mean?" Roya asked.

Seda's face blanched as she hesitantly said, "Kalon says that Feich is still alive."

"That liar!" Roya stood from her chair and slammed her hands on the table. "We saw him die."

"Well…" and the words tumbled out. When she finished, everyone's mouth dropped open in complete shock.

"There's no way," Ferona said. "Our brother would never go against Roya… against *you*."

"Think about it, Ferona. His body disappeared when the Mungder attacked him, and then it chomped on itself and exploded in anger when there was nothing within its tentacle."

Stunned silence echoed through the room. The only sound came from Askold's slow chewing.

Roya's eyes were wide with horror. The information was settling in deep within her, though, as she looked over Seda, focusing on the wall above, chewing on her lip.

The events Seda mentioned with the Mungder must be accurate.

"It's true," Vira, who spoke for the first time, said. "There are other Corvids who are hesitant toward you, Seda. I've heard their whispers. They spoke of someone gathering sources and people to their aid. It must be Feich."

"When did you hear this?" Ferona asked.

Seda's eyes snapped to the two new Corvids, as if seeing they were there for the first time. "I'm sorry, I didn't introduce myself. I've had quite a morning."

"I'm Vira," the tall Corvid woman said as she stood from her chair and bowed at the waist to Seda. "This is my sister, Sephyr." She gestured to the small Corvid woman beside her, who quickly stood and also bowed. "Our mother told us stories growing up of a queen who ruled over all Corvids. We knew you would return to us someday. We're here to serve."

"Um... It's nice to meet you both," Seda replied as she blushed bright pink at their displays of respect. It was obvious Seda wasn't sure how she felt about all of this.

The two women sat back down, but Vira looked toward Ferona and answered her question. "The other day, we heard some quiet whispers. Only a few have joined his cause."

Ferona and Roya pursed their lips in response.

"I don't trust anything that man says, Sed. He stole the moonstone and just took off into the night. How do we know he isn't lying again?" Ael growled.

"I don't think we have much of a choice right now. He said he's holding onto it and would give it back." Seda's gaze flickered between his. She obviously believed this story, and he gritted his teeth together as he refrained from arguing further.

He would kill this man, or god, or whatever the fuck he was when he showed his face again.

"You haven't told us why Suza's coming with us," Ael snarled as he looked pointedly at the petite maid sitting at the table, eating through a bowl of berries and cheese.

"Oh, yes. This is Suza. She works for Kalon," Seda replied as she looked at the woman. Suza's disguise flickered, and her serpentine form showed below the illusion.

Shock and disgust flared through him, and he quickly stood from his chair. "Abso-fucking-lutely *not*."

Seda also stood from the table and glared at him with furious, glowing irises. "She's coming with us, even if you don't want her to. She's coming with *me*."

Suza wasn't to be trusted, along with her piece of shit master. He wouldn't allow it.

Benny cleared his throat, and they parted their gaze from each other. "A lot of things are at play right now. We need all the help we can get, Ael. If Seda trusts her, I trust her."

Of course he did.

Roya looked over at Benny and smiled weakly at him. Then she also stood from the table. "It's settled. It's time to go."

"Yeah, Ael, pull that wedgie out of your ass. Wake up and stop being a dick," Luelle scolded.

Ael shot a sharp glare at Luelle, his oldest friend, who was the only person alive who could speak to him that way and still go unpunished.

"Fuck you, Luelle." He let out a sigh and stormed from the room, leaving the others behind.

Whatever Kalon was scheming, he intended to discover it.

And once he did, Ael vowed to kill him.

# CHAPTER 30

<u>Seda</u>

Seda could hear the roar of the ocean as they stood before the castle, the tumultuous waves crashing against the rocks below the cliff face. The sound was all-consuming around the group that had gathered at the tall, emerald-colored gates of the castle. The chilled wind swept through her hair, and she pulled her cloak closer to herself, thankful that Suza had thought to pick this for her.

"This is where we part ways," Benny said to her. "I don't like it, Seda."

She looked at her brother, her brave, loving brother who had stood at her side ever since they were children. For most of her life, he had been her only friend, and this was the first time they were willingly parting ways. It was clear he didn't want to separate from not only her but Roya as well, judging by the way he clutched Roya's hand tightly.

"Come here," she said to him as she held out her arms and stepped closer, pulling him into a tight hug. "Please be safe and let us know how things are going. Come back here as quickly as you can. We'll be back."

Seda looked over to Vira, who inclined her head at her. "We'll keep him safe, my queen."

She released Benny and stepped closer to Askold, hugging him as well.

"We'll be fine, Seda," Askold said as he hugged her back. "Benny's pretty smart when he wants to be."

Benny laughed, but Cahir growled at Askold, and he chuckled in response. "Chill, dude. She's my friend. Friend's *hug*."

Luelle smacked Cahir in the chest and muttered something about possessiveness before she swept past him, heading to Seda and hugging her as well. "I'll see you soon, Seda. Keep my friend safe," she said of Cahir. "I can see that man would do anything for you, no matter how stupid."

Everyone leaving was strapped with weapons, even Seda. She had a knife strapped to her hip, remembering when the Mungder had attacked them, and all she had was a stick to protect herself. The new weight of her wings felt heavy on her back, and they ached with the same soreness as if she had exercised for the first time in a long time, but she refused to let it affect her.

She mentally reassured herself that she was brave and strong, no longer the weak Seda of the past. Her fears and new feathers would not weigh her down.

"It's time to go," Cahir sternly said.

Seda looked at Askold, Benny, her new friends, Vira, and Sephyr, one last time before they set foot west. She watched them walk away, hoping that she would see them again soon.

THEY HEADED NORTH ON FOOT, away from the crashing sound of the waves, where the mountains and forests awaited them in the distant landscape. Hundreds of homes and buildings lay behind them as they pushed forward, away from the castle and city behind. They had walked past hundreds of Fae, who watched them with wonder and fear at the sight of Elco and herself. Many stopped to bow and talk to Cahir on their way out, but once they left that place behind, the familiar feeling of freedom sank deep into Seda's bones.

She was amongst nature once again, where mysterious animals, and possibly monsters, potentially lurked in the shadows. The last time she stepped into the unknown, she was scared, but her determination pushed her forward. And that same feeling rekindled again.

The floating orbs seemed to lessen in intensity the further they walked away from the castle.

Cahir walked by her side, Roya near him, and Elco followed closely behind with Suza at the far back. Wilted flowers dangled from Elco's mane, and he wore an expression of wariness that deepened the further they traveled.

"This land is unfamiliar to me, moon-flutter," he echoed into her mind. "I don't know what to expect on this trip."

She paused and looked back at him, at the way he looked into the darkened trees ahead. When he caught up to her, she reached out her hand and slid it across his scaled shoulder. "Thank you for coming, Elco."

He huffed, and smoke billowed from his nostrils. "I told you. I'm yours."

She smiled, feeling her heart warm for her friend. Elco was truly hers, and she was his. He was the steady ground beneath her feet, and they had shared horrors, both coming out stronger than they were before.

"Have you tried to use them yet?" Elco asked, eyeing her

glittering wings. Suza had helped cut a hole in the cloak she wore so her wings would be exposed, and she pulled the cloak closer around herself, feeling the cold, misty air sting her cheeks.

"No. I can barely move them. I struggled to sit in the chair earlier," she admitted.

"Practice flexing them," he suggested. He flared his expansive wings out and back in, showing her how to move them with ease. His movements were fluid and graceful, with an impressive power she longed to have.

She focused, biting down on her lip and straining the foreign muscles. They shifted, but not by much, as if they were seized up with tension.

"Relax," Roya said as she approached them. "Take a deep breath and relax as best as you can. Feel them, but don't strain."

Seda slowly breathed in and out, pausing her steps and closing her eyes. She focused on the new feel and weight on her back, and the memory of the dream came back to her—the dream of foreign muscles she didn't recognize as a battle rang out in front of her. She flexed the same muscles from her dreams, and her wings flapped vigorously, causing the air around them to stir.

Seda opened her eyes and saw Roya watching her, tears forming in her dark azure eyes as her hair blew around her.

"They're going to be sore. I'd suggest practicing moving them as much as you can while you walk. Maybe soon you can fly with me," Roya said with a smile that lit up her face.

"Thanks, you guys," Seda said to them, offering them a small smile in return. She didn't know if she could use them to fly any time soon, but what else were wings for? The thought thrilled her.

Roya shifted into her Corvid form and took to the skies, watching from far above and cawing loudly down at the group.

"How do you feel?" Cahir asked as she approached and began walking alongside him.

"Sore, confused, mad," she replied. So much was currently at play, and Kalon was right. She needed to refocus on what was important. She was tired of games and secrets. "When Kalon told me all of this, I started to feel... so angry, like it was all too much too fast, and all I could do was pulse with this fury."

He studied her, his eyes searching hers. "I'm sorry, Seda. I wish I had all the answers for you."

It felt honest, and a part of her ached to reach out to him. She offered a small smile and looked ahead on their path. The green, grassy landscapes stretched on endlessly until the darkness of the trees ahead stopped their cascade of color. They walked over a small bridge, over a trickling stream below, and Seda looked down, seeing a rainbow of small fish swimming around.

Everything appeared so peaceful in Umbrea. Why was Joro so vastly different? How had Tievel become this Monster King? He was just a short, snide-looking man who hosted the beginnings of each Wyrd. She never would have guessed he was behind all the torment down there.

It took them a couple more hours of walking through the peaceful landscapes before the roadway narrowed and the trees began to thicken, leaving the lush green fields behind them.

"We need to watch for wolves," Elco said to her, and she looked around at the vast pine trees, breathing in the fresh air and feeling the forest's tranquil silence.

If wolves approached, she knew they could handle them easily. She didn't feel scared at the thought. In fact, she almost embraced the idea. She hadn't used her powers much in the time she had been in Umbrea, and her palms began to itch with anticipation.

She flared her magic and looked down at her hands. A slight

feeling of pride washed over her. She was strong, and she could now feel that within herself—no more broken promises to herself and no more cowering in fear. The one thing her painful past taught her was that a person's sense of inviolability didn't develop overnight or even quickly. You had to grow into it and find it completely within yourself.

"The road seems to be cut off ahead by an overgrowth of those roses that were planted on the castle grounds," Roya said as she shifted forms and walked alongside them.

They walked forward until the roadway ended, leading into a dense thicket of rose bushes that blocked their path. As if on cue, all the roses turned their gaze to watch them, a rainbow of colorful eyes shifting and growing from dangerous stems.

Seda remembered what Neoma had told her. These roses were monsters, their tears like burning acid that could eat through your skin.

Cahir pulled his sword out, readying to use it as a machete to cut through the thick, thorn-filled bushes.

"Don't!" Suza ran in front of them, holding out her hands to stop them and blocking their path. "There's no need to hurt them."

Seda peered over at the flickering form of the snake, her eyes wide with fear. The roses had shirked away from them, peering back to watch them with wary eyes.

"Why not? I was told they were monsters," Seda asked as she watched the florals begin to quiver.

Suza glanced at Seda, her breathing ragged. "And what is a monster to you, Seda? Is Elco not a monster, despite his ability to breathe fire? Am I a monster because I'm an Amaru? Are you a monster because you have wings and magic that can kill? These plants harbor no ill will toward you. They thrive here. They're as much a part of nature as we are."

Elco huffed in annoyance. He really disliked being referred to as a monster, but so many had, and that made Seda reach over and place her palm on Cahir's arm, lowering his sword.

What truly was a monster? The Hailecs in the Heath Forest, the Gnashing Flora, and the Mungder... they all attacked them, resulting in the death of her friends.

But... they were only trying to survive in their own way... *right?*

She remembered feeling sorry for the roses when Neoma was chopping away at them, picking her stupid, fucking bouquet for her. A bouquet she didn't even want. They looked in pain, too. She recalled their quivering eyelashes and tears dripping down their curled petals.

Seda stepped closer to the bushes and knelt in front of them, causing Suza to move to the side with hesitation.

The roses continued to watch her, their stems trembling in fear.

These roses had no ill intentions. Their toxicity only appeared in their defence. They neither lashed out, lied, nor intentionally hurt others without reason; they just existed. A part of the world just as much as she was.

She slowly raised her hand and ran a finger along a large leaf, causing five of the roses to shudder, closing their eyes. The vibrations almost felt like a cat's purr, or like a dog rolling over as you rubbed its belly, its leg bouncing back and forth with happiness.

She stood and looked back at everyone. "Suza's right. We either go around or over." She glanced at Elco, requesting his help, but he huffed and looked away, showing no desire to carry anyone over the dense flowers.

"Then we walk," she said flatly, choosing a direction at random and beginning to walk, allowing the others to follow.

As she moved forward, she occasionally reached out her hand, gently brushing her fingers against the leaves and smiling as the foliage responded. Their eyes followed their movements with each step, as if they were just as curious about them as she was in return.

The sun began to set through the dark pines, their shadows breaking apart the slivers of sun that tried to break through. Seda continued to flex her new back muscles, slowly getting better at moving her wings in and out. Her movements were jagged, and she felt the strain in her muscles, but she continued practicing. These wings were now a part of her, and she wanted to be comfortable with them.

"We should make camp and rest. Tomorrow's going to be a long day," Cahir suggested, breaking the silence.

He had kept his distance most of the day, remaining near Seda, but not speaking much. She often felt his heavy silence and his eyes on her, though. She knew he was upset about Kalon's visit with her and was unhappy that Suza had joined them.

It wasn't the first argument they had ever had, not by a long shot. But it was the first one that didn't end in laughter and apologies. She briefly thought about their small apartment in Joro, and when she had thrown rice at the walls and wished for it to harm him. She didn't want any harm to come to him, not even in anger.

They needed to talk and smooth things out. More was at play here than just his loathing of Kalon and their ever-growing relationship. People's lives were at risk, and it was her responsibility to collect these stones, return to Joro, and find the doorway.

Cahir and Suza slid their sacks off their backs and started unrolling their blankets and other items, while Roya and Seda gathered sticks.

Elco helped light the fire, and they all sat down, listening to the peaceful wind blowing between the trees and the crackle of the flames. The roses observed their every move, as if studying them.

Cahir sat on the opposite side of the campfire from Seda, and she stood up and sat beside him. He glanced down at her, his seven-foot height towering over her own. She looked up at him and offered a hesitant smile, nudging her shoulder into his bicep.

"Are you okay?" she asked as she watched the firelight flicker across his strong jaw and cheeks.

He was silent for a long while before sighing and saying, "Yes. Come here."

He wrapped an arm around her and drew her nearer, her wings making it a bit awkward with their height difference. A feather brushed against his nose, and he laughed. "These are going to take some getting used to."

She flexed her back muscles and spread them out behind her, proud of how much she was getting better at moving them.

"I'm worried, Sed," he whispered.

"About?" She reached out and took his hand, rubbing her thumb back and forth across his palm.

"About all of this. Kalon and what he wants, La Uma, Tievel being the Monster King; Benny, Askold, and the others. I'm worried the Jotnar are planning to make their way to Umbrea, and I won't be there to help defend the city, but mostly... I'm worried about *you*." He looked down at her again, and she watched as the corners of his mouth pulled down.

"I'm right here," she reassured.

"I don't want to lose you, Sed. I don't know what I'd do if something happened." He lifted her chin with his finger and leaned in, softly pressing his lips against her forehead.

The rapidly beating pulse in his throat caught Seda's eye. She got to her knees, wrapped her arms around him, and pressed her lips to his, feeling her desire stir and remembering their morning together. He nipped at her lip in response.

Elco puffed smoke from his nostrils, blowing it heavily around them, and causing them both to cough and split apart. Seda had forgotten that others were around them, and when she looked over, they were all staring.

Roya shook her head, Elco gruffed, and Suza immediately looked away as she blushed.

She and Cahir nervously laughed, and she sat back down alongside him, running her hand along his arm.

"I'm not going anywhere, Cahir. We're in this together." She squeezed his hand reassuringly and looked at the others around the campfire.

"Sorry," she mumbled.

An unusual howl echoed through the trees, and Seda saw the roses start to quiver as they all turned their attention toward the sound at once.

Wolves.

The group quickly stood, their gazes mirroring the roses.

The darkness was a deluge, with only the firelight and the red glow of Elco's eyes illuminating the bases of the nearby rough pines.

A thick, nebulous fog began to weave through the trees, carrying a foul odor that lingered and clung to their clothing. The mist covered the camp, forming a damp layer that made the fire crackle.

Seda heard Suza gasp when a set of yellow eyes formed through the mist. She could feel the fear radiating from Suza, and she ground her teeth, not allowing herself to feel the same tendrils of fear crawl up her own spine. She focused on her will; she focused on her confidence, and her hands began to spark in response.

Elco growled and licked his lips as he approached Seda, forming a shield of red, warm scales around her.

The vibrant purple sparks flickered violently in her palms, and she raised her hands, aiming them at the haunted yellow eyes, waiting for the wolf to emerge.

To the right, a stick cracked sharply, drawing her attention away from the lingering stare. A large canine with rounded ears, roughly the same size as her, with elongated front legs, emerged from between two trees. Its fur was dark gray, and its nose resembled that of a boar.

Its deep snarl revealed darkened, sharp teeth.

More monstrous beasts began to circle the campsite, but Cahir quickly formed a shield around them, preventing the creatures from advancing further.

"These aren't wolves," Elco growled from her side.

Seda had never seen a wolf before. All her knowledge told her they were large, fierce, hungry canines that hunted travelers in the darkness of night. But these weren't dogs.

"We know who you are," a menacing, feminine voice rasped between the trees.

Seda turned to face the sound as the same glowing, yellow eyes slowly emerged from the fog, revealing a smaller, beastly form that matched the others. "Your friend has harmed one of my own." The beast looked between Elco and Seda. "We demand retribution. We demand *balance*."

Elco's red eyes deepened as he glared at the monster, a stark contrast to his mouth, which brightened with crimson behind a clenched, snarling maw.

"Give us the Lionne," the beast demanded.

# CHAPTER 31

<u>Seda</u>

"You can't have him," Seda snapped, feeling her anger rising, causing her chest to vibrate and pulse with a fury demanding to be unleashed.

No one could have *her* Elco.

She watched as the monsters licked their mouths and circled Cahir's magical shield, one lunging and being thrown back a few feet when its body collided with the transparent, green barrier.

Dark clouds began to swirl in the sky as a blanket of rain pelted the forest floor.

"The Lionne has lost its way and hurt one of mine. The Lionne must pay," the raspy female voice growled.

Seda narrowed her eyes at the form and raised her palms in the air. "Drop the shield, Cahir," she said to him. She was ready. She could kill the beast for thinking they could harm her friend.

"No," Cahir replied.

Roya looked at him sharply and seethed, "Do as she said and drop the *shield*."

"No. I won't," he yelled in response.

"Give us the Lionne!" the monster snarled once more. The beast turned her gaze to the others and nodded.

They lunged simultaneously, quickly pushed back by the force of Cahir's magic, but immediately rose and lunged again, repeatedly attacking the barrier.

Electrical shocks churned through the sky, darting across the tops of the trees, ready to strike down at any moment.

The speaking monster growled at their failed attempts and at the lightning sparking through the area.

Seda glanced at Cahir and noticed a bead of sweat forming on his forehead as he fought to resist the beast's assault on his magic.

He couldn't hold this for long.

"Drop the gods-damned shield!" Roya yelled.

Suza shrieked as she shifted herself underneath one of Elco's wings. He didn't flinch or shirk away from her. Instead, he tightened himself closer, protecting her as if she were one of his own.

Seda felt a flicker of pride well within her, but her focus was solely on the monsters ahead.

"Your friend cannot hold this for long. If you drop the shield and give us the Lionne, the rest of you may leave in peace," the beast purred.

"As I said," Seda replied coolly as a slow grin began to curl her lips. Electricity flickered across her face as ravenous thunder shook the ground. "You. Can't. Have. Him."

The beast's eyes widened before quickly hunching back and growling in response to the thunder.

Cahir fell to his knees, gasping for breath as he held out his hands, his magic beginning to sputter. Seda looked down and encouraged through a soft whisper, "It's okay. We have this."

He gazed at her with wild eyes, desperately trying to keep

the shield for as long as he could, refusing to put her in harm's way.

His eyes rolled to the back of his head, and he gasped as his body collapsed backward onto the forest floor.

The shield evaporated.

A menacing laugh escaped the beast in charge, but they stood firm and didn't move forward.

"As I said, we only want the Lionne," the monster cooed.

"He's *mine*." Seda tightened her fists, releasing lightning from the sky, striking the beasts around the campsite one by one.

Loud yelps screeched through the area. Roya lunged forward with her claws extended and danced around the monstrous forms, her body moving like liquid as she gouged deep cuts through their thick fur and through their flesh.

Elco roared, and fire erupted, engulfing one of them in molten lava that melted the fur from its body, leaving only a charred mass on the ground. The smell of burnt hair mingled with the foul odor of the mist.

Another ran from behind, and Seda attempted to strike down the beast, but missed as it quickly ran toward Elco. The monster lunged onto Elco's back and bit down, his torn red scales mixing with the crimson of his blood. A scream of panic burst from both her and Suza.

Elco flickered out of sight.

The monster fell to the ground as it attempted to tear into Elco once more. Rage flooded Seda's vision as her eyes glazed over, and she electrocuted it, focusing all of her power at once onto the beast as it writhed in pain and eventually stopped breathing. She felt exhaustion begin to weave its way through her nerves, but ignored it.

When she felt like the monster was charred enough, she

quickly looked around, trying to find Elco and Suza, but they were nowhere to be seen.

The roses began to shake violently, and thick, prickly roots emerged from the ground.

They wrapped around the remaining monsters, pulling them into the thorny bushes.

The beasts snarled, fighting against the roots, but were unable to break free.

Seda unclenched her fists, and the clouds parted abruptly as panic coursed through her. She looked around for Elco and rushed to where he was standing, feeling around for him, but the warmth of his skin was nowhere to be found.

"You have an Amaru with you?!" the female voice snarled as her body lay tangled amongst the thorny vines.

Seda jumped back as Elco and Suza reemerged a few feet from where they had been standing before.

"Elco!" She ran up to him and hugged him, feeling his racing heartbeat beneath her arms. Elco's blood seeped into her cloak, and she choked back a sob. He was hurt. She felt her anger begin to simmer once more as she glared at the tangled beasts in the bushes.

"He's depleted his magic," Roya said as she knelt next to the lying form of Cahir on the ground.

Seda gasped, remembering he had fallen, and ran to him. She dropped to her knees and brushed her hand over his damp forehead, pushing back the waves of his chestnut colored hair. The jade glow of his skin had faded, making him look almost human again.

"Will he be okay?" Seda choked out, feeling the tension in her muscles from the fight and their injuries all release at once. Her hands began to shake as she ran her knuckle down his cheek.

He was breathing.

"Yes. But he'll be out for a while," Roya replied. She looked over at Suza. "That trick would've been nice to get beyond the rose barrier. Why didn't you say you could do that?"

Roya quickly stood and marched over to Suza, glaring as she grabbed her by the shirt and forced their noses to touch.

"I can only do it once before my magic has to recharge! It's not an easy task. I'm not very powerful," Suza shrieked, trying to get away from Roya's wrath.

Roya roughly released Suza, causing her to stumble back a few paces. Roya marched over to the trapped beast. "You were warned, and you persisted! Now you have dead kin, you fucking fool!"

"There must always be balance," the beast huffed. "It's the way of this world since the beginning of time."

"What are you?" Seda demanded from Cahir's side.

The beast chuckled. "I know what I am. But you obviously do not know what you are. Refusing yanantin-"

"Shut the fuck up and answer!" Roya shouted, interrupting her and pointing a sharpened claw at the top of the beast's ghastly nose, drawing a small bead of red blood.

The monster growled in response, "I'm a Lobizon, a spiritual guardian of the forest, a member of the Coven of the Wilds, the first Lobizon of my kind."

A spiritual guardian?

"What happened, Elco?" Seda looked at him. She knew he wouldn't intentionally harm something unless he had to.

He was watching the Lobizon with narrowed eyes. "I protected the Fae girl you scared that day in the courtyard from one of them a couple of nights ago. She and I ventured out of the city walls. She wanted to find new flowers. And one of them approached, threatening her. I didn't kill the beast, but it did run away with a singed tail." He chuckled through a ragged, pain-filled breath.

Seda looked at the Lobizon. "He says he protected a child from one of your kind."

"Lies!" the Lobizon shouted. "We do not hurt innocents!"

Elco snarled, and his mouth began to glow, threatening to char the angry monster.

"Don't Elco!" Seda yelled, running in front of him. "You'll hurt the plants... They helped us."

Seda looked over at the flowers, their eyes warily watching as they held the Lobizon within their clutches. They didn't shed toxic tears that harmed the beasts. They only watched—and helped.

"Is this Lobizon of yours still alive?" Seda asked her.

The beast strained but nodded her head.

"Then I suggest you have a bigger problem on your hands. Elco wouldn't hurt one of your own without cause."

"Release me," the beast snarled. "Release me, and we will leave this place."

Roya spat back in response, "If we release you, the balance you are looking for has been paid. You came here over a misunderstanding, looking to hurt one of our own. The loss of your friends was your own doing."

The beast seethed, its teeth tightly clenched, but looked back at Seda. "You have my word."

Seda looked at the roses. She wasn't sure if they could understand her if she asked, but she walked closer and lightly touched one of their leaves. "Please release them."

They trembled at her touch and gradually loosened their hold on the remaining Lobisons.

Five of them jumped out from the bushes, growling as the thorns snagged into their fur. The female Lobizon broke free and shook her fur, flinging leaves and rainwater around them. Seda flared her magic again, readying herself in case the beast launched another attack.

The Lobizon chuckled as she looked at Seda's palms. "As I said, you have my word."

"What's your name?" Seda asked, eyes following her every move.

"My name is Sacha." Sacha howled once more and turned, then ran back into the darkness, the five others following.

The mist evaporated as they left.

# CHAPTER 32

<u>Seda</u>

The crackle of the fire surrounded them eerily as the last of the beasts left, leaving a scarred forest floor streaked with blood and fallen Lobison.

Roya, Seda, and Suza worked together to pull the dead monsters further into the trees and away from the camp. Cahir remained asleep on the ground, his eyelids thrashing back and forth.

Seda ground her teeth together when she heard Elco's whimpers as they worked. He whined like a hurt puppy as he lay next to the fire beside Cahir, softly crying with his eyes closed and body curled into a trembling ball.

The first thing Seda did when the monsters left was rush to him and smooth her palms over his back, avoiding the gnarled skin below. He promised her he needed time to heal, that he would be fine, and encouraged her to dispose of the bodies with the others.

When they pulled the last one into the trees, Seda asked

Roya, "How do you know Cahir will be okay?" She glanced at Roya before looking over her shoulder, watching Cahir's sleeping form on the ground.

Cahir tried to protect them—to protect *her*. But he didn't need to. He was repeatedly asked to lower the shield so they could handle the situation. But he refused.

Seda felt irritation envelop her as she recalled his panicked eyes staring at her, refusing to listen to them.

Did he not realize how powerful they were together as a unit?

"It's the way of magic. You can only use as much as you have before your body gives out," Roya replied as she wiped her face free of sweat. She looked at Seda, "This goes for you as well, Seda. You need to pay attention to how you feel as you use it. It's not endless. I saw how you focused your magic on the Lobizon who injured Elco. You need to learn to reserve as much as possible for when you need it in battle."

In battle? She hadn't thought about battling anyone, besides various monsters, but that was just protection. Why would she need to fight? Her goal was to collect the stones and open the door. That was it. What came after that, she wasn't sure. The Wisps never mentioned anything further.

She averted her gaze from Roya's and stared into the campfire in the distance, avoiding a response. That beast got what it deserved by hurting her friend that way. She would do it again, too.

They made their way back to Elco and Cahir, and Seda squeezed herself between them, reaching out to both and placing her hands on them at the same time. Elco's whimpering mixed with purrs, and she looked over at him with a small smile. He was slowly healing himself. She watched as his shredded scales slowly mended back together.

Her gaze shifted to Suza, who randomly played with a stick as she chewed on her bottom lip.

"Thank you," Seda said to her, watching as the woman idly began to poke the fire. "Elco would've been more injured if you hadn't gotten him out of there."

The Amaru's eyes flicked to Seda, and her cheeks pinked as she nodded with a pursed smile.

Seda glanced down at Cahir and furrowed her brows. *If he had only listened*, he wouldn't be out like this right now. What if something bad happened while he was down, and they couldn't take care of the Lobizons as they had? Cahir wouldn't have been here to help at all, or *worse*, he could have been killed and unable to defend himself. It was a lesson for them all, and she was sure as hell going to talk to him about it when he woke up.

*She held a diamond-shaped sapphire in her hand, the deep smoldering blue resembling the twilight depths. It was Somnium's color, the stone a part of him, representing the now failed promises they made together. The Mother Goddess gifted it to him for his harmonious intentions, a show of love that went beyond the creation hierarchy.*

*Their love flourished after uniting to stop Supay, the god of death, from usurping the Mother Goddess. Together, they transformed his flesh into a mortal form. Their defiance of Somnium's god led to his own death, marking the ultimate blow to his plunder.*

*"He is gone, child," a lullaby of a voice drifted through her.*

*She looked around, at the glittering of the river and the white deer that drank from its water. She dropped to her knees and pressed her hands against the base of the withering, massive purple-pulsing tree.*

*"I need him back. I cannot live this life alone." Sparking tears dripped down her cheeks as she pressed her lips against the base of the tree, begging and pleading for his return.*

"You are not alone," the voice echoed through the bark.

She glanced over her shoulder at Elco, who lay in the sun on his back in a deep bed of florals, with small, wing-borne kittens jumping on his stomach and biting at his toes. Her lips curled into a small smile as Elco's laughter rolled along the ground, but it wasn't enough to ease her pain. She needed to see Somnium's piercing gaze as he looked down at her. She needed to feel his gentle touch on her skin.

"I need him back," she said as she looked back at the tree. "I love him. Please, I beg you. Make this my one wish, the one wish you said I could have."

The Mother Goddess's whimsical voice chuckled through the tree. "I will grant this one wish and bend time and space for you, my child. It is my gift for containing Supay. But you will seek another one day, and only the Wisps will grant such a wish, as I will not be there to give it. Love knows no bounds or limits, but sometimes, over time, things change. I know what comes next, I know what came before, and I know what power you contain. Unity and balance supersede all. Never be selfish in your wishes, child, for darkness consumes and in its place only weeds will flourish. I will only grant this, for it is the love of another that you desire."

The wind began to blow around her, causing the white leaves of the tree to float down to the ground. Elco and the kittens looked up and peered at the tree, one kitten still gnawing on his toe.

"You know, once he comes back, it is his final life. The stone I gifted is now outside his form. Do not take this warning lightly..." Her voice paused before saying, "The stone you hold is as much a part of him as it is of you. Tell him to hold on tight to it, child, for you will need it someday."

A tornado of white leaves formed in the clearing, and the form of Kalon appeared, wearing his black, snakeskin armour and his bone mask.

The tree disappeared, only leaving a massive stump behind.

"What is this place?" Kalon asked as the leaves settled around him.

A sob tore from her lips as she stood and ran to him, wrapping her arms around him tightly.

*He ran his hands down her back and stared down at her.* "*I think it's time to celebrate,*" *he said with a wicked grin.*

# CHAPTER 33

Benny

The darkness of night had fallen as they walked down the path, gradually putting more distance between themselves and his sister and Roya with each step.

Benny didn't really want to go on this trip. Fucking Ojore. Why did he have to split apart from them like this?

He understood his wish to reach his people and protect them, but advancing without any plan? That was senseless.

He also could not shake the overwhelming feeling that something was wrong.

*Fucking fool*, he thought, and chuckled to himself, knowing those were Roya's words.

The scenery had slowly changed from green, rolling hills to semi-arid with strange, thorn-filled plants he had never seen before. Askold had—of course—been the first to touch one of them and had a welt on his fingertip now as a result.

Askold prattled on beside them, trying to flirt with both of the new Corvids.

Vira and Sepher were courteous to him, though their replies remained brief.

He hesitated to ask them to check in with Roya because, although he knew she was strong and capable, he still felt worried for her. He would ask them to check in later. He knew if something happened to the other group, Roya would say. Unless... Something happened to Roya, and they had no way to communicate.

They should have found another Corvid to go with them.

Benny realized he was smitten with Roya from the moment she appeared in his apartment and threatened him while he sat in that chair. She was incredible. He trusted her ability to handle herself, and her dedication to Seda made him smile as he walked.

"What are you thinking about?" Vira asked, pulling away from Askold and leaving Sephyr behind with the wooing idiot.

Benny felt the heat of a blush crest his cheeks. "Roya," he admitted.

Vira smiled. "Roya is quite special, isn't she? She's been the Corvid leader since her father passed away a long time ago."

"Yeah, she really is," Benny replied.

"You're lucky to have her as an ally."

He was. But he didn't just want to be her ally. He wanted *more*. He didn't just want brief moments of passion between them. Could he ever get more from being with her?

"We should stop before we reach the wall," Vira said. "In case the Jotnar are still lurking there."

"That's a good idea," he said and held his hand up, stopping the others. "We make camp."

They set up a small camp between two large cacti, as Sephyr called them, and built a fire. Vira and Sephyr shifted into their Corvid forms and circled the area, watching for any activity, as Benny and Askold sat down in the rough dirt.

"You should stop trying to flirt with them. They aren't interested," Benny suggested.

Askold chuckled and feigned shock by placing his hand over his heart. "I'm offended," he said. "My flirts are the best thing since sliced bread. I think Vira might like me."

"I highly doubt that," Benny replied and shook his head.

"Do you think they're okay? Do you think they'll be able to get the stone from the monster?" Askold asked of the others, his voice taking a serious tone.

Benny was silent for a moment before he admitted, "I really hope so."

Sephyr suddenly flew down and shifted into her small human form. She pointed to the far distance.

"Unipacas," she said.

A few miles away, they could see bright blue lights streaking through the darkness.

"W-What's a Unipaca?" Askold asked as he stood and reached for his sword.

She held her hand over his, lowering his sword. "Magical beasts with two-toed feet. They have a horn on their head. Not known for attacking unless provoked."

Benny watched the glowing blue lights streak across the distance. "We need to sneak past any Jotnar we come across. We're not strong enough to fight them," Benny said, shifting the focus back to their journey.

Sephyr nodded in response and sat between the two men, offering a hesitant smile to Askold. He perked up and puffed up his chest, readying himself.

"Don't," Benny said, holding up his hand. "I don't want to hear it anymore."

Askold deflated and muttered something like "jerk," then lay down in the dirt and rolled over to face away from them.

Sephyr chuckled and shook her head.

"I can only imagine how you feel," Benny said to her.

"I can hear you," Askold responded with a groan. "I'm literally *right here*."

Sephyr smiled at him and looked across the distance, watching the Unipacas move across the land. A bright beam of light made the darkness of night abate for a brief moment.

"What did it do?" Benny asked as he pointed.

"Who knows. But you don't ever want to be on the receiving end of that," Sephyr said.

He nervously watched as the light receded into itself, and darkness once more descended around their camp. But before the light was gone, a dark shadow in the far distance moved.

"Fuck," he said as he stood. "There's a Jotnar out there."

Vira swooped down from the sky and shifted forms, quickly stamping out the campfire. "Jotnar in the distance. No fires," she said.

Askold shot up and looked around warily. "Are we okay here?"

"Maybe... It was far off. One was fighting against the Unipaca herd and went down with that light. But another was closer to us. It's concerning that they're over the wall."

"*FUCK!*" Askold shouted.

"Shhh!" Sephyr scolded through a seething whisper. "We need to be quiet. The campfire might already have given us away. We're moving. *Now*."

They quickly grabbed their belongings and moved away from the blazing embers, quietly heading closer toward the wall.

# CHAPTER 34

<u>Seda</u>

The cold breeze brushed Seda's cheeks as she opened her eyes to the brightest full moon she had ever seen. Its amber light spilled through the trees' branches in a waterfall of golden hues. She pulled the cloak tighter with a shiver and scooted closer toward the warmth of the campfire. Cahir was sitting next to her, chewing on his inner cheek. He glanced at her and offered a hesitant smile. The luster to his skin had returned, radiant against the firelight.

She sat up and glared at him, the memory of the fight with the Lobisons coming back to her in waves.

"The sun didn't rise," he said as he looked toward the sky and stared at the twinkling stars visible through the trees.

She narrowed her eyes at him. "What are you talking about?"

He shifted his gaze toward her, his emerald eyes sparkling against the firelight. "The sun. It never rose. The sky should be turning blue right now."

She had no idea what he was talking about. Why would the sun not rise? It was obviously still evening.

"Roya told me what happened," he started before she could say anything. "And before you lay it on me, *I know*, and I'm sorry, Seda."

She didn't care if he didn't want to hear it again. She had things to say regardless. "You have to trust us, Cahir. You have to trust *me*. We're a team, and we're strong *together*."

He moved his eyes away from hers and looked at the crackling wood. "I..." He hesitated. "I know."

Silence fell between them, and Seda got to her feet, irritation flooding her. She could understand his reasoning, but he needed to trust that she was more than the meek woman he knew in Joro. She had power racing through her bones, and she knew how to use it. He didn't have to protect her at his own expense like that.

She looked around for the others, but they weren't near the campsite. She turned around toward the roses, and an opening was visible through the bushes, as if they had parted for them.

"What—" Seda began.

"They parted for us. Apparently, they were blocking the path intentionally, moving as we walked and taking us further into the woods."

Seda remembered how they had shifted their roots and snagged themselves around the Lobison. Why were they leading them deeper into the forest, and why had they now parted for them?

She left Cahir behind and walked closer to the flowers, watching as each rose's eye stared back at her.

*Whatever*, she thought in irritation. *At least it's open now.*

She walked through the opening and spotted Elco with Roya and Suza on the other side. "Elco!" she yelled, running up to him. His injuries had healed, and he was basking in a large patch of moonlight that glittered against his red scales.

"My moon-flutter. You're finally awake." He purred against her.

She hugged him close and sighed as his warmth seeped into her chilled bones. "I'm so happy you're okay."

"I always am," he replied with a huff.

"I had a dream with you in it. I know you mentioned you don't recall much from before the Camp, but I have a persistent feeling that this occurred. Can you tell me if you remember this?" she asked, starting to feel a bit foolish and nervous at what he might reveal.

"I can try," he said as he continued to purr under her touch.

She told him of the dream with the tree and the small flying kittens, and his purrs slowly stopped. He looked at her.

"I do vaguely recall that. That was the day you wished for Somnium back," he said.

Confusion swirled inside her, causing her to pull away from him and nervously fidget with her fingers. "How did you not know Kalon was Somnium when we traveled to the Wisps? How did you know it was me in the Camp?"

He huffed again, and smoke billowed from his nostrils. "I didn't know it was you at first. Only had a suspicion. And I had never seen Somnium without his mask. He was elusive toward me."

"But his voice?" she asked.

"It was so very long ago. I had been trapped in that dungeon for far too long. However, I do remember my kin—those tiny flying felines you mentioned. In the end, I did everything I could to protect them after you left."

"What happened to them?" Seda asked as she sat down beside him and picked at a blade of grass.

"I don't know," he whispered, staring up at the sky. He

sighed deeply and warmly through his nostrils. "Did you know the sun didn't crest the horizon this morning?"

Seda looked up at the moon once more. Cahir had pointed out the same thing. Why would the sun not rise? If the sun were missing, how would the moon still be ablaze?

"I don't understand," she said.

"Solios, the god of the sun and the Solar Sovereign, has lost hope." Elco's red eyes met hers. "We need the stones."

A deep, overwhelming dread took hold of her. Without the sun, life as they knew it would end. The world would perish if it were trapped in eternal darkness.

Cahir walked through the opening in the bushes and paused when his gaze met hers.

"The Fae only wanted to protect you, moon-flutter. He loves you," Elco encouraged. "I think more than you realize."

She ground her teeth together before releasing them and letting out a deep sigh. She stood from the ground and walked over to Cahir, who nervously ran his hand over his neck.

"Promise me you won't deplete yourself again trying to protect me?" she asked as she looked up into his emerald eyes.

His gaze flickered between hers, and his jaw clenched. "Can I talk to you in private, please? Away from the others?" He held out his hand for her to take.

She accepted his outstretched hand, feeling the warmth of it in her palm, and he led her back through the rose bushes to the campfire. They sat back down, and Cahir rubbed his thumb across her hand nervously. He placed a piece of datun in his mouth and offered her a piece. They both chewed in silence as his gaze continued to flick to her and away.

"My mom—" he started, breaking the silence. He let out a deep, ragged breath after spitting out the piece of datun. "My father murdered her. And since he was king, no one did anything."

Seda's eyes widened.

He continued, "My mother was my *world*, but my father was abusive. I'd often see her with bruises, and I was so young that I didn't understand. One day, she walked in on him having an affair, and he lashed out. Tahti was there, following my father's orders, and I never saw her again. So please, Seda... It's not that I don't believe you can handle yourself. It's that I cannot bear to lose someone I love so dearly again. I promise I won't deplete my magic again like that. But I cannot promise that I'll stop doing everything in my power to protect the person I love the most in this world." His eyes glistened as he stared down at her, his emotion breaking through. "You don't understand how devoted I am, how far I'm willing to go, and what I'd sacrifice for you. I'd give up my title, my kingdom, *everything*... for you."

Seda felt her heart ache at his honesty and openness. She spat out her own datun and reached up with a tender hand, cupping his cheek in her palm. "I'm so sorry, Cahir."

She shifted to her knees and pressed her lips against his. He inhaled sharply, holding back his emotion, and pulled her closer. She fell on top of him, kissing him as that tingly warmth began to simmer once more.

"I'd never ask for you to give up anything for me," she said, breathless with each kiss, wanting him to understand that her words were sincere.

The rose bushes shuffled and closed their open gap, closing their eyelids and not watching them as they embraced.

"Are you okay over there, moon-flutter?" Elco called from the other side.

She lifted her head and stared at the wall of closed flowers, shouting breathlessly, "Yes, Elco... Privacy, *please*."

She heard him gruff, "Just call for me if you need me. These flowers cannot hold me back. They forget I can fly."

She laughed as she bent back down and planted her lips

against Cahir once more, tasting the freshness of the datun left behind.

He growled, and she felt his desire press into her. She shifted and tugged at his shirt, wanting to feel his warm muscles under her hands. He pulled it over his head, and she ran her fingers down his defined abdomen, trailing them lower until she reached his pants and slowly ran them over his bulge below the fabric.

She understood his reasons for overexerting himself. He also promised he wouldn't do so again, and she trusted him. She had been safe with this man by her side for years.

No more arguing. She wanted him inside her. Now. She wanted to feel whole again with him by her side.

He slowly pulled her breasts out from her shirt, pulling the material down. She felt her nipples harden in the cool air, and he groaned when he looked at them.

"Seda." Her name escaped as a whisper, a plea, his desire bleeding through the hoarseness of his voice.

She unbuckled his pants and pulled his length out, wrapping her hands around it, and feeling the warm, smooth skin. She slowly began moving them up and down, watching him as his eyes hooded and his lips slowly parted.

"Take these off," he said of her pants, and she stood, slowly pulling them down her hips. His eyes followed the fabric as she lowered her pants, and he took himself in his hand, beginning to stroke himself as he watched her undress.

The cool, misty air did nothing to soothe the fire building inside her at the sight of him touching himself.

When she pulled them off her legs, she watched as his hand slid up and down his length, and she licked her lips. She had never done this before, but she wanted to try. She knelt down, feeling the damp ground seep into her skin, and slowly leaned forward between his legs.

He stopped touching himself, and she glanced up at him. His gaze was locked onto her, confusion swirling behind his emerald gaze. He went to stop her, but she placed her hand on him, just as he had done to her.

"Don't stop stroking yourself," she commanded.

He hesitated before slowly running his hand up and down, moaning through each steady, firm stroke, and she watched as a bead of cum began to form on the tip.

She bent forward and circled her tongue over the head of his cock, feeling the silky skin and the taste of him, so unlike anything she had ever tasted before.

"Fuck," he seethed as his hips trembled. She wrapped her lips around him and sucked him into her mouth. He growled low and heavy, pushing himself deeper into her throat.

"Just like that." His voice cracked, and she continued to pull him deeper, circling her tongue around each time she came up for air. His hand continued to move with her, and when she pulled him out of her mouth, he ran his palm over the head of his cock, moaning her name.

"No more. I need inside you, or I'll come undone all over your perfect, fucking lips." He pulled her onto him and quickly sank deep within her, growling when his cock was fully seated.

She yelped at the sudden sensation of him filling her through every inch of her body.

She shifted forward, running her tongue across his throat, feeling the soft hairs of his beard, and slowly began to move her hips. The feeling was all-consuming, with fire erupting from within. He rubbed his thumb over her clit, and she exploded in pleasure, releasing a small gasp at the sensation.

Nothing mattered anymore—not their argument, not the people waiting for them on the other side of the bushes, nothing except this moment, this feeling she got to share—with him.

Heat began to build as she moved over him, her movements

growing jagged and rough. He continued to circle his thumb, rubbing it around each time she sank onto him. She felt a phantom breeze in the air, and her hair blew around her. Her orgasm began to build, and she started moaning his name over and over as their eyes remained locked onto each other.

"Oh, gods, *Cahir*," she choked out as her orgasm crested through her in punishing waves. He pushed into her through muttered curses as he found his own release, pulling her down onto him and kissing her through each wave that rocked through them both.

As their heart rates decreased, they continued gazing into each other's eyes. Cahir remained steady inside her, and she could feel him twitching within, almost like he wanted *more*. He reached up and lifted her chin, running his thumb over her freckle.

"You're *mine*," he said.

A deep, menacing chuckle and a husky voice interrupted from behind, "Well, that was adorable. And no, *King Ael*, she belongs to no one except herself."

They both quickly looked over, and Kalon stood against a tree, leaning into it and picking at his fingernails. He looked up, and his pale, blue-green, almond-shaped eyes narrowed onto them. He pulled out the moonstone necklace from his pocket into the shaft of moonlight filtering through the trees, causing its prismatic cascade to shimmer across the area.

"Fun time's over," he teased with a wicked smile, the tone cold and mirthless.

# CHAPTER 35

<u>Benny</u>

They had walked for hours after, quickly losing sight of the path they were on, until finally giving up and resting on the cold, hard ground without a fire to warm them. Benny opened his puffy eyes to amber moonlight and sat up, seeing that the others were still asleep.

He quickly looked around in the darkness, searching for any signs of Jotnar nearby.

He heard a rustling behind him and jumped, fearing the worst. But when he hesitantly looked around, he saw a small, furry creature with a long neck sniffing at one of their backpacks. A sigh of relief escaped him.

It had a twisted, chrome horn that seemed to melt into the center of its forehead. Its fluffy coat was an inky, deep blue, and the creature's poofy tail wagged back and forth. Scattered across its chest, as if embedded, were patterns of silver colored flowers.

The creature was small, no taller than Benny's hip while standing, and Benny was reasonably short. It saw Benny shift and skittered into the bushes behind where they lay, nervously peering around at him.

Benny slowly stood and reached into his pocket, pulling out an old cracker and offering it to the animal. "Here you go, I won't hurt you."

The animal slowly stepped out and hesitantly walked over to Benny, sniffing the cracker within his hand. It moved its lips over Benny's palm and munched on the offering, its chrome colored eyes shifting up to meet his. When the animal finished chewing, it nudged Benny's palm once more, asking for another treat.

Benny reached into his pocket, pulled out another cracker, and offered it to the small animal.

"A baby Unipaca. How rare to see," Vira said in awe while lying on the ground.

The baby Unipaca startled and jumped back into the bushes, but it didn't run away.

Benny stepped closer and peered around. He slowly reached out and ran his hand down the Unipaca's back. It huffed and nudged the side of its head into Benny's hip.

"We won't hurt you, little one," he said. "Come out. I promise you're safe with us."

The little Unipaca took a hesitant step forward, walked over to the backpack it had been sniffing before, and nudged it. Benny picked up the sack and looked inside.

"You must want these," he said of Askold's apples and carrots within. He pulled an apple out and offered it to the baby, who quickly bit into it and yanked it away from Benny, chewing loudly and smacking its lips.

It let out a gentle humming sound and shook its head back and forth, stamping its foot.

"Whoa…" Askold said as he sat up. "She's a cutie."

"She?" Benny asked.

Askold looked at him as if he were an idiot. "Of course, it's a *she*. I can tell."

"Why do you think she's here? Where are her parents?" Benny looked at both the Corvids, who were both now awake and watching the exchange.

"Perhaps her family was in that fight last night with the Jotnar. Maybe she ran away?" Sephyr suggested.

"We should get moving," Vira interrupted as she looked up at the massive moon and the wall highlighted in an amber glow in the distance.

Benny reached into the pack and held out another apple for the Unipaca as a parting gift. She gleefully accepted it, swishing her tail back and forth, and crunched into its red skin.

"How long were we asleep?" he asked the others. The moon, before they had fallen asleep, had been crescent-shaped, but the moon above them now was full and glowing brightly.

"Not sure. Must not have been that long," Askold groaned. "I can use a few more hours."

"No, we need to move," Vira reiterated.

They packed up what little belongings they had taken out and began walking away. Benny glanced back at the Unipaca and saw that she was trailing behind them. He turned around. "You need to go find your family, little one. We're going past that wall, and your family is the other direction."

She shook her head at him and hurried over, stamping her foot again once she reached his side.

"She wants to stay with you." Sephyr smiled.

"That's what you get for feeding wild animals," Askold complained. "She's going to eat all my food."

The baby Unipaca stamped her foot repeatedly on the ground, releasing a huffing sound from flared nostrils, and narrowed her molten eyes at Askold.

"Do you think she can understand us?" Benny asked.

The Unipaca nodded at them, and Benny laughed. "She can understand you, asshole. You'd better stop being a dick, or else she'll stab you with that horn of hers."

The Unipaca let out a wheezing sound, almost like a laugh.

"If you come with us, you need to be *very quiet*. We're trying to avoid those giant beasts you ran into. We don't have the manpower to fight them."

The Unipaca nodded again and nibbled at the sack at Benny's side. Benny reached in and pulled out a carrot this time. She hummed and jumped up and down.

"What should we call you?" he asked her.

"What about Bluebell?" Askold suggested. "She has flowers on her chest, and she's blue."

The Unipaca glanced up at Askold and narrowed her metallic eyes once more.

"Don't like that name, I take it?" Benny asked as he laughed. "What about Aurora? That's a pretty name for a pretty girl."

She nudged him lovingly, and Vira said, "I think any name you said she would've taken. I don't think she likes Askold much."

They laughed, and Askold grumbled, "Of course not. Just wants to eat all my apples. I packed those for myself, ya know."

Aurora pranced over to Askold and quickly bit his thigh, leaving a hole in his pants. He yelped out in pain and jumped away from her. "Ouch! You heathen!"

She spat at him, and it landed directly where she had bitten.

The others laughed again, but Benny lightly scolded, "Okay, Aurora, you proved your point. But he's our *friend*, and we don't bite *or* spit at friends."

She huffed in response and made her way back to Benny, flicking her tail back and forth.

"She won't be small for long," Vira said. "They're only babies for a couple of days. She must have just been born."

"How's that possible?" Askold asked, rubbing his thigh. "I don't think my leg can handle this attitude when she's bigger."

"Probably not. You'd better get on her good side," Benny chuckled as he began walking once more, Aurora following his every step.

They walked for another hour as they approached the tall, stone wall. Sephyr was in her Corvid form, flying above, peering over, and watching for any movement on the other side.

"How do we get over it?" Benny looked to Vira before peering up at the hundred feet of stone face that blocked their path into the Lycanthrope realm.

"Please don't say we have to climb," Askold groaned. "We had to climb that damn mountain to get to the Wisps, and I never want to do that again."

Vira chuckled. "There's a door here somewhere, and I assume part of the wall is down too, considering the Jotnar are now on this side."

"Shit!" Benny said, remembering the Jotnar. "You should warn Ferona that the Jotnar are making their way to Umbrea. And Roya, too. Can you check in with them, please?"

Vira closed her eyes, focusing on her task.

Sephyr flew down and stood alongside her sister, waiting for her to finish.

"Done," Vira said.

"Umm... Did they say anything in response? Did Roya say she was okay?" Benny asked nervously.

Vira offered a small smile. "They're fine, Benny. We didn't say much, as our whispers can be heard by any Corvid interested. And with Feich and others possibly listening in, we have to be discreet."

Benny frowned. That made sense, but it was a letdown to say the least. He was glad that Roya and his sister were safe, though. He heard loud chewing and looked over at Aurora, who was happily chewing through dried grass. She looked up at him and stamped her foot, digging her two large toenails into the dirt.

"If I continue giving you all the carrots and apples we packed, there won't be any left to give, little one," he said to her. "Later."

She made a grumbling sound and went back to chewing on the grass.

Benny looked up at the wall once more. "Any ideas?" he asked as he pointed to it.

Sephyr answered, "There's a door about half a mile north. We should head that way. The Jotnar tore through the wall about a mile north of that. We need to be careful. There's no door south. We must head that way." She pointed north along the wall.

Benny sighed and started walking, as both Corvids took off again into the sky. Askold muttered beside him, while Aurora pranced ahead, her fluffy tail swinging back and forth in playful glee.

He sent a silent prayer to the sky, hoping they would make it safely past the door and find Ojore.

# CHAPTER 36

### Luelle

The throne felt awkward and cold as Luelle sat upon its emerald facade, looking down at her nails. She grumbled, realizing she had a chip in her red nail polish on her index finger. They were doing mundane tasks, listening to people ask for various things. She half-listened as someone ahead of her asked for more water rights to plant a new field of vegetables.

"Approved." She waved her hand in the air to shoo them away. She had approved everything so far. Is this what Ael had to deal with every day?

*Utterly boring*, she thought.

"I don't know why you get to sit on the throne," Praxis grumbled as he stood by her side, wearing armor like he was some strong, beastly male. She glared at his half-shaved head and cuffed ears and fought a laugh as she remembered how he tore into the dining room in a panicked state over the Jotnar, looking like a child who thought a ghost was in his closet.

"Because Ael said so," she remarked in a childish lilt with a slight curve of her lips, signaling to the next person in line.

An older man walked forward and bowed. When he stood, he said, "Advisor Luelle, as you know, the sun did not rise. What do you intend to do about it? Our magic can only go so far to produce our food without sunlight."

He was right. The sun didn't rise this morning. She swallowed her anxiety.

"I..." she started. This wasn't just a request to approve something. "We're doing everything we can to research the issue. Next." She waved him off. She had no fucking clue how to fix the sun. She ground her teeth together, wishing Ael were back.

Before the next person could speak, she said, "Approved," and pushed them along.

She desperately wanted to get back to spending time with Ferona. They had a quiet breakfast together this morning, not really saying much. Ferona seemed to be quite timid around her, but every time they spoke, Ferona's cheeks would turn a bright shade of pink. She was beyond adorable, and she couldn't wait to get out of this stupid chair—despite pretending she adored it for Praxis's sake—and back to Ferona's side.

As the last of the people left, the doors swung open, and Ferona rushed in.

*Oh, yay,* she thought, smiling as she watched her lithe form rush in. Her smile faded when she noticed that Ferona appeared out of breath, her eyes wide with fear.

"What happened?" Luelle asked, shifting forward on her seat.

Praxis stopped the complaining she wasn't even listening to as his gaze shifted to Ferona.

"The Jotnar have breached the Lycanthrope wall and are on their way here," Ferona gasped, clutching onto her chest to steady her breathing. "Vira just whispered to me."

"What!" Praxis shouted, spittle spewing from his lips.

*Fucking gross*, Luelle thought as she watched it fling down the dais steps.

"Get the guard together, Praxis. Watch from the towers. Sound the alarm when you see one approaching," she commanded. He looked at her with fear-stricken eyes. The fool was utterly chicken-shit over the damn Jotnar.

They were Fae for crying out loud.

She glanced at Ferona and asked, "Does King Ael know about this yet?"

"He should be informed at any moment," she replied.

Praxis turned to her, and she said, "Stop your complaining. We need to work together on this. While Ael is out, I'm in charge, Praxis. Fucking man up and assemble the gods-damned *guard*."

He nodded and, shakily, walked down the dais, stopping to thank Ferona before awkwardly leaving the room.

*At least he's loyal*, she thought as the door closed.

She shifted her focus back to Ferona. "Are you okay?"

"Um... Yes. Thank you," Ferona replied and started to play with her fingers nervously. "What will we do if they come?"

Luelle stood from the throne and walked down the steps, meeting her at her side. "We have a large guard, Ferona. They will not breach us. My nail polish is chipped, and I'd like to look *ravishing* when they arrive. Will you join me?"

Ferona nodded and nervously smiled at her. She held up her own hands, and the perfect, sharpened, baby blue manicure shone back at Luelle.

"Have you ever tried red?" Luelle asked, raising an eyebrow and offering a teasing smile.

"No, do you think it would clash with my hair?" Ferona asked, returning her grin, though nervously.

"Pink might be better. Let's go to my rooms." Luelle held out her arm, and Ferona hesitantly accepted it, her cheeks warming once more.

"And then I saw Meir's tiny ass cheeks! They were so squished together when he fucked her!" Luelle was gasping for breath through laughter as she and Ferona painted their nails.

They both sat on her bed, careful not to knock over the polish and stain the bedspread as they gossiped.

"That's so disgusting. How could that woman be with him? He was gross!" Ferona laughed and wiped a tear that had slipped free.

"Oh! Careful! They're still wet," Luelle said of Ferona's newly pink nails, her cheek now streaked with polish. They chose a shade of baby pink that Luelle had somehow purchased a long time ago and never used, realizing after she bought it that it didn't suit her attitude just right. She preferred that fiery red.

It was perfect for Ferona, though, and complemented her baby-blue-accented hair.

She reached out and gently took Ferona's moonlit hand, softly blowing on her nails. Ferona's laughter faded, and Luelle looked up while her breath continued to graze her polish.

Ferona's gaze flickered between hers and down to her lips.

Luelle felt her heart race. Should she do it? She didn't want to scare the beautiful bird or move too fast, but she was absolutely, completely, and utterly captivated by her.

She slowly stopped blowing on Ferona's nails and softly dragged her nails up her arm, making Ferona's breath catch.

She pulled herself closer and paused, asking, "May I kiss you?"

Ferona swallowed and nodded, and Luelle shifted closer,

softly brushing her lips against hers, feeling a soft gasp escape the magical woman.

"What about the Jotnar?" Ferona drew back just a fraction, breathless, her moonlit skin warming with a sudden flush.

"We're getting ready for them," she responded with a scandalized tone, before kissing her once more, feeling like she was coming alive as the softness of her lips caressed her own. She no longer cared as the nail polish tipped over between them and soaked into the silken sheets.

# CHAPTER 37

<u>Seda</u>

Seda quickly pulled her pants over her hips, grumbling through both anger and embarrassment as she squirmed into them. Kalon had turned away, glancing back through the darkened trees, while she and Cahir quickly separated and put their clothes back on.

"How fucking dare you!" she seethed at the back of his head, noticing that he had cut his hair. It was no longer in the long braid that ran down his back, but was trimmed above his ears now. Fuck his stupid hair. She wanted to fry his head. Now that they weren't in a dream, she could, too.

She remembered the memory and clenched her teeth. Why would she ever wish for this asshole to come back?

"All I did was appear at the wrong time," he replied, his shoulders rigid and unmoving.

"I'm going to fucking kill you," Cahir growled as he tucked himself back in. Seda saw the wet spot on the front of his pants and silently groaned. They should have taken them off before doing that, but they were so caught in the moment, they didn't even think about it.

Kalon turned around and stared at Cahir with a humorless smirk. "You had your fun, little Fae. Time for the grown-ups to get to work."

Cahir raced forward, quickly grabbing his sword from the ground and lunging for Kalon's chest, but Kalon flicked his fingers, and Cahir fell to the ground and writhed in pain.

"Stop!" Seda ran forward and fell to her knees at Cahir's side. "Stop, *please*," she begged him. "Don't hurt him!"

Kalon looked at her, and the anger in his eyes quickly softened, freeing Cahir from his magical nightmare. "Tell your little *plaything* to calm down. We need to talk."

Cahir snapped his eyes open, glaring at Kalon, and his magic erupted from his palms, wrapping around Kalon's throat and hurling him violently into the tree.

"Stop!" Seda yelled, drawing his attention to her in confusion.

"Why?" he asked through clenched teeth as he held his power tightly around the man.

"Because we need him. Pull back now!" she screamed, feeling her heart race.

Elco roared and flew over the hedges, landing behind Seda and growling ferociously, causing the ground to shake. Cahir pulled his magic back. Kalon's newly trimmed hair was ruffled and hung over his brow as he hunched over, gasping for breath.

"I deserved that one. But it won't happen again," Kalon rasped as he clutched his throat and inhaled a ragged breath. He coughed a few times before standing upright and dusting off the sticks on his armor. He brushed his hair back with his hand and looked at them once more.

"For you, Seda." He held up the moonstone necklace.

She took a hesitant step toward him, glancing at Cahir first, before accepting it from his outstretched hand. His fingers grazed hers, the contact sparking a quiet tingle. She quickly pulled away from him and placed it around her neck. The chain's familiarity and the weight of the stone settled over her, giving her a sense of comfort she deeply missed.

"Thank you," she whispered.

"What's going on here?" Elco growled, looking between the two men.

"Don't worry about it, Elco. It's over now," Seda said, walking closer and running her hands down his scales. "Thanks for coming. But it's nothing."

Elco narrowed his eyes at Cahir and Kalon and huffed when his gaze dropped to the spot on Cahir's pants. Seda felt her cheeks heat, but before she could say anything, he walked over to the roses, and they parted for him, forming the same pathway as before.

She looked back at the two men and cleared her throat, "Are you coming?

They looked at each other, and Kalon smirked, taking the lead. Cahir jumped to his feet and pushed in front of Kalon, trying to get closer to Seda. She heard him snarl at Kalon behind her, "Next time I won't let go."

She bit the inside of her cheek and walked alongside Elco, weaving their way through the bushes. She greeted Suza before seeing Roya opening her eyes.

"We have news," Roya said as they approached, but her gaze flicked to Kalon, and her brows furrowed. "Where did you come from?"

SEDA STOOD beside Cahir while Roya relayed Vira's words. How and why were the Jotnar attempting to reach Umbrea?

What could be the Monster King's reason for wanting to be here? She idly played with the chain around her neck with one hand, holding the stone firmly in the other.

She was surprised that Kalon actually returned it to her, as he had promised. She chewed on her lip as she watched the sparkling light from the stone glitter across the ground.

Suza had embraced Kalon when they first approached, but now she stood beside Seda, as if trying to show him that she was doing everything she could to stick to her word.

"You should tuck that into your shirt," Suza whispered as she looked down at Seda's moonstone. "A lot of people are after that now."

She tucked it into her top and refocused on the others, who were now arguing.

"I'm *not* leaving," Cahir shouted. "We get to La Uma and rush back to Umbrea."

"I can take you there now, Ael," Kalon suggested. "If the Jotnar are on their way to your kingdom, it's your responsibility to protect it."

"Can you take us to La Uma directly? We can jump in, steal the stone, and transport out?" Roya asked.

"I can get us close, but not within her lair. It's bewitched," Kalon replied. "And despite what you may think." He winked at Cahir. "My power isn't endless. If we transport there now, I'll likely need time to recharge before we can get away from her."

"How long?" Cahir asked as he glared at him. "And how do I know you won't just whisk Seda away from us?"

Kalon sighed and ran his hand down his face. "I swear I'm not here to *steal* Seda. If I wanted to do that, I could've just done it hundreds of times already." He looked at Elco and pointed to him. "This guy's massive. Normally, when I transport people, it's not magical beings of his size. I'd probably need an hour."

"How long do you think we need with La Uma?" Roya asked.

"No fucking clue," Cahir answered.

Roya looked at Seda. "What do you want to do?"

Seda felt her skin tighten as everyone, including Elco, watched her expectantly, waiting for her reply.

If the Jotnar were on their way to Umbrea now, they needed the stones as quickly as possible. She inhaled and looked at Kalon. "Transport us there. We go inside, locate what we need, and return to Umbrea after you recharge. If the Jotnar were spotted beyond the border wall last night, they'll be approaching the city soon."

She glanced at Cahir and saw his jaw flex, but he didn't argue her decision.

"Alright. Here we go," Kalon said as he raised his hands.

A blackened tornado began swirling around them as darkness swallowed the world.

# CHAPTER 38

<u>Benny</u>

The night sky burned brightly, a full moon illuminating the ground as they approached a large wooden door that met the path they had lost while wandering through the darkness.

Askold jogged up to the door first and jiggled the handle.

"It's locked!" Askold huffed, shaking the handle roughly, trying to open it.

Vira and Sephyr flew down and shifted forms.

"There's nothing we can see on the other side. The coast looks clear," Vira said as she watched Askold slowly freak out over the door.

"How do we get in?" Benny asked.

Aurora pranced up to Askold and nudged him in the side. He looked down at the little Unipaca and jumped back, his face paling.

"Shit!" he said, looking at the others. "Thought she was about to bite me again."

Aurora turned around and kicked the door as hard as her little body could, and the door splintered. She kicked it twice more, and it flew off the hinges onto the other side.

*Holy shit,* Benny thought as he cleared his throat.

"Damn, Askold. Be glad she didn't use her legs on you earlier," Benny said, chuckling when he saw Askold's gaping mouth. He reached into the pack and pulled out another carrot, offering it to Aurora. "Good work."

Aurora chewed the carrot happily as she waited for them to peer through the opening. Benny took a step forward and looked toward the other side.

A single raised gravel path ran through marshlands, flooded and stagnant. Bald Cypress trees were adorned with long, stringy moss that hung from their branches and pooled in the water. The air felt heavy here, smelling of decaying plants and algae. Benny looked at the water and saw the thick green slime floating in large patches.

"Smells like poop," Askold said as he gagged beside him.

Sephyr's piercing eyes scanned the area. "We didn't see any Jotnar from above. I thought Praxis said there'd be a dead one here, but we didn't see it. We need to be careful. I'll fly and watch for movement, and Vira will remain on the ground in case something creeps out of the water."

Askold muttered something again, but Benny walked through the door and ignored his complaints. He heard the owls hooting and saw a disoriented spoonbill in the distance, its long legs treading through shallow water and tripping, as if confused by the moon's bright amber glow.

What time was it anyway?

"How far is Tuath?" he asked Vira, watching the water for movement.

"About twenty miles," she responded.

They kept walking along the narrow trail, where in some

sections only two people could walk side by side. Aurora remained at his heel, her feet softly crunching through the gravel.

Benny walked behind Vira. "Do you have any idea how the Jotnar got here in the first place? You'd think with that wall, they'd have come through Umbrea first."

She quickly glanced over her shoulder at him before turning back and saying, "The gap between Dreadspire Crater and Tuath is crossed by water, but it's not a long distance. The Jotnar do not climb Mt. Ebenveil."

Benny recalled the treacherous hike up the mountain to reach the Wisps. Not only was it steep, but it was icy, and at the top... *yeah, no wonder they didn't go that route.*

"So they just... *swim?*" he asked, which earned him a chuckle in response.

"Possibly, but I doubt it. They may be large, but they're also pretty lazy. I'd wager they had a boat," she responded.

"Do you guys hear that?" Askold asked from behind. They paused and looked back at him. He stood frozen, his head tilted, listening to the surrounding area.

Benny realized that the owls had silenced, and in their place, a low buzzing sound vibrated through the air.

"Shit," Vira said, extending her claws.

"What is it?" Benny asked, slowly drawing his sword. He felt the hairs on his neck prickle as he listened to the buzzing sound that was slowly growing louder.

"Mosquitoes," Vira whispered, glancing up through the trees.

Mosquitoes? Sure, it was a swamp. They were bound to have insects flying around, but Benny hadn't felt a single bite yet. He lowered his sword.

"Don't lower that! Be ready!" she hissed at him.

His brows drew together as he looked at her. What the hell was he going to do with a sword and a mosquito?

"Fuck!" Askold shouted as he whipped around. A mosquito, the size of a dog, flew down from the trees and circled around him. It was dark, with white spots that shone brightly in the moonlight, and it had a long proboscis that dripped with clear liquid.

It knocked Askold back, throwing him violently onto the ground. He sprang to his feet and brought his sword down on the bug, releasing green fluid that splattered onto his shirt.

He held his sword up and looked at the slime stuck to the blade and then down at himself. "Yuck! I hate this place, you guys. Let's find Ojore and never come back."

"Good job," Benny praised as he lowered his sword once more.

Aurora nodded her head at Askold as if in approval and trotted over to him, nudging his side. Askold hesitantly patted her fluffy head in return. He looked up at Benny and smiled.

"More will likely come. Stay alert," Vira said, turning around and starting to walk up the path again.

Benny followed Vira as they wound along the winding trail, while Aurora trotted happily beside Askold. Benny let out a sigh of relief as the owls started hooting again.

THE SWAMPS FELT ENDLESS, and the musky air only thickened the further they walked. Benny's legs ached from this trip, and he scolded himself for wearing too heavy clothing as the humid air clung to his skin, causing sweat to bead down his neck. He had taken off his jacket an hour earlier and now had to hold the damn thing.

Askold wasn't doing any better behind him, as Benny kept hearing his muttered curses every few minutes.

The owls were increasingly loud and pounding against Benny's head until suddenly, they stopped.

Everyone froze, and Benny felt his blood run cold as the thrumming sound of buzzing began, growing steadily louder.

Sephyr flew down and shifted forms. "There's a swarm headed this way!"

"What do we do?" Askold shouted as he drew his sword and frantically looked into the trees. "Which way?"

Sephyr pointed, and the hanging moss began to sway as the wind picked up. "We fight with everything we have." Her claws extended.

Three mosquitoes blew through the swamp and surrounded Vira. She spun around them and sliced through the air, killing two of them quickly, green entrails splattering all over her.

More burst through and began swarming from above, darkening the already dim sky and watching, as if learning their movements. Benny held onto his sword, feeling it slip through his sweat-slicked hands.

Aurora screamed and kicked in the air as one tried to land on her back. Askold lunged forward and stabbed the insect, piercing it with his blade and pulling it back out with slick slime coating the metal.

The mosquitoes began to pulse in unison, as if angered by their fallen.

And then they descended.

Sephyr and Vira wove through the monstrous bugs, killing them one by one. Benny swung his sword around himself. He tried not only to protect himself but also Aurora.

The tiny Unipaca screamed and kicked her legs wildly, hitting the mosquitoes and producing loud crunching sounds as her feet made contact with them.

Benny struggled to see around himself, as everywhere he looked was blocked by brown, spindly legs with transparent wings. He heard Askold scream, and he wildly turned, striking through the bugs as he pushed himself closer to his friend.

Askold was lying on the ground as a mosquito pierced his chest. Benny heard a loud sucking sound and saw Askold's red blood sucked into its proboscis. He ran forward and kicked the bug off his chest, causing it to crunch on his boot and fly across the water.

Aurora let out another scream as a bright light blinded everyone, followed by a pulsing sound and a shimmering, high-pitched note.

The mosquitoes stopped attacking and buzzed around them.

Benny glanced at Aurora, whose horn blazed with a metallic blue beam shooting directly into the sky. The mosquitoes, as if lured by the light, flew into it and burned themselves to dust. Loud zapping and popping sounds erupted around them as grime rained from the sky. He held his hand over his mouth and nose, trying to protect his lungs from the dirty air.

Benny quickly reached for the jacket he had thrown onto the ground and tossed it over Askold's face, protecting him from the particles as he writhed in pain. Green gore surrounded them, soaking into the gravel pathway below.

He looked back at Aurora, her bright light shining like a beacon, and saw that she was beginning to *grow*.

"What's going on?" he heard Askold gasp from under the jacket.

Benny said breathlessly, "Aurora's saving us."

As the last of the insects flew into the light, the buzzing sound stopped, and Aurora's horn faded. Benny stared in awe at the fully transformed Unipaca. She was more than twice the size of a stag, and her horn had grown another few inches in length. Her chrome, floral patterns now scattered over her thighs.

She was breathtaking.

Askold started trembling violently. Benny pulled the jacket away from his face and noticed it was swelling. Sephyr and Vira quickly approached.

"We have to get him to Tuath before the poison fully sets in," Vira said.

Aurora neared and nudged her nose into Benny's side, making a chirping sound from her throat.

Benny glanced at her, momentarily surprised by her altered size and sharper features as she approached. "We need to get Askold to Tuath immediately. Can you carry him?"

Aurora nodded, her molten chrome eyes flicking down at Askold. She hummed and stamped her foot, throwing her head up, as if trying to hurry them up. She knelt to her forelimbs and waited, impatiently huffing through flared nostrils.

Benny, Vira, and Sephyr quickly placed Askold on her back. Aurora stood, and they began to run the rest of the way to Tuath.

Benny only slipped once through the mess they left behind.

# CHAPTER 39

<u>Jason</u>

The stars burned brightly in the sky, despite the time on his watch just striking noon. Each breath that escaped him sent a faint puff of steam from his mouth, rich with hypocrisy.

"Rebecca Halsy, you're the last Wyrd selectee. Please come forward for processing," Jason's voice echoed against the stone walls of the Palatium as he stared across the crowd, searching for the woman. He watched as she turned to her loved ones and embraced them in emotional goodbyes, their soft whimpers traveling across the dusty ground onto the stage.

He ground his teeth together. Unbeknownst to the Monster King, this was the last Wyrd that would ever be held. The sun was now gone, indicating that Solios had finally given up hope.

Portraying himself as their protector, wearing the sanctimonious mask of demise, worn through him with a slow and ravenous fury.

He couldn't do this anymore. His finger traced along the

device in his pocket, running it over the button. He wished he could press it now and let all chaos unfold. But it wasn't the right time.

About a dozen Corvid shifters stood alongside Feich and the Rozzers, who were lining the walls. When they revealed themselves at the beginning of this Wyrd, the people of Joro had a full-out panic. But, following Teivel's advice, Jason managed to spin the story as if they were compassionate protectors here to restore the cracked dome. Hundreds still flew from above, as if waiting to decide on whether they would follow Feich or his sister.

He looked up at the magical barrier, now broken into a spiderwebbed pattern of fractures that ran up the western side of the city over Cascade. The splinters through the magical barrier pulsed like heartbeats.

The citizens living on that side migrated to Orience, and what a pain in the ass it was to find homes they felt were livable by their standards.

A couple moved into Seda's old apartment and complained about the broken window. Jason had promised a new one as soon as possible. Little did they know he had never placed the order. He was tired of the classist divide amongst the citizens. Ignorance and biases tore through this city like a plague, infecting those who thought themselves better than others. It was disgusting. Especially since, in the end, they were all just food for the monsters anyway.

"Thank you all for a successful Wyrd. You are proving your love for our society every day by bearing more and more children. I bless you all for your efforts. Please don't forget to collect your food tokens on the way out," he numbly mumbled into the microphone and stared down at the exhausted citizens within.

He watched as people began to file through the doors in orderly lines.

Tievel stood beside him and patted him on the shoulder, whispering, "Good job, Lord Jason. As you know, I'm unable to return to the Camp tonight. See to it that things are in order there and return here once finished. Also, knock some sense into Mordred, please. Get him to talk. This has gone on long enough." His beady eyes studied him intently, watching for any signs of betrayal, obviously not concerned whatsoever about the lack of sun today.

When Jason showed no emotion, he patted him once more and walked toward Feich, who was waiting at the edge of the stage. Before talking to Feich, he turned around and said, "Shave the other half of that fucking ugly beard. I'm tired of looking at it."

"Yes, Sire." He approached the Palatium entrance, taking a deep breath of the stale air as he ascended the steps toward the mirrored doorway. He would shave his beard eventually, when he felt like it. The half-shaven mess was a silent display of defiance, an internal battle of courage, and it would stay until this mess was over... or it would follow him to his grave, whichever came first.

The rippled mirror flowed over him like water, seeping into every pore on his body. It had been a gift from the Oracle to Mordred years ago, allowing him access to the Camp and back, a way to smuggle inmates back into Joro. When Tievel figured out what it was, he stole it for himself.

That was the day Mordred lost the majority of his teeth.

Jason shuddered at the memory of seeing him ascend the steps and smiling with a jagged grin for the first time. Would the same become of him? He shook his head as the mirror undulated over him. He didn't care. He would prefer to eat sharp crackers against his gums for the rest of his life rather than live another day like this. What mattered was doing everything he could to help the Darkened descend upon the land and wipe the planet free of this corruption.

"Lord Jason," the Captain said when he entered the Monster King's office in the Camp. The slimy fool had been promoted once more after Jason's ascension to Lord. "Will our Monster King be joining us tonight?"

"No," he replied curtly. "He would like you to gather all the men and count them. *Do it now.* I must report back. Leave Mordred, he's a flight risk."

Jason knew that rounding up and counting all the men in the camp would cause chaos, and he needed this distraction.

"Yes, my Lord," the Captain replied through his slithery tongue and quickly left the room, barking orders to the other Dragors and Rozzers within the courtyard.

When the door closed, Jason quickly opened the Monster King's desk drawers, searching for the hidden key. He had not yet earned the Monster King's trust to gain his own.

A cold sweat broke out down his spine as he scattered papers across the table and checked through coat pockets in the wardrobe.

Where the hell was it? He heard shouting and a gunshot outside the door and panicked as he looked around. Time was running out. His gaze fell on the picture hanging above the desk, showing two young boys. He ran over to it and threw it to the ground, shattering the glass and tearing off the cardboard backing.

A silver key with a mushroom-shaped bow reflected back at him.

He wasted no time, grabbed the key, placed it in his pocket, and ran back to the wardrobe. He grabbed a cloak from within and walked out the door. A battle of desperation lay before him as the prisoners fought the guards, screams piercing his ears as chaos erupted across the sandy terrain.

He walked briskly, with practiced discipline, focusing on the scene ahead in case anyone looked his way, pretending to be invested in the count. When he reached Mordred's cell block, he quickly snuck in and closed the door behind him.

When he saw that no guards were within, a deep sigh of relief escaped his lips.

He rushed to the cell.

"Mordred," he hissed. "Wake the hell up."

Mordred was asleep, curled into a ball in the far corner. When he heard Jason, he popped his head up and began muttering incoherent words.

"He's not here to harm you. I found the key. We're leaving this place," he said, trying to encourage Mordred out of his panicked state.

Mordred stilled and looked up at him with red-rimmed, burning eyes that mimicked the sun.

"Get up. The Rozzers are performing a count now, and the distraction won't last long." Jason stuck the key into the lock, and it loudly creaked open. He threw the cloak at him.

Mordred's scarred, bloody hand with missing fingers shook as he reached for the material. Jason walked in and held out his hand for him to take. "We're in this together, friend. We always have been."

Mordred studied his outstretched hand. "How will we get out?"

"The mirror. Now hurry up." Jason flexed his fingers, hoping he would accept.

"Do you think that blood was from her?" Mordred asked as he turned away and stared at the bed covered in dried, dark blood.

She may have been Jason's daughter in this lifetime, but she was Mordred's one wish from the heavens. She was created in her grandmother's divine image, as a guardian between the heavenly and mortal realms, and as an offering of love to their creator.

"No. I don't," he replied. "She's strong. Stronger than we realized."

"I'm done, Jason. I cannot do this any longer," Mordred whispered with a sigh. "I'm of no use in this fight. It all started because of me, anyway. I wish for death."

Jason stood there for a long moment, listening to Mordred's ragged breathing and the chaos outside. He knew that Mordred had already surrendered, as the sun did not rise.

"The dome's about to collapse. You're not allowed to give up. We'll help the innocence of this world... *together*... with her," he encouraged.

A ragged laugh escaped Mordred, and he shook his head. "I'll never be forgiven. I accepted that long ago. Now I wish for eternal darkness."

"We need you. We need *Solios*," Jason pleaded. "We can't let the planet die in darkness."

His name. His real name. Solios, the god of the sun and the Solar Sovereign. He was the Mother Goddess's first creation, a Fae god to walk the mortal realm, and the first to *wish for more*, as the fairy tales described.

Mordred's eyes burned as they met Jason's, but he reached a hesitant hand out toward Jason and pulled himself onto shaky legs. He held his wrists out, and Jason slipped the skeleton key into the locks, uncuffing the bloodstone blocking his Fae magic.

The bloodstone was strong enough to block mortal magic, but not enough for the magic of the heavens. Teivel didn't know this, and it worked to their advantage. Teivel didn't know Mordred was Solios, after all.

Mordred pulled the dark cloak over himself, masking his face with the hood lowered over his brow.

"Walk alongside me casually," Jason said as he slowly opened the cell block door and peered out. He took a deep breath, feeling his heart race at what they were about to do. If they got caught, these plans could fail.

And not just that—his wife, the mother of his children, Sara, would be killed.

The guards were continuing their fight against the men, and somehow a fire erupted, lighting up the center of the courtyard in a blaze that rivaled Mordred's fiery eyes.

They walked quickly back toward the large door of the Monster King's office, and Jason opened the door. The rusty hinges creaked loudly.

Mordred walked in first, but a slithery voice called out, "Don't you want the numbers, Lord Jason?"

Jason looked over his shoulder at the Captain, "I'll be back in thirty minutes. Give it to me then."

He went to turn, but the Captain said, "No one arrived with you today. And yet... You leave with another." It was not a question.

Jason wasted no time, walked through the door, and locked it behind him. He stared at Mordred, his chest rising and falling rapidly.

The Captain knew.

He could hear the Captain rage as he shouted, *"Betrayer!* See if he took Mordred!"

"It'll take them hours to get word to Tievel, unless he comes here first. We must go *now*." Jason walked to the mirror and looked back at Mordred, holding his hand out for him to take. "Together?"

The door started banging loudly.

Mordred grasped his hand, and they walked through the mirror together. Like they were two halves of the same shield—one a simple human doing what he could to save the world, and the other a weakened god—leaving the angered screams of chaos behind.

# CHAPTER 40

<u>Seda</u>

As the blackness faded, they heard insects scattering as they opened their eyes to a dark ravine filled with dense plants. Mimicking a deep wound where sunlight could not touch, even in daylight, the cliffs surrounding them reached for the fog blanket above. The dark gray rockface was rippled and scarred with ridges, resembling a tomb that blocked escape for anyone who tried to flee. The only exit within this chasm was a steep set of stairs at the far side, etched into the rock.

They went rigid when a low chorus of moans began to echo through the narrow void from the opposite side.

"I don't like this, my moon-flutter," Elco said.

Seda walked up to him and pressed her forehead against his. "We have to do this, Elco."

"Which way?" Roya asked Kalon, slowly extending her claws as the eerie anguish reverberated around them.

"Toward the sound," he said, nodding his head in the direction of the moaning.

Cahir flared his magic at his palms and took the first step.

Kalon held out his hand, stopping him. "No magic works within her lair."

Seda felt the unwanted scales of fear wrap around her throat like a wet serpent.

"What do you mean? How's that possible?" she choked out. She knew only how to wield her power. She had no other defense besides the small knife she wore on her hip.

"Witchcraft," he replied. "There's a reason why I couldn't transport us inside. It's all blocked off."

"Knowing magic wouldn't work inside would've been nice to know before you brought us here," Roya seethed in response, causing the small form of Suza to bristle.

Kalon glanced at Roya before shifting his gaze to Seda. "Would it have made a difference? We need the stones."

*We.* Was he truly part of this with them?

Cahir growled. "You don't give two fucks about us getting the stones. How do we know you won't just steal it from us once we leave this place? What's truly in it for you?"

Kalon's eyes flicked to Seda briefly before looking away, focusing on the space ahead where the rock face curved, blocking their view of La Uma's entrance.

A long, quiet breath passed before he answered, "You'll just have to trust me." No smirk or joke lay hidden behind his words. His face displayed a quiet stoicism as he looked into the distance. Seda briefly admired how genuinely handsome he looked when he wasn't being an asshole. Not in the radiant, jade-hued way she'd felt with Cahir, but in something darker—sharp and rugged, created by evil rather than light. She silently scolded herself for the thought, biting the inside of her cheek with irritation. This was the same man who pretended to care for her and then disappeared into the night. He could have just *told her* what he was doing before breaking her trust like that.

Cahir scoffed, but Seda drew her knife and moved forward, pushing through the thick plants and getting closer to the keening sounds with each step.

The others joined her at her side. She reached out and ran her hand down Elco's scales, whispering more to herself than to him, "We can do this."

WITH EVERY STEP THEY TOOK, the moans grew louder, and when they reached a narrow cave entrance in the cliff face, the sound became so overpowering that it silenced all other noises.

The entrance was narrow and crusted with glowing amethyst gemstones sharpened like daggers.

Seda held her hands over her ears, trying to block out the cries from within, but Elco said into her mind, "I cannot fit."

Seda's eyes widened in realization. The entrance was just big enough for them to go through. Not only could Elco not make it within, but she also couldn't use her magic. This entire thing was already going wrong. She turned back to him, readying to leave this whole mission behind, but Kalon held his hand out.

"I know what you're thinking, Seda. Elco can stay here and wait for us. He can be our backup if things go wrong," Kalon said over the lamenting sounds.

She looked up into his seafoam-colored eyes. She didn't want to leave Elco here. She didn't even want to go into this hole anymore.

"Seda?" Roya asked, walking up to her and placing her hand on her arm. "You need that stone."

She glanced at Cahir, who watched her intently, knowing he would follow her lead. If she decided to leave, he would guide her away. If she went inside, he would stand by her side. Her eyes searched his, seeking confirmation.

He held his arms open, and she went into them, hugging him tightly. She felt the whisper of his breath in her hair and his rapidly beating heartbeat against her ear. "What do you want to do?" he asked.

"What I want and what I need are two separate things," she choked out. "I'm worried about you going in there." Her arm flew out in the direction of the crystallized hole as her face dug into his chest.

"I'll be okay," he said as he rested his hand against her head.

Her friends were right. They needed the stone this monster hoarded to help the people in Joro. This was more than just about her and her fears.

She took a steadying breath and stepped away from Cahir and walked toward Elco. She pressed her forehead against his, hoping this wasn't the last time she would embrace him. "If we don't come out in one hour, *leave*. Find Benny and make sure he's okay. Will you promise me?"

"I offer no such vow. I'll remain until the world exhales its last breath. Until the end of time. I'll not leave this place unless it's with you." His reply made her eyes sting, and she let out a choked sob.

"*Please*," she pleaded.

He growled and pulled away from her. "I promise an hour… *ish*," was his only reply before he focused his glowing, red eyes back onto the entrance.

She stepped away from him.

"Ready?" Roya asked with furrowed brows as she watched the tear roll down Seda's cheek.

Seda nodded and roughly wiped the show of weakness away.

"Ready," she replied in the strongest voice she could muster, looking at the others and steadying herself.

"You stay here, as well, Suza. Get word back to Noctrya if we don't return," Kalon said, looking at the petite woman.

Suza nodded in response as she bit her bottom lip nervously, looking between the entrance and her master.

Roya took the lead and stepped through first, with Kalon following second. Seda looked at both Cahir and Elco one last time before she stepped into the cavern.

She inhaled the strange scent of lavender once within. The jagged edges of the cave offered no support with the crystals. Seda avoided grabbing the wall and stepped cautiously across the rocky floor. As they descended, the narrow walls began to widen slowly, and the moaning grew painfully loud. The pungent floral smell, mixed with decay, made Seda cover her nose with her hand, suppressing a gag.

"What the fuck," she heard Kalon mutter over the noise. He paused in front of her, and she moved in between him and Roya.

She gasped when she saw the source of the wailing and tried to flare her magic in defence, but felt a sudden weight descend upon her, like a heavy blanket soaked in water; no magic came forward.

The cavern gradually leveled into a narrow corridor. The immense walls were adorned with severed heads staked to the crystals, their twisted faces moaning with pain. Various shades of blood ran down the amethysts they were staked upon, pooling onto the floor below and glowing against the light emitted by the stones.

The heads all turned toward the group, a variety of eye colors all fixed on them simultaneously, their distressed faces shifting into wide smiles when they saw them.

The moans stopped.

Cahir stepped alongside Seda and gripped his sword tightly, his knuckles white with tension. "They cannot reach us if we stay in the center of the path," he said as he stared at the too-wide grins.

Roya once again took the lead and descended further into the lair, taking careful footsteps through the center, some of the faces following her as she walked.

Kalon looked down at Seda and said before following Roya, "Stay close."

She looked at Cahir, whose face was pale with horror and disgust. "These are only the heads of men," she said to him. "Are you sure you want to continue?"

"Forever by your side, Sed," was all he said before he stepped in front and reached his hand back for her. She accepted it, feeling his warm palm within hers, and held the knife in her other hand as they began to walk through. She tucked her wings in closely behind her.

She tried to avoid looking at the eerily quiet smiles as they passed, but she made the mistake of glancing over, and the head of a man cackled at her in response.

"Do you know what I'd do to a pretty thing like you if I had my body back?" it said, licking its lips as its eyes rolled down her body.

Like a shadow of darkness, Seda felt her body tense as anxiety started to creep up her spine. It focused its energy on vivid memories of her past, of the men who had hurt her and diminished her confidence.

Cahir pulled his hand away from hers and brought his sword down onto the head of the man, breaking apart the amethyst it was staked upon. He repeatedly drove it into the man's face, crushing the mangled face into the wet ground below, wild fury blazing in his eyes.

When the man's face was pulverized beyond recognition, he reached for her hand once more.

Seda said nothing and accepted his outstretched hand.

None of the other heads spoke, but their smiles followed them as they moved deeper into the monster's lair. What truly awaited them ahead if this was the entrance? Why would this beast display these heads for anyone who entered in such a manner?

They walked for a few more minutes before the pathway widened further, revealing a vast, crystal-crusted cavern, covered in cobwebs, with alcoves of darkness in the walls, as if it split into a maze beyond.

"Disgusting," Roya said from ahead, and Seda tried to peer around Cahir, but he immediately froze in front of her, causing her to walk into his back.

She stepped around him and stared at the two amethyst stakes in the center of the path as if the items displayed on them were prized trophies. Propped onto one was the head of a man, and on the other, a flaccid male appendage. Seda stepped closer and stared at the face of the man, and his eyes shifted toward her.

She gasped at the resemblance.

"Father?" Cahir whispered hoarsely, his face twisted and nose wrinkling in disgust.

The temperature inside the cave dropped, and their breath started to billow out like ghostly plumes of air. They heard a skittering sound, like a massive insect scurrying across the walls.

A long, wet string shot out from the darkness and wrapped around Kalon, throwing him roughly onto the ground. He struggled to move. Roya immediately knelt and tried to pull the string from him, but also became tangled in the thick, gummy paste.

"Cahir, *darling*. What did I tell you about making faces?" a feminine voice echoed from the dark pits.

# CHAPTER 41

<u>Benny</u>

They ran until Benny struggled to breathe, and then they ran more. Askold lay atop Aurora's back and groaned through rasped breaths. Every time Benny glanced over, he saw that the swelling on his face was getting worse by the minute, and he no longer looked like himself.

Sephyr and Vira flew beside them like black shadows that blew the air around their faces.

"How much further?" he gasped, pushing himself harder with each stride.

Vira let out a loud caw, and Benny looked ahead. The marshlands were slowly abating, and in the distance, the wreckage of a town lay ahead, alight with massive bonfires that lit up the buildings.

Rooftops had been torn off, and houses smashed, but there were *people* there, slowly working to rebuild the devastation left by the Jotnar.

He ran harder, and Aurora picked up her pace.

As they approached the town, a large man stepped into the middle of the path, blocking their way. He had richly colored skin that shone against the firelight and graying, curly hair.

"Who the fuck are you? And why do you have a Unipaca?" he grumbled with a deep, growly voice as they approached.

Vira and Sephyr shifted forms, and the man stepped back quickly, unsheathing his sword.

Benny gasped through ragged breaths, "Please, sir. We came to find our friend, Ojore, but my friend was stung by a giant mosquito on the way here. He needs help!"

The man watched them with narrowed eyes, turning his gaze to Askold on Aurora's back. "Ojore, you say? Follow me."

They followed the man into the village. Dozens of people were within, doing varying tasks to clean up the town. Benny also noticed that animals were helping amid the chaos.

Bears helped to lift heavy beams. Large, fluffy-looking wolves helped to pull heavy loads on carts. One wolf transformed into a human next to them and snarled as he watched them pass, his hands fisted alongside his nude body, mismatched colored eyes boring into them.

The man led them to a makeshift tent, where he opened the flap and called in, "We have another sting." He looked back at them as he closed the flap and watched them, crossing his arms back over his chest.

Askold began to cough loudly. Benny felt his panic rise, and he looked at the man. "Will they be out soon?"

The flap opened to reveal a tall woman with long gray hair and mismatched eyes—one blue like the ocean in Umbrea, the other brown like the richness of the soil. When her eyes met Benny's, they carried the weight of wise years long lived. He looked down to see a syringe in her hand, noticing a freshly inked black moth tattoo on her wrist.

"Who are you?" she asked with a thick accent that rolled off her tongue.

"Our friend, please. He was stung by a mosquito," Benny pleaded, pointing to Aurora and Askold.

The woman's wrinkled eyes shifted to Aurora, and she gasped, taking a step back. "Impossible," she choked out.

Askold coughed once more, and the woman's eyes moved to Aurora's back. She took a hesitant step forward and asked Aurora, "May I approach, please?"

Aurora huffed loudly, flaring her nostrils, and the woman slowly walked to her side, peering at Askold. She looked at Benny. "I'll need to inject him, and he's going to pass out as a result. We'll need to bring him into the tent after."

Benny nodded before looking to Vira and Sephyr, who just watched the exchange.

The woman lifted Askold's sleeve and plunged the needle into his shoulder. He let out a pain-filled scream and immediately blacked out, slowly slipping off Aurora's back. Benny ran forward with Vira and Sephyr, and they caught him before his body slid to the ground.

They lifted him together and brought him into the tent. Benny looked over his shoulder at Aurora before the flap closed. "I'll be back out in a minute."

They set Askold on a makeshift cot of hay bales covered with a sheet. The woman placed her hand on Askold's forehead and looked at them. "He'll be okay. It's going to take some time. You're lucky you made it before his heart gave out."

Benny felt exhaustion weigh down on him heavily, and he let out a ragged breath of relief. He sat down on the ground beside Askold, his arms resting over his knees, and ran his filthy hands over his face. He was covered in gore, and now that the adrenaline was wearing off, he could smell just how awful the mess was on his clothing and skin.

"It's been a very long time since I've seen Corvids and a human in Tuath. What brings you here?" the woman asked from the opposite side of the cot.

"We came to find our friend, Ojore. Is he here?" Benny asked, looking up at the woman.

"Aye, he's here. You just met his cousin, Arzhel. I'm Yepa, pack leader of the Lycanthropes. Ojore had some friends arrive for him earlier today as well. Glad to see one of our own had fared so well living in Joro. We've heard awful things about that place." Yepa watched them with a worried smile forming on her face as she looked back at the tent flap. "As you can see, we've had quite the run-in with the Jotnar. But now with the Fae's help, we'll have more support."

Benny furrowed his brows. With the Fae's help? How did they manage that? He glanced at Askold and saw that the swelling of his face was receding, and he was beginning to look more like himself.

"Your friend will be okay. Let's get you to Ojore and check on your magnificent beast you have out there. May I ask, how did you befriend a Unipaca?" She looked back at Benny. "The Unipacas are very powerful, but they do not like mankind. They tend to stick to themselves."

Benny pushed himself back onto his sore legs and shrugged. "She found us."

Yepa walked to the flap and opened it, looking back at the others. "Coming?" she asked.

"I'll stay here with Askold," Vira said as she glanced back down at his sleeping form. "Sephyr will join you."

Benny and Sephyr followed Yepa back outside the tent. Aurora stood outside, huffing and stomping her front foot at people who walked by and stared at her for too long.

*Feisty thing*, Benny thought as he neared.

"Thank you, Aurora. You saved Askold," he said as he ran his hand over her fluffy back.

Her molten eyes met his, and she hummed in response.

They followed Yepa through the town, Aurora trailing behind them as she snorted at others watching them, her steps crunching into the dirt road.

"Ya know," Yepa started. "We're a community of shifters. The Corvids and Amaru were once considered our kin." She peered over her shoulder at Sephyr. "But that was thousands of years ago, before the world shifted."

"How do you know that?" Benny asked her, intrigue quickly slipping off his tongue.

The woman shrugged and chuckled. "We have stories that have passed down from generation to generation. They say angels were born for the Corvids and Amaru. Now we wait for our angel to find us, as well. All that remains of the Lycanthrope community are the Mauls and the Pack. We fear the world is shifting again, as the sun has failed to rise."

Benny looked up at the twinkling stars above. He didn't even know what time it was now.

"What do you mean?" he asked, looking back at her.

Yepa pursed her lips and said sharply, "Did you not realize? It should be early afternoon right now. But the moon lights up the sky, not the sun."

He cleared his throat. This town just went through a lot. Why would the sun not rise? He changed the subject, seeing that her irritation was growing. "The Lycanthropes... Are the packs the canines, and Mauls the bears? And you're a canine shifter, yes?" Benny asked as he stepped over lumber scattered in the middle of the road.

"Aye," she responded, her voice softening. "But we're a community nonetheless amongst our two shifter breeds." She looked at Sephyr. "Has your angel returned? I heard rumors. I wonder if she's the reason for the moon's everlasting glow."

Sephyr pursed her lips but didn't respond, instead choosing to look ahead at the dozens of people working.

They walked for a few blocks before stopping at a small house with a straw roof that looked like all the others. Yepa knocked on the creaky wooden door and stepped back.

"Who's there?" a deep voice gruffed through the door. "I said I didn't want to talk to anyone today."

"You have company, Ojore," Yepa replied.

The door swung open. "Sorry, Yep—" Ojore started, but froze when he saw Benny standing there. His eyes shifted to Sephyr. "Who the fuck are you?"

Sephyr's lips curled into a smile before she pursed them back into a scowl. "Sephyr," she replied.

"You one of those Corvid weirdos?" he asked, narrowing his eyes at her.

Benny interrupted, "Yes, she is. We came for you. Askold is with us also, but he was stung on the way here. He's healing now, thanks to Yepa here." He pointed to the woman with his thumb. "Why the hell did you leave like that?"

"Get in here quick. Yepa, you need to hear this, also." He held the door open, and they walked in, leaving Aurora right outside the door. He looked around a few times before closing the door behind them.

The small home was a disaster, greeting them with a thick animal smell. Mismatched furniture with tears and cabinets with doors hanging on hinges overwhelmed the space.

"Sorry for the mess," Ojore said. "I lost my temper."

Yepa gently smiled at him and sat on the small sofa. Benny sat in a chair in the corner that creaked under his weight, and Sephyr stood by the door.

Ojore paced back and forth, clenching his fists open and closed.

"What's wrong, lad?" Yepa asked as she watched his hands unfurl.

He looked at Benny. "Where are Seda and Ael?" he asked.

"They traveled north to retrieve the Stone of Peace from some beast called La Uma," Benny replied. "Why?"

Ojore growled and scratched at his curly beard, as if in irritation.

"Can you confirm that?" He looked at Sephyr. "Are the other Corvids with them?"

"What's going on?" Yepa asked, standing and glaring at him.

Ojore held his hand out. "*Please*, just hear me out."

"They set foot north as we headed west," Sephyr replied. "We communicated with Roya yesterday. They're fine."

"Fuck," Ojore said. He roughly sat down on the sofa, causing it to shift on the ground. He looked at Yepa. "The people who joined us today aren't who they say they are, Yepa."

"What do you mean? Who joined you?" Benny asked.

"King Ael and Seda did." Ojore looked at him and pursed his lips. "But, they *act* differently, Benny. King Ael is *nice* to me, and you know how much I dislike that grumpy asshole. I have reason to believe they're not who they say they are."

"Who do you think they are?" Yepa asked. "I swear, Ojore, you left our community years ago to go live amongst the humans, and you return to bring with you only chaos."

"I don't know," he replied with a bear-like growl. "But it's not them."

Benny's eyes widened. He recalled the others talking about Neoma using some potion to change Praxis into Ael. They had been sent away from Umbrea. "It's Meir and Neoma," he said.

"Who the hell are Meir and Neoma?" Ojore asked.

Benny sat straighter in his chair. It had to be them. "Meir's a Fae advisor, and Neoma is some woman he's along his side. They were sent away from Umbrea for impersonating King Ael."

"Can you contact your friends and check?" Yepa asked, looking toward Sephyr, her lips pursed and slightly crinkled with irritation.

"Only Roya's with them now. Ferona remained in Umbrea," Sephyr replied. "I'll try."

She closed her eyes.

"What do we do?" Benny asked the others, watching as Yepa chewed her bottom lip.

Yepa exhaled deeply. "We act as if they're who they claim until we learn more. I need to leave now. I'll check on your friend, Askold. Don't discuss this with anyone." She glanced at Ojore. "*Anyone*. Do you understand? No need to cause trouble until we have a plan."

Ojore huffed in response, "Fine."

Yepa opened the door and looked back at Benny. "There's a dinner tonight. Please join us." She didn't wait for their response as the door closed behind her, leaving them in silence.

Sephyr finally opened her eyes. "Roya's unreachable. Ferona says King Ael and Seda never returned, and they're prepping for the Jotnar to arrive. I fear I've said too much through the whispers."

Roya was unreachable? Benny's mind stalled as the news dropped into him like a pit of despair. What happened? Did that mean she was injured? They just reached out to her not that long ago. Did they reach La Uma and were now hurt… or worse?

An ache began to bloom within him, but he swallowed it down. His sister and the love of his life were okay.

They had to be.

"I don't trust Yepa," Sephyr said after looking around to make sure she was gone.

BENNY, Sephyr, and Ojore walked the path from the medics' tent to the courtyard where the dinner was supposed to be held. Askold was awake and seemed fine, though exhausted, and chose to remain in the tent with Vira rather than venture to the dinner. Aurora was apparently tired of people and decided to stay outside the tent as well.

They hadn't seen Meir or Neoma yet. He wasn't sure what he should do when he did see them, though. Just pretend to be happy to see his sister? He felt it was strange that Yepa wasn't more concerned with the news and wanted them to keep it a secret.

"Does anyone else have a bad feeling about all of this?" he asked the others as they listened to the loud yells and cheers coming ahead.

"Yup," Ojore replied. "I think we need to leave tonight."

Sephyr didn't respond, instead choosing to remain silent as she walked alongside them, her eyes scanning the area around them.

"So we eat, pretend things are okay, and then what? Take off after?" he asked.

Ojore only nodded in response.

Benny tried his hardest not to think about Roya being unreachable, but every time his mind wandered, his heart sank further.

*She's okay*, he reassured himself. *They're both fine.*

They approached a large gathering of people, merrily eating. Drunken laughter spilled from their lips as they cheered.

"To an alliance!" he heard someone say as they clanked together beer steins loudly.

Narrowed eyes met theirs, and Benny felt like they were all staring at them.

They made their way to an open table at the far end of the gathering. Platters of food lined the center of the table, but Benny couldn't bring himself to make a plate. He looked over at the random Lycanthrope watching them warily.

A loud cheer rang out, and Benny looked up. Yepa's tall form ascended the far stairs alongside the replica of Ael and Seda, who were holding hands and smiling brightly at everyone.

Seda didn't have her wings, and Ael's bright smile seemed uncanny, like it stretched a little too far.

"Fucking A," he said under his breath. "It really isn't them."

They watched as Yepa made her way to the center of the stage, Ael and Seda following. Wild cheers rang out as she turned to the crowd.

"We need to leave. *Now*," Ojore snarled as he began to stand.

Yepa raised her hands, calming the crowd, and Ojore's eyes snapped to hers.

"It's been hundreds of years since the Fae and Lycanthropes have had an alliance. I want to thank our friends here." She pointed at the impostors. "For helping us to bridge the gap between our societies. The Fae have promised to join us in revenge against the weakness that has descended upon this world! Lycanthropes! We've found our divine angel!"

The image of King Ael transformed into Meir, and a wicked grin spread across his face. His eyes were solid black, like endless puddles, sucking the life out of anyone who looked.

The ravenous crowd began to cheer wildly with deep howls and growls echoing across the area.

"But…" she started. "We have some among us who do not wish to join us." Her mismatched colored eyes shifted to Benny,

Sephyr, and Ojore. "And instead, choose an alliance *with the weak*."

Benny saw Seda's replica grin as she looked at them.

An arrow shot through the crowd into Ojore, piercing his throat and causing blood to run down his shirt. Ojore's heavy body crumpled onto the ground with a loud thud.

Benny froze in fear, his body failing to respond.

"Ojore has not been one of us for a long time. He chose to live amongst the humans and befriend that imposter Monster King of theirs." Another arrow shot through the crowd and impaled Sephyr's chest. She tried to shift into her Corvid form, with feathers expanding around her, but remained partially human.

"The Corvids, also, have chosen to go against the balance of this world. Their kind left us a very long time ago. They're not one of us! Their angel only brings darkness!" Yepa's eyes shifted to Benny. "And the humans. So weak and pathetic. They do nothing as the Jotnar eats their people."

A loud cheer rang out among the crowd, and Benny felt his body start to respond. He shifted out of his chair quickly and ducked under the table as an arrow flew over his head, landing with a loud crunch into a tree behind him.

"We have a chance now to unite and work alongside our angel! The angel of death, the Black-Crowned King! We'll no longer be seen as weak! We will defeat the frailty of the world with our new brethren!"

Benny could hardly believe what was unfolding. He crawled toward Ojore and Sephyr, their blood seeping into his hands and knees. Ojore's motionless body lay on the ground, while Sephyr was gasping for air with ragged breaths.

He asked her in a panicked whisper, "We have to get out of here. Can you reach the others?"

"Come out, human. We do not allow weak, pathetic people amongst our kind," Yepa's voice purred.

Sephyr's anguished eyes met Benny's. "I'll try," she gasped, shutting her eyes. He saw her eyelids flutter briefly before they became still.

Her chest stopped moving.

Benny's blood ran cold. He didn't know what to do.

*Fuck, Fuck, Fuck,* he thought. He began to crawl through the trees behind him, fear racing up his spine. He had to get away and had to find Aurora, Askold, and Vira.

"Oh, human..." Yepa said. "You cannot escape us. You and your friends will die tonight. I may have wasted an antidote on your friend earlier. But he'll not leave this place either. Thank you for bringing us a Unipaca, though. She'll be instrumental for our cause." He heard her chuckle.

The trees began to close around him as he quickly crawled through. A feral howl ripped through the darkness from the shifters, and Benny's panic crested like a tsunami crashing into him. He jumped up and ran, feeling his chest rise and fall with each unsteady breath. He didn't know which way to go, but he pushed himself forward.

The sharp hiss in the air met him before the impact did. He collapsed to his knees and stared down, seeing an arrow protruding through his chest.

Howls and roars began to close around him as he looked up and saw dozens of Lycanthropes surrounding him with snarling faces. Seda's replica walked up to him and placed her hand on his shoulder. He looked up and was met with a smile that looked exactly like his sisters'.

Tears began to roll down his cheeks as he stared into her violet eyes. He felt no physical pain, but the same ache in his heart from earlier returned with a vengeance and began gnawing upon his soul, eating him from within.

He could feel the darkness slowly encroaching on his vision.

He had nowhere to go and no one to rescue him. Ojore was gone, Sephyr was gone, and his sister's face loomed over him with a cruel amusement that tormented his soul.

This wasn't her. He wouldn't allow this false image to tarnish the love and memory he had of her.

His mind wandered to the memories of his mother's smile, at the way she would cradle him in her arms. He reflected on his father's defiance against injustice, which sparked the Rising. Yepa was wrong about humans. They had endured the most and still survived. Images of Aurora flashed through his mind, of the small Unipaca who happily munches on apples and stamps her foot in irritation.

She needed to flee before they got to her.

He felt his body fall backwards onto the ground as he stared up into Seda's eyes, seeing the trees sway behind her. Slowly, he started to see himself as if he were floating above, staring down at his body lying in the cold dirt.

He thought about Roya and how he loved her, how he never got to say those words aloud, and how much he wanted one more chance to hold her tightly in his arms. He thought about how he could break down her walls and see the beautiful smile she always kept so hidden, and how strong she always managed to be.

She was okay. She wasn't gone from this world. He could feel it now; he could sense her magic out there somewhere, burning bright with that beautiful vengeance he loved so much.

He heard a caw in the distance. Vira maybe?

"I love you," he pushed the words out for the first time, feeling the softness of his voice echo into nothingness as he stared down at his body, his lips unmoving.

His vision blurred, replaced by an overpowering brightness that surrounded him, as if the sun had finally risen.

He didn't feel like he was here or there, like time didn't matter anymore. A saturation of loving warmth bloomed from within, flowing outward as he took in his surroundings. The feeling of serenity draped itself around him, and the realization dawned on him that everything was going to be okay.

He was safe.

He was returning to a home long forgotten.

A soothing voice called to him, *"Come to me, my child."*

# CHAPTER 42

### Luelle

The piercing sirens blared as Luelle and Ferona ran through the halls, exiting the throne room doors and meeting Praxis on a patio outside that overlooked the kingdom.

"There are two of them in the distance," Praxis said to them as he pointed toward the distant mountainside. Luelle looked out and saw the dark shadows of two Jotnar standing far off, watching Umbrea. Their massive, disgusting forms, lit by moonlight. They weren't moving forward, as if they were waiting for others to arrive and biding their time. The green orbs evaded them, as if a thick barrier covered them and prevented them from touching.

"What do you want to do?" Praxis asked, honoring her given position.

Ael wasn't here to give the orders, and a fierce determination grew within her to prove to Ael that she could do this.

"I want us to kill those fuckers," she replied, staring up into his eyes. He only nodded approvingly in response, a nervous smile curling on his lips.

She looked over at Ferona, who was looking ghostly pale.

"Are you o—" she began to ask, but Ferona fell into a chair beside her, eyes closed and rolling to the back of her head. She rushed to her side.

"What's happening?" Praxis asked as his eyes widened.

"I don't know!" Luelle shouted as she ran her hand over Ferona's forehead, seeing the nail polish still under her eye. She looked back up at Praxis. Could it be a message from someone? Usually, the Corvids didn't pass out like that when they whispered to each other.

Ferona's eyes snapped open, and she jumped up, yelling, "The Lycanthropes have allied with Meir and Neoma. Benny, Ojore, and Sephyr are dead! Meir and Neoma are pretending to be Ael and Seda! Vira's headed here with Askold. They've escaped! But the Lycanthropes have gathered and are making their way here!"

"What the fuck?" Praxis shouted. "How do they know it's Meir and Neoma?"

Luelle looked at the damn fool sharply. "Because that fucking woman turned you into Ael, idiot! Remember? Can you reach Roya?" Luelle asked, turning her attention back to Ferona as her panic rose. Were the Jotnar with Meir? How could that have happened? She silently scolded Ael. He should have had Meir and Neoma killed for conspiring, not sent away as he had.

Ferona shook her head. "Roya's unreachable."

Luelle gasped, unsure of what that signified. Was Ael alright? She narrowed her eyes and glanced back at Praxis and the distant Jotnar, feeling a surge of resolve grow within her.

"Kill them, Praxis," she said calmly. "We need to protect Umbrea at all costs."

Praxis gave the orders, and the Fae guard began to form. Luelle stood over the gathering crowd and looked down, seeing both the citizens and the guard look up at her with a mixture of fear and determination. Umbrea had never been attacked like this before, and their king was not here. It was her responsibility to speak on his behalf, even though she didn't want to.

She had no idea what to say, but she ground her teeth together before saying, "Citizens of Umbrea. Today marks a day in history. We've never had an attack on our soil before. We'll do everything in our power to prevent the Jotnar from advancing." She looked over the crowd, feeling like she was doing a shit job at this. "We move forward and kill those fuckers!"

The crowd responded loudly, a mix of cheers and cries. Maybe that wasn't the right thing to say in her position, but she had no other words. She really wasn't cut out for this.

"Captain Praxis!" she shouted and pointed down at him. "Fire on those assholes!"

Praxis raised his sword in the air and turned around, giving the command of the guard. Loud bangs erupted from dusty canons that Ael's father had installed during the first monster war as a preparation, and shot across the green grass beyond to where the Jotnar stood. They didn't move as blasts exploded around them, one meeting its mark on the Jotnar's arm.

Luelle turned to Ferona and asked, "Are they idiots? They aren't moving away!"

Ferona's eyes widened. "Look!" She pointed out to the Jotnar. They slowly walked beyond the range of the cannons. They sat down and stared at the city once more, watching as the blasts rained down ahead of them.

Luelle shouted down at the guard, "Form a protective barrier!"

The Fae guard awkwardly assembled and made their way through the city gates, forming long rows of lines that shielded the entire city in a magical glow.

Luelle bit her nail, chipping the polish, and watched the scene as nerves wrapped around her throat.

Why weren't they advancing?

# CHAPTER 43

<u>Ael</u>

Ael saw a large cloud of his breath escape his lips with each gasp. His father's head, alongside a piece of his body, had been staked to the center of this cavern, on display like a prized possession.

He felt no remorse for his father's fate. Though it was revolting and malevolent, he wasn't here to save that asshole. Let him rot in this cold, unforgiving purgatory for the way he treated him and countless others.

"Don't go in, Ael," his father's tormented face said. "She died. That's not her!"

Ael averted his gaze from his father toward the glow from the amethysts, the light unable to reach into the dark network of alcoves that extended beyond this lair. He heard a chuckle coming from a recess along the ceiling, and his eyes shot upward.

"I've missed you, my son," the voice said, sounding just as

he remembered. He felt a sudden surge of sorrow at the sound of the voice.

It wasn't her. It couldn't be.

Uncontrollable emotion began to blur his vision as memories of his mother flooded through him—her tickles and laughter, and her pain-filled eyes as she watched him being torn from her for the final time.

Roya and that asshole, Kalon, were trapped on the ground in a thick, gummy paste, desperately trying to escape, but only tangling themselves further. He saw Seda kneel to help them and reached out to stop her, shaking his head as he pointed up toward the dark pit. If she touched it, she would get trapped, also.

Ael blinked away his tears, slowly unsheathed his sword, and stepped further into the cavern, distancing himself from his father's mangled head.

"My Cahir..." the voice cooed.

The amethyst stones began to pulse vibrantly, partially highlighting the darkness beyond. A long, pointed tip, like the end of a black widow's leg, wrapped around the edge of the opening.

"Show yourself!" he demanded of the monster within, straining to see through his blurry vision. "You're not my mother. She *died*." The final word broke in his throat, feeling his emotions tear through him like a wicked storm. What kind of cruel beast took pleasure in mimicking the despair of loss?

Seda held her knife by her side, her hand shaking as she gripped it firmly. He stepped in front of her. He would not allow this beast to hurt her in any way. He brought her here. This was his fight to finish.

Another spider's leg wrapped around the ledge, and slowly, the darkened shadow of La Uma crawled into view.

Ael tightened his grip on the sword and anchored himself, waiting for her to strike. The rapid pounding of his heart beat wildly in his chest. He didn't know what to expect when they set out to find La Uma, but it wasn't this.

La Uma appeared. A giant spider emerged, blacker than night, with a large emerald green stripe down her back. Eight legs like sharpened needles connected to a rounded body in the center, with two extra arms on the front of the arachnid body. But her head... her head hovered above her form, hanging on nothing but air. Long black hair with a familiar white stripe cascaded wildly in the air.

The face of his mother stared down at him.

Ael's sword clattered to the ground, and he sank to his knees as a painful cry escaped his lips at the sight of her. That same painful ache from years past when he lay by her casket burned through his chest.

"Don't believe her!" his father screamed.

"Silence!" La Uma hissed in response, expelling a thick paste from her body onto the staked head, leaving only muffled sounds behind. She shifted her gaze back to Ael and slowly crawled along the walls, whimpering as she descended.

Seda bristled next to him. He could see her body shaking from the corner of his eye, but the pain tearing through him was too much. He couldn't do anything. He couldn't react. It *was* her —the person whose loss molded who he became, leaving an open wound on his heart for hundreds of years.

La Uma slowly crawled toward Ael.

"How?" he choked out.

The monster reached out and ran her cold hand across his face, lifting his chin, and staring into his eyes. He gazed into her familiar, emerald eyes and cried out once more.

Tears that matched his own trickled down her cheeks and landed onto the spider's body below.

"Your father tried to kill me, my darling. But like all things in his life, *he failed*," she said as her voice deepened with rage and she spat in the direction of his father's head.

Her eyes widened when they snagged on Seda, and she hissed wildly in response, shirking back into the recesses of her cave and growling.

Ael's gaze shifted to Seda. Wild fury burned behind her eyes, and they were glowing vibrantly. Beads of sweat dripped down her forehead as she struggled against the magical depression of the cave.

How was her magic getting past the barrier?

"You..." La Uma said as she slowly uncurled her body from the corner. "You're finally here."

Dark clouds began to form in the cavern as electrical shocks radiated across the ceiling.

Seda raised her arms, and her eyes narrowed on the covered head of his father.

"Stop!" a familiar voice screamed from behind them. Ael's awareness came rushing back to him, and he shot to his feet, grabbed the sword, and quickly turned around.

Tahti and the same Lobison, Sacha, barreled through the macabre tomb behind them, carrying the head of another Lobison.

"Don't hurt her!" the witch screamed as she hobbled forward.

Thunder roared through the cavern as lightning danced across the ceiling. Seda looked furiously between Sacha and Tahti, narrowing her eyes once more.

She slowly lowered her arms, releasing the magic within, and began to pant as the magical barrier once more descended, blocking her storm. A loud zap sound erupted, and the clouds quickly dispersed.

"Explain," Ael demanded of the witch. He pointed to his mother. "Explain now!"

Tahti held her hands up, words quickly tumbling from her wretched lips, "The day you were torn from her arms—that was the day your father demanded I kill her and erase her magic from this world." She took a deep breath, quickly looking between him and Seda. "Your mother was once the most powerful Dark Witch in all of Xyberus. Your father only married the poor girl from the north to use her for his own gain. But once she had you, her dark magic turned into something stronger, something *pure*. She channeled that love and became the most powerful witch in the Coven of the Wilds—The White Witches."

"But she's alive!" he snarled in response, feeling the anger surge forward. He wanted to kill this witch. She had played enough tricks on him over the years, and this was the fucking cherry on top.

"Yes. She is, King Ael. I faked her death, but my magic had its limits, and I accidentally turned her into what she is now. When we left Umbrea to bring her here, we stole the Stone of Peace. Your father wanted to collect all of them, and we stopped him from having this one."

A feral growl rumbled in Ael's chest. All these years, Tahti knew his mother was alive, and she never told him. "Why did you never fucking tell me? And why did you leave your house? You play too many fucking games!"

The witch shrugged. "I had more important things to do. But I left my book for Seda to find—"

Kalon cleared his throat, and they all looked at him.

"Hello, Tahti," he said from the ground with a broad grin on his irritating face. "How have the millennia of nightmares been since you stole from me?"

Tahti seethed and pointed a bony finger at him. "You! Why are *you* here?"

"Oh, you know... just here to collect the stone for Seda. The stone you stole from *me*," he said. "Do you recall? Or has your mind finally given out after all these years?"

"The stone isn't yours, asshole," Ael replied, his irritation with Tahti now doubling with Kalon's voice in the mix. He was right. Kalon wanted the stone. Why wouldn't Seda just allow him to kill the man?

Kalon winked at him.

"You two know each other?" Seda interrupted, looking between Kalon and Tahti.

"Tahti and I used to… be friends," Kalon said with a pause and a chuckle. "Get me out of this mess, Fae witch, and I'll forgive your transgressions and no longer haunt you when you use your magic."

The witch's eyes narrowed as she looked down at him. She spat on the ground and smiled widely, showcasing her dark, sharpened teeth.

"You should really get those checked out," Kalon said as he grimaced at her rotting mouth.

"Enough!" Seda snapped, glancing at him before turning her attention back to Tahti. "Release my friends from this hold. We'll not harm her. We're here to collect the stone and leave. The stone *you* told me I needed. Where is it?"

Tahti waved her hand in the air, dismissing Seda. "We have things to discuss first. The stone belongs to Misandra, or as you know her, La Uma. You came here looking for a fight, thinking you needed to kill a monster, but that's not the case, child. Not everything in this life is brute force or fear." She looked to Ael's mother and motioned her over.

The spider's body gradually moved closer, her eyes fixed on Ael. He swallowed hard. How did he not realize she was still alive? All this time… he could have spent it with her, could have come to her when she needed him. She didn't need to be alone in this cave like she was. She had been here for hundreds of years, wasting away in this cold cavern.

Tahti grabbed the severed head from Sacha and tossed it toward La Uma. "This one betrayed the balance. This one tried to hurt an innocent. We offer him to the Amethyst Wrath."

Both Tahti and Sacha bowed before his mother, and her emerald-colored eyes began to change, swirling into a white hurricane.

The severed head's eyes shot open, and it began to moan loudly.

"Find a place for him. His pain will continue to power the yanantin," Misandra softly said.

Ael looked at her in confusion. Why did she bring these beings back to life only to condemn them to eternal pain and suffering?

Sacha grabbed the beast's head from her maw and backed into the entryway, telling it through muffled words, "You brought this upon yourself."

Tahti wiped her hands on her worn dress. She looked at Seda and sighed. "You are powerful, child. You've gotten past our suppression spell. I'm quite pleased. You'll need that to move forward."

"What do you mean?" Seda asked.

"To defeat the evil in this world, we need strength. But not only that—we need *compassion*. The world is unbalanced, and malevolent beings with sinister plans are rising. Not everything is what it seems. Some of the beings you call monsters are just part of nature. Have you seen that yet?" Tahti took a deep breath and pointed to Misandra. "You set out to kill a monster, but what happened? She isn't a monster at all. She's a testament to perseverance. She was wronged and torn from her child, and now devotes herself to our cause. You must do the same. You must return the yanantin to this world. It's why you were created, why you were *reborn*."

*What the fuck?* Ael thought, looking at the woman like she was bat shit crazy.

"Hold up," he interrupted. "What do you mean by 'reborn'? I swear if this is another trick of yours..."

A long pause followed, and Tahti glanced up at his mother. She nodded at her.

His mother walked into a dark alcove and returned, holding the same dark-blue, diamond-shaped gemstone he remembered from his childhood.

She spoke, interrupting the silence, "This is not her first life. She's a *guardian*, my Cahir—the key to the Celestial Vault, Bearer of Moonlight, and Arbiter of Eternal Justice. The crystal is hers to take, to bring her wrath upon this imbalanced world. We, the Coven of the Wilds, are mere subjects to the cause, spanning across a multitude of species. Doing what we can to aid the Mother Goddess. And you, my Cahir, were born to help her."

She smiled at him and held the stone out to Seda. The rippling blue light cascaded around the room, highlighting everyone in dancing blue ribbons.

Seda reached for the stone, and as her fingers made contact with the solid surface, her eyes rolled back, and she collapsed onto the ground.

Ael rushed forward and pushed his mother away from Seda, crashing onto his knees and picking up her limp form. "What did you do?" he choked out as he clutched her close to his chest, looking wildly around the room.

"Her memories are returning to her," Kalon whispered.

# CHAPTER 44

<u>Seda</u>

They stepped outside of the cavern, passing the tormented souls who deserved their fate on the way out. Seda didn't look at them once as she marched through. She felt her power reemerge as they exited, and she inhaled the fresh air, free of decay and lavender.

Elco and Suza stood near the entrance, their wary eyes watching them.

"What happened in there, moon-flutter?" Elco anxiously asked as she neared him.

"We have the Stone of Peace," she whispered. "You promised me an hour. How long has it been?" She looked up at the darkened sliver of sky above, moonlight casting its empyreal shadows across the jagged edges of the rock face.

"I promised an hour-*ish*. It's been about three," he said with a huff.

"No one was hurt?" Suza asked as she ran to Kalon and looked him over, crinkling her nose at the spider's goop still attached to his clothing. He smiled down at her, but his gentle gaze shifted toward Seda.

"No," he said, his deep voice sending shivers down her spine and making her heart tingle. She remembered now. He *was* the Guardian of the Last Sleep, created in the Deathly Sovereign's image, and the first to capture her heart.

A wave of discomfort washed over her when their eyes met, but she quickly looked away, noticing his posture stiffen as she diverted her gaze.

Words crashed into her, tearing through her mind, ripping apart her soul. She fell to her knees and gasped as her head pounded in pain. She heard Elco growl and approach her, but she couldn't focus on anything but the words.

*"The dome will fall soon."*
*"Where's our queen?"*
*"The dome is weak."*
*"Tonight marks one thousand years since its true creation."*

Roya tensed before shifting her focus to Seda. "Do you hear the Corvid Whispers?" she asked, stepping closer as she and Cahir knelt beside her.

*"Her brother…"*
*"Our queen. We need our queen."*
*"I feel her! She's here! She has come!"*
*"Find her! We need our queen!"*
*"Roya's back! I can sense her!"*

Seda gasped and pressed both hands to her forehead, screaming out in agony as the words tore through her mind.

"Steady your breathing," Roya suggested.

Seda inhaled a ragged breath and blew out through parted

lips, trying to exhale the pain from her mind with each small breath that escaped her.

"You can close yourself off. Try to think of a brick wall between you and them." Roya placed her hand on Seda's shoulder.

Seda knew this. She remembered this now. She imagined a brick wall slowly being erected. With each brick she placed, the whispers grew quieter. She set the final stone in place and slowly pulled her hands away from her head. She looked up at Roya. She could still hear them, but they were muted now.

"I can now," she rasped. "The dome over Joro is about to collapse."

She heard Cahir's gasp, and her eyes met his. Pain filled her heart for her friend. He just discovered the terrible truth about his mother, and she... *she wasn't who he thought she was.*

"You need to send a message back, Seda," Roya said as Seda stood once more. "They need to hear from you."

"I don't remember how," she replied with a strained sob.

"Close your eyes and remove one of the bricks you just placed. Only one is needed. Call out to them. Let them feel you, my queen. Let them *hear* you."

She closed her eyes and took a deep breath, mentally removing one of the bricks once more. Whispers began to filter through her, but she blocked their messages out.

She hurled her words into the void, channeling her anguish into each syllable, igniting her inner fire of revenge.

*"I am Seda, the Guardian Angel of the Celestial Vault, Bearer of Moonlight, Arbiter of Eternal Justice, the Corvid Queen—and I have returned with vengeance."*

# CHAPTER 45

### Ael

Ael hated needing Kalon's help to transport, and hated the feeling that something had shifted in Seda after she awoke in the cavern. She didn't tell them what she learned and what she remembered.

He ground his teeth together. He wanted to talk to her, but they had now left his mother's catacomb—that was an entirely different set of emotions he couldn't process right now—and entered the Amanita Copse.

It was a place he never thought he would see in person. He only knew of this from whispers and rumors before seeing Seda here on her voyage north through the clear stone Tahti gave him.

Seda had insisted they come here before pushing forward into Joro. Why? He wasn't sure.

It felt like too much was happening all at once.

Roya said the Jotnar were encroaching on Umbrea, that the Lycanthropes had murdered Benny, Ojore, and Sephyr, and that

Askold was fleeing with Vira. He felt torn between staying with Seda or leaving to protect his realm, but he couldn't be in two places at once. The fucking Lycanthropes. Benny was his friend, and he felt immense sadness for his loss alongside Sephyr and Ojore. He also knew Seda was taking it hard. She had fallen to her knees when she found out and cried to the heavens, electrifying the sky so brightly it lit up like an explosion. Roya wasn't faring much better, but her pain seemed more reserved, as she hadn't said much since the news.

He made a promise to Seda, and he couldn't break it. He had to stay by her side, no matter what. He would help her find the stones and tear the fucking world apart if that's what she needed.

She meant everything to him.

Seda fluttered her starlight wings behind her. She was getting better at moving them. He saw her look up at the darkened sky, further shaded by the massive mushrooms that blocked the moonlight and the stars beyond.

"Don't touch them," she said in a monotone voice about the mushrooms. "The Vatte are this way."

She took the lead and led them through the forest of giants. He noticed Kalon's gaze flicking to her often and bit his cheek, refraining from arguing with the man.

As he glared at Kalon, he noticed the man silently hiss in pain and grab his neck.

"What the fuck is wrong with you?" Ael asked him.

Kalon's gaze shifted to him, and he dropped his hand, revealing a red mark on his neck over his stupid tattoo. Kalon pursed his lips in response and kept walking.

In the distance, small twinkling lights and cheerful music echoed through the vast forest. He could smell roasting meats and the smoke of veilroot, and hear children playing and singing along to stringed instruments.

He had never met a Vatte before. They were a powerful species of being, relying on their earthen magic to navigate this world. They remained hidden deep within the Amanita Copse for a thousand years, sheltering themselves from the chaos outside amongst the poisonous fungi.

The merry sounds of the Vatte grew louder as they walked closer to the twinkling lights. He heard Elco whimper a sound and lunge forward as a tiny boy came into view.

"Elco!" the little boy shouted, running up to him and hugging him tightly. "You're finally back!"

"It's nice to see you again, Orion," Seda said to the little boy as she bent down to hug him as well. Ael could see the pain on her face through her smile. "Are your mother and grandfather around? We need to talk to them."

"Oh, yes, pretty lady! *Wow!*" He paused, staring up at her wings with awe. "You grew sparkly wings! Do you think I might grow some someday? Also, did you notice the sun didn't come up? So *weird*."

Seda smiled again in response. "I did notice. As for the wings, nothing is impossible in this world, little guy. Can you please take us to them? This is very important."

Orion jumped up and down, clapping his little hands in excitement. He led them through the town of merry folk with bright cheeks. Everyone was drinking from small mugs. Ael could smell the scent of mead strongly in the air as the people cheered for Elco and Seda's return, falling over themselves in drunken stupor.

Why were they here? How could these small, happy people help them?

Orion knocked on a small, rounded door. "Papa! Seda and Elco are back!"

Ael heard an older man's voice grumble through the door, "You say this all the time, Orion. You know—" The door swung open, and a small, older man who looked familiar stared at them with wide eyes and a slack jaw.

"Hello, Chief Vidar," Seda said to him with a smile. "It's nice to see you again."

They sat around a campfire. A small woman with rosy cheeks, like peaches, handed each of them a thick mug filled with mead.

Ael took a drink, and the rich taste exploded in his mouth, burning down his throat as he swallowed. The Vatte mead was much stronger than he was used to.

"It's so nice to have you guys back. What did you need to talk with us about? I do so hope you know what happened to the sun," the woman, named Lucja, asked as she sat down on a thick log covered with moss. She stared at Seda intently.

Elco had wandered off with the little boy, and they found other children who began to climb his stomach and jump off, attempting to fly, and pretending they had wings like Seda's.

Seda took a deep drink from her mug and softly moaned after, licking her lips. Ael watched her tongue slide across her mouth, wanting to cherish the taste of her lips on his.

Kalon cleared his throat next to him, and he looked over at the asshole.

"Now isn't the time, King Ael," Kalon scolded, as if he were a child.

"Fuck you," Ael replied. He hated that this intrusive prick could hear his thoughts.

Seda cleared her throat at them, and they both looked back at her.

"I know who's responsible for the sun, and he's in danger."

She paused. "Chief Vidar, your brother's still alive," Seda said as she looked at the small man.

He heard Lucja choke on her mead, her face becoming brighter than a cherry, but Vidar stood from his seat.

"Impossible," he angrily said. "My brother is long gone from this world. I do not appreciate—"

But Seda interrupted him, "He stole the Dark Stone from Supay and is now going by the title, the Monster King. His name is Tievel."

The realization came tunneling into Ael like a storm. That's why Vidar looked so familiar. He and Tievel were brothers. It explained so much, and how this Monster King had been around for so long. The Vatte could live for thousands of years.

Vidar sat back down onto the large stump with a loud thud. He pressed his hands to his shaking face, disbelieving what Seda was saying. "But my brother died when the war restarted. He's the reason we left. He told us to come here. Why would he keep us safe, just to hurt others?"

"The Dark Stone's powerful. It once belonged to the Mother Goddess, but when Supay stole it from her, he used his dark magic to turn the stone wicked. When Kalon and I—" Her eyes flicked to Kalon, before quickly looking away, and she cleared her throat. "When we cast Supay into a mortal soul, Tievel found the lost stone and used it for his own gain."

A heavy silence followed. Ael could hear the wood crackling in the fire in front of them and the merry sounds of the Vatte behind, but the quiet around the campfire was so overwhelming that he felt like he could hear his own heartbeat.

"Your brother wants to collect all the stones and destroy the dome. If he succeeds and makes it to the Mother Goddess's tree, he believes he'll attain eternal life. It's what he's been working towards for millennia. He wants me to open the door to the Celestial Vault so that he can enter." She looked at the chief with softened eyes. "The citizens of Joro were mistaken about its creation date. Today marks one thousand years. It will fall, Vidar. We need your help."

"We cannot help—" Vidar started, vehemently shaking his head.

"Hobberwash!" Lucja stood from her seat and pointed a small finger at her father. "Abso-fucking-lutely-*HOBBERWASH*! We help these poor souls. It's *we* who have created this imbalance in this world. It's our own kind who banished us to live alone in these blasted mushrooms! I'm over it, Father! *We help them!*" Her chest heaved through every breath, and her eyes bore into her father's.

"Um," Vidar started, looking around at everyone in the campfire's circle, eyes begging for help. When none came, he sighed. "Ugh, *blasted*. Okay. We help, Lucja. We help. Anything for you, my dear."

Ael noticed the wide smile spreading across Seda's face, and for the first time since hearing of her brother, it looked genuine.

She was stunning, flawless. She was strong and clever, more remarkable than anyone he had ever encountered.

*I love her*, he thought as pride welled within him.

Kalon bristled next to him.

"What's the plan?" Roya asked with a hoarse voice. Her gaze remained unblinking and fixed on Seda.

Seda smiled once more and took a deep drink from her mug before saying, "I've *always* loved this stuff." She set the mug down and stood. "The Rising foretold of the Darkened. For this to work, I need to remember how to fly."

# CHAPTER 46

<u>Jason</u>

J ason and Mordred made it back to Jason's apartment unseen. He knew that the Monster King would soon wonder where he was and travel through the mirror looking for him. They didn't have much time.

"Sara!" he shouted as he opened the door. "We need to go."

Sara walked out of the bedroom, looking like she had been crying. Her hair, usually pristine in a tight braid, was now wild around her face. She looked like she had seen a ghost.

"What happened?" he asked as he ran up to her and held her in his arms. "What's wrong?"

Sara was a White Witch, a member of the Coven of the Wilds. The day he met her, he knew it was fate. He knew she was the one the Oracle spoke of. She carried verdancy magic deep within her bones, passed down from her mother. Only women could bear such magic, a trait that skipped generations until a baby girl was born.

"It's Benny," she replied. "He's no longer with us."

"What—" he began as an ache tore through his chest. His son, his baby... it couldn't be true. "How do you know?"

She raised her dirt-covered palms in the air. "I was spoken to." She cried out and buried her face in his chest, painful sobs breaking through whimpering moans.

He ran his hand from the back of her head down her back. "Do you know what happened?" He tried to stay calm and composed for her, even though he felt like everything was collapsing around him, as if he were drowning in rapid waters—unable to swim up or breathe.

She pulled away and looked at him with watery eyes, burning with rage. "There's a force stronger than we know building north of here. We need to escape, Jason. The magic of the dome is crumbling tonight."

He looked at Mordred, settling his face into a neutral, calm expression. "Let's go to the woods past the Gardvord. Our girl will return soon. She has to."

THEY MADE it past the Guardvord, into the woods, where the hidden doorway was covered in vines and shadowed by trees. The city limits stopped just beyond, and the vast border wall blocked their exit.

All of the main exits were now guarded, and it would be any moment that the alarms would ring out, indicating that the Monster King knew he had escaped with Mordred. But he had a plan, one devised and set up long before Mordred was thrown in that dungeon. A way to help free the people once the dome fell. All he had to do was click that button in his pocket. It was his one way he knew how to help save as many lives as possible until the Darkened arrived.

Jason pulled the device out of his pocket and looked at Sara and Mordred.

"Ready?" he asked. "Once the wall crumbles, we hide. I don't know how strong these will be. Be prepared to run."

Sara and Mordred nodded, panting through ragged breaths from their journey here.

The city's piercing alarms began to pulse through the air, manic and desperate, matching the frantic heartbeat in his chest.

The Monster King now knew he was betraying him. He knew Mordred had escaped with his help.

The world shuddered as a crashing sound erupted against the dome, shaking the ground violently and echoing through the sky. Jason looked up and saw the magical barrier quiver, releasing a loud, resonant sound that pierced the air.

The Jotnar were attacking the dome. It was about to fall.

They ran as fast as they could back into the trees, ducking behind and readying to push the button. They slipped when the dome wailed in the sky and shook the ground beneath their feet, causing Jason to drop the device in his palm.

A deafening, piercing sound knocked Jason unconscious as the world shook once more.

He felt someone shaking him, and he opened his eyes to see Sara over him. *"Please, please.* Jason!"

Mordred pulled him to his feet, and he stumbled. He held onto Mordred as he glanced over his shoulder and looked up at the sky.

The glittering dome had vanished, bursting like a bubble. All that remained was the clear sky above, lit up by the vast full moon and twinkling stars. The air felt cooler and fresher than it did before.

He reached for the ground, picked up the device, and finally pressed the button.

A loud barrage of explosions blasted across the city walls in quick succession.

The dome had fallen, but so had many portions of the border wall, no longer blocking people's escape from the city. The magical dome may no longer be protecting Joro, but the citizens could now find freedom if they made it out in time.

The sound of screams echoed through the trees.

*Please save us all*, he prayed.

They concealed themselves behind the enchanted stone facade that marked the entrance to *Her* realm, taking cover under the thick vines.

# CHAPTER 47

<u>Seda</u>

The blackened tornado of darkness gradually dissipated around them, revealing the sounds of chaos and destruction beyond. They landed in the woods past the Gardvord, next to the once mysterious wall she discovered with Roya. Seda resisted the impulse to open it, longing to reconnect with her roots.

She didn't have all the stones yet, but she would soon.

Instead, her gaze shifted farther and saw that the border wall had collapsed, creating a wide opening into the Heath Forest beyond.

Her vision trailed up to the sky above Joro. The magical dome she had created upon her death was now gone. The last dying breath of her previous life, her desires, and the gift of her protection no longer existed.

Her one gift was gone.

She looked to Kalon, suppressing her fury that the dome had fallen without her here. "Thank you for transporting us here," she said, still unable to meet his eyes, and instead focused on the group that had gathered. She wasn't yet ready to face him; she wasn't ready to confront the thing she did that probably tore him apart.

It felt strange to be in Joro once again and to see the trees she used to stare out at on her way to work. This life she had spent living in fear and conformity. It now felt strange and foreign to her. That wasn't the real Seda. That version of herself died the moment she left Alexi a charred mass on the dungeon floor.

Chief Vidar, Lucja, a few other Vatte, and her friends stood alongside her. They looked around them with wide eyes as screams echoed in the distance.

Cahir reached his hand out and brushed it against hers.

An offer of support—of love and devotion, through thick and thin, through life and death.

His touch felt different to her, knowing more now than before, and the thought made her heart wrench in confusion. She held his hand in hers and gently squeezed it in return.

Kalon's eyes shifted toward Seda and Cahir's intertwined hands before glancing up at her.

"We got it from the ground," he said to her, his voice tight and controlled. He nodded at Cahir with pursed lips.

"She's here!" Seda heard a voice call from behind them and turned around.

Her mother, Sara, rushed out from between the trees, quickly followed by her father, Jason, and... *Mordred*.

"You're back!" Sara hugged her tightly, her body shaking as she cried. "Your brother—"

Seda interrupted, "I know." She couldn't hear the words again. The pain was too much, like a knife to her heart. She felt her anger simmer with fury, but kissed her mom on the cheek.

She planned to seek revenge on the Lycanthropes, but for now, she had to finish Tievel's rule.

She pulled away from her and dipped her head at her divine father. Modred once told her he needed her for 'retribution'. She understood why now. But she still didn't understand his role in all of this, and why he felt like he needed excess at all. He was Solios, the first god to be created in *Her* divine being, the first magical creature to walk through and experience the grasses and forests of Xyberus—the first to experience the beauty of this world. He was granted eternal life, and yet he longed for something else.

Jason hugged her tightly next, saying, "I'm so glad you're safe. We did what we could to get people out of here by taking down sections of the wall, but many are still out there. They need you, Seda."

She pulled away from him, trying not to allow her rolling options get the best of her, and spread her wings wide, lifting herself into the air and feeling the ache of sore muscles strain her back. She immediately felt the familiar freedom of flight blowing around her, and she pushed the muscles that had been untrained harder, not allowing weakness to hold her back any longer.

She looked down once more at both Cahir and Kalon, saying a silent prayer for them. Her eyes snagged on Cahir's, and he smiled at her in response, revealing his dimples, but his smile felt forced. She offered one in return, before looking away and flying higher into the sky.

Roya and Elco followed her lead, trailing behind. She flew above the tree line and looked into the distance.

Jotnar were tearing through the city as people screamed and ran in fear. The evil creatures smashed into buildings and snagged at innocent people, unable to flee from their insatiable hunger. Their eyes swarmed in crimson clouds as the Dark

Stone's power radiated through their being. The scene before her was so similar to that day, when she gave all of herself in exchange for protection.

*That won't happen again*, she said to herself.

*I am here. Come to me.*

She called to the Corvids and pushed her wings further, flying up higher into the night sky, as if reaching for her moon, trying to feel the kiss of her source.

When she summoned her power, she clenched her teeth, fueling her inner fury. She would do this. They would end this nightmare.

Storm clouds began to churn wildly above her.

A sea of loud caws echoed through the distance, and she called to them once more, feeling their love descend upon finally seeing her.

She looked to the dark swirling storm circling the Palatium, and her eyes narrowed. Tievel stood upon the tall tower's battlement, laughing as he watched the destruction around him. He clutched the stone in his hand tightly, holding it up in the air with his fist.

Seda's palms tightened, and lightning began to descend from the sky, striking the top of the Palatium, missing Tievel by mere feet.

She flew closer to the faux Monster King as thunder roared so loudly across the land that the Palatium shook, releasing the loosened, crumbling bricks onto the ground below.

Seda could see the Jotnar falling into painful nightmares from Kalon's magic. Long strands of green mist erupted from Cahir and wrapped around them, choking them to their deaths. Massive vines snaked up from the earth from the Vatte, coiling around the Rozzers and Dragors tightly and choking them to the ground.

Tievel looked up at the sky, his face darkening as he let out an evil laugh when their eyes locked onto each other.

"Seda! You have returned!" His laughter echoed through the oily magic and slammed into her, pushing her back.

The Corvids began to circle, flying around her in a hurricane of feathers, lightning, and rain.

It was time to end him.

It was time to give them the Darkened.

# CHAPTER 48

<u>Ael</u>

The Jotnar were massive beings, and the quantity of magic needed to take them down was quickly burning him out. Ael had promised he wouldn't overexert himself again and switched to using his sword, driving it into the Dragors and Rozzers with ease.

Kalon fought alongside him, taking down the Jotnar one by one with nightmare-inducing pain, then rushing up to them and slicing their throats to save his magic, his moth tattoo on his neck glowing a fiery red.

Suza, Jason, Mordred, and Sara, unable to fight, were guiding the frantic citizens toward the openings in the nearby walls.

Suza occasionally used her ability to transport people more quickly, but her magic was weak, and she could only use it every few minutes.

She and Sara ran back to them after transporting a mother and her child to the nearest exit, away from the destruction.

"Look!" Suza yelled, pointing to the sky.

Ael drove his sword into a Dragor carrying a bloodstone blade and kicked the body away from him before glancing up.

The sun began to rise rapidly, shifting the sky from the moon's amber glow to pinks, reds, and burning-ember hues.

It came to rest just behind the moon, and the land below smoldered beneath a solar shadow edged in flame.

The storm clouds parted, as if making way to the magical retribution of the heavens.

"The Darkened," Jason said in awe as he looked up. His mouth hung open, and his eyes were wide as he pointed to the sky.

A swarm of Corvids flew, rising as one, creating a living vortex of shadow and feathers. They transformed into a dragon form, Elco at the forefront, matching the Rising members' tattooed design.

High above the Palatium's silhouette, Seda unfurled her wings, and her beats sent glittering motes of starlight into the air, pulsating from her very being. She flew above like divinity itself, the storm clouds bowing to her command of justice.

A jagged arc of lightning struck Tievel, combining his dark magic with a blazing voltage that illuminated the sky in a sudden flash of blinding violet.

Thunder violently shook the earth as the fire-breathing dragon swooped down from the sky, focusing on the Palatium tower and engulfing the moss-covered stones in incandescent flames. The once proud banner bearing the years of the 'victory' smoked as it fell to the ground, exposing the lie it always symbolized.

Ael felt a stabbing pain tear through his side and spun around, diverting his gaze from the heavenly retribution above to see a Rozzer pulling a bloodstone blade from between his ribs. He looked at it in shock, adrenaline pumping through him and numbing the pain. His anger surged, and he wrapped the bits of magic left within him around the man's throat, coiling and squeezing so tight the Rozzer's head fell to the ground.

The tendrils of weakness clouded his vision. He was nearly out of magic and couldn't go on, so he fell to his knees, wrapping his palm over the hilt, and pulled the knife out. Blood quickly soaked into his shirt.

Kalon held out a hand to him. "Will you be okay?"

Ael looked from his own hand to Kalon's, recognizing the gesture of help from the man he had sworn was his enemy.

His hesitant hand reached out to Kalon, dizziness clouding his vision, as Kalon helped him stand on shaky legs.

"Look!" Sara yelled from behind, pointing to the Palatium.

Tievel was high above, laughing manically as the dragon descended once more. He held the Dark Stone in the air, pointing it at Seda, and suddenly, all the guards and Jotnar shifted their focus from the fight below toward Seda in the sky.

A small group of Corvids began to circle the firelit tower, swarming like swallows, but they quickly disappeared.

"That's probably Feich and those who chose to follow him," Kalon said as he held firmly onto Ael.

Tievel, with wild hair and clothes burned across his body, pointed the stone at Seda once more, and Ael saw her falter, saw her body jerk. Dark, incoherent words from Tievel pulsed through the city, vibrating the ground beneath their feet and causing black oil to rise from cracks in the earth.

A ragged yell tore from Ael's lips as he saw Seda begin to fall from the sky, her bright radiance burning in a crimson glow.

He could see her battle the dark magic, her silhouette flickering between reds and violets.

Kalon vanished, and Ael collapsed to the ground, desperately looking up as Seda fell from the heavens.

There was nothing he could do.

Kalon reappeared on the landing at the top of the Palatium, catching Seda's vibrant red body within his arms.

# CHAPTER 49

<u>Kalon de Somnium</u>

He once thought that the eclipse of darkness descended the heaviest when loss consumed the heart.

But he was wrong.

It doesn't just descend. It consumes. It annihilates. It slowly eats from within without mercy, changing a person and burning through their very soul. It makes happiness transmute into velvet voids of despair, suffocating the joy you believed you had.

But love. Love transcends. It doesn't just end when things change or loved ones pass; it continues to *smolder*. When you finally open your eyes, that small spark's metamorphosis finds its tinder and spreads like a forest fire, burning through the tops of trees and fighting to compete against the mighty sun's wrath. That's what Seda was to him before she sacrificed herself. That's what she brought into his dark world over a thousand years ago.

But when she left, he allowed the ease of darkness to return and consume him. For twenty years, he allowed his own evil urges to resurface once more, only granting himself the breath of fresh air—*of hope*—when he thought she might someday return.

That wasn't what love was supposed to be. Love wasn't selfish; it wasn't only about allowing yourself to find that spark within when it benefited you.

Something sinister was stirring, something they believed had disappeared long ago. It was more than just this Monster King and this city. He could sense it deep inside him; he could feel it in the way the tattoo on his neck called him northward.

The sanctity of their world rested on all the guardians' unity, bound as one in a harmony of good and evil, nature and divinity. The civilization and army he had created for her would soon become essential.

But not yet.

He had changed, and he saw that now. He was light with or without Seda's embrace, with or without her love to wrap around his heart and ease the pain.

And in the here and now, he caught his guiding light in his arms before her body made contact with the crumbling bricks of the Palatium's battlement, staring down at the crimson glow of the Dark Stones' power radiating through her and highlighting his olive skin in a scarlet glow.

He didn't let her go.

Not even as wild fury burned through his stomach, and his gaze shifted toward Tievel.

Tievel clenched his fist tighter around the stone, and Seda started to pulse with angry waves of crimson. Her eyes flared open, and she snarled at Kalon like a beast, raking her nails across his face and drawing blood from her fingers. But he held her tightly, not allowing her to succumb further to the dark power.

"You think you can defeat me? I have become the darkness that breathes. I *will* become a god, the first to be ascended in history! I may not be able to control you with this magic, but I can command *her* fury! And through her you will die! You will finally fucking die!" Teivel shrieked as his sickening, wicked grin spread wider across his face.

Seda began to writhe in his arms, storm clouds churning and brewing above her as bright flashes lit up their faces.

"I won't let that happen," Kalon replied coolly.

He didn't let her go as lightning descended and hit him in the shoulder. He held her body tightly against his as he fell to his knees against the edge, pain flaring through his body, vibrating through every nerve. Through the pain, he clenched his fist and poured the last bit of his magic into a pain-filled nightmare, channeling it into the Monster King.

The Monster King's eyes widened before he fell backwards, emitting a scream that tore across the land, funneling through the dark, oil-slicked magic and shaking the earth.

He didn't let her go as the stone slipped from Tievel's hands, landing and turning a dull shade of gray.

His own smile crested his once-evil lips as he saw the megalomaniac Monster King on the floor, writhing in convulsing waves.

He didn't let go as the electrical shocks receded and Seda's radiance changed from crimson to violet starlight, and her burning eyes met the pain-filled tears dripping down his face.

He did finally let go when she shifted out of his arms and turned her slitted gaze toward Tievel, lightning sliding up and down her form.

Seda unleashed her divine electrical storm upon the man. Her fury focused on him as she watched his burning body thrash and his back arch off the floor in a mix of Kalon's nightmares and her own rage.

With her magic, Seda lifted his body high into the sky, over the Palatium battlement's edge, and released him, allowing the charred body to fall to the rocky ground below.

Kalon gasped at his weakened state when he pulled back his magic, as if the last tendrils were a flickering candle, clinging to nothing but the wick as the wax had evaporated into thin air.

His vision blurred, and his body gave out, toppling backward and falling over the battlement's edge. The air enveloped him as his body fell, and he watched himself drift farther from the divine being from the heavens who had absolved him long ago.

Kalon closed his eyes, waiting for the impact that would finally claim him.

He heard a roar and felt himself land on something warm. As the warmth spread through his body, he cracked open his eyes and saw Elco's burning red scales, rescuing him—a man who had given up hope to see another day, a man who barely deserved to inhale the air around him.

Elco dropped him back onto the battlement, and Seda rushed to him, kneeling by his side. Her exhausted eyes met his, and she held him tightly in her arms. He allowed the wholeness to swell in his heart as he inhaled her lilac scent, his nose brushing against the top of her head.

"I'm so sorry. I never meant to hurt you. Not today and not a millennium ago," she choked out, pulling away and brushing her hand across his bloody face. "Thank you for never giving up." Her words were soft, but he could feel the love in each syllable—something he believed had vanished long ago.

He watched as she nodded to Elco before brushing away a tear, and glanced at the stone. The dark, pulsating magic beckoned his weakened body forward, flaming through his dark tattoo, and urging him to succumb to the darkness's addiction once more.

He looked away as she picked it up.

# CHAPTER 50

### Seda

Seda felt nothing as her fingers brushed against the cool stone and looked at it in her palm. It looked like any other rock, dark and jagged. She expected something grand, like a tornado of Wisps or an explosion when her skin made contact, but there was nothing. It was just... a rock. A rock once so pure with motherly love, now tainted by the evil magic from Supay.

She looked at Kalon, at his handsome face and chiseled jawline that she knew so well. She could see the torment in his eyes, the way the dark magic called to him, attempting to lure him into the recesses of corruption once more.

She placed the Dark Stone into her pocket and reached a hand out to him, an offer of friendship, a plea for forgiveness.

His seafoam-colored eyes met hers, and she saw him swallow before reaching out and taking his hand into hers.

The sounds of screams returned as they looked over the

banister, seeing the Jotnar and Dragors resume their torment on the land.

The Vatte were below, doing what they could to take down the monsters, but the Rozzers stood still, as if confusion swirled through their minds.

Her gaze shifted to Kalon's once more. "Stay here. Your magic is almost gone. We'll end this."

Her wings splayed wide, and she took to the skies again, allowing her magic to churn and darken the horizon, blocking the slivers of sunlight that tried to break past the eclipse far above.

The Corvids flew around her.

*To the ground. They need your help.*

The Corvids descended as one, all shifting into their human forms and fighting against the monsters below. Fire charred the massive beasts as Elco dove down.

Lightning began, once more, to rain from the sky, striking the demonic beasts in deathly blows.

SILENCE FOLLOWS BLOODSHED.

Victory doesn't shout from the rooftops; it gently releases a long-held breath. It amplifies your senses, making the most minute sounds the loudest, like the distant chirping of a bird or the soft crunch of gravel as someone you love steps by your side.

Seda looked up into Cahir's emerald gaze, at the green blood soaking his shirt, and released a ragged cry as she wrapped her arms around him carefully. She could feel how drained her magic was, like the last drop of water trying to drip from an empty glass. Tears of joy and exhaustion slipped free as she pressed her ear to Cahir's chest and listened to the soft thumping of his heart below, steady and strong.

They did it. They defeated the Monster King and his malevolent power over the land.

They finally possessed the Dark Stone, the Stone of *Power*.

She closed her eyes as Cahir gently placed a warm hand at the nape of her neck, holding her close, then leaned down to kiss the top of her head.

She opened her eyes to see her friends and what was left of her family surrounding her.

They were alive.

A whimper escaped her lips when her eyes landed on Elco, and she slowly pulled away from Cahir and walked toward the one friend in her many lives who had stuck by her side the longest. He was the guardian of the mortal realm, the keeper below the stars, part of her divine *family*, and together they brought peace once more to their world.

"Thank you, Elco," she said into his inky mane.

"Look around you," he said in response, and she pulled away, looking through the destroyed streets of Joro at the hundreds of Corvids, waiting for her command.

Roya stood closest, and she bent down on one knee, placing a hand over her heart and the other toward the still-heavy moon in the sky.

"To the Guardian of the Celestial Vault! The Bearer of Moonlight, and our angel, *The Corvid Queen!* " Roya shouted.

Like a vast wave flowing through the ocean, the hundreds of Corvids lining the city streets followed, bowing before her and chanting her name.

It was then that she began to feel the quiet happiness take root in her heart. It was then that she pulled the Stone of Power from her pocket and held it aloft as a symbol of hope, smiling as everyone cheered around her.

And it was then that Feich emerged out of thin air, stabbing into her chest with a claw sharpened like a blade, and stole the stone from her hand.

"This belongs to Supay," he shouted, his eyes flashing crimson as the dark power surged through him. He quickly disappeared, vanishing out of sight.

The very last of her magic surged through her, a violent storm rumbling across the skies as she tried to strike back, but that last drop of water fell from its cup, landing onto the parched earth below.

Seda collapsed to her knees as she heard the echoes of chaos surrounding her, felt the earth shake from Elco's mighty roar, and saw shadows begin to blur her vision before she closed her eyes to nothingness.

She had, for the first time, depleted all of her magic.

# CHAPTER 51

<u>Ael</u>

When her body fell to the ground, it felt like Ael's world had ended.

Both he and Kalon had rushed to her side, and Ael fought the urge to push him away, biting the inside of his cheek in irritation.

"She'll heal," Mordred said. "It isn't a fatal wound. The armor protected it from being worse."

Ael looked up to the scarred face of the man before him, at the way he looked down at Seda with fatherly love.

"I'm going to find her a place to rest," Ael said, and he gently picked her up into his arms, cradling her against him, and stared down with love at that small freckle on her chin.

The Vatte had picked up the charred remains of Tievel and wrapped him in a thick layer of vines, saying they were going to return his body amongst the Amanita Copse. Lucja, furious as she was, had vowed to let his body decay where Tievel had sent them. She insisted that their people would no longer live in fear and hide far away, letting his remains decompose alone—just as he had done to them.

Ael clutched Seda to his chest as he and Kalon walked the shattered remains of the city. They passed the familiar roads he knew so well in silence until they saw a still-standing building that he once called home… with her.

They ascended the winding steps until they reached the locked door.

Kalon kicked it down, gaining them entry.

Ael walked through and inhaled the familiar citrus scent of the room. His eyes shifted to the still-broken window, and he smiled, remembering the day Roya had broken in and kick-started this entire thing.

He quickly looked for the rice stuck to the walls, but someone had sadly cleaned it up.

They entered the bedroom, and he placed her on his old bed, with the same linens that thankfully were still there. He bent down and placed a tender kiss on her freckle.

"Check the bathroom for antiseptic, please." He looked to Kalon, who nodded and left the room.

Roya and the others remained within the city limits as they figured out what to do with the remaining Rozzers and citizens, but a vast majority of the Corvids flew in search of Fiech and his small cohort of betrayers. A brief moment of hesitation passed through him at the citizens who had fled into the Heath Forest, fearing for them amongst the Hailec who roamed those woods, but they didn't matter right now—not with Seda in the condition she was in.

The only one who mattered in his eyes was Seda, and unfortunately, he had to share this moment with Kalon.

Ael saw what Kalon did and how he saved her from Tievel's

dark magic, and he swallowed down the jealousy from within, erasing it entirely from his feelings.

She was safe, that's what mattered.

Kalon returned with antiseptic and a few bandages, and together they quickly dressed her wound and left the room so she could rest.

They sat on opposite sides of the old couch, staring at the broken window as silence filled the room. A strange sense of resignation washed over him with this man by his side. He had *saved* her.

"I—" Ael started, but closed his mouth.

Kalon looked at him. "I forgive you, too," he said with a smirk that highlighted both the scratches on his face and his reddened tattoo. He closed his eyes and leaned back against the couch's headrest.

Ael rolled his eyes and stared at the cracked bedroom door. She would be okay, she was alive, and he would continue to stand by her side.

They could figure out who Supay was and how to handle him later. They had also heard no further updates from Umbrea regarding the Jotnar, who remained idly outside Umbrea's city walls.

He could afford this night of rest.

Ael closed his eyes and quickly drifted off to sleep, with his sleeping adversary lying beside him.

# CHAPTER 52

<u>Seda</u>
(One thousand years ago)

"We did it!" Seda shouted as she stood on the dais, looking down toward the hundreds of Corvids and Amaru within the Noctrya throne room. Elation hummed beneath her skin, and she held her hands aloft, creating a vivid, electrical depiction of the battle against Supay in detailed violet hues for all to see.

An explosive cheer burst from the crowd, the loudest coming from Elco, who stood to her left on the dais and shook the walls with an earth-shattering roar.

"We pushed his soul into a mortal. Our lands are now free and balanced once more!" she yelled as a broad smile lit up her face.

No real method existed to kill a god, but they found a workaround together. They cast aside his soul, and when that body failed him, the demonic embodiment would float aimlessly around for millennia.

She looked to the man sitting on the throne to her right, at the dark snakeskin armor and bone mask, and saw the piercing eyes she loved so much, *focused solely on her*.

As the cheers died down and the drinking began, she held onto Kalon's strong arm as they conversed with others, laughing through mouthfuls of cake and glasses of mead.

They neared the end of the gathering hall, and Kalon pulled her into a dark alcove, ripping the mask from his face and pinning her against the wall with his knee between her thighs.

"What are you doing?" she teased through ragged breaths, knowing full well what he wanted, what *she needed*.

His full lips met hers with unmistakable hunger, and he bit her tongue, causing a slight sting before caressing it with his own.

He growled as her electrical spark danced across his lips, and slid his thumb into her mouth for her to suck, touching it to the back of her throat. "I'm going to fucking hunt you down, my lunita. And I'm going to *fuck* you when I catch you."

She felt a surge of excitement ripple through her as his intense eyes burned into hers.

"You better fucking run," he growled, releasing her from his clutches.

She didn't hesitate and ran from him, knocking into other guests as her legs flew through the room and into the long, dark halls. She felt her heart pounding above the feel of her bare feet striking the stone floors. She grabbed onto the corner of the wall, and she sharply threw herself around the edge, hearing the dining hall's doors crash open behind her.

The stairs to the exit were over a hundred steps long, and she pushed herself harder, flapping her wings to increase her speed as she descended.

She could hear his armor rattling behind her, and she fought the urge to look back. She needed to get outside, where she could fly, and where he would have to work harder to reach her.

The doors flung open, and the cool night air wrapped around her body. Her feet hit the grass outside, and she took to the air, flying toward the distant tree line on a rocky hillside. She heard his growl as he exited the castle, and she smiled at herself.

*Good luck,* she thought as her wings pushed her forward.

She landed and pressed her feet into the dirt, looking back, only this once, to see how far back he was.

He wasn't there.

*Fuck, fuck, fuck,* she thought as she scanned her surroundings, her pulse quickening, and anticipation shivering up her spine.

She saw a small cave of rocks in the distance, and she ran to it, quickly ducking inside and holding her breath.

The wind blew through the dark opening of her hiding place, and she heard Kalon's armor clatter.

*Cheater,* she thought of his magical transport, but she kept herself hidden, fighting against her rapidly beating heartbeat, trapping her breath tightly in her chest.

She couldn't exhale; it would be too loud, and he would hear, snaring her in his grasp.

"Come out, come out wherever you are," Kalon's growly voice purred, causing her core to throb. "You can't hide forever."

She began to feel dizzy, and slowly released the breath she was holding through pursed lips, praying he wouldn't find her. She peeked through the rocks and saw him standing nearby.

*I'm in the trees,* she thought, hoping her racing thoughts would misguide her location.

He walked away, and when only the soft sound of crickets echoed, and her heart was pounding too hard to bear, she slowly crawled out from between the rocks and looked around.

Like the prey-driven black leopard he was, Kalon pounced

with a low growl, grabbing her with his thick hands and pinning her to the ground.

"You cheated!" Seda screamed, and Kalon smiled back at her with an evil grin.

"Play smarter, not harder." His words brushed her ear as he took her lobe between his lips, exhaling softly, and igniting a fire within her.

She tried to wiggle free as he wrapped one large hand around both her wrists above her head and ripped apart her dress. She felt the sting of the cool air hit her skin as his warm mouth claimed her nipples as his own, painfully slow, one at a time.

His other hand pulled his cock free from his pants and pushed her legs open, driving himself into her and filling her in one swift movement.

"I think you like this little game," he purred, groaning through the slickness that now coated him.

He held her firmly, devotion and want blending until nothing else existed. He began to move with a steady, ardent rhythm, and she shifted her hips to take him in deeper, wanting to feel it harder, loving the ache that his thick length created from within. Shudders passed through her body as he claimed her in ways no one ever could.

"You feel so fucking good wrapped around my cock," he growled as a bead of sweat formed on his forehead.

Her tension began to build as his movements quickened, fucking her with primal force into the soft ground below. She looked into his eyes, at the way they were hooded in the pleasure of his own, the pleasure she gave to him, and she came undone. Her orgasm ripped through her in punishing waves, and she screamed into the darkness as her body exploded into a violet glow.

His fevered movements became jagged, and he groaned, sliding in and out firmly as he sought his own release.

"Fuck," he growled as his body tensed and he spilled into her, wrapping his palm around her throat and squeezing it tightly, causing her to gasp from the pressure.

When his body finally stilled, and she inhaled the fresh air around them, he slowly pulled out of her and wrapped her in his arms.

"That was fun," he purred into her ear. "But I did find you rather fast."

She smacked his chest. "Next time I get to find you."

"Deal."

They both stared up at the glowing moon above. A shooting star flew across the sky, its trail reminding her of the magic of the Wisps.

She couldn't evade the emotion that began to form within her chest, and she held back a small sob.

"What's wrong?" he asked as he pulled her face toward his, staring into her burning violet eyes.

She tried to look away, but his firm grip held strong.

"Why do you want to be with me when I cannot bear children?" Seda choked out the words, closing her eyes to avoid the look he might offer in return. She knew it wasn't the right moment to ask this, not after the victorious battle, where they were supposed to be celebrating, and especially not after he just came back for her. It made her look weak, and she hated that she placed herself in this position.

"Open your eyes," he commanded, and she obeyed, staring through her teary, blurred vision at his face, so close to hers. "I know this pain is something I can't fix, but your worth has never been tied to what your body can or can't do. We have each other until the end of time. That's more than I've ever felt worthy of, Seda." His words were steady and calm, but she knew they carried sadness, as well. How could it not? The Wisps told her that they would not grant that one last wish, the wish the Mother Goddess said she could have.

Even Elco, whose warmth held the arcane embodiment of love and fertility, was powerless to alter her destiny.

"I'm broken," she whispered as she pressed her face into his chest, releasing a ragged cry.

The air shifted, and an Amaru appeared beside them.

"Now isn't the time!" Kalon gritted out.

"Kalon de Somnium," it said. "The war is still ongoing. Someone has recovered the lost stone and is now attacking the humans."

DARKNESS SURROUNDED Seda as the wind tore through her hair. She could see the glimmer of the stars in her wings above, harmonizing with her frantic heartbeats through the feathers.

She could hear the sounds of innocent people screaming and Corvids cawing in the distance, and pushed her wings further into the center of the chaos.

When she landed, she saw fires enveloping homes, and children clutched tightly in their mothers' arms as Jotnar tore through the small village of Joro, snagging people with wild fervor and eating them whole.

Their eyes were blazing red, as if controlled by the Dark Stone—a stone they believed they had lost.

She felt the burning sensation of rage radiate from her chest, and pain tore through her soul. She thought they ended this. They were supposed to be free from this darkness.

She glanced back, seeing Somnium a few steps behind, clad in his armor and skull mask. He was taking down the Jotnar two at a time, tormenting their minds and making their bodies writhe on the dirt roads. Blood seeped from their noses, death pulling them back into the pits of hell from which they came.

This was supposed to be over. She watched children cry out for their families and felt their sadness seep into her soul.

The world was still cruel and unbalanced.

She could offer this one sacrificial, parting gift.

Somnium looked over at her, at her chest pulsating violently and her hair alight.

Seda heard him scream for her to stop and saw him rush toward her, ripping off his mask and revealing wild eyes with fear etched into his features.

But it was too late. She had made her decision.

With the mighty moon's ancient strength, a bright purple light erupted around her, forming a vast, magical dome above that instantly killed all the demonic beasts created by Supay within. Only those remaining within were blessed by the Mother Goddess.

Kalon ran to her side and clutched her to his chest.

"Why," she heard his muted voice ask. "I cannot live this life without you, and I don't have wishes I can seek. Please, *please*... don't leave me. You are my light, Seda. *Please don't leave me.*"

But she did, and it was a mistake she would regret.

She whispered a final plea as her eyes fluttered closed, "Save the children."

She knew she would someday return; she knew she had one life to give, for her stone was still within.

But she didn't expect the evil of the world to lurk and intensify while she was away, and she didn't expect to return to a shattered world, tilted on its axis. She also didn't expect to be reborn with no memories.

But most importantly, she never anticipated that Supay would rise again.

# EPILOGUE

### Supay

It had been over a thousand years since his soul was placed inside that weak, mortal body. A body that tried to fight with Supay's consciousness time and time again. The mortal repeatedly used Supay's ancient magic against him by gaining entry into the Royal Alcove, aiming to sever the connection of the darkness's caress. But, to Supay's delight, none of the scrolls that he had examined described the dark power needed.

Meir's time was over, and Supay would never allow himself to be cast aside again.

The foolish Corvid man before him handed him the stone, and he felt his magic resurge with a vengeance, shedding the skin he wore into who he was before. Meir's pathetic, lifeless body collapsed to the ground, revealing his true demonic self underneath. The seven-foot, muscular figure with cadmium-colored skin and hair, matching coiled horns, and solid black eyes took form. The ecru shredded robes he wore a millennium ago wrapped around him, exposing his broad chest and comforting him within a blanket of destruction.

He had spent far too long failing with Meir's pathetic body, working his way through the ranks of Fae royalty, and luring the old king to marry a Dark Witch in an attempt to collect the stones.

But Supay had finally returned, and his dark magic swarmed like ripples of oil suspended in the air, igniting into flames around him and expelling black moths of death from the ash.

As he stood high on the cliffside, gazing down at the distant city he had pretended was his home for too long, he smiled broadly, relishing the loud cheer that erupted at his divine transformation.

He raised his flame-charred fist in the air, holding the stone as his barbed tail swung around him, and laughed loudly for all to hear. He kicked the dead body over the edge, loving how the deepness of his voice echoed from his godly chest across the land, causing the floating green orbs to quake in his wake.

Those stupid, fucking orbs. His death moths would eventually consume them all.

"Our Dark God has returned!" Neoma screamed from his side down to those before them. "He's no longer Meir, advisor of Umbrea, but is our Deathly Sovereign! *Bow before your god!*"

The Dark Witch had helped him get to where he was, pretending to be a Fae lord's daughter. He had promised to make her a queen, and if he was good for anything, it was keeping his word to those who remained loyal to him.

Besides, she felt too good to throw away, and he couldn't wait to experience her in his real form.

His vast army of faithful Jotnar, Dragors, newly appointed Lycanthropes, and returning Dark Witches before him bowed and chanted his name. Their cheers shook the ground beneath them. The loudest came from the Lycanthropes, who believed the sun had returned in his honor—the fucking simpletons and their ignorance.

*Supay, Supay, Supay.*

He inhaled the praise exploding below him and looked once more toward the tall emerald towers of Umbrea, the wicked grin spreading wider across his sinister face, revealing the fangs meant to suck the life out of anyone who stood in his way.

This realm was going to be the first to belong to *him*.

Once, long ago, he solely ruled the underworld, but that title alone was never enough. Supay was resolute to finish what he began years ago—eliminating his counterpart from the divine realm. The Mother Goddess's reign over both the heavens and the earthly realms would finally come to an end.

Only he alone would remain, forged from corrupted divinity itself, wielding absolute power and dominion.

From the ashes of destruction, Supay was destined to enslave all creation to his will.

And this time, the world would know what it meant to be powerless against him.

# A History of Magic's
# Divine Family Tree

**THE MOTHER GODDESS**
THE DIVINE CREATOR

**SUPAY**
THE DEATHLY SOVEREIGN

**SOLIOS**
THE SOLAR SOVEREIGN

**UNKNOWN NAME**
GUARDIAN OF THE MORTAL REALM & FERTILITY

**SOMNIUM**
GUARDIAN OF THE LAST SLEEP

**UNKNOWN NAME**
GUARDIAN OF THE CELESTIAL VAULT

Seda's journey continues in *CORVID WRATH*.
Estimated late 2026.

# Acknowledgments

I want to thank the readers who dared to read Corvid Whispers, my debut book, and chose to continue this journey.

A big thank you to my ARC and beta readers, who have been there since day one as well.
You're seriously the best.

Thank you all for supporting a new indie author. <3

# About the Author

Dee Mannine is an indie author who loves storytelling and enjoys reading fiction, particularly fantasy, romance, and dark gothic genres. She works full-time in the tech industry, but her genuine passions are in the arts—such as painting, drawing, and baking. She has two daughters who love anything that sparks their creativity, which helps keep her motivated on her personal journey. Dee has been happily married for 10 years and lives in beautiful Northern California, running a small homestead with her husband. She has always had vivid dreams and ideas, so she chose to write some of them down, turning them into this story.

Find out more at:
deemannine.com
TikTok: @author.dee.mannine
Instagram: @author.dee.mannine

Cover character art illustration created by:
Anas Arzaq — Instagram: @anasarzq